SECRETS
THRILL RIDE MAGAZINE
BOOK NINE

BLAZE WARD   ANNIE REED   REBECCA BUCHANAN
OTIS JOHNSON   KIM MAY   MARIE SUTRO
DAVID BOOP   MATTHEW HELLMAN   NORA B. PEEVY
ALISON MCMAHAN   E. CHRIS AMBROSE
RACHEL AMPHLETT   DAVID H. HENDRICKSON
M.L. BUCHMAN

KNOTTED ROAD PRESS, INC.

Secrets
Thrill Ride Magazine, Issue 009
Copyright © 2025 by Knotted Road Press
Edited by Blaze Ward and Richard ED Jones
All rights reserved
Published by Knotted Road Press
www.KnottedRoadPress.com

Cover art:

ID 8825315 © 3desc | Dreamstime.com

Cover and interior design copyright © 2025 Knotted Road Press

This book is licensed for your personal enjoyment only. All rights reserved. This is a work of fiction. All characters and events portrayed in this book are fictional, and any resemblance to real people or incidents is purely coincidental.

No part of this book may be reproduced in any form or by any electronic or mechanical means, including information storage and retrieval systems, without written permission from the author, except for the use of brief quotations in a book review.

Essay: Under New Management © 2025 Blaze Ward

Same Worm, Different Day © 2025 Annie Reed

The Goddess and the Mad Friar © 2025 Rebecca Buchanan

From Watts © 2025 Otis Johnson

Alexandria Has Fallen © 2025 Kim May

You Oughta Know © 2025 Marie Sutro

Impact © 2025 Shells Legoullon

Shell Games © 2025 Blaze Ward

The Spy Who Stabbed Me © 2025 David Boop and Matthew Hellman

$100,000,000 © 2025 Nora B. Peevy

Sister Secrets © 2025 Alison McMahan

The Purloined Legacy © 2025 E. Chris Ambrose

The Back Nine © 2025 Rachel Amphlett

Mcuse and the Fate of the World © 2025 David H. Hendrickson

All Eyes Face Inward © 2025 M.L. Buchman

ALSO BY BLAZE WARD

The Science Officer Series (Season One)
start with *The Science Officer*

The Science Officer Series (Season Two)
The Bryce Connection
The Alien Suns

The Jessica Keller Chronicles (series complete)
start with *Auberon*

Shadow of the Dominion (series complete)
start with *Longshot Hypothesis*

The Star Dragon (series complete)
start with *Birth of the Star Dragon*

Star Tribes
start with *WinterStar*

ESSAY: UNDER NEW MANAGEMENT

Hi there. I'm Blaze, and it's all my fault.

Background: On that long drive down to Oregon to watch the eclipse, the Fabulous Publisher Babe™ and I came up with the ideas that would turn into the Boundary Shock Quarterly (BSQ) science fiction anthology magazine. Issue 029 just came out in Jan 2025 and we're going strong.

In an effort to convince others that it could be done easy, cheap, and fun, I wrote a book (How to Launch a Magazine for Professional Publishers) and handed ebook copies out to random strangers at writing conventions.

My wife liked the idea so much that she started Mystery, Crime, and Mayhem (MCM), which has gone on to place stories in various Year's Best collections and be nominated for various things.

Then it was Matt's turn. He and I were on the phone on our monthly mastermind call, talking about various things, and he lamented (bitched, really) about how there wasn't any sort of dedicated short form magazine for Thriller, as the genre came out from under Crime and Mystery to become its own category.

So I suggested he start one. That was Wednesday. On Friday morning, I got an email with the subject line "I hate you" and a five page white paper explaining how he could do it. Worse, he went ahead and did it.

Because I helped (and blackmailed him some), I knew the themes and his editorial preferences. I was lucky enough to place stories in the first eight issues, when he was doing a semi-open call. Not widely blasted, but telling folks in the field or adjacent. Still got a little slush, but also recruited some heavy hitters to play.

Fast forward two years, and Matt's life took a radical left turn. Summer of 2024, he told me that he didn't have the bandwidth to keep doing the magazine, and was going to shut it down after issue #8. That's the usual fail point for projects like this, by the way. Somewhere around two years.

Except that I was having fun. And writing a lot more Action-thriller stuff, both long and short.

And it was all sort of my fault.

Thus, I volunteered to step in and take over as Publisher and Editor.

First up, I recruited Jones. He's got the chops as an editor from other fields, and will be picking that part up pretty quickly, but doesn't know much about the publishing side, so I figure he'll be a year sorting that out and learning how he wants to do it.

Next, I changed the magazine from an open call to a Syndicate, which is how both BSQ and MCM are run. Small, set number of previously vetted folks who promise to send me two stories per year. They get editorial freedom, as long as they hit theme and give me quality. In 400-some stories for BSQ, I have rejected five.

From there, recruiting the people. When I started BSQ, I had to ask fifty people to get 15 names. This time around, it took twenty, which was gratifying to me. Means people respect my rep in the right ways.

Matt is still involved. And still writing. I'll be Publisher for a time, even after Jones takes over as Chief Editor (presumably later in the year when he's more comfortable with the structure I'm building) and then I will ramp down my direct involvement some and become more like a Chairman of the Board.

Running two magazines and maintaining a full-time writing career takes a lot of effort. BSQ is profitable enough to make it wort doing. TRM should be as well.

And I've got several years experience at this, so I should make new mistakes in the future. That's always the key. Fail originally.

With that, this is your formal announcement that Thrill Ride Magazine is under new management, starting officially with issue 009.

Got some changes planned, but you won't see those until probably 2026, because I'm only slowly modifying Matt's old structure instead of tearing it down and rebuilding it. (See Chesterton's Fence.)

This issue is **Secrets**.

We all have them. Sometimes, they are worth a life. Or were. Might get you killed. You might even have it coming.

Maybe you're playing both sides against each other, and one side might kill you when they find out. That's the genesis of my story in this issue, *Shell Games*.

You previously met Boston the Wheelman in Issue 004, with the story *Right Hand*. I had fun with him, basing a lot of the mannerisms and vocabulary off a very English friend of mine. When looking at the upcoming themes for **Thrill Ride, Year Three**, I saw a pattern I could exploit to write more Boston.

In Year Two, I wrote a whole set of Chace Haig stories, and

will circle back to him at some point. That's the fun of themed issues. Finding that sweet spot where the same cast of misfits can come back again and again.

Issue 010 will be **Fast Cars**, and I've already written *Barn Owls* (another Boston caper) for it. Then 011 will be **Sidekicks**, and I decided to explore more of what makes Humboldt tick, because she's interesting and it's her chance to shine.

Issue 012 will be someone new, **Spies**, but someone that I'm already writing assassin novels about, and this was a chance to explore Rory in a small setting and learn who she was.

Plus, Year Four is mapped. And I have notes on Year Five already, but Jones is likely to have opinions on that, so I haven't written anything in pen. He'll take over that aspect of things at some point, and I want him to have that freedom, even as I run things with something of an iron fist for a bit now, because otherwise it would have stopped entirely.

Can't have that. At least not without a good reason, anyway.

So welcome to **Secrets**. And the new Syndicate of authors dedicated to keeping this dream and this magazine alive. Some will be names you recognize from previous issues. Some are newcomers to the fold that I recruited to give us the widest possible reach of fans and interested parties.

All of us have turned in some fun stories, guaranteed to entertain you and make you think. And maybe worry about your own secrets and what costs you might bear.

So fix yourself something to drink, settle into a comfortable chair, and let's dive in.

And thanks for being there for us.

Blaze Ward
West of the Mountains, WA
January 2025

SAME WORM, DIFFERENT DAY

ANNIE REED

SAME WORM, DIFFERENT DAY

ANNIE REED

Danny Griffin got the same question thrown at him over and over again his whole life.

"What the hell is wrong with you, man?"

The first time he'd been eight. He'd eaten a live worm, dirt and all. The thing had been disgusting, but he'd choked it down.

Then he'd laughed about it.

The neighborhood bully who'd dared him to eat the damn thing—double fucking *dog dared* him—had puked up his lunch, right there in the schoolyard in front of the whole class.

The bully's buddies, Frick and Frack, Danny's best friend called them, had turned green around the gills. Then they ran away.

None of them bothered Danny again.

The whole thing had been a revelation. He'd just learned the biggest secret in the universe. The secret every bullied kid in the world wished they knew, and Danny *knew* it.

Doing disgusting shit made people think he was wrong in the head, and that made even the bad kids leave him alone.

All learning that secret had cost Danny was the gritty, slimy feel of the worm sliding down his throat.

Cool.

~

When you knew from an early age that most people thought there was something fundamentally wrong with you, putting up with all the weird, disgusting, and downright disturbing shit life threw at you became second nature.

So when the nutjob with the crazy eyes and dreadlocks ripped open the passenger door of Danny's car while he was waiting for the light, threw a duffel bag inside and dove in after it, Danny just blinked.

As strange shit went, this didn't even ping Danny's personal *You Gotta Be Shitting Me* meter. Life had been throwing weird at him for years.

He just shook his head and laughed.

Then the nutjob pointed a gun at Danny's head and ordered him to drive.

Danny laughed harder.

"What the hell is *wrong* with you?" the nutjob screamed at him. "I said *drive!*"

Danny tried to bring the laughter under control. It wasn't the first time someone had pointed a gun at him. It *was* the first time somebody crazier than he was had done it in his own car.

Same worm, different day.

"Sure thing," Danny said. "Where to?"

"I don't give a fuck," the nutjob said. "Just get us out of here!"

The light hadn't turned green yet and Danny was three cars back from the intersection. Commercial street. Two lanes on each side. Danny was the last in line in the right-hand lane. No cars next to him on the left.

His car wasn't quite a junker. The door locks didn't work.

The radio was toast. The headliner had rips big enough to put his fist through, but she had a good engine under the hood.

Did she purr like a kitten? No. She roared like a tiger. She was his go-fast baby. That's why he'd kept her for as long as he had, dents and rusted out paintjob and all.

He spun the wheel and stomped on the gas.

The car shot across the left-hand lane and into oncoming traffic. Panicked drivers screeched out of the way. Cars jackknifed and smashed into cars parked at the curb.

Danny drove through the mess like a pro.

His baby accelerated through the intersection, narrowly missing a delivery truck that locked up its brakes trying to stop. Danny spun the wheel hard, rear wheels fishtailing as he laid rubber into the skid.

For a split second gravity failed. His baby threatened to tip into a roll, then she righted herself.

The road ahead was clear. No traffic till the next light, a quarter mile away.

Danny whooped and laughed like a maniac.

Now, this was *living*.

Girls didn't much like him, but that was okay. By the time Danny turned sixteen he had a job working for Louie the Large—never, *ever* Louie the Lardass—and Danny didn't have much time for girls.

He'd grown up lean and lanky and about as average looking as a white kid of questionable heritage with stupid hair and bad skin could look. With his low-rider jeans and dark hoodie, he could have been any one of dozens of kids jiving down the streets in the bad part of town in their hundred-dollar sneakers, trying to look cool.

Danny didn't try to look cool. He *was* cool.

He knew how to eat the worm.

"You gonna grow up to be a leg breaker for me, you know that?" Louie told him. "You got the balls. You got the crazy."

Danny wasn't violent by nature. Leg breaking wasn't his thing, but he'd do it if Louie asked. Louie paid him good. Louie gave him a place to stay with an actual bed when his mom was falling down drunk. Louie trusted him.

So when Louie sent him to rifle through the pockets of a dead bagman whose head had been half blown off by a shotgun blast, Danny did it.

He climbed into dumpsters reeking of week-old restaurant garbage, fighting off rats while he looked for something that belonged to Louie. Something that somebody had tried to ditch in all that muck.

When Louie needed someone to slice open a dead mule's belly to get the balloon of drugs the mule swallowed to get across the border? Yeah, Danny did that too, and laughed while he had his hands inside their guts.

Same worm, different day.

The guys Louie sent along with Danny to take possession of whatever Danny had been sent to retrieve always said the same thing.

"What the hell is wrong with you, man?"

Inappropriate affect.

That's what the high school counselor had called it. Back when Danny had still been going to high school. The counselor had suggested his mom send him to a shrink.

She took him home and got drunk instead.

Nobody knew Danny's biggest secret. They didn't understand that laughter was the way he swallowed the worm. Laugh and he wouldn't have to think about the slimy, disgusting, gritty taste of it all.

At least at first.

Later laughing became a habit.

Later, it became a problem.

~

The nutjob with the gun didn't like the fact that Danny was laughing. He told Danny to shut up.

Danny ignored him.

Then the nutjob yelled at Danny to shut up.

Danny ignored that too. He was just having too damn much fun. He hadn't driven like this in years.

Then the nutjob shoved the business end of his gun in Danny's ribcage and told him if he didn't shut the fuck up right now, he'd blow a hole through Danny's guts and take his chances.

Danny didn't think the nutjob would actually shoot him. Not while the car was clocking close to a hundred.

Not unless the nutjob was as crazy as Danny.

That was a possibility he'd never considered. He'd never met anyone as crazy as he was. That's what made him so valuable to Louie the Large, and to other people after that.

So Danny did his best to stop laughing.

He clamped his jaw shut and tried to think serious thoughts. Not about swallowing the worm. Thinking about the worm triggered his laughter, just like impossibly crazy situations did.

They sailed through two more intersections, the lights in their favor. Danny steered around the cars that didn't try to get out of his way like he was trying to take the lead in the last lap of the Indy 500.

His luck ran out at the next intersection. The light had turned red, and cross traffic was clogging up the intersection. It seemed like nobody could find a gas pedal to save their lives. Like they were all part of a caravan of little old ladies out for a Sunday stroll.

Danny couldn't see any gaps between cars he could exploit.

Jumping the median into oncoming traffic was out of the question. The city in its wisdom had planted the median with mature trees surrounded by spiked iron cages. Car versus one of those caged trees would kill the tree and his car.

Not optimal. Danny was crazy, but he didn't have a death wish.

He let up on the gas.

The nutjob jabbed the gun into Danny's side. "Why are you slowing down?" he said.

A giggle tried to bubble up from deep in Danny's chest. He fought it back down.

"You're kidding, right?" he said.

He shot a quick look at the nutjob. The guy's eyes were wide, whites showing all around, but the pupils weren't blown.

The nutjob wasn't high.

He also wasn't wearing a seatbelt.

Danny always wore his. A long-established habit that had saved his ass from time to time. Maybe it would again.

He took a split second to consider his options.

His side of the street was lined with cars and trucks parked against the curb. If he cranked the wheel to the right, he'd either roll the car for real or slam into the parked cars. Or both.

He'd survive. The nutjob? Danny didn't like the guy's chances.

The question was whether the nutjob would have the time or the brainpower to pull the trigger before the crash.

Only one way to find out.

Danny let out the laugh he couldn't hold back any longer.

He gripped the wheel hard and prepared to swallow the worm.

Danny got busted the week after he turned seventeen. He should have known something was up. Louie's right-hand man, a big hulking bruiser named Buttons—stupid name for a big man, but nobody told him that just like nobody called Louie "Lardass"—was supposed to go along with Danny to dig up a bag someone had left for Louie in a dumpster.

Buttons backed out at the last minute.

"Bad oysters," he said, arms held tight against his considerable belly.

As far as Danny was concerned, all oysters were bad. Worse than worms. Buttons ate them because he said they made him a stud in bed.

Danny'd just discovered what made him a stud in bed.

Her name was Phoenix. She had gorgeous red hair halfway down to her shapely ass and wore tight skirts that barely covered that ass. She worked the corner two blocks from where Danny lived.

She always gave him a discount. Said he was sweet. Said he was hung like a racehorse. Danny knew better on both accounts, but it was nice to hear just the same.

Danny figured he got to do the dumpster pickup by himself because he was seventeen. Seventeen was better than sixteen. Seventeen was almost a man. Seventeen meant he might not have to do stupid shit anymore to make people think he was wrong in the head so they'd leave him alone.

The something that someone had left in a dumpster for Louie turned out to be a paper bag half full of greasy twenties and a solid lump at the bottom that Danny didn't look at too closely. Only after he was busted did he find out it was cocaine.

A lot of cocaine.

Enough to go from simple possession to possession with intent to sell.

Or so the cops told him.

"We can charge you as an adult," they told him. "Put you

away for a good long while. Or you play nice, we charge you as a minor. You go away for a year. When you come out, the slate's wiped clean. You start fresh. What do you say?"

He knew what the cops were after. He wasn't about to play nice and rat on Louie. Rats had a way of getting themselves exterminated.

Besides, Louie had been good to him. Gave him a place to stay. Work to do. Louie trusted him.

When he said no, one of the cops gave Danny a look like he'd grown two heads.

"What the hell is wrong with you?" the cop said. "We're offering you a sweetheart deal here. You know what life's gonna be like in prison for a kid like you?"

Danny had a good idea.

He wondered if they had worms in prison.

That probably wouldn't be enough. He wondered what else he'd have to do to make everyone think he was crazy enough they'd leave him alone.

It turned out to be a matter of making the right kind of friends. Friends who had friends on the outside. Friends who had powerful friends on the inside.

Friends who appreciated Danny's kind of crazy. He didn't even have to get his hands dirty.

Much.

While he was inside, Danny thought long and hard about Buttons. About bad oysters and the big man's decision not to go with Danny at the last minute.

About how the cops had been watching that dumpster, hoping to catch someone from Louie's crew with the goods they'd planted.

Someone they could get to flip on the big man.

Someone they could exploit.

He came to the conclusion that Buttons had set him up. Somehow Buttons had known about the cops. He'd sent Danny because Danny was crazy. Danny was also crazy loyal. He'd eat a worm before he'd flip on the man who'd taken him off the streets and away from his alcoholic mom.

Danny did eight years, released for good behavior and the state's need to alleviate overcrowding.

By the time he got out, Phoenix was gone.

So was Louie.

Buttons had taken over Louie's territory.

Danny paid Buttons a visit late one night. Danny had new skills thanks to his time inside. He would have made a good leg breaker. Louie would have been proud of him.

Buttons had gotten fatter. Slower. More complacent. He didn't even have a bodyguard. Nobody messed with Buttons.

Nobody who wasn't crazy.

Buttons never stood a chance. Danny cut through the big man's belly, spilling his guts out on the man's satin sheets. He laughed the entire time.

Same worm, different day.

Danny caught sight of an alley at the last possible second.

The alley wasn't much wider than a suburban driveway. Just a service alley between two commercial, brick-sided buildings on Danny's side of the street.

Could he make it?

Would it really make a difference?

If he smashed the car into a line of parked cars or into the side of one of the buildings, he'd still be a wreck and the nutjob might still end up dead.

But there was that one slim chance he wouldn't crash. Danny was just crazy enough to take it.

He slammed on the brakes, tires squealing. The rear end of the car fishtailed into a skid as Danny worked the wheel.

The seatbelt kept him from kissing the steering wheel.

The nutjob had no such protection.

He flew forward, dreadlocks flying as his body slammed into the dash and his forehead starred the windshield.

The gun went off, but Danny barely heard the shot over the sound of tires laying rubber on the street and the symphony of horns blasting as other drivers fought to control their own cars. A line of fire erupted across the top of his left thigh as he double-footed the brake and the gas, aiming his car at the mouth of the alley while he tried to control the skid.

The nutjob was screaming, calling Danny all sorts of names. Calling him crazy.

Danny laughed at him.

He almost made it into the alley, but he'd been going too fast. Zero to sixty wasn't the same as ninety to nothing.

The rear end of his car slammed into the building on the left side of the alley. Metal crunched and the car shuddered, not quite stopping.

The impact threw the nutjob against Danny. Blood was running down the nutjob's face from where his head had hit the windshield. His eyes weren't wild now. They were starting to roll up in the sockets.

Danny shoved the nutjob away.

He punched the gas.

The car screamed as the rough brick exterior of the building tore through the side panel, but the car responded, shooting down the alley.

The alley dead-ended in another alley that ran behind the buildings. Danny made a hard left. The nutjob slammed against the passenger door.

The lock on the passenger door failed. The door flew open, and the nutjob scrambled for something to grab to keep himself in the car.

Danny wanted him *out*. He shoved the nutjob toward the

open door. The man flailed at him, but Danny was wearing a seatbelt and the nutjob wasn't.

Danny won.

When the nutjob fell out of the car, he was still holding on to the gun like it was glued to his hand. He got off another shot. It didn't come anywhere near hitting the car or Danny.

A dumpster loomed large near the end of the alley.

Danny couldn't reach the passenger door to shut it, so he aimed for the dumpster. If he hit the dumpster just right, the impact would slam the door shut.

His left leg was starting to hurt like a bitch. It put him off his game just enough. Instead of shutting the open door, when Danny hit the dumpster it ripped the door clean off.

Danny laughed and kept driving.

He'd have to ditch the car. People noticed when you drove around in a car with the kind of damage his had. At least he'd been smart enough not to use his real name when he'd registered the thing. He'd learned a lot since he'd been seventeen. Not all of it was crazy-ass shit.

Then he'd have to take care of his wounded leg. In the back of his mind he heard a cartoon character say, "It's just a flesh wound," and he laughed harder.

A flesh wound he could deal with. He'd dealt with worse in prison.

He drove down a warren of side streets until he came to an abandoned strip mall. Storefronts were boarded up. Garbage had accumulated in the empty parking lot.

Danny drove around the side of the strip mall and parked the car next to the building. He opened the glovebox and grabbed the few belongings he cared about.

A burner phone.

An envelope with five hundred dollar bills in it.

A scrap of paper with a phone number he'd never used.

He glanced at the duffel bag that had belonged to the nutjob.

It was still on the floorboard on the passenger side where the nutjob had thrown it. The thing was dirty and stained and might have been olive green in a previous life.

Danny needed to get out of here. Find a drugstore where he could buy some supplies to wrap up his leg. But he was curious.

He lifted the duffel onto the passenger seat. A breeze kicked up some of the garbage that had accumulated at the side of the building. A stained paper menu blew in through the empty passenger door followed by a fast-food wrapper.

Danny unzipped the duffel and looked inside.

Cash.

Not a huge haul. Nothing rubber banded together. Just wads of paper bills and some coins at the bottom.

And a pepperoni stick, the kind sold at counters in convenience stores everywhere.

Danny laughed.

The nutjob had robbed a convenience store, but he didn't have a getaway car. So he'd decided to co-opt Danny's.

Danny laughed harder.

Bad choice, dickhead.

He grabbed the pepperoni stick and zipped up the duffel bag.

When he walked away from his ride, he had the duffel bag slung over his shoulder. There was enough cash inside to buy himself a bus ticket. He wouldn't have to touch his own cash. First he'd have to fix up his leg and buy himself a new pair of jeans.

He might even call the number on the piece of paper.

The woman who'd written her number on that piece of paper was someone he'd met at the halfway house where he'd lived in the first couple months after he got out of prison. She hadn't called him sweet. She didn't have red hair and she'd never had an opportunity to tell him he was hung like a horse. But she'd been nice. He hadn't needed to be crazy with her.

For the first time in his life, he'd been able to be himself.

He'd even thought about telling her his biggest secret. That he wasn't really crazy like people said.

He wasn't. He just liked to laugh.

He unwrapped the pepperoni stick and took a bite.

It wasn't great.

But one thing was certain.

It tasted a damn sight better than the worm.

THE GODDESS AND THE
MAD FRIAR

REBECCA BUCHANAN

THE GODDESS AND THE MAD FRIAR

REBECCA BUCHANAN

L*ittle is known about this band of revolutionaries, though they would have collectively objected to the term revolutionary. They saw themselves as preservationists, as the spiritual descendants of the great philosophers, poets, and artists of the classical world, dedicated to the arts of mind, soul, and beauty. Most of their names have been lost, and the ultimate fate of only one is known, but even that has been called into question. What is known with absolute certainty is that the world owes them a debt that can never be repaid ....* **Lost to the Fire: On the Destruction of Culture and the Culture of Destruction** by Dr. H.C. Roberts

"I swear by the Virgin's holy tits, Bonino, if we have to stop one more time so you can piss, I'll leave you behind and you can *walk* the rest of the way to Florence!"

As Nencio's irritated shout rang in her ears, Riguardatta sighed and rolled her eyes towards the heavens, praying to that same Virgin — and a few others — for patience. Patience and strength. Patience and strength and a dignified tongue.

Balanced on the edge of the wagon seat, Nencio leaned around her so he could continue to glare at Bonino. He gripped the reins too tightly. Horses would have pranced in agitation; the pair of donkeys just ignored Nencio and his undignified tongue to munch on the late winter flowers that grew along the sides of the road: bright red carnations, frilly purple irises, burnt yellow calendulas.

She took that as a sign, a blessing. Beauty marking their path.

Or something. Sappho would have said it better, and she was certainly no Sappho.

Nencio opened his mouth to yell again.

She clapped her hand over his lips, earning herself a glare that she ignored as adroitly as the donkeys did everything that bored them.

"Bonino?" she called out.

He was only twenty feet away. Though he was crouched behind a hawthorn tree, she had a clear view of his pale bottom and legs. He half-turned his head to peer at her around the trunk.

"Bonino, darling, we really must arrive in Florence before the midday bells."

He frowned. "One cannot hurry art."

Nencio knocked her hand to the side and shouted. "You're *pissing*. There's nothing artistic about it!"

Bonino sniffed. "Well, maybe not the way *you* do it."

Nencio sucked in an offended breath. She could see the ugly retort forming on his lips.

No. There would be no patience or dignified tongue courtesy of the Virgin and the virgins this day.

"Bonino!" she snarled. "Pull up your pants and get back in the wagon! Now!"

He thrust out his lower lip in a pout, but complied. He hopped awkwardly through the grass, tying his pants, smoothing his knee-length shirt back into place, and straightening the laces on his vest. He even tapped the dirt from his boots before settling onto the back of the wagon again.

At least Riguardatta assumed he was back on the wagon. It creaked slightly with the change in weight, but she couldn't see him over the barrels and crates and bags of dried meats, onions, garlic, turnips, and carrots.

Peasant food.

A useful lie. One that would hopefully gain them entrance to Florence.

Another lie would have to get them out.

Nencio snapped the reins. The donkeys flicked their ears, glanced at one another, and decided to walk.

One lie at a time.

As the wagon rolled forward, Riguardatta pulled her shawl higher over her shoulders, straightened her braided hair, and tucked her heavy skirt around her legs. Far down the road, beyond the forest and hills, Florence glittered in the morning light and mist.

From the center of the city, a column of thick black smoke rose into the air, looming, spreading, threatening to block out the sun.

Farms large and small, villas vast and modest lined the road, interspersed with creaking vineyards and arbors of sleeping fruit trees. Here and there, a shepherd cajoled herds of ornery sheep and goats out of their pens to graze on old grass, or a huddle of laborers wandered a field, kicking at the dirt, poking at the ground with their spades and hoes. Winter vegetables had already been harvested. In a few weeks, God and the Virgin willing, spring planting could begin.

It was said that Botticelli, the master artist himself, had lived in one of those villas for a time, playing at being a farmer. God had granted him a gift: to create such beauty as to make men weep. And he had squandered it, burning dozens of his works under the influence of the mad friar.

It was unlikely he would set brush to canvas again in his remaining years. And, if he did, Riguardatta doubted that his work would ever again capture that essence of divine beauty.

The Muse did not appreciate being cast aside.

As they drew closer to Florence, the fields and vineyards gave way to clumps of cottages, and the road that had been nearly empty began to fill. Other wagons loaded down with barrels and crates, and horses carrying mercenaries and merchants, and beggars and pilgrims.

So many pilgrims. Chanting their prayers, weeping their prayers, crawling on their knees.

And the members of too many holy orders to count, distinguishable only by the colors and fabric of their frocks and the cut of their hair. Among them — frustratingly, ominously — were the Piagnoni. The Wailers. Thugs in holy robes. Completely devoted to the mad friar and his cause, they patrolled the roads leading to and from Florence, and the roads and alleys and rooftops of the city itself, hunting for anything the friar had deemed *a vanity*.

Paintings, sculptures, collections of poetry, musical instruments, cosmetics, mirrors. Even playing cards. Bonino had been quite put out when informed that he would have to leave behind his favorite deck.

Though Riguardatta suspected he had the cards secreted on his person somewhere.

"Eyes down, dear wife," Nencio muttered beside her. "Don't give the thugs a reason to stop us."

She twisted her lips, eyes on her lap. "Remind me again why I'm married to you, and not Bonino?"

THE GODDESS AND THE MAD FRIAR

With her gaze unfocused, she could see a clump of Piagnoni moving through the crowd to grab the reins of a horse. The mare pranced in alarm and the merchant riding the horse shouted in surprise, then immediately quieted. He said nothing as the Piagnoni pulled the bags from his saddle to spill the contents all over the road. They pawed through the clothing, dried food, rolls of vellum, and books. Grinning, one of the Piagnoni finally lifted a small hand mirror in triumph.

Still smiling, he stepped to the side of the road and smashed the mirror on a rock.

Riguardatta saw the merchant hunch his shoulders, the mare continuing to strain against the unfamiliar hand on its reins; but they were quickly lost, absorbed by the crowd.

His back stiff, Nencio finally answered her question. "Because no one would ever believe that your father married you off to *him*. I make a much more plausible bridegroom."

She huffed a laugh under her breath, still watching the crowd from the corners of her eyes. Outwardly, Nencio certainly made a more appealing husband, but in reality he would make for a lonely marriage bed.

But that was a truth she would share with no one.

At the back of the wagon, Bonino began to sing. A humble hymn, not one of his usual soaring ballads. A quiet tune meant to reassure the Piagnoni that this little wagon was of no consequence; just more poor farmers come to deliver the last of their humble harvest to the hungry city.

Within moments, the merchants, soldiers, beggars, and priests around them had picked up the song. A little girl peered at Riguardatta through a carriage window, shyly mouthing the words. A monk thumped his walking stick, matching the beat, and an old man with most of his teeth missing clapped his hands.

And so they rode into Florence, a city in thrall to a mad friar who would gleefully throw all three of them onto a bonfire if he knew what they planned.

~

Florence had outgrown two sets of walls in the centuries since the first cornerstone of the first building was set down. The guards posted at the third, outermost wall barely paid them any mind at all. They were far too busy dealing with an arrogant (and quite drunk) German mercenary captain and his company of heavily-armed foot soldiers, and casting worried glances at the company of English mercenaries loitering on the opposite side of the road.

The wagon rumbled on, through the gate, Bonino still singing.

Scattered buildings on this side of the wall, and small plots of land ready to plant. Scattered vineyards, smaller than those located beyond the outer wall. Chickens squawked and a goat broke free of its pen to join the caravan, its caretaker shouting curses in its wake.

The second gate loomed over them. Through the tunnel, beyond the portcullis and the mass of travelers, Riguardatta could see many more buildings, white- and yellow-walled, with roofs of blue and red tile. Further yet, the inner wall, and the soaring clock tower of the Palazzo Vecchio, and the dark red dome of the Duomo; Brunelleschi's miracle.

And the cloud of black smoke, grim and seething.

The guards at the second gate were a mixture of Florence's own soldiers and the mad friar's Wailers, bland robes belted with plain rope. Much more diligent and attentive then their brethren at the outer gate. They stopped every traveler, whether on foot, on horseback, or in a wagon or carriage. Every bag was searched, contents pawed through or dumped. Silks were seized, pages ripped from books, packets of playing cards scattered and trampled into the ground. Those who protested the confiscation were pulled aside by the Piagnoni to be prayed over — or worse.

As they drew closer to the gate, the donkeys twitching their noses, Riguardatta cast up her own prayer: that Bonino was as clever as he thought and his deck of cards was well and truly hidden.

The wheels of the wagon turned. A guard held up his arm. The wagon creaked to a halt as Nencio pulled back on the reins, the tall stone walls rearing over them. Piagnoni swarmed around the vehicle. They grabbed the reins from Nencio, shoved Bonino to the ground, and scrambled into the back; the wagon shook and creaked alarmingly. The Wailers dug through the barrels, cracked open the crates, tore open the bags. Vegetables flew through the air. One of the donkeys twisted to snatch a turnip tumbling past its hooves.

A Wailer stopped beside Riguardatta, glaring up at her. She kept her eyes on her lap, one hand clasping the shawl around her throat. After a long moment, he turned his attention to Nencio.

"Business?"

Nencio cleared his throat, fidgeting in his seat. His voice shook just a bit. "Produce for the market, sir. We were hoping to hear the holy friar speak, too, if he should so bless us."

A grunt in response, eyes still studying them.

The wagon rocked and creaked again as the Piagnoni climbed down. At a look from the Wailer beside Riguardatta, they shook their heads. He grunted again and waved his arm towards the wall. "Be on your way. The Virgin and all the saints keep you safe and pure in the eyes of our Lord."

Nencio dipped his head. "Amen."

Riguardatta whispered her response, Bonino's hearty "Amen, amen" echoing as the wagon rolled through the tunnel and into Florence.

The midday bells clanged and rang from the tower of the Duomo as Nencio guided the wagon around a corner and down a narrow street. Ahead on the left lay their first stop: a produce seller who would no doubt offer them far less than the value of their onions, garlic, turnips, and carrots. Nencio, of course, would humbly accept the offer. As an ignorant peasant, he could not possibly know better.

And he would not dare to argue, anyway. They did not want to be unusual, unexpected. Remembered.

Nencio tugged back on the reins, pulling the wagon to a halt. The donkeys snapped their ears, twisting their noses in irritation. They did not like the noise and smells of the city, and Riguardatta could not blame them. This work was valuable, necessary, holy even, but she would be grateful when they returned to the Villa Stella dell'Alba, and their fellow thieves and heretics, and the treasures they had made safe.

Bonino bounced off the back, skipping around the wagon to grin and wave at her. Playing the fool. She smiled at him indulgently, climbing down to join him as the produce seller stepped out of his shop. Narrow-eyed and blustery, he ogled the vegetables; he could sell them for a tidy profit in a city as hungry as Florence.

Nencio turned towards her with an irritated frown. "Sylvia, take the idiot and fetch that cloth for your sister while I speak with the good signore."

Riguardatta dipped her head, looped her elbow through Bonino's arm, and led him down the street.

Bonino grinned, waving at the produce merchant.

Just another dumb peasant.

She could hear Nencio apologizing for his brother's behavior. Not respectful enough for a man such as this fine merchant.

And on and on it would go, until Nencio had succeeded in selling off the entire load of onions, garlic, turnips, and carrots. Even the barrels and crates and bags. Nencio would ride away with a pittance, leaving him only an empty wagon.

Such a clever merchant.

Riguardatta suppressed another smile, her arm stretching as Bonino stepped around the corner and led her onto a wider, busier street. They moved faster, steps quick, but not running. They were already late, but there were soldiers and gangs and Piagnoni and other ardent followers of the mad friar filling the streets of Florence.

I am no one. I am nothing.

Beggars called out, waving wooden bowls and cups. Monks chanted and paced silently, bare feet dirty. Roving bands of rival Bigi and Arrabbiati lobbed insults at one another from opposite street corners (grabbing their cocks for emphasis), skipped into the road to exchange punches and kicks, and shout their allegiance to either the Medici or the republicans, then stumbled away to find a new corner and new targets. Prostitutes warily eyed potential marks, watching for those who were not as they appeared to be, melting through doorways and closing windows whenever the Piagnoni appeared. The Wailers frowned and glared, moving through the city as they willed. They ripped the fancy silk hat off one woman's head, snarling and berating her for her immodesty; one Wailer tossed a dirty linen cloth back at her and told her to cover herself.

Riguardatta tightened her grasp on her own shawl, pulling it higher over her chest and neck.

The closer they drew to their destination, the more the air tasted of rough ash.

Up one street, down another. Up and back and down, making their slow, circuitous way through the crowds towards their rendezvous point.

At last, nearly an hour after the bells had tolled, they reached the square. Piazza della Signoria, the heart of Florence. The fortress-like Palazzo Vecchio, with its soaring clock tower, bordered one side, while the elegant arches of the Loggia dei Lanzi formed another side of the square. The crowds here were even denser, angrier, louder. Shouting, cheering, circling the flames.

The bonfire in the center of the piazza roared, alive and hungry. It consumed everything fed to its flames, willingly or otherwise: paintings, clothing, music and the instruments to play it, poems, books of philosophy. Statues of metal melted to slag, while those of ceramic or stone cracked and exploded, sending bits of rock flying into the crowd. The dark cloud roiled and heaved above, spreading, filling the square with the stink of burning paint and silk and vellum.

Riguardatta could only stare, fury and frustration scorching her chest.

A sob caught her attention, dragging her focus away from the massive bonfire. An old man hobbled past her, assisted by a younger woman; their clothing was fine, but their expressions were of raw devastation.

The old man's voice trembled, his eyes glassy. "My liuto. He took my lute. She burned. Oh, she is burned!" He wailed, tearing his fingers through his thinning hair. Snot ran from his nose. "She is burned!"

His knees gave out and he crashed to the ground, half-dragging the young woman with him. She was weeping now, too, face pressed into his shoulder.

Riguardatta's feet had stopped, stuck to the ground.

They wept, and no one reached out to help them.

Something tugged her arm.

A lute.

A fucking *lute*.

The friar truly was mad. To cause this kind of pain, this much grief ... for what?

A harder tug that had her body leaning and one of her feet sliding to keep her balance.

So that Florence could regain its "lost glory"? Take back a few miles of forest and farmland surrendered to rivals? Send the French and Germans fleeing back across the Alps and the English back to their grey little island?

Because surely God would listen to their prayers, fill the city's coffers, and hand them rousing military victories if the people would just ... stop playing lutes.

Stop painting. Stop sculpting. Stop shuffling cards and tossing dice. Stop smiling into mirrors and wrapping their bodies in silk.

The tug turned into a hard yank and she found herself stumbling along, smashed up against Bonino's side by the press of the crowd.

"They are not why we are here." Bonino's words were hard to understand, spoken through gritted teeth. The play-acted fool was gone. His face was harsh. "We cannot help them. We have other duties."

Bonino pushed around a huddle of white-robed monks who had begun to strip down to their waists. Each held a flail of knotted ropes, and the flesh of their backs that Riguardatta glimpsed as she passed was covered in welts and bruises.

She sucked in a breath, choked on the ash from the bonfire, and wrapped the edge of her shawl over her nose and mouth. Her eyes stung.

Bonino was right.

She blinked rapidly, refusing to shed tears of her own. There had been enough weeping in Florence.

Straightening her shoulders, she lengthened her steps to match Bonino's stride. Twisting and turning, edging around lumps of pilgrims, they let the crowd carry them along, gradually making their way around the perimeter of the Piazza della Signoria. Closer and closer to the Loggia dei Lanzi.

Closer.

The mad friar himself stood there, in the shade of that graceful gallery, hood drawn up over his tonsured head, grim-faced Wailers gathered around him in a protective crescent. His sharp eyes remained fixed on the bonfire, taking note of every book, mirror, deck of cards, and other vanity cast into its flames. He never wavered in his focus — and yet Riguardatta could not help the shivers of fear and uncertainty that climbed up and down her body the closer they drew to the shadowed bays.

I am no one. I am nothing.

Was he watching them, the mad friar?

No, of course not. That was silly. They were two figures — poor, unimportant peasants — in a mass of hundreds of people. Not worth noting at all.

Closer and closer, moving with the crowd. Close enough for her to see the sweat that beaded along the edges of the mad friar's face.

His head turned, his gaze sweeping across the mass of humanity. For just a moment, his eyes settled on Riguardatta.

Even a moment was too long.

Dirty. She felt filthy. Condemned. Corrupted and unworthy. Desperate to be clean, to be saved.

She blinked, dropped her head. Shuddered, forcing the feelings away.

No wonder the friar had won so many to his cause.

Riguardatta wished she had the heart of an assassin, not a thief. A knife, an arrow to the throat, a bolt to the chest. How much pain could she spare the world, how many treasures could she save, for just his life?

And then his head turned away, his eyes touching others, studying them, reviling them.

Finally, her ears ringing, her nose prickling, they reached the low wall and soarings columns of the Loggia. They squeezed through the mass of humanity that chanted for the mad friar, or screamed at him in frustration, or just gawked and whispered. Following the line of the low wall far to the left and around the corner, there, in the shade of a soaring stone column, they found Fra Tommaso.

At least that was the name they had been given.

He sat on the hard stone, wooden bowl at his knees, a staff leaning against the wall beside him. A thin, plain Psalter bound in blue leather lay open in his lap. He read aloud, lips moving, though she could not hear the words over the chants and screams of the crowd. Only when she bent to drop a lira into his bowl — two sides of the coin subtly shaved to give it a peculiar and unique shape — could she make out the specific words.

... gloria tua et decore tuo decore tuo prospere ascende propter veritatem et mansuetudinem iustitiae ...

Bonino nodded solemnly. "And your glory is that you will pass and ride for the sake of truth and righteous humility." When the friar paused, eyebrows raised, Bonino continued, "*Et docebit te terribilia dextera tua.*"

Fra Tommaso tipped forward, bowing from the waist. "And it shall instruct you so that your right hand shall perform terrible things." His eyes quickly flicked left, right, behind them, and back again. He raised his voice slightly as he clambered to his feet, tucking the Psalter and wooden bowl into deep pockets. "Yes, my children. I believe I can counsel you in this time of need. Come."

Staff in hand, he turned, making his way towards the near edge of the Piazza della Signoria. Away from the bonfire and the mad crowds and the mad friar who watched over it all, zealous and sharp-eyed.

"I was told there would be three of you." Tommaso's staff clacked against the street. His head moved constantly, side to side, up and down, his eyes seeming to take in everything all at once: see, analyze, dismiss; see, analyze, dismiss.

Riguardatta wondered if he had once been a soldier or mercenary; someone trained to grasp the entirety of a scene down to the smallest detail with only a quick glance.

"There are," Bonino answered. His hold on her arm had loosened since they left the heart of Florence. There were still many people in the streets, but they could move — and speak — somewhat more openly. "Our compatriot awaits us near the statue of Santo Cristoforo."

Fra Tommaso snorted. He sounded simultaneously amused and annoyed. "A logical, if obvious, choice. Through here."

He led them down a short alley and beyond a narrow door, its blue paint clinging to the wood in thin stripes and flakes. Tommaso closed the door behind them, then set aside his staff and carefully placed a metal rod across the door's width. The rod thunked as it slid into brackets on either side of the frame.

Tommaso dusted off his hands and made for a tall wooden armoire along one wall. Aside from a narrow bed and a single table and chair, it was the only furniture in the small room. "We can speak freely here, but we haven't much time. She has become suspicious of her father. He may know what she plans, and he likely does not approve."

Riguardatta felt her eyebrows jump in question. "She?"

Tommaso swung open the armoire, revealing a nearly empty interior. He pressed his hand against a slat of wood in the back, and another piece of wood in the bottom popped up.

"You will see," he answered vaguely.

Lifting the slat out of the way, he quickly removed two more pieces of wood. Reaching into the hidden storage space, he pulled out three hooded monks' robes. "We will only need two of these now, yes? I have sandals, as well. Hopefully they will all fit." Tommaso held one up to Riguardatta.

She nodded silently, took the clothing, and looked around. Taking in the tiny space, she sighed and flapped a hand at the armoire. "May I?"

The corner of Fra Tommaso's mouth twitched. He dumped the extra robe back in the hole, restored the slats to their place, and waved her to enter.

Stepping up into the armoire, she swung the doors almost closed. The crack let in enough light for her to see what she was doing, and to catch hints of movement out in the room.

Bonino's boots thudded onto the chair, followed by his vest and shirt. Clothing rustled as he wrestled with the monk's robe, pulling it over his head. She caught the flap of a sleeve, even as she tugged off her shawl and dress. Her elbow banged into the back of the armoire. Her knee hit the door and she swore, catching it before it could swing open.

Bonino's voice was muffled. "So what brings you to once-fair Florence, Fra Tommaso?"

The other man grunted. Riguardatta caught a sliver of him as he gathered up Bonino's clothing from the chair. "Aristotéles," Tommaso answered. "I had the good fortune to serve in a monastery where a palimpsest of Aristotle's *De Virtutibus et Vitiis Libellus* was found. Heh. Partly hidden under a hagiography of Santo Columba, appropriately. My mind was cracked open." Tommaso paused. He rolled his shoulders, seeming to throw off a weight. "I became quite a nuisance after that. The abbot took great pleasure in punishing me for my questions. So I left."

A shrug, a small smile.

Riguardatta lost sight of Tommaso for a moment as she tugged the robe over her head. When she pushed the door open and stepped back into the tiny room, she found Bonino also dressed, pulling on a worn pair of sandals.

Tommaso nodded when he saw her, eyes narrowed. "That will do. Though the hair, I'm afraid, will not do at all."

Riguardatta held out her bundle of clothes to him, then tugged her hair loose from its braid. "You have a knife?"

She had sacrificed much more than her hair in the past, and no doubt she would do so again.

~

Nencio was waiting for them near the statue of Santo Cristoforo. It was an ugly piece of marble with disproportionate arms and a weirdly bent knee. The Christ Child sitting astride the saint's shoulders looked to be a shrunken adult rather than a toddler.

No wonder Florentines hurried past it, rather than offering a prayer and a coin.

Riguardatta shifted the hood of her robe. The fabric was scratchy against her freshly-shorn head. Only stubble remained. And the sandals were slightly too big, slapping against the stones. She skipped to keep up with Bonino and Fra Tommaso as they approached Nencio, who was quietly feeding a handful of carrots to the donkeys. The animals nipped at his fingers, impatient and ever hungry.

Tommaso made a show of hiring Nencio. They haggled, came to an agreement, coins were exchanged, and they were on their way.

Fra Tommaso led them further and further from the center of Florence; away from the stink and ash of the bonfire. Riguardatta only knew where they were, vaguely, by the occasional glimpse of the red brick dome of the Duomo down streets and over tiled roofs.

And then he motioned for them to stop. The wagon creaked. Nencio remained in the seat, reins loose in his hands. He looked around, wide-eyed, like a peasant awestruck by the height and grandeur of the buildings.

Though this was hardly a grand building. The walls needed to be patched and there were tiles missing from the roof. Wide double doors on the ground floor had been flung open to reveal a goldsmith's shop. Pots of hardy herbs clustered around the front door; one of the donkeys stretched its head towards the nearest pot, sniffing hopefully. Laundry hung from the windows above, and Riguardatta could hear children chattering.

A face appeared in a window on the third floor. The woman leaned out, her messy reddish-gold hair dancing, waved to Fra Tommaso, and disappeared.

Tommaso deftly moving around the pots of herbs and whacked his stick against the door. It opened to reveal a sour-faced man with thinning yellow hair and pieces of a mustache and beard clinging to his face.

The man's nose wrinkled. "You are here to offer my daughter prayers and condolences again, Fra?"

Tommaso half-bowed. "I come to offer comfort and good news, Signore Filipepi." He waved a hand towards Bonino and Riguardatta, hoods still half-hiding their faces, and the wagon where Nencio waited. "These holy men have consented to escort Signore de Fiedricis' body to the church of Santa Lucia in Arezzo, that he might be laid to rest beside his parents and grandfather."

A slightly breathless voice echoed out of the room behind Signore Filipepi. "Oh, thank the Virgin and the virgin martyr, Santa Lucia." The woman Riguardatta had seen in the window pushed her way past Filipepi. Tears shimmered at the corners of her eyes. One hand grasped the frame of the door, while the other rested on her swollen belly. "My prayers have been answered. Come. This way, please. We have my husband — the Virgin watch over him — laid out in the cellar. Come. Please."

Her hands flapped as she turned away, still babbling.

Riguardatta caught the shadows of old bruises on her arms as her sleeves tumbled up and down.

Fra Tommaso half-bowed again to Signore Filipepi, who grimaced and stepped away, allowing them entrance. Tommaso motioned for Nencio to remain with the wagon; the latter awkwardly hopped to the ground, bobbing his head and continuing to gape.

The woman, who could only be Signora de Fiedrici, led them across a room stuffed with furniture, goldsmithing tools, half-finished weaving projects, incomplete canvases, bits of paint-stained cloth, cups of brushes, and more; the cluttered, disorganized mess of a genius who had been abandoned by his muse. On the far side, the Signora yanked open a heavy wooden door and waddled down a set of stairs. The pale light from below must have provided just enough illumination to keep her from falling or she knew those stairs by heart.

Her voice echoed back up. "Close the door behind you, please. We must keep the cellar cool."

As she moved down the stairs, Riguardatta reached back for the handle. She caught a glimpse of Signore Filipepi, his arms crossed, glaring at them in suspicion. Dipping her head, expression serene, she pulled the door closed and carefully descended to the cellar.

The space was almost as large as the room above. Shelves filled with pots lined the walls, and bundles of herbs, onions, and garlic hung from the ceiling. A pile of white cloths sat to one side and there, in the middle of the cellar, lay a human form draped in a white sheet.

By the smell of him, he had only been dead for a few days.

Riguardatta frowned. Word had arrived at Villa Stella dell'Alba six days ago that some of the Master's works had been rescued and needed to be secreted from the city. Yet Signore de Fiedrici had died ... three days prior, perhaps...?

Riguardatta clasped her hands inside the wide sleeves of the robe and cleared her throat. "My condolences on the passing of your husband, Signora."

The other woman paused, the hells of her hands pressed to her lower back. She tilted her head, holding Riguardatta's gaze. "A brief illness. God was merciful and spared him much suffering."

"... Indeed."

A short silence filled the cellar.

"I am not certain how much time we have." Signora de Fiedrici turned brusquely and moved across the room, ignoring her husband's corpse. She reached for a pot on one of the far shelves. "Help me with these."

Bonino hurried over, pulling out one pot after another and setting them on the ground as the Signora continued. "My uncle left not long before you arrived. He took a dozen of his paintings with him." Her jaw clenched. "Sacrifices for the bonfire. His studio has been chaotic, of late. He has not noticed yet that these are missing, but he will soon."

Bonino finished clearing the pots. The Signora reached around him, her fingers digging to tug loose a stone from the cellar wall. It thudded onto the shelf. A moment later she stepped back, holding a stiff, waxed cloth tube. Untying the top, she pulled out a roll of canvas.

"Just these three," Signora de Fiedrici said. "I wish I could have saved more."

With a flick of her wrists, Signora de Fiedrici unrolled the canvas.

"This is what you will be saving from the flames."

Riguardatta's mouth dropped open and she gaped, stunned.

A master artist blessed by the Muse. There was no doubt.

The painting was life-size, but incomplete. Minerva stood in the center, nude, one hip canted to the side as she took a step forward. Hair the color of night tumbled down her back and over one shoulder and across her hips. A pillar to one side supported her shield and spear, and her shining silver armor. Medusa glared horribly from the breastplate, tongue lolling.

The goddess' hands were raised, holding her helmet above her head. Was she putting it on? Or taking it off?

Eyes an intense and otherworldly grey stared out at Riguardatta. Studying. Considering. But not condemning. No. Welcoming. Inviting Riguardatta — inviting everyone — to accept the gifts of holy wisdom.

With her attention fixed on the goddess, it took Riguardatta several long moments to notice that there were more figures in the background. Unfinished, though; only charcoal outlines, not fully realized. To one side, Vulcan with his hammer. To the other, Mercury with his caduceus.

Wisdom attended by the incarnations of industry, creativity, and communication.

Fitting. And, somehow, their ghostly appearance focused the eye and mind even more firmly on Minerva.

Riguardatta suddenly realized that she had been holding her breath and inhaled sharply. The stink of decay filled her lungs. She grimaced, her mind wrenched back to the mission at hand.

Bonino was speaking. "And these other two?" He held up the smaller canvases that had been tucked inside the larger painting. One in dusky rose, dull gold, and evergreen; the other in bright, brilliant reds and blues and yellows.

"The Three Graces." The Signora took the first gently, holding it against the top edge of the painting of Minerva. "And the Virgin with the Spirit of Florence." The second was tucked atop the first and the Signora carefully, reverently rolled the canvases back into a tube and then tucked them inside the waxed cloth.

She looked at them each in turn. "Now, who wants to help me wrap up the corpse?"

They tucked the tube with the Master's treasures underneath the body, right along the line of his spine and legs. They packed extra cloth on either side, evening out the corpse and taking its weight off the cloth tube, then wrapped the death shroud round and round. The dead man flopped ungainly as they worked, flesh sunken. Riguardatta breathed through her mouth, quick and shallow, pausing now and then to turn her face into her sleeve.

By the time they finished, the late Signore de Fiedrici looked as though he had eaten quite well in life. Or he had bloated in death. Not disproportionately large, but Riguardatta still wrinkled her nose in concern.

Perhaps the smell would help dissuade the gate guards from looking too closely.

Fra Tommaso fetched a long piece of wood that might have been a shelf at some point, and they hefted the body onto it.

With one last look at one another, and a firm nod, Riguardatta and Bonino lifted the wooden plank. Fra Tommaso led the way, softly chanting prayers for the soul of the deceased as he climbed the stairs. Signora de Fiedrici came last, sniffling and scrubbing at her cheeks as tears tumbled from her eyes.

The main room was empty, but Signore Filipepi had not gone far. He was outside, face to face with Nencio. The latter stood beside the wagon with hunched shoulders, twisting his hat in his hands, answering the elder man's questions in trembling monosyllables.

As they emerged from the house, the Signore turned towards them, his mouth pulled into a disapproving grimace. With Filipepi's attention diverted, Riguardatta caught the expression Nencio quickly directed towards her and Bonino — *Caution. Be careful.*

"I do wish you would reconsider, Foscharina." Signore Filipepi followed them around to the back of the wagon.

"Mariano can be buried in chiesa di Ognissanti next to my parents."

The Signora shook her head, still weeping. "No, Papa. It was my husband's fervent wish to be buried with his own family in Arezzo. You know this."

But the elder man wasn't really listening. Riguardatta kept her head down and her gaze averted as she and Bonino slid the plank and body into the wagon. But, from the corner of her eyes, she could see the way he was studying all of them. His forehead wrinkled in suspicion. He knew something was wrong, something was different....

She dropped down onto her knees, blocking his view of the corpse as best she could, and clasped her hands in prayer. She moved her lips, silently reciting the Padre Nostro as Nencio climbed into the front seat. The wagon groaned, Bonino joining him a moment later.

Fra Tommaso moved to stand in front of Signore Filipepi. "We must be on our way, Signore. God protect you. And you, Signora. May the Virgin bring you comfort in your time of loss."

Signora de Fiedrici sniffled again, nodding silently. She lifted her hand to wipe away her tears, and Riguardatta could see the bruises on her arms even more clearly.

With a final nod of his head, Fra Tommaso moved up to stand beside the donkeys. Nencio flicked the reins. The donkeys twitched their ears, looked around for food, didn't see anything tasty within reach, and decided to walk.

Riguardatta could feel the Signore and Signora watching them as the wagon made its way down the street, but she did not dare to look up. The wood was hard beneath her knees, the vehicle jostling over ruts in the street.

Finally they rounded a corner, joining the denser crowds on a wider street, and the grieving widow and her father were out of sight. Fra Tommaso adjusted his stride, moving back so that he walked beside Nencio and Bonino. He said something

Riguardatta could not hear. The other two men nodded. As they approached the next intersection, people hollering to one another and cursing and haggling, Fra Tommaso stopped. When Riguardatta, at the rear of the wagon, reached him, he clasped the frame and followed along for a few more steps.

"I leave you here," he said. "You have supplies waiting for you on the road?"

She nodded. "Yes."

"Good. I suggest you change your clothes outside the city as soon as possible." He raised an eyebrow at the corpse. "And find a river to dump that in. I did not like the way Signore Filipepi was watching us."

"Nor I. And what of you?"

"They did not see me entering the city. They will not see me leaving. At least, not *this* me." He smiled up at her. "It has been an honor. God grant you the wisdom and strength to do what must be done."

"And you."

He turned away. The wagon heaved around the corner and through the intersection. Within moments, Fra Tommaso was lost to the crowd.

It took them hours to reach the south-eastern gate. The sun had already slipped behind the Duomo, casting the dome's shadow across the city. The ash of the bonfire hung low in the sky, giving the late afternoon light a haunting, reddish hue.

Piagnoni continued to patrol the streets. Riguardatta could only watch, mute, as they turned over one merchant's cart, spilling crates of food and pots of oil. They dragged a well-dressed man from his horse, ripping and cutting the fine silks and furs from his body. They surrounded a prostitute, knocked her to the ground, spat on her and screamed at her to repent.

Nencio flicked the reins. The donkeys trotted faster.

They reached the Arno River, the stone bridge arcing beneath them. They squeezed past a carriage holding a beautiful lady and her dogs. Pedestrians snarled at them for taking up too much room, for blocking the way. Nencio just smiled stupidly and tipped his hat.

Shouts ahead, and then violent screams.

Rival mobs of republican Arrabbiati and Bigi, chanting their loyalty to the Medici, swarmed one another right in the middle of the bridge. Riguardatta grabbed the side of the wagon as the crowd surged, moving back and forth. Someone shrieked and tumbled over the low wall, into the churning river below. She could see cudgels raised in the air. Knives flashed red. The wagon lurched. Rocks flew, cracking skulls.

Riguardatta flattened herself against the floor of the vehicle. The wood smelled faintly of turnips. The corpse shifted as the wagon lurched again, sliding against her back. Something made a squishing sound. She could feel wetness welling up through the shroud to dampen her robes.

She tried not to gag.

More shouting. Another shriek and a splash.

Feet thundered over the stone. The crowd heaved, parting. Riguardatta peered over the frame of the wagon as Piagnoni surged around them, a horde of the grim-faced thugs racing to quell the battle.

Although apparently not in the way they had intended. As soon as the Bigi and Arrabbiati saw the Wailers, they turned from one another and fell on the Piagnoni. Bones broke, bodies tumbled, blood splattered the stone.

Bonino twisted around in the seat. "Cover the body!" he yelled.

Grimacing, Riguardatta curled over the corpse, doing her best to hold it in place without touching it. She dug her fingers and toes into the floor as the wagon pitched forward, following the horde of Piagnoni. A rock crashed down beside her hand. Another struck her hard on her hip.

A shriek and a splash.

Wood cracked. Bone cracked. Blood splattered her back and the floor of the wagon. The donkeys stumbled forward, the battle around them so loud that Riguardatta's ears rang.

And then they were through, joining the flood of pedestrians and horses that were fleeing the bloodshed, making for the relative safety of the far shore of the Arno. The road branched there, splitting into three routes. Nencio gripped the reins, pulling hard to force the donkeys around and to the right. Southeast, towards the gate to the road to Arezzo.

Riguardatta lifted her head, looking back. The bridge was in chaos. She could only watch in horror as a body was tossed into the river, falling in bloody silence.

Her ears were still ringing. Only when Bonino reached back and grabbed her shoulder did she realize that he had been speaking.

"Safe?" he was asking.

At least she thought that was the word.

She nodded, then blinked as she came to fully understand his question. She slid one hand under the corpse, grimacing at the odd wet spots; past the pads of cloth; to the tube along the line of the dead man's spine. It felt solid; round, not flattened.

Hopefully the wax would protect the Master's works against any dampness as the body continued to decompose.

Riguardatta looked up and nodded to Bonino. He returned the gesture, looking relieved, and sank back onto the bench.

Riguardatta curled up against the frame of the wagon, facing the body. Her hip hurt. Her toes and fingers ached from gripping the floorboards. And all she could smell was turnips, decay, and the ash of burned beauty raining down from the sky.

The first gate. The inner wall of Florence loomed over them. There were fewer travelers now then there had been when they entered the city through the north gate earlier in the day. The roads were dangerous at any time, but even more so at night, and the sky was rapidly growing dark. The later they set out, the more attention they would attract. They needed to get out beyond the third wall, beyond the city, and quickly.

Riguardatta crouched behind the bench, hood up over her head, watching between Nencio and Bonino as the gate drew closer and closer. Standing torches burned on all sides, and more rested in brackets screwed to the stone wall. In that flickering light, she watched the short line of carriages, wagons, and travelers on foot move closer and closer to the gate.

A wagon passed through. Then a couple of women pushing handcarts.

One lie had gotten them into the city.

A second wagon was stopped, inspected, and waved on.

Another lie would have to get them safely out again.

Closer. Just a carriage, a handful of pedestrians, and one man with a donkey stood in their path.

The carriage pulled up the gate, one of the city's soldiers raising a hand for it to stop while a Wailer moved around the vehicle, his eyes narrowed. A passenger inside poked his head through the window. He spoke rapidly to the soldier, his words darting and lilting with a Venetian accent; demanding that he be allowed through the gate. The soldier just listened. The Venetian disappeared back inside his carriage, his head and one hand bobbing out again a moment later. Gold flashed, and coins tumbled through the air into the soldier's waiting hand.

The soldier grinned.

Then he reached out, tore open the door, and dragged the Venetian from the carriage. The man cried out in surprise as he tumbled across the ground. The pedestrians whimpered and backpedaled towards the far edge of the road. Wailers surrounded the carriage and, within moments, it had been dragged off to the side. They pulled out the two other passengers, kicked the boxes off the roof, and attacked the interior of the carriage with knives and hammers. Ripping. Smashing.

Hunting.

Nencio spoke so low that Riguardatta had to strain to hear him. "Bonino, give me your cards."

There was a sigh, but no hesitation as Bonino reached deep inside his robes. "I'm about to lose my third best deck, aren't I?"

A grunt as Nencio held out his hand, low, down between their bodies.

"Try not to lose your life, as well." Bonino set the pack in his hand.

Without looking back, Nencio slipped off the side of the wagon. He grabbed a bag that Riguardatta hadn't even realized was under the bench, tossed it over his shoulder, and ambled past the man with his donkey to slip into the huddle of pedestrians. He blended in perfectly, his head down, gaze averted as the Wailers continued to tear apart the carriage.

Only a handful of guards were left at the gate. As the pedestrians scuttled towards the looming wall, their faces etched with fear and exhaustion, those remaining guards waved some through with barely a glance. But others they stopped; the younger women in particular; hands grabbing, pulling at scarves and hats, pawing through bags.

And then cards flew through the air. Brightly painted, images of half-nude goddesses and nymphs and amazons fluttered through the torchlight.

The guards gaped, mouths open. One grinned and seized a card drifting past his nose. He pulled it close, laughing and nodding. But a second guard, his face hard, spun towards Nencio.

He pointed and yelled, but it was too late. Nencio had bolted. He had dropped his bag and run, feet churning. The guards piled after him, following him along the wall for a short distance before he arced away, skipping down a side street, into the shadows between buildings.

Leaving only one guard, half-crouched as he scrambled to collect every card he could reach — preferably before the Piagnoni realized what had happened, and abandoned the Venetian and his carriage to return to the gate.

The pedestrians scrambled past that one remaining guard, followed by the old man with his donkey, through the gate, through the wall, onto the road on the other side. Walking quickly, casting worried glances behind them.

Bonino slapped the reins. The donkeys, eager to be away from the city, trotted forward, their ears perked. Through the gate, through the wall, to the road on the other side. The Venetian wailed behind them as his carriage was torn apart, piece by piece, and the guard grinned down as his handful of naked goddesses.

The middle gate was manned by guards who took one look at the squishy corpse and beat a hasty retreat. The guards at the outer gate were asleep or huddled around a fire against the oncoming night, leaving only one man to give their wagon a cursory glance.

And then they were outside the walls.

Three hours outside of Florence, full dark settled around them and the road empty of other travelers, they found their stash of supplies. Tattered lepers' rags, worn sandals, and hollowed walking staffs, water skins, and a small bag of dried meat, cheese, and figs. They flipped over the corpse, cut loose the waxed tube, and stuffed it into one of the staffs. The body of

Signore de Fiedrici, squishy and stripped naked, was rolled into the Arno River; the waters quickly carried it away, along with their monks' robes. The wagon was driven deep into the brush and trees that surrounded the road. They unhooked the donkeys, smeared mud on the animals' hides and their own torn clothes, and returned to the road.

They started walking.

An hour later, hooves thundered behind them. Shouting and cursing, a party of Piagnoni and Florentine soldiers drove past them. One hit Bonino in the head with the flat of his sword, sending him sprawling.

Riguardatta knelt at his side, waiting to speak until the riders had climbed up a hill and out of sight. "It appears Fra Tommaso was correct. Hopefully Signore Filipepi has not taken his suspicions out on his daughter."

She wondered if he had told his brother, the Master himself, that his own family may have conspired to save some of his work from the flames.

Shaking her head, she clasped Bonino's arm. "Can you keep walking?"

Bonino groaned, one hand pressed to his skull. "That was extremely unpleasant." He stumbled to his feet, dragging on the reins. The donkeys grunted unhappily. "Only another hour. Another hour, and we can rest."

They kept walking. The moon rose high, and then higher. A priest walking from the other direction gave them a wide berth, covering his mouth with his sleeve. Exhaustion settled into Riguardatta's limbs, making her feet drag. She tripped once, and then again.

She was almost too tired to see the rocks when they finally arrived.

The tumble of boulders made a natural rest site, large enough to create a shallow cave. Clusters of carnations, frilly irises, and burnt yellow calendulas grew in the shadow of the rocks. A fire burned there, other travelers already huddled inside. The guard they had set to watch stood, hand on his sword. He pointed around, up and behind the boulders, away from the fire and the other travelers.

Riguardatta and Bonino bobbed their heads, pleaded for a single burning stick from the fire, and then hastily retreated. They collected what wood they could find, built their own fire, and settled down on the bare, cold ground.

With Bonino to one side of her and a donkey to the other, Riguardatta fell asleep almost immediately. She dreamt of burning goddesses and playing cards.

They waited at the boulders for two days. Most of the other travelers who stopped to rest ignored them, but a group of nuns returning home from a pilgrimage to the Eternal City shared what food they had, even offering Riguardatta and Bonino extra blankets.

And then, late on the second day, Nencio walked into the camp.

Or limped.

His feet were dirty and bare, and he wore different clothes. One side of his face was swollen, and a nasty cut on his forehead had just barely begun to heal.

Riguardatta hugged him hard. She knew he had been frightened because he hugged her back just as tightly.

Bonino tossed Nencio a water skin, waiting as he dropped down beside the fire and guzzled the bag nearly dry. Eventually, when Nencio tossed the bag back, Bonino flicked a finger towards the other man's wound. "How did that happen?"

Nencio shrugged. "A tile broke."

Riguardatta frowned, reaching into the supply bag to pull

out some cheese and figs. Nencio took them gladly, stuffing his mouth. "A *roof* tile?"

Another shrug as he chewed. "They were very persistent. I finally lost them at the Duomo."

Bonino stared at him. "Do not tell me that you *climbed the Duomo* to get away from the guards?"

"No. I scaled the outside wall of the cathedral, ran across the roof, climbed around the dome, then down the other side."

"At night." Bonino's tone was flat with disbelief.

Another shrug as Nencio stuffed most of a block of cheese into his mouth, then a grin. "You piss artfully. I escape artfully."

Riguardatta snorted a laugh, clapping a hand over her mouth.

Bonino chuckled and reached into his ragged leper's robes. He pulled out a deck of brightly painted cards. "Who's up for a game of ronfa?"

The next day, three lepers and their donkeys could be seen walking the road to Arezzo, tall staffs clutched in their bandage-wrapped hands. A company of Piagnoni and soldiers gave them a wide berth as they returned to Florence, empty-handed, to face the wrath of the mad friar.

[A]uthor's Note: history nerds will note a number of discrepancies in the above tale. For example, Florence is not Florence in Italian, it's Firenze. Sorry, but this is historical fiction, and the average reader's knowledge and lived experience has to be taken into account.

. . .

Also, some of the people in this story are figments of my imagination, while others were quite real. Riguardatta, Nencio, Bonino, Fra Tommaso, and Signora Foscharina de Fiedrici? Sorry. They came out of my head. But, yes, Botticelli created dozens of luminous works of art with mythological, spiritual, and theological themes, and there have been rumors for centuries that he burned some of them himself under Savonarola's influence. As for Savonarola — well, it's not just art and books that were burned in the heart of Florence.]

FROM WATTS

OTIS JOHNSON

CHAPTER 1

"Who killed 'Suspect A'?" Hey, man, I swore I'd take that secret to the grave.

Well, the doctor gave me a week to live, so that's close enough for me.

A lot of people have theories, and those are the conspiracy kind: They say it was rival gangsters; they say it was East Coast rappers, or that it was cops that he pissed off. Some even say it's the motherfucking Illuminati, whatever. And of course, some say it was Brutus, from Brutal Records. As for me, I'm just about gone from this world, and he can't touch me — not from his cell, anyway — so I feel I can finally talk freely.

Nobody can rhyme anymore, not like they used to. My grandson played me some of the new shit they're listening to nowadays, and I had to laugh. The songs are two minutes long, and the rappers all want to kill themselves or take Xanax. I'd never thought I'd miss hardcore, down to earth, rapping about the neighborhood. Times have changed.

The first rap group that actually told it like it was, was 'The Lineup.' Their debut, *From Watts,* was certified triple platinum.

Can you believe the record company remastered it from cassettes the group recorded on a four track? They used to sell tapes right out of Mastermind's trunk. That album changed the whole world.

Almost immediately, the Lineup was dubbed "The World's Most Dangerous Group." Riots started whenever they came to town. "Gangster Lifestyle" and "Dope Dealer" were street anthems, but their biggest hit of all was "All Cops are Bastards," a crossover hit single that hit number one despite being banned on pop radio. *From Watts* should have made every last member of the group millionaires, but fast fame was intoxicating, and nobody was paying attention to their contracts. It was greed that tore apart the Lineup. Everybody was angry and resentful, and the trust that had once bonded them like brothers, was lost.

That was exactly the climate a man like Brutus was born to exploit. Nobody was ready for him. He was an invasive species, the apex predator of the music industry. After the Lineup split up, Brutus swooped in and grabbed the exclusive contracts for Mastermind and Suspect A, the Lineup's producer and lead rapper, respectively. It's long been an industry rumor that he acquired the contracts by dangling their former manager, Meyer Wolfsheim, by his ankles from the top of the Bonaventure hotel.

Brutus was used to getting his way. Standing a shocking six-foot-eight inches tall, and weighing maybe 400 pounds, he was the most physically imposing person I ever encountered. He had hands that could hold a basketball, the way most people held a baseball.

Brutus was always with Black people, and he was accepted as such, but he was at least part-Samoan. It was whispered that he was related to those Samoan wrestlers you'd see on Saturday morning television; that this was the source of his cash flow, and his media instincts. He had brown skin and long, curly hair

— members of the Lineup spent a fortune on activator to get what Brutus had naturally. His arms were covered in tribal tattoos, way more than were popular at the time. He always wore mirrored sunglasses, the shape of which reflected a squished rendition of your own face whenever you talked to him.

Can you imagine interviewing for a job with this monster?

After the first Desert Storm, I demobilized and was back on the street, working as a security guard at a mall in Beverly Hills. It was a fun gig, but the pay was atrocious. I'd get wired at the new Starbucks, and flirt with women I met on the job. I got to talk to celebrities every day — David Duchovny, Joe Pesci, Uma Thurman.

One day, I spotted Suspect A, or Alonzo, as I knew him later, walking around alone. You'd think he would have had an entourage, but he was solo. Maybe he was just getting away from everyone. He was an insanely popular rapper, but he had a degree of anonymity here in this upscale enclave. I was about to ruin that for him.

"Suspect A!", I shouted, a little louder than I meant to. He looked around, worried, and I tried to disarm him with a smile. I realized I had him at a disadvantage. He was all of five-foot-ten, so I towered over him, and I was wearing a vaguely police-like uniform.

"What up?", I asked, and we slapped hands together.

"Just walking. Sometimes you gotta get away from motherfuckers and think. You know what I mean?" He was surprisingly candid, as if we'd already met.

"I can imagine."

"This what you do? Dress up like a cop and try to bone all these white girls?"

"Whenever I can." We both laughed at that.

"This ain't no job for a brother." He reached into his pocket and handed he a business card. "Brutal Records" was embossed on the front, surrounded by some crazy, tribal tattoo design, like a forest of thorns.

"Go to that address about six on Friday. Fuck your rent-a-cop bullshit. Come get you a real job."

CHAPTER 2

I knew I could do much better than a mall security job, but it was honest labor. I quit the military because my work was getting sketchy and intense. I was a low ranking airman, but once I won the Air Force Small Arms Expert Ribbon, I got pulled for special missions. Instead of joining the invasion, I was escorting intelligence types around Iraq. More than once, I followed Captain Dennis McCurdy as he met with locals in his network, exchanging duffel bags full of cash for the latest intelligence. McCurdy was a cynical asshole. He was a patriot once, but something got twisted up inside of him. His name came up a few times on CNN in the Iran-Contra scandal, but he wasn't brought up on charges.

When my time came, I chose not to reenlist. I needed a break from looking over my shoulder. I could tell the constant ambushes and betrayals were messing with my head, too. I left the service with an 'honorable' and returned home to LA, a city that hadn't waited for me, or anybody else.

After a year in the civilian world, I was struggling to eat and keep the lights on. SoCal Edison really doesn't care if you protected oil fields in Iraq. When Suspect A made his offer, I was close to eviction, so I almost had to take him up.

I wasn't sure what to expect as I walked up to the glass doors of an office building on Wilshire. I gave a wide berth to two young men in green that were shooting dice on the stairs.

The lobby was covered in tasteful marble and there were expensive leather couches and cherrywood desks. A pair of men wearing green, (the colors of the local Dollars gang) were slap-boxing in front of an enthusiastic group of gang members and scantily-clad party girls.

The area reeked of alcohol and marijuana. I nearly left as soon as I smelled the pungent odor, as I was used to random drug testing in the Air Force. They told us secondhand smoke could show up on your test and end your career.

The fighting men saw me and backed up. A woman threw down her joint and stamped it out, while another man shoved a mirror with lines of cocaine into a drawer.

"Good morning, officer," said one of the fighters.

"It's okay, I'm not a cop." I guess to them, I looked like a cop. I'm a lean six-foot-three, 220 pounds, with a clean shaven face and head, handsome mixed-race Black and Asian features. I was looking for a job, so I wore a navy suit with a tie and wingtip shoes. Dressing well is a sign of respect. You get the job you dress for.

"Are you a cop?" asked the other combatant. "If you don't tell me, and you are one, that shit's entrapment."

"I don't think that's true," I said, "but I came here about a job."

"Aw, you want Brutus, then. He in his office. Go on back."

CHAPTER 3

Brutus was a giant behind an equally massive mahogany desk. He sat in an elegant leather-and-oak chair that had clearly been custom-made to handle his weight and frame. He raised his eyebrow above his mirrored sunglasses.

"Shit, they sent you to check up on me? That motherfucker said seventy-two hours." Brutus snorted and wiped powder away from his nose.

What the hell was I getting myself into?

"Suspect A gave me your card," I said. "He said you might have some work for me."

"Oh, shit," said Brutus. "He said he met his future bodyguard. That must be you. Markus, right? You ever done high-profile client detail?"

"You could say that," I said.

"I seen you before," said Brutus, "Where you go to school?"

"Jordan," I said.

"I was in CIF wrestling, with your cousin."

"That's right. You took us to the championship." I said, remembering.

"Did you do sports?"

"Nah, I was in ROTC," I answered.

Brutus laughed.

"You from the neighborhood, though," said Brutus, "You ain't no snitch, right?"

"No, not even under torture."

"You a little square for this crew, but maybe you can keep Suspect A out of trouble. You start today, are you strapped?"

"No, I don't have a weapon."

"We don't got any time for a waiting list." Brutus produced a business card. "Call this number, my boy will set you up." He tossed me the keys to a Cadillac Escalade. "When you got your shit, get SA, and get him to the studio. The Mastermind is waiting to lay down some tracks."

CHAPTER 4

The LA river was really just a stream, with concrete inclines on both sides. Nobody hangs out there, which makes it perfect for shady deals. Red, Brutus' weapons contact, displayed his wares from the back of a van, hidden under a bridge.

Red was a tall, wiry, light-skinned black man, named for his kinky, red hair. He wore a green flannel and jeans. I got the feeling that he was once in the military as well.

He had some choice pieces in there, actually. It was going on Brutus' tab, so I was just getting what I would be comfortable with. Red had brought a whole arsenal: a couple M16 assault rifles, a Desert Eagle, some .45s. I was looking down the sights of a SIG Sauer P229. The Swiss Industrial Group produced precision firearms.

"That's cool for a backup," said Red, "but I could see you with this. Check out this John McClane shit." Red held a Heckler and Koch MP5. "All you looking at is little baby shit." Red laughed, his buttery, crooked teeth showing.

"This is all I need," I said, checking the weapon before I

handed it back. "Just aim and shoot, you don't have to spray shots everywhere."

"Y'all dragged me out of bed to sell a fucking pistol?"

"I'll take some magazines and that vest right there, too. And one of those Maglites."

"I got all this gangster ass shit, and you just want to play cop. Whatever."

CHAPTER 5

I banged on the door of Alonzo's West LA Condo.
"What you want, motherfucker?" A voice came from inside.
"I need Alonzo. I'm supposed to take him to the studio."
"Fuck you, pig!"
"I don't have time for this bullshit!" I yelled. "Don't make me call Brutus!"
Silence from inside. I'd give them a minute to consider what I said.
The door opened, and I walked in to a scene of debauchery. The room smelled of sex and weed. The coffee table was littered with beer bottles, a bong, and a cocaine mirror. Two young Black men and a young woman were on the couch, watching Scarface on a huge TV that must have cost ten thousand dollars in those days.
"I need Alonzo," I announced, clearly and assertively. "Someone get him." I was getting impatient. These losers were sponges. I would have loved having rich friends so I could get wasted and bang hookers all day. At least Alonzo earned his money.

"He ain't here," said the woman.

"Don't tell him shit," said the man next to her.

"Then, do you want to explain to Brutus why Alonzo isn't coming to the studio to record?" I addressed the man directly.

"He in church," said the woman.

"Bullshit," I said. "It's night, and Suspect A doesn't go to church."

"No, *Church*" she said, emphasizing the word derisively and rolling her eyes, while her compatriots laughed. "*Church* is a club."

CHAPTER 6

The First Baptist Church of Christ the Redeemer had fallen on hard times. They survived by renting out their basement to an underground club promoter named Angela "Disco" Jones.

I walked up to the church, looking for tell-tale signs of a club. I could barely sense the throbbing of bass, vibrating underfoot. I saw a well-dressed man out front that had the look of a pastor. He seemed out of place this time of night.

"May I help you?" he asked, with a smile.

"I'm looking for Church."

"Right this way," the man signaled, waving me to an alley next to the church building. Down the alley and some stairs, and I wound up face-to-face with another doorman. He was only a little taller than me, but much heavier.

"Password, please?"

"I'm here for Alonzo."

"Password, please?"

"Brutus sent me. I'm Alonzo's ride to take him to the studio."

The doorman scrutinized me, nodded, and let me in.

Church was like nothing I'd ever seen. Sensuous beats

throbbed as I entered, with ethereal female vocals lilting across trip-hop rhythms. At one end of the room was an elevated stage, on which a woman in a leather nun habit sat in a chair, paddling another woman in a schoolgirl outfit on her bare bottom. Two more leather nuns danced in go-go cages flanking the stage. Huge, stained glass windows depicting sex acts hung suspended in the air. They reflected and refracted the club lights, drenching the floor and dancers in rich jewel tones. Velvet couches in those same jewel tones lined the walls, partitioned off by gossamer curtains, not at all hiding the figures within. The air was thick with sweat and smoke and sex.

I scanned the dance floor, then looked around the sides of the room. I spotted Alonzo with another hip-hop dude, getting lap dances on a couch. Alonzo had a gorgeous Asian woman, and his friend a blonde. As I watched, the Asian lady poured white powder from a small vial on the web between her thumb and forefinger, and lifted it to Alonzo's nose. He snorted deeply.

"Alonzo!"

"Oh, shit, my dude!" Alonzo slurred drunkenly, "Yuki! This my man, uh…"

"Markus."

"Don't worry, baby, he's not a cop!"

"Brutus sent me to get you," I said. "Mastermind is ready to record."

"Fuck that, man. Have you met Yuki?"

"She can come with us."

"That my boy Drunken Master, from Eastern Assassins. He here for a guest spot on the album."

Without looking away from his blonde, Drunken Master fist bumped with Alonzo. Sensing his distraction, the blonde proceeded to grind harder.

I really just wanted to knock Alonzo's ass out and throw him in the car. I was getting a bad feeling about this place. I scanned around to see what bothering me.

I didn't like the look of a dude I saw wearing a Raiders hat and an oversized black jacket, watching the club goers. He had the style of the Los Angeles "Spooks" gang, but his bearing was off, like a military stance. I spotted another on the other side of the room. He was a white man in black with a bandanna. Wrong race for the Spooks. His lips moved as he was talking into his hand.

The hat dude opened his coat, and raised a rifle. I dove for Alonzo, knocking Yuki away and taking Alonzo to the floor. The hat dude fired, and red wounds erupted on Drunken Master and his blonde companion. I rolled and drew, took a beat to line up my sights on the shooter's hat, and squeezed. His hat flew off, revealing a black dot on his forehead as he dropped.

The club erupted into chaos. Amid the screaming and running, I saw four people in black, calmly advancing. They were spread out and moved in formation. This was no good.

Alonzo shouted and drew a Glock pistol. He stood and fired like an idiot, holding his pistol sideways, spraying shots everywhere. His bullets hit one of the stained glass windows, showering the crowd with stained glass fragments.

I grabbed Alonzo's wrist, shook the pistol from his grasp, and dragged him towards the back of the room. Alonzo fell, but slid across the floor on his butt as I ran with him.

One of the assailants was in my path. I must have missed him in my scan. As he raised his rifle, I released Alonzo, managed to grip his weapon, and wrench it away from me. As we struggled for control, I stomped his foot, breaking his instep with my heel. As he fell, I took his carbine away, and fired a short burst into the assailant's torso.

"Come on!" I shouted at Alonzo, getting him on his feet and shoving him ahead of me.

I spotted two of the leather nuns, going over a bar in the back. I followed with Alonzo. We went over and discovered an open trap door. I pushed Alonzo down the hole and followed. I pulled the trap door shut behind us as gunshots erupted above.

We were in some kind of dark tunnel. I heard the clacking of heels as the nuns made their escape.

"Now fucking what?" asked Alonzo. "We can't see shit in here."

I shined a Maglite down the passage, and we made our way to a ladder. We climbed and found our way to the street, not far from the Escalade.

The leather nuns piled into a BMW and peeled out, screeching.

I clicked off the alarm on the key fob, and Alonzo and I pulled away from the church in the SUV.

CHAPTER 7

"Who the hell wants you dead, Alonzo?" I asked, now miles away from the church.

"Spooks. They was in black. It had to be, cause I'm with Dollars."

The Spooks and Dollars were Los Angeles largest gang affiliations. Not like street gangs, but alliances that were composed of smaller gangs across the city. The Spooks wore black, and Raiders paraphernalia. The Dollars wore green and money motifs. They were known rivals.

Towards the end of the LA Riots, the Spooks and Dollars actually declared a truce and there was peace on the streets. The war was back on, inflamed by skirmishes over drug territory, and increasingly violent rhetoric from rappers.

Alonzo pulled a vial from his pocket and poured white powder on the back of his hand.

"Alonzo," I said, "Could you possibly…"

I was interrupted by a loud crunch, as the Escalade was rammed by a black pickup. Cocaine flew everywhere in a white cloud.

We fishtailed, but I kept control as we sped down the street.

Our pursuers followed. I saw a man in black aiming a rifle out of the passenger window. I swerved to make us a difficult target. The shooter missed, making sparks in the road.

"Do you know a safe spot?" I shouted to Alonzo.

"Go left at the stop sign!"

I did.

"Turn right in the alley!"

I did, and sped down an alley between between the backyards of one story houses. The pickup was close.

"Turn right! And go up that driveway!"

I followed Alonzo's directions and we sped up a driveway, avoiding several men in green, standing around in a front yard. We crashed a party, it seemed. As I braked, Alonzo jumped out of the vehicle.

"Yo, Dollars!" yelled Alonzo, "Spooks!"

The pickup pulled up, and the occupants saw Dollars in the front yard, diving into the front bushes and coming up with rifles. The pickup went full reverse, and sped off into the night. The Dollars fired parting shots, sparking off the fleeing vehicle.

CHAPTER 8

Alonzo was treated like a hero by this pack of Dollars. Some of them followed us to the studio to record. If Mastermind didn't like the extra company, he'd have to cope — at least he was getting Alonzo alive, and in one piece.

On the drive to the studio, Alonzo and I had a rare, peaceful moment. He lit up a pungent, cigar-sized joint. I opened the windows.

"Those weren't gang members in the club," I said, remembering their moves, "They were actually trained. Military."

"You don't know these streets. They wanna kill me cause I throw up Dollars," said Alonzo, making a 'D' sign with his fingers.

"I wouldn't go around announcing what happened until we find out more."

We arrived at the studio for Alonzo to record.

The Mastermind laid down a beat. It was all distorted bass and weird, dark synth. Hard hitting, but creepy.

Alonzo, captivating storyteller that he was, rhymed a tall-

tale version of the last night's events. According to these verses, he was attacked by Spooks, and he shot his way out.
"3AM in the club
You know I'm faded
But Alonzo gettin' love
I got these hoes just grinding

M ind on my money
On this Chinese honey
They caught me slippin'
Didn't even see the Spooks creeping

B lap-blap!
They all in black
Motherfucking bastards
Sprayed Drunk Master

I had a gat
And you know I shot back
Pulled out the chrome
And shot three to the dome

A nd now it's on sight
Now it's on sight
If I see your Spook ass
You gonna die tonight."

. . .

Just great, I thought. If he wasn't enough of a target, before, he definitely was one now.

We were all dragged in for questioning, and nobody knew anything. The guys I shot were never found, and I'm assuming that the same ops team that attacked us recovered their bodies. Nobody was ever charged with anything.

The murder of Drunken Master was big news, but the facts got twisted around by the time they got to the street. People said that Alonzo had set him up to die. The bad blood led to East Coast rappers beefing with West Coast rappers, while the Spooks and Dollars conflict also ramped up. News of drive-by shootings and kidnappings dominated the headlines, and the whole city was charged with fear and anger. It was total anarchy.

It was whoever hired the squad that hit Church, that was behind it all. I had to wonder: Who benefited from throwing the city into chaos?

ALEXANDRIA HAS FALLEN

KIM MAY

ALEXANDRIA HAS FALLEN

KIM MAY

Henry Bastone clicked on the video call link. He had mixed feelings about these weekly calls from SIS headquarters in London. While they were the sort of meeting that should have been an email, they were also one of the few times he was able to see and speak to a real person. Henry was the Lord Captain of the SIS Archives. He even had a badge declaring him thus on the back of his wheelchair. He'd made it himself from the lid of a tin of soup but little details like that weren't important.

"Hi Henry," Emilia Steward said with a cheery tone. Her dirty blonde hair was pulled back today and her faux tortoiseshell glasses made her look like an innocent librarian instead of a woman with few scruples when it came to protecting the commonwealth. "How are things at the archives?"

"Still archived." Henry said. "There's only been three hacking attempts this week and none of them got past the first firewall. If they don't step up their game soon I'm tempted to let them through just so I can play with them."

"Henry," Emilia glared. "We've been over this. You can't compromise security because you're bored."

"Just one?" Henry did his best sad puppy impression. It didn't seem to be working because Emilia's glare deepened. "Fine. I'll be good."

"Thank you. Your restraint is appreciated."

"My restraint only lasts until I get bored again. Please tell me you have a big research project or hell, I'll even take an inventory at this point."

"Not quite. An inventory isn't required until next quarter. There are some files that have been approved to be declassified. I'll email you that list when we've finished."

Henry whistled low. "Ooh, who did the royals piss off this time?"

"Surprisingly, no one."

"Ah, the PM needs a smoke screen for an upcoming scandal?"

Emilia narrowed her eyes at Henry. "Something like that."

"Don't give me that look. When something marginally juicy gets declassified, it's usually for one of those two reasons. I don't need to know what's on the list to surmise that much."

"Yes, well," Emilia pushed her glasses up. "I'll be sending that to you soon. I'm afraid that the only other item I have to mention is that today's supply delivery is running a little late. Traffic delay from what the driver said."

Henry nodded. "Barry knows the gate code. He can let himself in whenever he gets here."

"Apparently Barry is out sick. There's a new driver. I don't have a name I'm afraid, but they should have all the necessary verification information at hand."

Henry nodded again. "Standard protocol. Got it."

An email notification popped up on the bottom corner of his screen. "Looks like the de-classification list has arrived. Gimme a sec..." He opened the email and skimmed the identification numbers. Most of what was on the list was so old that they'd only have hard copies. Those could be a challenge.

After the SIS archives were moved to the manor that was internally known as the Chancery House, despite that not being the manor's actual name, many improvements were made to make the estate not only secure but up to code. While every part of the house and cellar were wheelchair accessible, the physical archives were still on rolling shelves. It was difficult to turn the wheel to move each unit and once he did get the aisle he needed open, if the box he needed was on the top shelf, he was out of luck. He did have an assistant but she was on maternity leave for another six months and the head office had yet to send over someone to fill in.

"Will you be sending someone over to help me pull these? Most of the list are physical records."

"We're still looking for someone willing to accept the temporary assignment."

"Did you tell them I don't bite?"

"Why would—"

"I think it might make a difference if they know I haven't become feral during my time in the wilderness. That's all," Henry said with a nonchalant shrug.

Emilia froze, her mouth hanging open. It took her a few seconds to regain her composure. "I'll try that."

"Great." Henry gave a thumbs up.

"I won't keep you any longer. Do let me know if the delivery is missing anything."

Emilia ended the video call without bothering to say goodbye, which was how these calls usually ended. She didn't do it out of a lack of professionalism or patience. She wouldn't have risen in the ranks like she had if that were the case. Best he could figure, it was because his jokes threw her off balance and she wanted to return to her normal staid existence as quickly as possible.

Henry pushed away from the desk and wheeled himself out of his office and to the bedroom down the hall to freshen up. While the charcoal grey jumper he wore was nice enough for a video call, the blue plaid pajama pants were not what he wanted a visitor to see. He wouldn't have even bothered for Barry but a new delivery person deserved to see him in proper trousers. He listened for the gate buzzer while he changed.

Living on site wasn't his favorite part of the job but there were times like the present when it was very convenient. It was also a bit of a godsend after the car accident that took the use of his legs. He was in hospital for so long that he lost his flat. His last handler arranged for him to be transferred to his current role and live on site so he wouldn't have to worry about navigating public transport in a wheelchair.

There hadn't been a single beep from the gate while he changed into khaki slacks so he went back to his office and to the mind numbing task of fulfilling research requests from various departments. All of these requests was for information within the past five years, all of which was in the digital archives. After double checking their credentials to verify it was an authentic request and then sending them a pass code to an internal drive that contained the requested information and nothing else.

A buzzer rang. The jarring sound sent a jolt through him. Henry took a deep breath to calm his heart and pressed the intercom. He pulled up the security camera feed on his main screen. There was a nondescript white van in the long driveway, idling at the gate. He could see the driver's face as he leaned out his open window to get closer to the speaker. They were a young man in their mid twenties with shaggy curly hair and wiry frame. It was hard to tell but it looked like there was someone in the passenger seat. They had a smaller frame. A woman perhaps? *That's definitely a break in protocol.* It could be that they're still in training or being reviewed by a manager, but it was enough to make him wary.

"State your business."

"I've got a delivery," the driver said.

"What's your name and driver number?"

"You've got to be kidding me. It's just a delivery."

"Not kidding. Name and number please, for you and your companion."

The driver didn't answer right away. Instead they turned to their companion. Henry couldn't hear what they said, not even a mumble came through the intercom. They must be whispering. A minute later the driver leaned out the window again.

"Look, I'm already behind schedule. Can't you just let me in so I can unload this and get on with my route before I get in trouble."

"Not my problem. I can sit here all day. I got nowhere to be."

Henry watched the screen, waiting to see what they would do. His gut said he should call for a security team. That this was a breach attempt. But he didn't want to jump to conclusions. *Just breathe. They've got to make their intentions clear. This might be nothing.*

The driver leaned over to the passenger again. It was a more heated exchange this time, more from the passenger than the driver. The driver pointed with his thumb to the road behind them while the passenger emphatically pointed forward.

Henry picked up his phone and typed "Alexandria has fallen" in a text to Eliza. His finger hovered over the send button.

The van backed up in the driveway. Henry watched as it reached the junction with the main road.

Keep going. Keep going. This isn't going to end well if you don't.

Smoke emanated from the rear tires and the van bolted forward. Henry pressed send and watched the monitors.

Henry's phone rang and he picked up before the third note of his ringtone.

"Stop being dramatic."

The van hit the gate. The hinges twisted with a sickening screech that made him shiver. The barred gate itself slid over the hood and onto the roof of the van as it sped into the courtyard.

"What was that?" Eliza exclaimed.

"Does that sound like I'm being dramatic?"

Henry started a video call and centered the gate and courtyard video feed on his screen. Eliza watched with him as the van went up the steps and crashed through the front door.

"Backup is on their way. ETA 20 minutes," Eliza said.

"Twenty? This will probably be over in 10."

"It's rush hour. Even with sirens there's only so much they can do."

"Can't they take a helicopter?"

Eliza shook her head. "Budget cuts."

Henry cursed.

"Hold out as long as you can. It's your call whether or not to go full Alexandria."

Henry nodded and ended the call. He opened the bottom desk drawer. Inside was the Glock 17 and shoulder rig he used during field work. He loaded a new magazine, put both the gun and shoulder rig on his lap, and hurried out of the office.

Henry pushed hard on his wheels to get some speed in the long hallway that led to the foyer. He coasted down the hallway at a swift pace while he put on the shoulder rig and secured his gun in the holster. Thankfully the floors were hardwood. There was no way he'd be able to do this on carpet.

Henry slowed down as he neared the end of the hallway. There was a large landing at the top of the stairs that led down to the foyer. He stopped at the edge of the wall with his chair parallel to the wall and as close to it as the wheels allowed. In order to have the sight line he needed he had to push forward a bit. His chest and head were shielded by the wall but his legs were partially exposed. The carved wood railing gave his legs a little cover. It was more exposed than he liked but it was the best he could do.

Below in the foyer, pieces of the double doors were scattered across the tile floor. The front of the van was past the door frame and both people inside had climbed out. Henry was surprised that not only did it appear that both of them made it through the impacts without any serious injuries but the van's engine was still running. The windshield had more spiderwebs than an abandoned warehouse but it looked like it was still driveable.

The passenger turned out to indeed be a woman. She was a head shorter than the driver with a slim frame and short black hair that was pulled into a pony tail, revealing an undercut in the back and she had a small black nylon backpack slung over one shoulder. Both had a hand gun out, pointed toward the rooms below the landing. The woman had a Ruger of some sort. He couldn't tell what the driver had but he looked uncomfortable holding it. Not surprising since his large hands dwarfed the weapon. He probably couldn't afford anything better suited for him from the neighborhood dealer.

"What now, Ms. Mastermind?" The driver asked.

"It got us in, didn't it?" The passenger said. Her voice was low and husky.

"Yeah, and nearly killed us in the process." The driver rubbed his neck.

"Too bad it didn't. Would've saved me a load of bother," Henry said as he sighted on the driver's thigh. "Since you won't identify yourself, do you mind telling me what you're after?"

The pair looked up and around trying to locate him. The high ceilings in the foyer caused his voice to echo and they were having trouble spotting him. Henry fired. The bullet hit the driver above his right knee. The driver bellowed and fell to the floor, clutching his thigh.

It would have been an easy shot to take him out but killing civilians, even those trespassing on government property, brought on a lot of questioning and paperwork that he'd rather avoid if at all possible. Besides, they needed to know what they were after and how they found out about it in case there was a leak.

The passenger retreated back to the van and hid behind the door she'd left open. She looked through the rolled down window, continuing to search for him. "You really think we're dumb enough to tell you?"

"You were dumb enough to force your way onto a secure facility. It seemed logical to me."

Her eyes widened the moment she spotted him. Henry leaned back as far as his chair would allow. The passenger fired twice. Both shots skimmed the top of the railing and hit the wall on the other side of the landing. Henry took a deep breath to steady himself and leaned forward again. The passenger had taken advantage of the moment and was running for the rooms below the landing.

Henry cursed. One of those rooms was his assistant's office and her computer had full access to the digital archive. All she had to do was get past the log in screen. Henry thrust his Glock into the holster and turned his chair around. He pushed on the wheels harder, propelling himself faster than ever before, racing for the elevator across from his office.

His assistant's office wasn't one of the rooms below the landing. It was further down the hall, closer to the elevator. That gave him a little bit of time to get there; hopefully before the passenger. The thought didn't give him much comfort. He had no idea if she'd locked the door before she went on leave but there was a name placard on the wall so there was no chance the passenger would walk by thinking it was a supply closet.

"This would be a great time to have an assistant," he grumbled, "but no, they had to drag their arses."

Henry had too much momentum to stop in front of the elevator so he pressed the down button as he passed the doors. He stopped his chair as quickly as he could without toppling himself onto the floor. By the time he'd made his way back to the elevator the doors hadn't opened.

"Oh, come on!"

A minute later the doors finally opened. Henry spun his chair around and backed into the elevator, mashing the first floor and door close buttons before he came to a stop. The doors closed at a leisurely pace and the long pause before the motor engaged and started lowering him must have given him a few white hairs. It wasn't fear of losing his job or having to incinerate the archive - Go Full Alexandria as Eliza called it. Every second that passed was another second they had to get past the system's security.

The elevator slowed and crept to a stop. The elevator dinged, making him wince. This had to be the most indiscreet pursuit in the history of His Majesty's Secret Intelligence Service. Henry pointed his gun at the doors.

The doors opened and Henry checked the hall for the passenger. What little of it he could see was clear. He returned his gun to the holster for a moment. Before he left the elevator he paused to listen. Perhaps it was his imagination but there seemed to be a slight shift in the air to his right.

Trusting his instincts, Henry backed his chair to the rear of the elevator. He pushed forward, not letting go until he was bent over. He pulled his gun out one handed and fired, high and to the right.

He heard a second shot a heartbeat after his. Henry braced for the bullet to hit. It never did. However, a loud shout confirmed his instincts were right and he'd at least hit his target. Henry used his free hand to turn his chair in an arc. He kept his gun aimed at the target and let his chair come to a stop. It wasn't until then that he realized that he hadn't shot the passenger.

Leaning against the wall clutching their right shoulder, was the driver. Somehow he'd managed to pull himself together and find the strength to hobble his way here. His gun fell from his limp right hand.

If he's here, where is the passenger?

Henry looked at the door to his assistant's office. It was ajar.

Henry aimed and fired two rounds into the driver's chest. Couldn't have him following, after all. Besides, the gun he'd dropped was still within reach and there was no way for him to kick it out of reach or take it with him. *You did what you had to do to eliminate a risk,* he told himself. It didn't make him feel better about it but it did allow him to steel himself for the next part of this impromptu mission.

Henry returned his Glock to the holster and pushed himself to the office doorway. He could hear typing inside and the whir of the hard drive's fan. Henry pulled out his phone and brought up the control panel for the building's security system and pressed to lock the place down.

The sound of metal grating against the stone facade reverberated throughout the archive as steel grates slid down, barring all of the windows. He couldn't hear the exterior door locks click into place but his screen confirmed that everything was locked tight. The system automatically sent a notification to Eliza about the lock down. She could pass the access code along to the back up team.

"There's no way out and no one to interrupt. Are you sure you don't want to tell me what you're after?"

"What are you going to do if I don't?" she scoffed. "Burn the place down?"

"Actually, yes."

Henry pushed the door the rest of the way open with his chair and held up his phone so she could see the screen. She turned to him and eyed his phone suspiciously.

"Alexandria? You couldn't think of anything more original?"

"Being original isn't part of the job description." Henry brought his pointer finger closer to the activation button which was a fire emoji.

"You're bluffing. You wouldn't set this place ablaze with you still inside."

"You see, that's the funny thing about almost dying. It makes you less afraid to do it again."

"I know."

"I — wait, what?"

The passenger sat in the desk chair and crossed her legs. "I know you almost died last year. My dad was driving the car that hit you."

"And you want proof he was innocent? You could've just bribed a court clerk to get that footage."

She shook her head. "No, I'm looking for proof that he was under orders." She turned back to the computer and typed a few commands into the search algorithm she'd loaded from a thumb drive. "He died from cancer a few months ago. Right before the end he was delirious, thought he was at work, but instead of talking about the office football betting pool or deadlines he kept saying, 'Wasn't my fault. Had to run him over...following orders.'"

Henry's hand fell from the phone screen. The loyalist in him was angered that anyone would divulge details about an operation, even unintentionally. But he also sympathized with her. Deathbed confessions aren't the easiest to hear. There was no way to know how much was true and how much was delirium.

What puzzled him was that she hadn't mentioned a nurse or

doctor trying to convince her to pay him no mind or someone from the home office giving them a debrief with a NDA chaser. There was no hesitance in her expression and movements. Something happened to convince her this was not only true but important enough to risk a life sentence or worse to acquire.

"What made you believe him?"

"Mum. She has no poker face." The algorithm finished its search. A window popped up with a single file. There wasn't a name on the file, but the ID number showed it was from April of last year — the same month the accident that paralyzed him happened. The passenger opened the file and clicked on a video. "When he started saying these things all the blood drained from her face. After the funeral, a bottle of Johnnie Walker and I talked her into sharing what she knew."

The video started to play. It showed a four lane street in London, one he was familiar with. There was a tea shop around the corner he used to frequent. It was late at night and there was only one car, a white Vauxhall Corsa, on the road. The video switched to another camera further down. This view showed a crosswalk at an intersection. In the distance the car's headlights were visible.

A man came into view. He was dressed all in black and walking toward the crosswalk. When the man was nearly at the intersection the car sped up. There was no sound but he could hear in his mind the screech of tires and roar of the engine as it launched toward him.

That's me. This is from that night...

Henry turned his head away. He couldn't watch this any more.

"I haven't figured out which news outlet to send this to but if I can find the man—"

Henry lifted his head. She was looking at him with an expression that was a painful mix of awe and horror.

"Oh my god."

There were so many questions in his mind, spinning around like a merry-go-round. Why was the order issued? He hadn't blown a mission. His record was clean. Why hadn't he overheard whispers about this? Did Eliza know? Was she the one responsible for the order?

Henry dropped his phone in his lap and gripped the arm rests of his wheelchair as he shoved all of those questions to the back of his mind. Even though his mind was a flurry of confusion, there were two things he could be certain of. The first was that his superiors must have been confident that he didn't know or suspect. Otherwise they would never have posted him here with full access to every shred of proof.

The other was that he needed to proceed cautiously. If they suspected he knew, they wouldn't hesitate to finish what her dad had started.

"Um...I'm glad you survived."

"Yeah...yeah I did." Henry said with a half-hearted laugh that he couldn't be sure wasn't hysteria. "I'm afraid you won't though." He drew his gun and pointed it at her.

"What are you doing? Shouldn't you be thanking me or something?"

Perhaps he should. He tried to form the words but failed.

She looked longingly at the doorway behind him. "I promise I won't leak it. I won't tell anyone about Danny getting shot. I swear!"

The calm confidence she had a few minutes ago was gone. Now there was nothing but wide-eyed fear and desperation.

"You know what? Keep the video. Keep the file. I don't need it. You can have the thumb drive."

Had she already forgotten that even if she got out of this room, there was no way out of this building until the electronic locks were disabled from the outside? Henry tightened his grip and aimed for her chest.

"Why? You could be free from the people who did this to you. You don't owe them your loyalty."

Henry pulled the trigger twice. Her body slumped backward in the chair, her head falling limp.

"Because some secrets are only valuable once," he said to her body. "Best to wait until I'm in control of the price." Henry put his gun back in the holster.

Backup would arrive soon to clean up the mess. That didn't give him much time to make a copy and scrub the system of all trace that the file had been pulled at all. He pushed forward, shifted her and the desk chair to the side a bit so he could reach the keyboard, and got to work.

YOU OUGHTA KNOW

MARIE SUTRO

YOU OUGHTA KNOW

MARIE SUTRO

The Norse gods didn't give a damn about Noah's prayers. If they had, he wouldn't have been battling to keep the contents of his stomach from exploding all over the backseat of one of the world's largest vehicles. *So much for the local deities.*

He dutifully placed each of the orange safety helmets on their respective seats. All the headgear bore Valhalla Ice Cave Tour logos identical to the one on his jacket.

"You okay?" Sigur called out in heavily accented Icelandic from the driver's seat of the super jeep.

Steeling his stomach against the oily smell of engine exhaust drifting through the open door, Noah forced his gaze to the rearview mirror. The bigger man's icy blue eyes were full of concern.

Keenly aware of the sweat breaking out around his collar, Noah lied. "Yeah. Almost tripped."

"So much for Iceland's most requested guide!" Sigur replied, mimicking the laudatory tone their boss reserved for Noah.

"Bullshit."

Except it wasn't. Noah always scored the highest in

customer feedback and was the tour company's gold standard when it came to adhering to safety protocols. *Until today.*

"Thanks again for helping Helga." Sincerity replaced levity in the deep baritone.

"Huh?"

"This weekend...tutoring her in mathematics. I know you don't have a lot of free time..."

"No worries, dude. She's a good kid." Noah turned away from the mirror and looked out over the parking lot. In the distance, Iceland's world-famous Jökulsárlón Glacier Lagoon sprawled across the horizon. A flotilla of turquoise icebergs lazily crowded the surface of the glacial meltwater.

Under the nausea, the piercing headache, the sweats, and the occasional spins, Noah felt far worse about showing up for work hungover. It wasn't just unprofessional, it was downright dangerous.

Noah had never been prone to callous or irresponsible behavior. Back in Colorado, his parents bragged about their generous and conscientious son, lovingly referring to him as their *perfect boy scout.*

As of late, he hadn't been so perfect. He'd bailed on work twice this month. Golden boy or not, his boss would never accept another last-minute cancellation.

Hopefully breaking the rules this one time wouldn't hurt.

"Hi, we're here for the ice cave tour!" A thick Australian accent accompanied the perky greeting.

Sucking frigid air into his lungs, Noah forced a smile and shoved his face into the open doorway. A brunette north of fifty stood close to a stocky man of the same age. She smiled broadly up at him.

"Welcome! You've come to the right place."

"Thanks! We can't wait to get into the cave!"

Praying he could keep whatever wanted out of his stomach in it, Noah blurted, "Great. We'll wait to board until the rest of the group arrives." His gaze slid over the couple. "Glad to see you followed the dress code."

"Oh, yes. Waterproof pants, jacket, hiking boots, gloves, and backpack with water." She spun around to prove the last point as her companion looked on dolefully.

"Us too!" intoned a choir of distinctly Mandarin accents as three twenty-something women pranced in to stand beside the couple. Decked out in almost identical cream-colored winter gear, they looked as if they had just walked off the cover of a magazine.

Instagrammers.

Seemingly dead set on proving Noah's suspicion, the three set about touching up each other's hair in preparation for a group selfie. Their ministrations caught the attention of two men in their early forties who hovered just at the edge of the group. Clad in the most expensive labels on the globe, their bored expressions were laced with the type of condescension that festered under the weight of excessive wealth. The taller of the two whispered to his companion, prompting a lascivious smirk.

Assholes.

"Load in time," Sigur announced from behind the steering wheel.

Noah sent up a silent prayer. What he was about to do violated all his training as an AIMG certified glacier tour guide.

"Let's go," Sigur urged, passing the clipboard back. Accepting the offering, Noah addressed the small group.

"Hello everyone! Welcome to Vatnajökull National Park." He did his best to ignore the sweat pooling in his crotch.

"Today we'll be traveling into an ice cave inside one of the country's largest glaciers. Your biggest priority on this tour is to stay safe. That means following instructions and watching out for yourself, as well as others. Do you understand?"

Only the Australians nodded.

"If anyone can't follow directions, we will not risk going up on the glacier. So, I'll ask again, do you understand?"

Noah wished like hell they didn't. A last-minute tour cancellation was the only thing that could send him right back home to bed. Exactly where someone with a killer hangover should be.

If Emeline knew about it, she'd have told him to bail. Then again, Emeline didn't think too highly of jobs or responsibility. She'd come to Iceland with her last boyfriend looking for adventure and found work as a server for one of the posh local hotels.

When she'd discovered her boyfriend was cheating with a chick from Vik, her casual friendship with Noah had escalated at light speed. The blonde bombshell with the sultry French accent and the pouty lips that had oh so many uses, moved in with him the day after their first night together. That had been eight months ago, and she hadn't left or paid rent, since.

Last night had been different. Emeline hadn't come home after her shift. A series of texts just before dinnertime claimed she'd be working late.

Noah had stayed up all night texting into the void. Beside himself with worry, he'd opened the bottle of whiskey his boss had given him last Christmas. He'd awakened this morning next to a nearly empty bottle with a mouth full of cotton and a stomach ready to purge. Crawling out of the bathroom, he'd discovered another painfully brief text claiming she'd crashed with a friend and would see him later.

The adults outside the super jeep shifted back and forth like chagrined five-year-olds. Almost as one, their voices lifted in a rousing chorus of agreement to the safety question.

"Good," he replied, thinking it was anything but. "Please

board the vehicle, and as you enter, initial your name on my form so we can make sure we have an accurate count on today's tour. Any questions?"

Like in open water diving, a successful outing meant maintaining the same count going onto the glacier as coming off it. *At least I can get this right.*

Staring at the smiling faces, he could feel his moral compass spinning out of control. *It's wrong to hide how sick I am! Wrong to even attempt this tour!*

He lifted the attendance sheet and glared at the form below. It was the cave pre-tour safety inspection he'd helped create as part of his initiative to increase safety protocols. He skimmed over the date, his name, and the checkmarks in all the right boxes. The entire form was a lie.

By the time he'd been able to drag his ass out of bed, it had been too late to go up to inspect the cave. Instead, he'd filled out the form in his car and broken every speed limit on his way to meet Sigur.

Noah had hated lying to the single father of two who worked seven days a week to give his kids everything they could want. *But Sigur had accepted the form. After all, it was only one missed inspection. And if he got fired, how would he ever save up for an engagement ring good enough for Emeline?*

Mentally waving off the deafening clamor of inner alarm bells, he raised his hand and waved the expectant faces inside.

"Then let's get started!"

The world outside the windshield seemed better suited to the setting of a postapocalyptic planet in a SciFi disaster flick. Scarred by the glacier's taciturn advances and retreats, the exposed earth was blanketed in black, volcanic ash. In the distance, the massive hunk of ice presided over all, its resplendent aqua tones contrasted with dribs and drabs of dark ash.

It was all Noah could do not to vomit all over the front windshield. Despite letting some of the air out of the tires when they'd exited the highway, the last twenty minutes had been a hellish rollercoaster.

Thankfully, the group seated behind him seemed relatively sedate. Chatter had died off after the first ten minutes as they did their best to hide varying degrees of motion sickness.

Grunting, Sigur turned right between two small hills and brought the vehicle to a halt. "All right everyone," he called. "Time to go. Grab your helmets and put them on as soon as you step out."

Noah shoved the door open, relishing the blast of cool air. He secured his helmet and came to stand before the group as Sigur made his way around to the trunk.

Trying to ignore the sensation of oily sweat seeping down the small of his back, Noah watched Sigur emerge with a lidless container. He placed it on the ground before them.

Visually confirming all helmets were in place, Noah gestured to the box. "Here are your ice cleats for the trek up the glacier."

Desperate for more cool air, he unzipped his jacket before retrieving a set of steel chains sprinkled with spikes. The spins threatened at the edges of his vision as he righted himself.

"Affix these to your boots. Dig those spikes into the ice, and you can walk safely. The trick is digging the spikes in the right way so they'll hold you.

"Serious safety tip. Only hold them by the plastic grips. Understood?"

Affirmations all around. *At least they were paying attention.*

"Good. Now Sigur is going to demonstrate how to safely put these on."

The bigger man lifted an eyebrow. Equipment show and tell had always been Noah's job.

Deciding the best defense was a good offense, Noah smiled. "Please show everyone how easy it is to put their toe in first and then pull the grip over the heel."

Without a word, Sigur did as instructed.

"Easy, right?"

Grumbled affirmations.

"Come get your pair. And if one-legged balance isn't your thing, you can sit on that pile of rocks when you put them on."

Sigur's gaze narrowed as Noah embarked on another first—taking a seat next to one of the Instagrammers. When Noah was vertical again, he clapped his gloved hands together. "Time for a quick inspection to make sure you're all set."

Inspecting gear is important, but it'll all be for naught if the cave is compromised. I've got to stop worrying. Yeah, the temperature is a little warmer today than normal, but nothing drastic.

The words rang hollow against the weight of his training. Pieces of instruction resurfaced in his mind, one chasing another.

Never trust Mother Nature.

A wall that's structurally sound one day can be compromised the next.

Reaching into his pocket he checked his phone. A new text from Emeline:

Will be moved out before you get back
Met someone new
Don't make this weird

The words swirled in his head, spinning into a vortex that threatened to swallow him whole.

She can't be serious!

He'd already sacrificed so much for her. The days he'd taken off to party with her in Reykjavik…last night's terror fest.

Doesn't she love me like I love her? Did she ever love me?

"Is this right?" the Australian guy asked, holding out his foot for inspection.

"What?" Noah asked.

"Are they on right?"

"Yeah, they're fine," he shot back without really looking.

A tap on his left bicep. Sigur pointed to the rest of the group. Some were beginning to tread gingerly across the ashy earth.

"Hold it," Noah called out, trying to give a damn about anything other than getting Emeline on the phone.

All sets of eyes fixed on him.

"Those spikes can easily get caught on a pant leg and tear right through the fabric, so pay attention."

Devastating heartache added to the rest of the symptoms afflicting his body. It was all he could do to make it through the rest of the training and safety spiel. When he finally led the group up the glacier a few minutes later, he'd forgotten all about the dangers of being a distracted guide, or the fact that he'd missed the pre-tour inspection.

Despite the early hour, the sun hung low on the horizon as the group approached the cave entrance. A large trap door was visible in the roughly hewn wood cover which lay flat over the earth.

Somehow, the steep hike up the glacier had worked wonders on Noah's hangover. Forcing more blood through his veins seemed to have done what promised hangover remedies never could. Instead of wishing to bend over and purge, he wished he could reach inside and tear the wreckage out of his chest.

Crossing the last few yards to the entrance, Noah stopped and stared off toward the ash-littered main body of the glacier looming above.

"Is this it?" One of the forty-somethings asked, eying the blackened surface around the structure with disdain. "I thought this was an ice cave tour, not a dirt cave tour."

Gloved hands balling into fists, Noah took a deep breath and turned around to face the arrogant asshole.

"I already told you, it's ash from the volcanoes. If you don't believe we're on ice, take off your damn cleats and see how long you last."

Awkward laughs echoed through the rest of the group. Catching a warning look from Sigur, he forced a smile. "Just kidding!"

Sigur inserted the key in the padlock and motioned for Noah to help him prop the door open. Dusting off his hands, the tour leader addressed the group. "Remember, stick together, be mindful of your spikes, and never take off your helmet."

A little voice called out from beneath the heartache, imploring Noah to at least perform a cursory inspection before letting anyone else in. Sigur answered it with a simple question. "Ready?"

The other man's eyes bore right through Noah. *Could he tell Sigur he needed more time? A moment alone to double-check all was okay inside?*

The group decided for him. Crowding the entrance, their cheers crashed over him. *Shit!* All he wanted was to get through this damned tour and find Emeline.

What're the odds that the one time I cut corners is the one time something goes wrong?

Noah turned on his helmet light and addressed the excited audience. "Go ahead and turn on your lights. There's a set of stairs here with a rope railing. Hold onto the rope at all times and be sure to plant your cleats firmly. Listen for the crunch and take the steps one at a time. It is beautiful inside, but no stopping for pictures until you reach the bottom of the stairs and join me in the first chamber. Ready?" He was greeted with the most exuberant affirmations of the day.

Nodding at Sigur, he began the descent into a world of mind-blowing beauty. Cut and polished by melted water moving through the glacier, the walls were crystal clear and more beautiful than anything created by man. Alternating hues of turquoise, midnight blue, and everything in between reigned in breathtaking majesty throughout the icy palace.

Fanciful beauty eroded the jaded veneer of adulthood from his charges. Their excited chatter ebbed to hushed, awe-filled whispers as they descended behind him.

Unlike his charges, Noah was barely aware of his surroundings. Each step prompted another question in his mind.

Was there really another guy?
Was she just pranking him?
If there was another guy, had they kissed...or worse?

By the time he reached the floor of the first chamber, he was entirely lost in thought. When everyone had assembled, and the oohs and aahs began to ebb, Sigur cleared his throat.

Noah looked at his coworker blankly for a second. Spotting confusion in his co-worker's eyes, Noah forced himself to focus. A series of safety precautions spilled from his lips. Eventually, he released his charges to explore and take pictures.

After another agonizing ten minutes, he announced it was time to move to the next chamber. Noah had just turned toward the opening at the far end of the room when a scream tore through the cave.

He spun back around. All but one of the group was still standing. Two of the Instagrammers stared in shock at their fallen friend. She was sitting on her ass, preparing to let out another wail.

Both guides were beside her in an instant. Noah took the lead, taking inventory of her fallen form. No limbs appeared out of normal alignment and there were no detectable signs of blood visible on the cream-colored ensemble.

"Don't move. Tell me what happened and what hurts."

"I was backing up to take a pic, but I stumbled," she responded shakily.

"Did you hit your head?"

"No, just my butt." She lowered her dark lashes before pinning him with an excessively grateful stare.

As Emeline always said, Noah wasn't the best-looking guy in the room, but he had a way of making a woman feel she was the only woman in the room.

She placed a hand on his arm. "I think I'm okay, but I'm scared to stand. Can you help me?"

"Sure." He snaked an arm around her shoulders. "Plant your spikes and come up slowly."

When she was fully upright and able to return to her friends, he turned back to the group. "A good reminder that we have to be aware of our surroundings at all times. Always move forward, never backward. Got it?"

Clocking each of the nods, he headed back for the corridor to the next chamber. "If everyone's ready, it's time to enter the very best part of the tour. Get your cameras ready. This next room will blow your minds."

He ducked into the opening. Swirling glassy walls rose around him, like ocean waves frozen by a jealous magician in mid-movement. Leaving the group to discover the fascinating air bubbles trapped in the ice for themselves, Noah hurried forward.

Emerging into a chamber with far higher ceilings than the one he'd left, he didn't bother to scan his new surroundings. Noah had seen it all before.

Sunlight spilled down from a small opening in the roof, reflecting off the glassy floor and bouncing about the room. Turquoise and navy blue waves encircled the chamber. Within the ceiling, bits of trapped ash added fanciful arcs and swirls to the panoramic mural.

Noah pulled out his phone and checked the display, praying a message had made its way inside the cave. Something like:

Sorry, Babe!

JK!!!

Despite the opening in the roof, there were no service bars on the screen. He tucked his phone back in his pocket as the last of the group filed inside. Those around him fanned out, moving with the reverence of novice nuns during an introductory visit to the Sistine Chapel.

"Holy shit, is that...?" Sigur whispered pointing at a wide crack running from the entrance they had just come through. It arced from the floor up to the ceiling. Water leaked from the bottom third, pooling on the floor just to the right of where they had come in.

Noah's next thoughts came in choppy flashes.

The crack is new.

The structure is compromised.

It isn't safe!

The last thought screamed through his brain, flooding his body with adrenaline. His heart thundered in his chest as his throat constricted.

Forcing a deep breath, he announced, "I'll lead everyone back to the stairs now. Don't run, but we need to get out as quickly as possible. Sigur will follow behind."

"But we just got here..." the same forty-something asshole whined as if he were a hooker from whom Noah had enjoyed more services than he had cash to cover.

"Out now!" Noah power walked to the entrance. He couldn't tell if the groan that followed came from the asshole, or the glacier itself.

In the next heartbeat, the groaning rose to a high keening. It was chased by the sound of crashing thunder.

"Hurry!" Noah implored as he stepped into the opening.

The world shook violently, forcing Noah to his knees. Multiple voices screamed out as giant blocks of ice came crashing down all around. Shards of ice sliced across Noah's face. Plumes of pulverized ice washed over him and filled his lungs.

More screams pierced the madness as he struggled to rise to his feet. Ahead, the corridor was rapidly filling with ice boulders. Ignoring the impulse to run while he could, he turned back to his charges just as the shaking stopped.

It took a moment for the icy dust to settle, but amidst the sobbing and sounds of terror, he was relieved to find the entire group huddled in the small space around him.

He waved the flashlight in broad arcs. Beyond their little band, the chamber had virtually disappeared into a mess of icy rubble. The devastation elicited another series of desperate cries from his companions. Light flashed briefly across Sigur's face, illuminating an expression Noah had never witnessed on the other man—fear.

One voice grew louder, hiccuping and screeching so violently that Noah was afraid it would trigger further collapse. He waved the flashlight back over each group member in turn until he came to the Australians.

The husband stared in horror at his wife who trembled as if in the throes of a seizure. She squeezed her eyes shut under the bright beam and braced herself against the newly fallen rubble.

The Instagrammers' voices joined in rapid-fire Mandarin as Noah swept the light down, dispelling the shadows on her body. The right leg of the older woman's pink waterproof pants hung in jagged tatters, the fabric drenched in crimson.

Inside the ruins of the material, a nine-inch gash lay open in the blueish-white skin of her calf. Blood flowed freely from the wound, pooling across the floor. Steam rose from the morbid stain.

Noah began shrugging out of his backpack. "I need you to stay calm. We're gonna get you patched up and ready to move. Then Sigur's going to call for help on the satellite phone. But the rest of you need to be quiet. *Now!*"

Sigur helped him lower the woman to the ground. Noah pulled off his gloves and seized her panic-stricken face between his hands. "We're going to get you out of here, but we need to stop the bleeding first."

Her pupils frenetically dodged from side to side.

"I know it hurts, but you just need to be tough for a little bit while we fix you up. Alright?"

Tears coursed down her cheeks as she nodded.

"You're an impressive lady, now let's get that closed up."

As bad as the blood bath had appeared, the wound was not life-threatening. "It's going to need stitches when we get out of here."

Confirmation his spouse was in no real danger flooded life back into the husband's face. "It's okay, babe. It'll be a great story to tell when we get back home."

Another cascade of tears accompanied an uncertain nod. Once pressure bandages were properly applied, Noah and Sigur helped her to stand.

"Think you can put weight on it?" Noah asked.

She took one careful step and exhaled. "It hurts like hell, but I can walk."

"Good."

Sigur pulled the satellite phone out of his backpack.

"This is Sigur Jonasson with Valhalla Ice Cave Tours. We've had a cave-in at site A Four. We are trapped. Repeat trapped. Requesting immediate evacuation for ten people."

"Evac team is on its way," The efficient tone was heavily accented in Icelandic. "Any injured?"

"Minor injuries only."

"What is your exact location and is it stable?"

As if wanting to answer for itself, deep groans erupted from the rubble around them, prompting bits of ice to drop to the floor.

Sigur's gaze shifted to Noah who shook his head as he shouldered his backpack. Frowning, he replied gruffly, "We're in Chamber 2. Sights and sounds of movement. We don't believe it's stable. Repeat not stable."

"Possible to move to a safer spot?"

Noah hurried back to the corridor. He ran the light over the diminished opening. "Corridor appears blocked, but there are pockets. I'll see how far I can get."

Sigur relayed the information.

"Only if you question the stability of your current position." The disembodied voice was thick with warning. "Help is on the way."

An ancient creaking sound from somewhere in the darkness set off another chorus of panicked exclamations.

"Listen..." Noah looked at each of them in turn. "...we are going to get out of this, but I need you all to stay calm. Wait here with Sigur and do not move or make any sounds."

He turned back to what was left of the corridor. The roof had dropped from nine feet to four. Mammoth blocks of ice lay piled up at odd angles. They didn't appear to be very stable, but it was no longer about how long the structure would hold, it was about whether they would all make it out alive.

Ducking into the opening, he dropped to his knees and began crawling between the unevenly stacked ice. The way narrowed within a few feet, forcing him to shimmy sideways to avoid dislodging any part of the delicate house of cards.

Bright light from his headlamp reflected off the icy blocks around him, blinding in its brilliance. He squinted his eyes against the glare just as his progress suddenly halted.

Ice pressed against his chest and back, pinning him. Afraid of dislodging anything, he rocked back and forth gently, but nothing gave. He was trapped.

Doomsday scenarios shot through his mind as his breath came in shorter and faster bursts. *What if the cave collapsed?* His pulse pounded in his ears. *What if I have a heart attack...am I having a heart attack?*

"Don't worry..." Sigur's voice sounded from somewhere behind him. "Noah is Iceland's most requested tour guide. If there's anyone who can get us out of this, it's him."

The words were a salve for the riot in his head. His next thought never would have occurred to Emeline. *They are counting on me.*

Slowing his breathing, he opened his eyes and shifted his thoughts to problem-solving. *If only I could reach my backpack... Oh shit, my backpack!*

He made a series of micro-movements to determine exactly how he was pinned. Slipping his left hand to his belt, he pulled out a utility knife and sliced through the left strap of his pack. When he'd done the same to the right, he sheathed the knife. Exhaling, he gently tugged on the loose straps while gingerly shimmying backward.

Seconds later, he was free. He slid the ruined pack back toward the entrance. "Sigur, pull out my pack. Tell everyone else to take off theirs. It's too tight in here."

"Okay. Did you make it through?"

"Still working on it. Need another minute."

"Hearing more shifting here. Make it quick."

"Got it."

Noah returned to the spot where he'd been stuck. He eased himself back in, keeping his breathing shallow.

It was tight, but he made it through. A few feet more and the way opened up again. Seconds later, he emerged into the first chamber. Robbed of its awe-inspiring beauty, it was now one-third of its original size. What remained evoked the despondency of a Berlin neighborhood after an Allied bombing raid.

Light from his headlamp crept toward the stairs. He steeled his stomach, bracing for the worst. A fresh dusting of ice dulled their shiny finish but they looked no worse for wear.

We're going to get out! Everyone will be okay!

Tears of gratitude sprouted in the corners of Noah's eyes. He poked his head back into the broken corridor.

"The way's clear," he announced. "It gets a little tight in places, but it's easy. Just don't hit the walls and come through as safely and quickly as you can. Ladies first. Guys bring up the rear."

He heard a muffled argument, then the sounds of movement in the corridor. Light rode up and down the walls, punctuated by angry grunts. Plunging back into the corridor, he spotted the lead asshole's terror-filled face.

So much for ladies first.

The idiot hadn't left his pack behind and was as tightly wedged as Noah had been. Worse yet, he was using all his might to force his way through.

"Calm down!" Noah soothed. "You don't want to risk…" The block upon which he'd caught his pack earlier began to shift under the pressure.

The cave rumbled to life again. More boulders rained from above, one pummeling Noah soundly on his right shoulder. The older dude began to scream, his voice joining a rising chorus of fear echoing from the other chamber.

Noah lunged forward seizing the dislodged block. "Stop moving," he hissed as he threw his weight into wedging the ice back in place.

The asshole froze. Two breaths later, the rumbling stopped. Still holding the ice, Noah pinned his eyes on the older guy who looked like he had just soiled his pants. The acidic tang of urine filled the tight space, confirming the suspicion.

"I...I'm sorry...I..." the guy mumbled.

Noah scooted closer, pinning his shoulder against the weak spot. Retrieving his knife with his free hand, he thrust it toward piss pants.

"I told you! I'm sorry!" his eyes were wide with contrition.

Without a word, Noah sliced through the straps. "Listen to me. It's the backpack. Let all the air out of your lungs and slowly try to slip backward. Tiny...movements...backward. When you're free, shed the pack and go back. Give it back to Sigur and try again."

The man nodded, working gently until he was free. When he returned without the pack, Noah eased away from the wall and backed out to give him room.

The guy emerged moments later, accompanied by the stench of urine. Keeping his eyes averted from Noah, he stood and caught sight of the stairs. Without so much as a thank you, he made a beeline for the exit.

"Wait! We need to help the others..."

The dude was already halfway up the stairs, and Noah had more people to evacuate.

"Sending the next one..." Sigur's deep voice purred through the ruined corridor.

Having followed the instructions, the rest of the group made it through without incident. When Sigur finally stood and caught sight of the stairs, he nodded to Noah. "Let's get the hell outta here."

"Wait!" The second half of the asshole team pinned Noah with a wounded puppy look. "Where's my buddy? I thought he came out right after you."

"He did. And he kept going." Noah turned to address the group. "We don't know how long this part of the cave will stay standing. Go carefully and quickly up the stairs. When you get to the top be sure to stay to the right of the entrance and immediately start making your way back down to the super jeep. Sigur will go up first. Ladies follow after him. Guys bring up the rear."

Sigur shook his head at the change of protocol. "You're lead. I bring up the rear."

"Not this time," Noah insisted.

Something shifted in the bigger man's expression but he did as instructed.

Noah emerged from the cave to the thrum of helicopter rotors. His gaze drifted over the group, tallying a quick inventory.

Where the hell is...?

He spotted the cowardly asshole off to the left, about twenty yards away. Despite or perhaps because of his soiled pants, the jerk was bounding up and down, waving frantically at the helicopter.

Oh shit...

Sigur caught the movement and bellowed out a warning. "Noah don't!"

Having failed to listen to his conscience earlier, there was no way Noah could ignore it now. He ran toward the panicked tourist, keenly aware of the danger of running in ice cleats and the fact that the ground beneath his feet might give way any moment.

Above, the helicopter banked southward toward the flat, open space near the superjeep. The asshole's movements stilled as the bird veered off. Now only a few yards away, Noah saw the flush of indignation spread across the older guy's face.

"Stay still!" Noah called as he slowed his pace.

"Screw you!"

"This whole area is compromised! It could..."

Another loud rumble rose from the ground beneath them. The asshole whirled around, watching in horror as a giant crevasse opened up behind him. Ashy ice collapsed in on itself, creating an ever-widening maw in the hungry earth. It stopped within ten feet of the pair of overpriced hiking boots.

Noah reached out a hand. "Come toward me carefully..."

The asshole looked over his shoulder, his mouth going slack at the sight of the deep opening. Noah started to repeat the warning, but the fool set off at a mad dash.

Noah extended his hand. The designer glove was only a few feet away when the ground dropped out. Noah lunged forward, but the man was gone.

Easing to the edge of what was now a twenty-five-foot drop, Noah called out again and again but was met with silence. The sight of a dark crimson pool creeping out from beneath two massive chunks of ice caught his voice in his throat.

Guessing at the sudden silence, the guy's friend screamed, imploring Noah to do something. The rest of the group huddled around their distraught fellow traveler. Eventually, his cries faded and the group began moving again. Easing back to his feet, Noah headed after them.

There would be an investigation into the collapse. Questions about whether the accident and ensuing death could have been averted. Noah knew he would tell the truth about what he'd done and what he'd failed to do. No matter the consequences.

While he didn't know what the future held, he was certain of one thing—that stupid bitch Emeline, could rot in hell.

Up ahead, Sigur pulled the pricey cell phone out of his back pocket and checked the display. The text from Emeline was steamy enough to melt five glaciers. The pics accompanying it could melt the polar ice caps, too.

Tucking the device back into his pocket, he made a mental

note to slip it into the trash later. It wasn't like Sigur needed an extra phone—especially one that smelled faintly of urine.

He'd come across it wedged into the corner of the corridor on his way out. From a practical standpoint, the owner was never going to need it again. And Noah sure didn't need to know what his girlfriend had been up to last night, or with whom.

IMPACT

SHELLS LEGOULLON

EMILY

Emily Minton has no intention of avoiding the accident. Brake lights cut through the rain, splintering the darkness. The BMW in front of her slows for the approaching stop sign. She checks her speedometer. Ten miles per hour. They'll live.

She braces for impact, indifferent to the possibility that the collision and crunching of metal may trigger some sort of post-traumatic episode.

Wham!

Although her airbag stays intact, the jolt whips her head forward, and something flies from the passenger's seat, clunking against the glovebox. A visceral flashback of her near-fatal car accident two years ago roars like a ravenous beast in the back of her mind. It's there and gone, her brain too focused on making sense of her neon pink electric toothbrush on the rubber floormat. She pulls her attention forward and unclenches her teeth, the muscle behind her jaw throbbing from the tension.

Thrusting the gear shift into park, she throws her door open and tugs the hood of her raincoat over her head. As she approaches the sleek black coupe, an inner warning chides her with every step. *This is a dangerous game.*

The wiper blades fly back and forth against the BMW's windshield, making zero progress in the downpour. Emily bangs on the driver's window with an ironic hope the driver is unharmed. A flood of light fills the interior as the door opens, and a dazed man in mint green hospital scrubs peers up at her.

Gooseflesh crawls over her body, but she stays put.

He tips his head to the side. "Are my taillights not working?" He's not angry so much as confused.

Emily wags her head, unable to find her words. Then, "It was my fault," she exhales. "I looked away." She can only pray he mistakes the tremble in her voice as a result of the accident.

When their eyes meet, Emily waits for his recognition, but it never comes. This small win somehow gives her strength. She forces a coy smile, and an ounce of flirtation is all it takes.

His eyes sparkle mischievously. "I'm Randy," he says, squaring his posture against the leather seat.

Yes, I know who you are, and if I'm right about you, you'll be dead by morning.

"Alice Stone," she lies as she looks around the sleepy neighborhood. It's close to eleven on a weekday night. The houses are dark. Not a soul has seen them. Slipping into her well-practiced script, she says, "Maybe we should exchange insurance information somewhere dry and warm?"

The look behind his intrigued blue eyes confirms he's nibbling at the hook. Emily bends forward, presenting enough cleavage to make his decision simple.

"There's a pub a block up," she suggests. "Let me buy you a drink." She looks up from under mascara-laden lashes. "It's the least I can do."

He hesitates, eyes flitting to her chest, then runs a hand through his thick black hair. "Sure," he says, oblivious to the baited invisible barb he swallowed whole. "I've had a long shift, and a drink with a pretty girl is just what the doctor ordered."

She smiles back at him. "I'll follow you."

Five minutes later, they rush through the drizzle into Joe's Bar. Randy didn't even peek at the damage to his car. Emily's not surprised. He's a man, one thing on his mind. She scans the crowded college pub. Her homework paid off. Thursday nights are two for one. They'll be faceless and forgettable in the sea of bargain drinkers.

Emily removes her raincoat and hangs the drippy nylon on a coat rack by the front door. Randy loops his coat beside hers and stares for a lingering beat. The slinky red dress, cut low at the bust and short at the hemline, has his attention.

He sucks in an audible breath. "Wow, Alice, you're all dressed up."

She tips her chin upward, blonde waves hanging over one shoulder. "I had a date," she says with pouty disappointment. "It didn't work out."

He scoffs, "Is he stupid or blind?"

Annoyance flushes her cheeks. Randy puffs out his chest, surely thinking his compliment has made her blush.

"Lucky me," Randy says, motioning to a dark booth in the back corner.

Another reason why Emily chose a place where the clientele is young and full of liquid energy. Most of them have no desire to sit and talk. She weaves past the noisy patrons with a sinister twinge in her belly.

Randy Wilcox honestly doesn't know who she is and why would he? He had met a woman with a disfigured face, bruised and bandaged, four front teeth missing, half of her head shaved. The other half was covered in dark raven curls like her brothers. Even after healing, when she was released to go home, Emily didn't look like she does now.

She glances back at him, and he beams. Had this encounter been authentic and this man a stranger, she might have been attracted to him. Tall, fit, with a boyish demeanor. But all Emily sees beneath that soft green cotton is his pulsing black heart.

RANDY

Randy can hardly believe his luck. He could care less about the Beamer. It's his sister's car. Besides, this fucking, drop-dead gorgeous creature inviting him for a drink tonight after a really shitty shift at the hospital is like a gift from the universe. He'd be dumb not to take it.

They order their drinks—his, a whiskey neat, and hers, a vodka tonic with lemon, not lime. There's something familiar about her, but he can't pinpoint where he knows her from. Maybe that's why he agreed to the drink. He laughs at himself, hiding it with a cough. Who's he kidding? All he does is work, and he can't recall the last time a beautiful lady hit on him. If he plays this right, she might be up for more than a drink.

"So, what do you do for a living, Alice?" He hates small talk.

"I'm a chef," she says easily. "And you're a doctor?"

"I am," he says before he can stop himself. He's not ashamed of being a nurse but wants to impress her. What's the harm in a little white lie?

She shakes her head and chuckles. "Oh my gosh, I rear-ended a doctor."

The waitress sets their drinks on the table and turns away. Randy lifts his glass in a toast.

Emily follows his lead, raising her tumbler.

"Here's to the best rear-ending I've ever had," he says, and she visibly blushes again. He's killing it tonight.

They clink rims and sip their cocktails.

She winces. "Wow, that's strong." Her mouth puckers slightly upward to the right, and a spark of déjà vu hits him so hard he can't breathe.

She sets the drink down and absently brushes her hair off her shoulders. "Something wrong?"

His gaze fixes on the jagged scar peeking out from her hairline, then to the dimpled skin on her right wrist from an undeniable third-degree burn. Then he meets those brilliant green eyes, and the picture comes together.

Her name is not Alice Stone. It's Emily. He can't recall her last name. Five-car pileup on Interstate 10. She was one of four survivors. Three broken ribs, a fractured collarbone, and a traumatic head injury. Room 202.

"What could possibly be wrong?" Randy grins. "I'm having drinks with the most fascinating person I've ever met."

EMILY

They order another round, then another, the time consumed with flirting and lying. Even if she doesn't know everything about Randy Wilcox, she knows enough to know he's blurring the truth tonight. She's done her fair share of research.

After disappearing for years, Randy moved back to Springfield, where both he and Emily grew up, a city big enough they moved in different circles. Now, he lives with his sister and her husband in their guesthouse, mostly because he spends all his money at the strip clubs. He has zero social media presence, has never had a long-term relationship that she's aware of, and has held the night shift as a CNA at Maplewood General for half a decade.

Emily will never forget the evening she was released from the hospital. The doctor and head nurse had just stepped out of her room. Her father was pulling the car around, and her mother was gathering her discharge papers at the nurse's desk.

Randy had stepped into her room wearing a pair of blood-red scrubs and a devilish grin. His inky black hair was slicked back with some kind of pungent pomade. It was the first time she'd seen him without the haze of medication.

"You get to go home," he'd said, his mouth twitching up and down as if in debate over the subject.

His voice caught her off guard. Emily had just stared at him from her bed, her brain connecting the cadence and rasp of his tone. She'd always been good with voices.

"I'll miss you around here." He'd winked, striding past her mother with a warm smile as she entered back into the room.

She should have paid more attention to the chills spiking up the back of her neck, the hum of danger in her gut, but she hadn't understood the gravity of her instinctive response to him at the time.

The nightmares would tug at the seams of her mind much later when she was home in her childhood bedroom, safe and coherent. Her certainty grew stronger with each passing night, alone with her thoughts. The distinct scent of Cinnamon Altoids on his breath. His profile. The gritty tenor of his speech. It's funny how life brings certain people into your orbit, for good or bad. Either way, Emily considers it a blessing. Thanks to a drunk driver, she'd been reunited with a monster she never thought she'd see again.

Now, she sips her vodka and straightens her spine as her mother's voice fills her head. *That dark imagination of yours will get you into trouble one day.* It's true that sometimes her brain spins stories until she's too dizzy to decipher what's real and what isn't. She's gotten things wrong before. She's reactive. But this time, she's positive.

Randy excuses himself to use the restroom and Emily takes the opportunity to strain her cocktail through the ice into a planter above the booth. She pulls a bottle of water from her purse and refills her glass. This next part is crucial and hinges on precision.

He slides back into the bench seat across from her as Emily

tips her drink to her lips and guzzles it down. He raises an eyebrow, throwing back his whiskey in a single gulp.

"Want another?" He leans forward onto his forearms and strokes her hand, running his finger over the scar on her wrist.

Although the skin is dead, an irritating prickle shoots up Emily's forearm. She pulls her hand away.

"What happened?" His warm voice is laced with concern, and if Emily didn't know he was the devil, she'd be in trouble.

"Grease fire at my restaurant," she says, then changes the subject. "To answer your question, yes, I'd like another drink." She bites her bottom lip. "Let's go to my place."

RANDY

Rain pelts the roof of his car, lightning shocking the sky as Randy follows Emily home. All the while, he wonders why she gave him a false name and lied about where the burn on her hand came from. He wanted to question her back at the bar when he realized who she was, but instinct told him to keep his mouth shut. He doesn't know her life. Maybe she's hiding from something or someone. Hell, he knows what that's like.

And she clearly doesn't remember him, which is understandable given the cocktail of narcotics in her drip line during her stay at Maplewood. That'll mess with anyone's head. And who knows, she might really believe her name is Alice Stone.

Either way, he's curious, and if he's truthful with himself, he likes how she sees him—a wealthy, young doctor with a shiny sportscar and personality to match. He hopes that's not the only reason she invited him home with her. He likes this girl. She's smart and funny. Different from the women he usually goes for. Would she still be interested in him if she knew he was only a nurse? Or that he was her nurse and didn't mention it?

Randy ignores the pinch to his conscience and parks his car

against the curb outside her condo. He slides a tin of mints into his pocket, feeling optimistic. Maybe tonight will work its way into something. What a great story it would make years from now. *She hit my car in a rainstorm, took me for a drink, and the rest is history.*

He climbs out of the car and approaches the house. Emily waits for him by her front door, and he can't place the look on her face beneath the porch light, but it sends a spike of apprehension through him. Something's off. His gut urges him to be cautious, but his feet move him forward, disregarding the warning.

Randy forces a light expression as she bolts the door behind them. He swallows the jagged lump in the back of his throat. His instincts are rarely wrong. Maybe he should go. But when their eyes lock and a deep, dormant desire stirs, he decides to stay.

Because whatever this mysterious, sexy woman has in store for him might be fun, too.

EMILY

Emily shrugs out of her coat, hangs it on the wall hook, and reaches for his.

"Nice place," he says, sliding out of his rubber hospital clogs and bending over to neatly line them side by side. When he straightens, he hands her a shiny slotted spoon with the tag still on it. The one she purchased at the chef store last week and promptly misplaced. "Is this where you keep all your professional tools, Chef Stone?"

This time, the heat that spreads across her face is from authentic embarrassment. She reaches for the utensil. "I'm in my head a lot and get distracted easily. Forget where I put things." Just one of the many residual perks from her near-fatal collision, along with paranoia and, per her therapist, an unhealthy fixation on death.

Randy flashes a consolatory grin. "Happens to all of us," he says, and Emily's struck by his compassion.

She takes another long look at him. He seems harmless in loose-fitting scrubs and thick white socks, his cheeks pink from drink and the weather. She hesitates, doubting. Could she be wrong about him? He's been a gentleman tonight, considerate and charming even.

No. Stay on track.

She smiles. "I promised you a drink. I make a mean Old Fashioned?"

He nods to her delight, and Emily breezes into the living room, motioning for him to make himself comfortable on the couch before rounding the corner out of sight. Emily's professional scope is food, not cocktails, but how hard could it be? The man at the liquor store convinced her the pricy bottle of Scandalust Whiskey, with its spicy undertones, would blow the cobwebs off the dusty, overdone recipe. She's counting on it. After all, she'll need something to mask the additional ingredient in Randy's drink.

"Do you live here alone?"

She's in the kitchen, reaching for two tumblers. "Yep, just me." She opens the freezer and grabs the special ice tray she purchased from Amazon. Who knew a giant ice cube was so vital to the experience? With her back to the kitchen entry, she plunks a frozen block into each glass, then slides her hand to the back of the silverware drawer, where she pulls out a baggie of white powder.

"I like the idea of a condo," he calls. "You've done a great job with decorating. Shabby Chic, right?"

"Thanks," she says, surprised by his knowledge of design. Shabby Chic is precisely what she was going for. Uncertainty wriggles deeper in her belly as she examines the crushed Ambien she's hoarded since her hospital stay. A little whisper nags in the back of her head. *It's been ten years. Are you really betting this guy's life on a few details?*

"Are you hungry?" Emily asks, buying herself time to think this next part through. She's gone over this a million times, bordering on obsessive. But now that he's here in her home, acting like a normal guy who clearly wants her to like him, she wonders if she's crammed pieces that don't fit into this vengeful puzzle.

"I could eat," he calls back. "You want some help in there?"

"No," she says too quickly. "Trust me. It'll be worth the wait."

"Mind if I look through your vinyl?"

The collection of albums and vintage record player belonged to her dad. He loved music. "Sure," she calls back, unsure how she feels about him touching her things. She snags an orange from the fruit bowl and reaches for the paring knife in the wooden block. The slot where it belongs is empty. Damn, it could be anywhere, considering her toothbrush on the floorboard of her car and the brand-new spoon under the foyer mud bench.

She chooses the utility knife instead, which is longer and narrower but will do the job just fine. Her wrist works with expert accuracy as a slice of peel spirals from its protective hold on the fleshy interior. She cuts the garnish in half and sets it to the side.

Marvin Gaye's soulful voice fills the condo as *Let's Get It On* takes Emily back to her childhood, her parents dancing in their tiny kitchen. She used to spy on them from the dining room corner when they thought she was tucked in and fast asleep upstairs. She loved how her dad stared into her mother's gaze and wondered if a man would look at her the same way one day.

She pictures Randy back at the bar, how he leaned in when she talked as if she were the only person in the place. It's been so damn long since anyone's paid attention to her like that. Her recovery was brutal. Slow and isolating. And she can't remember the last time she felt seen. Before she left the house tonight, she studied her reflection for a long time in the hallway mirror. With her hair and makeup done, she looked beautiful.

Now, between the music and Randy's relaxed behavior, Emily is second-guessing everything.

Her lips curve upward in betrayal at the thought of him in

her living room. Maybe Randy isn't her monster after all, the one who comes for her in the dark. Maybe she's let time manipulate and confuse her mind like it often tends to do.

Wake up, that condescending inner voice snaps. Even if she has it wrong, he lied about his profession—a red flag. But can she really hold that against him? She's given Randy a fabricated name and orchestrated an entire encounter around her revenge. She returns her attention to the recipe, adding a teaspoon of sugar, three dashes of bitters, and a teaspoon of water into a mixing glass.

Focus Emily.

Her eyes shoot to the baggie. Randy's much bigger than she remembered. Three tablets might not have the right effect. She glances over her shoulder before reaching into the cupboard for her prescription. She removes two additional pills and tosses them into her mortar, using the pestle to grind them into a fine consistency. She lifts the Ziplock, and the pad of her index finger brushes against something hard inside. Several small chunks linger in her pre-crushed bag. Shit. Shit. Shit.

"Almost finished," she calls as she pours the contents into the mortar and combines the new and old batch. She tosses the used baggie in the garbage and works quickly, terrified of getting caught. Or is she worried she's got it wrong?

"Is that a picture of you and your dad on the mantel?"

Emily freezes, pestle clenched in her fist. Her dad's recent heart attack is fresh and still stings. She pictures the photo Randy's referring to. Her mother had the snapshot framed for Emily's birthday.

"Father-daughter dance." Tears threaten in the backs of her eyes as she rinses the pestle. "I was twelve," she chokes, remembering that night fondly.

It had been an unforgettable evening. Her dad had taken her to a fancy dinner place where the plates of food were almost too pretty to eat. It was that very night that Emily decided she would be a chef one day.

She examines the powder and lifts the mortar over his glass.

"You're glowing," he says, and warmth floods Emily's chest. "Looks like you two have a great relationship."

She sighs. *Had.*

"You're lucky," he says. "My father and I...well, let's just say he's never liked me very much."

The disappointment in his voice nearly breaks Emily. Her brother, Cody, didn't have a great relationship with their dad either, and he never got the chance to change that.

Her response is genuine. "I'm really sorry to hear that." He's quiet as the song ends. She holds her breath, anticipating the next on the album track.

In the minuscule stretch of silence, she glances at the stone bowl in her hand. She has no problem drugging a guilty man, but this man is empathetic and thoughtful. There doesn't seem to be an evil bone in his body.

Her decision is swift as she flips on the faucet and rinses it down the drain. All that wasted time and energy. Years of anger. Her therapist warned her more than once about watering poisonous weeds. Shame devours her. The only thing worth killing now is that menacing trickster who hides in her head and plays with her emotions.

Emily sighs, stirring the whiskey into the mixing glass, then straining the concoction over the ice cube. She twists a ribbon of orange peel, citrus zest bursting above amber, then wedges it between the ice and rim.

"Should we order pizza?" Randy asks from the other room.

This simple suggestion of normalcy sends her spinning. She and her brother home alone, fighting over Hawaiian or pepperoni, then ordering a half and half. She pictures Cody's broad smile as he devoured a hot cheesy ham and pineapple slice. It's been a long time since she's shared a pizza with someone.

"Yes," she says, her benign answer like a mallet against fogged glass, shattering delicate shards of all her inaccuracies. She's floating as she mixes a drink for herself—the heft of her burdens scattered on the kitchen tile. Emily lifts the tumblers and turns, nearly bumping into Randy. She startles. In those soft socks, she hadn't heard him come into the kitchen.

"You scared me," she stammers.

There's a strange look on his face that she can't read. How long has he been there?

His eyes taper, and she follows them to the counter where the open prescription bottle rests next to the safety cap. He reaches forward, and Emily's heart leaps behind her ribcage.

Randy grabs the tray of warming ice. "The key is keeping these as frozen as possible." He winks, opening her freezer and sliding the tray back inside.

Emily's rigid body relaxes. She thrusts her right hand forward, offering him the cocktail.

He stares at the sweating glass as his eyes dart back to the counter and then to her. "You know you never want to mix Ambien and alcohol, right?" Randy takes the glass from her left hand.

Of course, he recognizes the pills. He's a nurse. And, if he's seen the mortar and pestle, he must think the worst. Which he should.

"I couldn't sleep last night," she lies.

To break the tension between them, Emily lifts the glass intended for him to her lips and takes a sip. He watches her with interest. With a flirtatious grin, she says, "I promise, Doctor. I'd never mix drugs and alcohol."

This elicits the desired result. "Cheers," he says, endearing, thin crinkles cupping his eyes. "Mm. It was worth the wait." His eyes draw above her head to a shiny magnetic knife bar where a dozen lethally sharp knives are suspended in place.

She follows his gaze, taking in the gap where her butcher knife belongs. She shakes her head. "They are a little scary looking, aren't they?"

Randy grits his teeth, and Emily laughs, the sensation both foreign and pleasing.

She takes another sip and leads him from the kitchen. He's right. The cocktail is delicious. Emily eases onto her sofa, feeling like her old self as her chef's brain conjures up a recipe using the unique new whiskey. A sauce for the pork ribs at her restaurant. She'll serve it with smashed red potatoes and warm garlic kale.

Randy thumbs through the albums in the box on the table. "No way. Elton John? I grew up to his music."

"Me too," she says, appreciating how careful he is with her father's collection. "What's your favorite song?"

Randy tips his drink back, seemingly thinking through the plethora of hits. *"Levon,"* he says without looking back at her. He removes Marvin Gaye and slides it back into the protective sleeve. "Yours?"

"Rocket Man," she says without a second thought. "We'd blast it in the car on the way to school and sing at the top of our lungs." In her mind's eye, she sees them in the front bench seat of her father's classic El Camino, her brother nestled between her and her dad, belting out every word as if he wrote the song himself. That was before. When they were all innocent.

A familiar piano chord hums through the speakers as the lyrics to *Rocket Man* unfold. Emily's heart takes flight. That's how it happens: a song, a smell, or even a phrase can release a feeling palpable enough to render a person helpless to the memory braided through it.

This particular song makes her so sentimental she doesn't

notice Randy pulling out the photo album from the back of the record box until it's too late.

RANDY

Emily bolts from the couch and snags the red leather keepsake from his hands. He's already seen the beginnings of an obituary behind the plastic sheath. The headline, *Beloved Son and Brother*.

She snaps the book shut without even a glimpse, clutching it to her chest.

There was no picture or name, no age of the boy. "I'm sorry," Randy says. He's never been good at knowing the right thing to say.

Emily squeezes the book so tight her knuckles go white. "My brother," she says, those two words like a kick to his teeth.

He wants to tell her he understands. He lost a brother, too. But Randy holds his tongue.

She exhales a shrug. "It's been a long time."

Same, he thinks. "What happened?"

Emily's eyes well up, and the pause between them is like a vacuum sucking all the oxygen from the room. Then, her cupid bow lips twist.

"Bad choices," she deadpans, sliding the scrapbook back where it came from.

It's vague, but Randy speculates, staring at the severe edges of her shoulder blades peeking through her blonde waves. He's seen his share of overdoses working in the hospital. "Drugs?"

She shakes her head. Thunder cracks outside, rattling the windowpane. Emily doesn't seem to notice. Her body's still and quiet when she says, "He was murdered."

Like an infectious rash, fine, erect hairs spread up Randy's forearms. He and Emily have more in common than she knows. The only difference is that she seems content to tuck the sad memory of her brother's death away in a box. Not him. If Randy ever found the dirtbag who killed Bubb, he'd cut them up into little pieces and feed them to his sister's Rottweiler.

He takes control of his dark mood, not wanting to ruin the night with her. "It's hard to lose a brother," he says, keeping his tone even. "Do they know who did it?"

"Mm-hmm," she says, turning to face him, and Randy's struck by the fury in her eyes. Maybe they're more alike than he thinks.

Bubb's killer is still out there, free to live their life. Randy grinds the back of his teeth, then recites the words he wishes someone would tell him. "May the guilty Fucker rot to death in a prison cell." He holds his glass up in toast.

Emily lifts an eyebrow and smirks. "Oh," she says cooly. "They're rotting all right." She taps the rim of her tumbler to his, gulps back the last of the whiskey, and wipes her mouth with her silky sleeve. "Want another?"

An uneasiness grows in Randy's gut as he takes her in. He doesn't know anything about this woman, not really, and he has the strongest feeling that the new hair color, dress, and makeup are part of a costume she's created for this Alice Stone character. Because Emily is more complicated than he imagined, and if he's honest with himself, it frightens him a little.

Then again, he's never been more turned on.

"Yeah, I'd love another drink," he says. "My turn to play bartender." He takes the empty glass from her hand. Their fingers brush, and a shiver zips between his legs. What would it be like to be her person, with all her complexities? She smiles back at him, and an unfamiliar sensation tips him off balance. It's been a long time since a woman made him nervous. Randy rattles the ice inside the glass. "You order the pizza. I'll try to measure up."

EMILY

Emily puts in their order with Rokos as Randy makes another round of cocktails.

He calls from the kitchen. "Do you have a paring knife?"

"Misplaced it. The knife I used is in the sink," she says, placing the needle against the vinyl groove as a familiar static introduces the beginnings of a beloved song. Neil Young's *Harvest Moon* opens up with a melody designed for swaying. The song sends her reeling back in time, her mother playing this song over and over, dancing with her fussy baby brother to calm the colic.

Randy returns with their drinks, and like a pesky mosquito, hesitation buzzes in the back of her mind. Wouldn't it be a cruel plot twist if he crushed the Ambien and laced HER cocktail? She'd deserve it for being an idiot and letting her guard down. She stares at the glasses in each of his hands, comparing if one is cloudier than the other. Once again, she's allowing deception to burrow holes in her mind and distract her.

Randy must notice her caution. He smirks and takes a swig from the glass in his right hand, then thrusts it forward. "Not quite as good as yours, but I think you'll like it."

How did she not get this right? Again. He's not the first man she's stalked and nearly killed over her brother's death. And if it were him, the third boy that night in the alley, she'd handed him the perfect opportunity to share that he'd also lost people he knew to murder. But he didn't even flinch.

Her therapist's words are so loud in her ear that it's like he's standing next to her. *Sometimes, we turn the little things into big things to squelch our desperation for closure.*

Closure is all Emily's ever wanted.

She reaches for the glass and takes a long pull. It's stronger than the one she made but tasty all the same. She shoos away the menacing hum, wanting to lose herself in him. Randy sets his cocktail on a coaster and extends his hand as if he can read her mind.

"May I have this dance?"

A shudder whips through Emily's middle, her inhibitions loose from alcohol, those familiar childhood dreams close to the surface. His expression is almost bashful, and she's drawn to him like a magnetic charge.

She sets down the tumbler, and her eyes fall on the shiny coffee table book she bought at Barnes and Noble. *A Girls Guide to Shabby Chic.* Hmm? She thinks back to his comment about her decorating style. Her skeptical brain screams. *He's pretending to be someone he's not.* But her heart thumps excuses for him. *He's trying to impress you. Hardly devious.*

Emily's so tired. The rage and incessant drive for revenge have worn her down. She exhales a loaded breath and takes his hand. With her heels still on, she's almost as tall as him. He wraps his right arm around her waist as they float over the hardwood, their bodies close, and he looks at her the way she'd always hoped someone would. It's the first time in a very long time that Emily feels safe and cared for. She leans her head on his shoulder. For once, her thoughts are quiet.

"Tell me a secret," he says close to her ear, the heat from his breath sending chills across her neck.

"You go first," she says.

He sighs, and she swears she can feel its weight. "I'm not a doctor."

She pulls back to look at him, feigning surprise. "But you're wearing scrubs," she says, his honesty unexpected.

"I'm a Certified Nursing Assistant," he says, studying her reaction. "Disappointed?"

His admission and vulnerability are disarming. This innocent man has been earnest, even sympathetic, when she shared her brother's tragedy. Not once has he crossed the line with her.

She lifts her head from his shoulder and peers into wanting eyes. His transparency is something Emily isn't used to. She's either starving for love, or it's plain simple lust, but she can't help herself. She tips up onto her toes and kisses him, the taste of whiskey and spice heavy on their tongues.

At first, the kiss is soft and sweet. But within seconds, their desire grows fierce, a feral hunger in how they cling to the other. Emily finally breaks away. Her breaths are shallow and fast. She threads her hand in his and leads him down the hall, never once looking back. No question of what she wants until she opens her bedroom door and stops short.

With the wall-to-wall paint tarp covering her plush bedroom carpet, it looks more like a glistening body of water. Her queen-sized bed, with its bulky wood headboard and matching nightstand, anchors like a ship in the center of the room. The plastic taped to her windows distorts the moonlight filtering in.

Emily got swept up, distracted by the unfamiliar sexual energy brewing in her pelvis. Now, she's mortified.

Thinking fast, she says, "Sorry, I forgot all about my little painting project." Her apologetic grin expands all the way to her eyes. Heat pops on the balls of her cheeks. "Try to envision satin burgundy walls."

Randy clears his throat. "God, Alice, if I didn't know better, I'd think this was some sort of murder room."

She sucks in a breath. He has no idea how right he is.

"The bed looks comfy under that plastic, though." He lifts a shoulder.

She exhales her shame and bends over to release the straps on her heels. Padding across the tarp, her bare feet making crunching sounds with each step, she rips the clear covering away from her comforter and crawls onto the mattress. Randy climbs onto the bed beside her, and they pick up where they left off, an urgency between them.

"Hey," he murmurs, breathless. "Do you have condoms?"

She nods, pulling her mouth from his. Flipping over, she opens the nightstand drawer but pauses, struck by the incongruency. Her brain does a quick inventory of the contents. Nail file, Chapstick, a bottle of Melatonin, several square condom packages, and two items that definitely don't belong.

She snags one of the shiny foiled wrappers and slides the drawer shut. She turns to face him. Laying the condom on the bedding between them, she's sick to her stomach. Sometimes, she really scares herself.

The seductive way he looks at her sends a quiver straight up Emily's middle. He's waiting, patient and polite, for her to make the next move in this intimate chess match. But no matter how hard she tries, she can't unsee what's only an arm's length away in that drawer.

Four extra-large zip ties and one deathly sharp butcher knife.

RANDY

Fuck, this is really happening. He studies every detail of her perfect face. So different from the first time he met her, bruised and damaged, one side of her head covered in matted dark curls. Even then, he'd been attracted to her. He could have never dreamed he'd be lying next to her. In her home. Her bed.

Sliding his hand into her hair, Randy glides the pad of his index finger along the scar on her scalp, where he knew it would be.

"You're staring," she says, noticeably uncomfortable.

"You're beautiful, and you still owe me that secret."

She plays with the sleeve of her dress, and the idea that she's anxious pleases him. It means she likes him, too, and cares what he thinks. Maybe she'll tell him why she uses the name Alice Stone or explain why she lied about the burn on her wrist. He really can't believe she doesn't remember him from the hospital. Then again, his shift started at midnight, an hour before her sedation break, where he'd rotate her shoulders and legs to help with atrophy. He was usually finished before her pause in medication. Besides, if she had remembered him, she would have said so.

It's probably better this way, anyway. He'd be embarrassed if she remembered him bearing his soul while he worked with her, complaining how much he hated living with his sister. How much he missed Bubb.

Randy isn't sure why he held back the fact that he, too, lost a brother to murder. Maybe it's his guilt. That night was all his fault. He'd riled Bubb and Kyle up about Angelica cheating on him. They'd just wanted to teach that kid a lesson. But it didn't end the way they meant it to, and what did Randy do? He ran away like a coward, and still, his brother and Kyle protected him, denying that anyone else was involved despite the statement the kid's sister gave the police.

Randy never got the chance to make it up to Bubb. Provide an alibi or testify at the trial. Because there was no trial, his brother and Kyle were brutally killed the day they were released on bail.

EMILY

Randy wants a secret from her, and his eyes are so sincere she longs to confess. Not even her therapist knows this truth, and it's eaten her hollow for ten years. Wouldn't it be nice to let someone else hold it for a minute?

She sucks on her bottom lip as he slides a faded tin of mints from his pocket and pops two into his mouth, then offers her some. She shakes her head, contemplating the idea of her big reveal. Randy might leave if she tells him her darkest secret. Or worse, he'll see her differently.

How could she ever tell someone like him, a nurse, that she poisoned two of the three men who beat her brother to death, then used the carving knife her father gave her as a gift when she graduated from the Institute of Culinary Education, gutting them from chin to scrotum as easily as slicing a Christmas ham?

That would definitely scare him away. She meets his understanding gaze.

Randy leans in and kisses the soft spot between her clavicles. "You can tell me anything you know."

Like a punch to her senses, the strong smell of Cinnamon Altoids on his breath, mixed with his gravelly tone, sends her spiraling back a decade. She and Cody were walking home from a party. It was his freshman year in high school, and Emily's mother had tasked her with chaperoning. Most brothers would be pissed about their adult sister tagging along, but not Cody. He adored her. So did his friends, and she looked young for her age.

They'd stayed at the party until neighbors called the police. Emily had found her brother on the back porch making out with a pretty red-haired girl Emily had never seen before. She'd given the lovebirds one minute to say their goodbyes before they headed out the back gate. Cody couldn't shut up about Angelica. She was a cheerleader at Wilsey High across town, and supposedly, they'd met at a basketball game. They'd been hooking up ever since, regardless of Angelica's having a serious boyfriend.

Emily will never forget the moment they passed the Ford dealership and cut down the alley toward home. It was there that two guys jumped Cody. A third grabbed Emily from behind, one arm wrapped around her waist while the other threaded behind her neck, covering her mouth with his sweaty hand so she couldn't scream. His profile was so close in her peripheral that their cheeks almost touched. Cinnamon mints stung her nose as those raspy words sent prickles across her scalp. *"He can't fuck with another guy's girl and get away with it."* Emily struggled against his hold, tears trailing down her cheek while she watched helplessly.

Now, her body shakes uncontrollably, and the visceral reaction is so overwhelming that it has to be him.

"Hey," Randy soothes. "It's okay."

The mass of his body is heavy on hers, like a suffocating weighted blanket—her brain works fast to sort facts from feelings.

He interrupts, slicing through her thoughts. "I have enough secrets for both of us." He kisses her forehead. Once, then a second time. "I lost a brother too," he whispers into her hairline.

Brother? Emily nearly laughs out loud with relief, this grain of information somehow quelling her doubts. Randy Wilcox can't be the third guy. She's certain because the names of those men she sent to hell on that warm July night did not share Randy's last name.

She exhales hard, brushing her fingers up and down his arm, going through the motions of comforting another. She has to get off this crazy train. Stop fixating on the past. In the stillness, Emily makes a decision. It's time to act normal, healthy. Start a relationship even.

"He was my half-brother," Randy sighs.

It doesn't mean anything. Her heart says. *It means everything, you idiot.* Her brain retorts. Emily squeezes her eyes shut. She needs the noise to go away.

Randy chuckles. "I couldn't say his name when I was little, so he was Bubb since I could talk."

Emily's eyelids spring open, those words forever etched in her mind. *"Kick the shit out of him, Bubb."*

Her blood runs cold despite the heat radiating from his body. He's clueless, pressing his mouth to hers, wedging his tongue between her lips. Emily's revulsion is instantaneous. She bites down hard.

"Fuck," he growls, ripping back from her, pressing the tip of his finger to the bloody wound. "What was that for?"

Words bubble up and out of her like a chemical reaction. "That was for my brother," she says. "Remember him? Cody Minton. Fifteen-years-old. His biggest crime was kissing the wrong girl."

Randy winces, swallowing hard enough that his Adam's Apple bobs beneath his pale skin. He knows the name. It's written all over his expression.

He shakes his head. "I was young," he murmurs, looking

away from her. "A hot head." As if this is an adequate explanation for the part he played. Emily glares at him. He's silent, seemingly lost in thought. He runs his hand through his dark hair, his chin quivering, and he speaks so low Emily has to strain to hear him. "It was an accident."

Really? Not even an apology. Her tone is cold and brittle. "I. Was. There." She sees the spark of recognition now behind his eyes. "You egged them on until my little brother was no longer identifiable," she snarls. "It was no accident."

In the muted light, the muscle in Randy's jaw clenches. "We just wanted to scare him," he says. "They didn't mean to kill him."

"But they did."

Emily wants to hurt him. Recklessly, without a thought of the position she's in, she delivers the next bit with a level of satisfaction she would have missed had she drugged Randy Wilcox and killed him the way she was going to in the first place.

"And when I cut out your brother's rotten heart…," she pauses, letting it sink in. "That wasn't an accident either."

The tension between them is charged, and she can practically see Randy's tiny man brain at work. He's putting it together, remembering how authorities found his brother, Benjamin Roth, and Kyle Morgan. Two empty husks slumped behind a dumpster, vital organs neatly severed from their cavities—the work of a professional.

A savage smile spreads across Randy's face, his teeth stained with blood from the bite to his tongue.

"I knew there was something off about you," he scowls.

Lightning flashes beyond the covered window, and Randy's boyish features morph into a demonic mask. Maybe the trick of distorted light or possibly his true essence bleeding through. Thunder follows. Booming like an exclamation mark.

Emily never sees it coming. He slaps his hand around her slender neck and narrows his eyes.

"I swore if I ever found the person responsible for killing my brother..." He squeezes her windpipe, working his fingers into the grooves of her esophagus. "They'd die regretting it."

Specks of light dance in the corners of Emily's vision. She claws at his clenched fingers. It can't end like this. Randy is the bad guy. In her mind's eye, she pictures the butcher knife in her nightstand. He releases his grip just enough to allow her to catch a breath. She holds his gaze while she stretches her left hand toward the drawer. There's no way she can open it at this angle.

Randy repositions on top of her so that his knees lock against her sides, pressing his thumbs into the flesh beneath her chin. Emily digs her heels into the mattress and, with every ounce of strength, bucks her hips upward. Randy's bulk doesn't budge.

He smirks, his voice void of emotion. "I actually pictured tonight ending differently."

He's going to kill her. She cannot win.

Yes, you can. Her brain screams.

Randy toys with her some more. Applying pressure to her throat, then releasing pressure. It would spoil his fun if she passed out. She gulps for air. Her heart goes silent, defeated and powerless. *Finally*, her brain says smugly. *Your heart is the reason we're in this mess.*

Emily blinks rapidly. She has to fight.

Randy leans close to her ear. "I think I'll do to you what you did to my brother," he says, letting her take another breath. "Don't worry. I'm a nurse, not squeamish in the least."

A toxic mixture of adrenaline and panic swirls in her veins. She searches her room for something, anything.

He sits back now on her upper thighs, his hands removed momentarily from her neck. He cracks his knuckles one at a time. "I won't be as kind as you were, though. I'm going to keep you alive while I do it." Then, as if he's just remembered her low-cut dress, he runs his fingers along her throat, trailing them slowly down her chest.

Another flash of lightning makes her jump. Something glints from the top of the headboard above them.

Randy licks his lips and slides his hand beneath the soft fabric covering her breast. With the pads of his fingers, he twists her nipple so hard she cries out. He laughs, as the vein in the side of his neck pulses like the second hand of a clock.

Emily's reach is quick, and like a Viper's strike, she's accurate with the tip of the paring knife.

Randy smacks at his neck as if he nicked himself, shaving. A stream of blood shoots from his Carotid artery like a pressurized hose. Deep red plasma splatters Emily's cheek, the bed, the nightstand, and the wall.

She pushes from underneath him, shimmying up against her headboard. The knowing in Randy's eyes that he's dead already and cannot be saved should produce some sort of emotion inside of her. But all she sees is a monster who deserves his punishment. She wonders what he's thinking. If he's sorry, he went for that drink with her tonight.

It's strange, but as each one of his heartbeats produces another spray of dark crimson on her pale walls, Emily decides a rich burgundy is exactly the right color for this room.

The doorbell rings—the pizza. Glancing at Randy, limp and lifeless on her comforter, she exhales and slides off the bed, releasing the paring knife. She pads into her bathroom and studies her reflection in the mirror. There's no time to rinse the blood from her hair, so she tips over and quickly secures a bath towel around her head.

She uses a wet washcloth to clean her face, then slips on a fluffy robe over her dress. Closing the bedroom door, she tip-toe runs down the hall and retrieves a bill from her purse. Emily squares some dignity back into her shoulders and opens the front door.

"You're a lifesaver," she says, thrusting a fifty-dollar bill forward and smiling at the delivery boy. "Keep the change."

The pimply-faced kid hands Emily the warm box. "Thanks," he says, studying the large bill.

She's already closing the door when he calls out, "Enjoy the pizza."

Emily turns the lock and opens the cardboard cover. A blast of smoky steam fills her nostrils, waking her senses. Her stomach growls. She heads into the kitchen, lays the pizza on the counter, half pepperoni and half Hawaiian, then pops a coffee pod into her Keurig. She grabs a plate and a few napkins as her eyes land on the knife block and the blessed empty slot where her paring knife should be.

Plunking onto a barstool, she slides her fingers beneath a saucy slice and takes a tentative bite, careful not to burn her mouth. "Mm," she moans audibly, picturing her younger brother across from her, devouring his half. It's finally over. The score settled.

Emily sinks against the back of the chair. Well, it's almost over. She has a long night of cleanup ahead of her.

Glancing at the magnetic knife bar above her stove, Emily's eyes land on the polished black handle of the carving knife her father gave her all those years ago, then on her vacuum sealer. Emily once won a competition in chef school for carving up a roasted chicken: bones and meat. Although things got a little sloppy tonight, her original plan will work just fine. After all, Randy Wilcox is just bones and meat.

It won't be easy, but Emily's thought through every detail. She knows exactly how she'll get away with her closure.

Because Emily Minton has no intention of getting caught.

SHELL GAMES

BLAZE WARD

SHELL GAMES

ANOTHER BOSTON JOB
BLAZE WARD

Boston didn't like secrets. Especially not the kind that could get him killed.

Same same, wasn't like he had a lot of options. Feds had boxed him in pretty tight in letting him not take the rap for a string of murders by his ex-partners, even if that had been Scarlet trying to kill him and the rest of the gang to eliminate all witnesses and keep all the money for herself.

He was still owned in fee simple by the American government. Not necessarily the worst thing, until the phone rang yesterday and it was one of those calls you take, even if you're driving the getaway car in the middle of a hot pursuit.

So here he was, dressed in his nicer duds. Thank God they didn't do ties in Seattle, or he'd have had to go shopping, but at least today he could pass for a techbro's employee or something. Walk the streets downtown and not draw attention to himself or look like a panhandler.

His name had even been on the reservation list at the restaurant, though the fancy pants guy at the door had sniffed at him anyway.

Boston ignored it and focused on table manners. Not for

himself, but because he didn't want to get killed today. The latest episode of his current binge show series was dropping in a few hours and he didn't want to miss it.

Italian joint. Old place. Pictures on the walls in here of famous people who'd probably been dead before he was born. Boston was from Leeds, in merry old England. Got called Boston because too many Americans had a tongue-twister trying to say Boswell Worthington.

That, and criminals were generally smarter not to go by the names on their passports.

The bread was warm and fresh. Dipped in spiced olive oil and balsamic vinegar. Boston had grown up poor in Leeds. Almost any good food was something novel. Especially in America.

Table was back in a corner. Away from the few other folks in here mid-afternoon. Less witnesses or something.

Then trouble walked in.

Boston knew he'd watched too many old movies, because the private detective was always in trouble when a leggy dame walked into his office. Today, he was probably in hers, and she was never Chinese in those movies, but Maggie Chan was absolutely trouble. Gorgeous, but trouble. Rumor had it that she'd been a tong killer when she was young. And forty-whatever wasn't old, but she had all that deadly maturity on top of it.

Three goons with her. One stopped by the front door, two stood a respectful distance and glowered at him and everybody else.

Boston rose. Even a dumb git like him knew that. Nodded to the woman as she approached. Caught her smile go from professional to almost nice for a moment before she gestured him to sit again.

Neither of them had a back to the front door, but Boston

figured he was the second safest person in Seattle this afternoon with Ms. Chan around.

"I'm glad you could join me," she began, as someone delivered a bottle of wine, opened it, and started pouring.

"Ma'am," Boston nodded.

She was Hong Kong British Chinese money. The old stuff, dating back to the 1840s when the pirates went legit. Better schools and accent that a mutt like him.

Boston sipped the wine when he got a glass and watched her face for clues. Astonishingly beautiful. Like, Old European Masters competing to render her in marble or oil. Rich. Smart.

Utterly, fucking deadly woman.

"I need you to steal a car," she said without preamble, voice pitched low enough that he barely heard her.

Boston nodded. That was kinda his thing in this town.

Or had been.

Since watching his ex-girlfriend try to kill him in route to blowing up the entire previous team last week, he was a bit at loose ends. Worse, those ends were a leash and the cops held the other end, but they had instructed him IN NO UNCERTAIN TERMS to continue to pretend to be a car thief, wheelman, fence, and whatever else the criminal underworld around here needed when it came to transportation.

One whisper of that around this woman and they'd never find his body. Not unless she left his head on a post as a warning or something.

Maggie Chan had that kind of reputation, too.

"Which one?" he asked politely.

You did everything politely around this woman.

"A blue 1972 Ferrari Dino 246 GTS," she replied with a smile.

Boston pursed his lips and nodded while gathering his thoughts. Weren't like there were that many of them around here. Not like Los Angeles, where a complete car culture had intersected with a lot of money to make pretty collections, like the one that TV talk show host had accumulated.

Boston didn't even have to ask which one. Well, maybe he did.

"The Russian gentleman should no longer be in possession?" he asked obliquely.

Boston knew all the car collections in this town. Which meant that he'd dealt with almost all of the collectors at some point, usually finding them obscure parts.

Or stolen cars they could hide in a private, underground museum.

There were certain questions one didn't ask, especially when surrounded by crime bosses.

Ms. Chan smiled. Warm again, like he was a brighter pupil guessing right on a teacher's question.

Not entirely off-base. He did cars. Not much else.

The fact that she'd called him spoke volumes about risk. Her. The government. The Russian mafia in town.

"Where should it be delivered to?" he asked, pretty much already accepting the contract.

You did that when Maggie Chan asked. Like you always took her call and invitation to lunch. The money would be good. The potential for favors, better.

"I don't really care," she said, nose scrunching up cutely. "Merely that he no longer has it. It is, after all, his pride and joy."

Boston nodded. Any fool would love that car.

"Not really easily disposed of, unless we put it through a crusher," Boston hazarded.

She paused, then nodded.

"That would be destroying a piece of art, wouldn't it?" she asked.

"Yes, ma'am," Boston nodded. "Can be done, if necessary, because I'm not entirely sure who I might arrange as a buyer for such a thing, considering its provenance."

"That's why we're talking, Boston." The smile was back. The charm. The trouble. "I'll put a million cash up, half now, half on completion. You let me know if you have strange expenses unexpectedly, and I might cover them as well."

"And the car simply vanishes?"

"I agree that only another player might be willing to take that risk," she nodded. "And that might be asking too much."

Yeah, that about summed it up. Two crime lords fussing? And her asking him to steal a car from a guy, like a jealous ex-girlfriend?

A waiter suddenly appeared, delivering plates to both of them, in spite of him never ordering.

But then, like the rest of it, Boston wasn't sure he had a lot of options here anyway. All his secrets were likely to get him killed.

Boston completed his explanation and watched the emotions play out on Rollins's face. None of them good.

After a moment, the man nodded.

"This was not exactly what we had in mind in running you, Boston," Rollins replied quietly.

They were in a back room of an office building across the street and down from the federal courthouse downtown. Boston didn't exactly know which agency owned the pink slip on his soul. He also knew it probably didn't matter.

Rollins felt a little older than Boston's thirty-three. Short hair dark. Tan and muscles. Tattoos and scars. Hard years. Presumably a military background of some sort, doing things he wasn't legally allowed to discuss with a foreigner. Even a friendly one.

Not much more than that, other than the man knew guns.

Shooting them. Fixing them. Finding them. About as well as Boston knew cars.

Nuff said, guv'nah.

"Not a lot of options here," Boston countered. "Worse, I could probably pull it off."

"How's that?" Rollins asked, suddenly sharp as a razor.

"Because I stole it for Atorov in the first place," Boston grinned grimly.

Gari Atorov. Russian gangster. Folks that had emerged after the old Soviet Union imploded thirty-some years ago. As crude as Chan's people were subtle. Heavier presence in Tacoma and such these days, but Seattle kinda stretched from Olympia to Marysville, depending how you judged it.

"You what?" Rollins barked.

"Full disclosure and all that?" Boston nodded. "You demanded that I account for various crimes when folks asked. Your folks. I did that one. With some friends."

"We'll circle back later," Rollins retorted after a moment. "Can you steal it again?"

Boston shrugged.

"I'd have to turn into some sort of criminal mastermind," he barked rudely at the man. "Run a team like a proper caper, and all that shit."

Rollins studied him. Nodded in a way eerily reminiscent of Maggie Chan.

"I can handle armaments," Rollins said. "Who else do you need?"

Boston blinked at him like a drunk owl.

"Are you utterly daft?" he asked.

At least Rollins had a smile on his face.

"Probably," the man replied. "What would it take for you to build a caper team?"

Well, shit. Worse, he had a pretty good idea.

And the apparent backing of the United States of America in

doing it?

How stupid *could* he get?

∽

Money talked. Boston knew that. Even in Seattle. Maybe especially here, as it had always struck him as a much more mercenary town than any other he'd lived. Even London.

Couple of calls and he had people. Him. Really.

Edgar called himself the **Grey Welshman**, which was a load of hokum, as he'd been born in Yakima, Washington to Mexican parents, but had inherited some big Iberian genes, a lot of moxie, and enough money to go into business for himself as a teenager. Man owned, among a bunch of other things, a pick-a-part car yard, which was how Boston knew him. And owned a string of laundromats and dry cleaners through various fronts. Also knew folks who owned vacuum trucks for cleaning parking lots. And pig farmers.

Boston didn't ask.

Man didn't do field work, but made an excellent fence when you needed to acquire things. Stuff that other folks maybe wanted to disappear.

Jones was the black bagger. The Penetration Expert™ who knew how to nullify security systems of all sorts. What Scarlet had done before she'd tried to burn him. Rollins had grumbled quietly in private about the number of times that Jones had been arrested, but Boston had countered him by pointing out how amazingly often things got pled down to misdemeanors or dropped for inability to prove anything.

Slippery.

Last team member was **Humboldt**. Real name, as she'd quietly admitted when it was just the two of them, was Nayeli Garcia. From Eureka, California by way of Mexican parents who worked their asses off in various fields to get their girl through college and out of that life.

She'd turned into a criminal anyway, but Boston had to admit that the money was good. And he'd made the mistake of calling her Hispanic exactly once, after which he'd gotten a lecture, in better English than he spoke, about the Nahuatl language and how she was a pureblood Nahua.

He did understand that she was the smallest adult person he'd ever met, coming up to barely four foot eight, yet built exactly like a woman a head taller.

Lineman. Woman. Something. Spotter was the usual nomenclature, but didn't really encompass someone who spoke fluent English, Spanish, Nahuatl, several other Aztec dialects, and Mandarin. He also didn't ask. Cute enough to be a face on the team but so striking as to be memorable, which you really didn't want.

Plus, he wasn't running a con or a bluff on this one. At least he didn't think so. The day was young.

"Why not drive it away?" Humboldt asked as he laid out all the details of the job.

"Personally, I'd've disable the damned thing while I had it in the garage," Boston replied. "Pull a wire somewhere or just add a kill switch. Something he could undo in a heartbeat, but you had to be him or his mechanic to know. And I don't want to try suborning a mechanic here, because we'll get one chance at this. We fuck it up and we might as well move to Cleveland. And I wouldn't wish that on my second worst enemy."

"Second worst?" Jones asked.

"First one's dead," Boston smiled, then nodded to Rollins. "He killed her for me."

Which was rude. Technically correct, though, which was the best kind of correct, since Rollins had shot Scarlet before she could kill either of them.

Did make old Boston the Wheelman look a bit more

dangerous than some folks might have expected in this town. Might be necessary, if the feds were about to turn him into some sort of criminal mastermind, however utterly deranged that idea was.

Rollins nodded, but he'd gone all in on being the heavy for this operation. Man knew guns. Knives. Fists. Possibly explosives, but Boston hadn't asked. Yet.

The other three sobered a bit. They had known some shit had gone down recently, with a whole raft of criminal scum all dead in a single day a few weeks ago. Boston didn't want the rep, but also wouldn't refuse a little respect if he was about to accidentally relegate up a league.

"So," Humboldt said, getting all the boys back on track with a growl. "Warehouse. Alarm system. Guards?"

"Haven't checked yet," Boston said. "Your job as Spotter. Want Rollins or Jones along?"

"Not on your life," she said, then turned to Jones. "You want video or stills of the setup?"

"Video," he said. "I can pull images out easy enough if you shoot at a decent frame rate with a modern cell phone camera."

Humboldt nodded, then turned to Boston.

"Who's driving the getaway?" she asked.

"Rollins," Boston replied. "We're going with a shell game here, so I want to carry the motif as far across the board as I can. You'll be a date in the front seat of his beater pickup."

She nodded. Looked at all of them, but it was the look of a younger-than-anyone woman who happened to be rather attractive, surrounded by a bunch of old farts, with Boston being at least a decade her senior and second youngest. She nodded.

"Welshman, you deliver the parts I need at my shop," Boston announced. "From there, I'll set the schedule, but it will be at least another week."

"Time for me to acquaint myself with things," Jones nodded.

The Grey Welshman shrugged.

"Trailer, too?" the man asked. "I have one with a winch on the front for hauling junkers."

"Perfect," Boston said. "I'll need to rent it for a week. Anything else?"

There being none, the group departed.

Boston was on his way.

Probably to hell, but weren't they all?

~

The knock on the workshop door was immediately followed by it opening.

Boston hadn't bothered locking it after he'd come in this morning. He had space behind a proper business, and anyone skulking about would cause a call to someone.

Rollins walked in, grabbed an empty, five-gallon bucket, and inverted it to sit. Because who uses chairs?

Boston nodded to the man and went back to welding the frame of steel bar stock into a shape he had in his head. Didn't have to be exact. Merely close enough for the things the Welshman would be delivering in the next day or so.

"Boss wants to meet you in person," Rollins called.

Boston reviewed that phrase, killed the welder, and lifted his blackout mask to stare at the man.

"Capital idea!" he snapped. "Let's just go ahead and get me killed, right up front."

Rollins bit back some profanities by the way his lips pursed.

"You don't think that *someone* is watching this place?" Boston continued, snarking at the man pretty hard. "Watching me to see what I do?"

Rollins shook his head and grimaced.

"Told her that," he said. "She might overrule me."

"Do you want this to succeed or fail?" Boston asked bluntly.

"You set me up into some genius of crime. I'd like to get out alive."

"You honestly think it can?" Rollins asked. "Succeed?"

"I stole the car in the first place, mate," Boston said, softening his anger. "Know the system there enough to describe it to Jones and Humboldt. Pretty sure we can steal it again. Not entirely certain what happens to it at that point, since Ferrari owners are an incestuous clique of toffs and probably can't keep a secret for long."

"You not keeping it?" Rollins asked, surprise evident.

"Where would I store a thrice-stolen Ferrari?" Boston growled.

"Well, it belongs in a museum, like…"

"Like what?" Boston pursued when the man suddenly stopped talking.

"I am not at liberty to say," Rollins said formally, saying a lot.

Man finally come clean about having been US Special Forces until injuries got him retired from active duty, to turn right back around and get a badge from…*someone*. Boston hadn't looked close then and didn't want to know now.

Peelers of some flavor. That was all that really mattered.

"Museum?" he pressed anyway, already dreading knowing.

"Crime bosses frequently do art collections," Rollins offered in an almost diffident tone, hinting at things Boston really didn't like contemplating. "Usually paintings, but a few do cars, as you know."

Boston's grimace felt painful.

"Start my own private stolen car collection?" he asked his cop friend dryly.

Rollins nodded.

"The team has a space in SoDo," he replied, referencing *South of Downtown*, beyond the stadiums into the old area that used to be warehouses and light factories, before turning a little yuckier recently. "Storage. We kept a few things there."

"We?" Boston asked.

Rollins nodded.

Could cops keep their mouths shut? Possibly. Otherwise, Rollins had the same sorts of secrets that would get him killed just as quickly.

Did he want an old classic Ferrari? Not the sort of thing Boston could ever drive while Atorov was alive. Or his close killers. Still, better than trying to find a buyer in the short term.

Start a museum of stolen cars?

Yegads, the thought of it had him cackling. What better way to stick it to more than a few folks that might deserve it?

"Not meeting with your boss," Boston circled back. "Unless it looks like a date and she's dressed all slinky in public."

"Pretty sure that's a deal-breaker for her," Rollins nodded, grinning. "Will ask anyway. Mostly to watch steam come out her ears."

Boston nodded. He'd only met the woman the once. Generic looking brunette that reminded him of a spy. In all the bad ways. Best not to spend too much time around her, in case something rubbed off on him.

"How close are we?" Rollins asked, nodding to the frame taking shape.

"Couple of days," Boston replied, tapping the nearly-done metalwork. "Then the shit will get silly."

Rollins rose, so Boston flipped his mask down and got back to work.

Boston still lived in Kent, but not at this end. Long town. Third biggest in the state by population. Used to be farms, but all that had long-since been filled in with warehouses.

Including the one he wanted.

Wednesday night, because quite a lot of god-bothered folks

went to church in this town, so there was more traffic than usual. That worked in his favor, since this job was supposed to be quiet instead of a bloody car chase.

Rollins's 1999 Ford F-150 Extended cab. Looked like a lot of old beaters. Bondo and rust. Boston had redone the engine, though. Space for four, with Boston having parked an old Toyota Camri nearby that he and Jones would use to bug out later.

Trailer was in place behind them. Lump on the back that looked remarkably like a 1978 Pontiac Firebird under a tarp. Welshman had supplied the panels from his yard.

Humboldt was watching the night through compact binoculars.

"Unless there are guards inside, that's it," she announced quietly. Truck windows were down on a warm night, so outside sounds could be heard, including highway 167 in the near distance. "We're ready to go."

Spotter. Literally her job to know who was where and when. Warehouse on a Wednesday night, but not too late. People moving around, which would make it harder to spot them on the road.

Rollins turned in place to look back. Boston nodded.

"Jones, you ready?" he asked.

"Was wondering if I should take a nap," Jones muttered.

"Go," Boston ordered.

Rollins dropped the beast into gear and started rolling. They were across a sidestreet in a closed dental office parking lot, halfway behind the building. Quick shot down and across, and Rollins was in front of a generic warehouse door.

"Just past, stay to the right," Boston reminded him.

Rollins grunted and did, parking and leaving the engine purring quietly as Humboldt bailed out of her side and walked around the trailer in back. The rest of them stayed still until cleared by the Lineman. Spotter. Her.

Because if you're going to hire someone for their expertise, why the hell aren't you going to listen to her?

Humboldt turned and nodded in the open window. Boston opened the door and followed her, with Jones sliding across to join him and Rollins coming up last.

If all went well, they wouldn't need superior firepower. Best to have it anyway. Too many people thought of guns as magic wands you waved to get people to do what you wanted. Boston knew better.

Same same, if you were expecting gunplay, best to have experts on staff there, too. Folks like Rollins.

They were around on the side of the warehouse. Place had an office up front that wasn't used, but had glass looking out. And lots of extra security there to keep tweakers from getting in. Less of a trouble spot than Fife, but still a risk.

Humboldt planted her butt against the side of the building and started scanning all directions, including up. Boston stayed out of her way. Rollins was about as tactical as Boston had ever seen.

Jones went to work.

Man knelt and pulled out a small bag of gear. Roll-up garage door with a ten-key next to it that also took a fob none of them had. Boston looked left while Rollins watched right, but he did steal glances as Jones *fiddled*.

It was a technical term.

Wires from a doohickey got attached to the box. Signals got traced. Jones grunted occasionally and nodded to some unheard rhythm.

At one point, he stopped and locked eyes with Boston over his shoulder.

"Russian gangsters?" he asked bluntly.

Boston nodded.

Jones did something more and the wall thunked pretty hard as the locks retracted. Boston wanted to ask what the hell that meant, but time was literally of the essence at this point.

"Cameras were on," Jones said. "I've killed them, but it's only a matter of time before someone realizes that. We need to move quickly."

Boston grabbed the handle and lifted. Rollins would be ready to shoot. Jones was busy disconnecting things. Humboldt was watching.

It was a team effort.

The interior was a vast cathedral of cars, stretched out and diagonally parallel parked. Lights were low enough inside to make everything dim, but visible.

Boston led, immediately turning left and going up that side's long corridor.

Place was a long box, with fast cars tail in diagonally and ten feet apart so you could have both doors open at once and not touch.

Wouldn't do to so much as scratch the paint in here. He'd heard rumors that the mechanics employed weren't allowed to wear blue jeans, on account of the rivets that some brands put in. Cars were not driven about, but instead lifted like newborn babies on powered roller carts.

Boston fought to keep from drooling at the collected wealth in precious antiques Atorov had accumulated. Not the Old Masters, but maybe close enough for a gearhead like him.

The 1953 Mercedes Gullwing that he had lusted after for so long. That Jensen-Healey Mark I from home. The 2012 Ferrari 458 Spider in arrest-me-red. The midnight blue '96 Porsche 911 GT2. Older Alfas, Bugattis, and BMWs from the racing days. So much iron he'd happily liberate and haul off.

Pity, as Atorov was certain to seriously upgrade his security around here, once he realized that being a crime boss with a reputation for abject brutality wasn't enough.

And Ms. Chan wouldn't protect him. Merely cover for this,

because there had to be some bad blood between those two if she'd sent hunters after the man's favorite auto.

The Dino had never really done it for Boston, but he liked his Blue Zip, the 2005 Toyota MR2 Spyder right-hander that he'd tweaked. Most of the cars Atorov owned could beat him on a straight track. Nothing in here could touch him in a slalom.

Boston moved quickly. The cart he wanted was tucked away in a corner. Hydraulic pallet lifter, basically, only much bigger. And covered with cloth so it didn't scratch the underside. He hopped on and drove it rather like that standing mower that one chap had in the park. Helped that it was fully charged and top of the line.

Like so much of what Atorov did, except for having better security around his system than obscurity and a few locks.

Maybe Boston really did need to turn himself into a criminal genius, after all...

Jones was there when he got back to the Dino, standing to one side and guiding him in, but this was almost automatic for Boston, though he'd never owned such a toy. Too busy rebuilding and selling things. Or fixing up getaway cars for others to burn after use.

Never a collector.

He could see where that might have been a mistake on his part.

Or maybe his greed was getting the better of him.

Boston drove forward and settled the beast. Just to be sure, he hopped off the carrier and walked over the driver's door. Window was open. Keys were in the ash tray.

Idly, he wondered if the car might actually start on the first go.

It was Atorov's favorite. Did he take it out for the occasional spin? Beast like this was meant for the track east of town, but pushing a race car to its limits took skills that he doubted the average Moscow goon had ever learned in a Lada.

Probably just took it through the coffee shop drive-thru to show off.

Still, Boston leaned in and made sure that the parking brake was set to hold things in place before getting back and lifting the Dino off the concrete with a whir of hydraulic power that sent a chill through his soul.

Turning, he patiently pulled out of the parking slot and lined up with the stripes, a small dump truck hauling an extra trailer in his mind. Jones backed away quickly, but Boston was moving at a sedate walk.

Honestly, Ms. Chan probably would have been satisfied if he'd dropped a Molotov cocktail in the driver's seat, but let's face it, there was a certain lack of subtlety to such a thing, and that behavior should be reserved for Thatcher statues.

Outside, he found Rollins standing on the front of the trailer, with the winch cable ready to deploy. Humboldt watched from close by. Jones moved to the side of the truck, out of everybody's way because he'd done his part and didn't do automobiles like the rest of them.

Boston drove like a valet delivering the PM's car to the front of the restaurant on the tellie. Rolled it all the way around to his right and began to line things up with the trailer, but didn't bother getting too straight just yet.

Instead, he lowered the lifters and sat the Dino back on pavement. Parking brake would hold it in place, so he backed away and drove the little cart just inside the doors and pulled it down.

First person in tomorrow would discover the theft, but Boston expected that whatever Jones had done to the systems would show up first.

And there was no way to hide a missing Ferrari.

Chuckling to himself, Boston walked over to the Dino and hopped in. Keys? Why the hell not?

He put them in the ignition and dropped the clutch,

expecting nothing to happen, so it surprised the hell out of him when the engine turned over and purred. This would make it so much easier to get it onto the trailer, as he'd been expecting to sit here as Rollins winched him up.

Movement on his right was Humboldt exploding into motion, running right towards him.

"We're blown!" she yelled, slipping around the ass end of the Dino and sliding into the passenger seat. "Jones, in the truck. Rollins, move!"

She was looking over her shoulder, so Boston glanced up at the rear view. A big Jersey tractor of a blacked-out SUV was barreling up the street behind him and turning into the parking lot without slowing down, hammering the undercarriage hard enough that Boston actually saw sparks underneath.

Normally, big rigs like that had a lot of clearance, the kind you needed for snow and such. If it was riding that low, someone had armored the shit out of it, so nothing Rollins was carrying would do much to even scratch the paint.

Boston glanced over at Humboldt, even as he automatically found first gear.

"You're going to need a spotter," she told him.

One hundred percent correct, madam.

Rollins was moving. Jones was halfway in the pickup.

Boston popped the clutch with enough rev to throw smoke from the back tires as they leapt into motion.

Time to drive like a madman.

Boston blasted the gap past the pickup and trailer like a rabbit going into a woodpile, pretty certain that the shiny element would draw the beast after him if they had to only choose one. After all, this was the boss's baby, and somebody was stealing it.

Worse, he remembered the machine from before. Factory standard everything, which made it so valuable, but it also meant that the engine was *significantly* underpowered compared to modern vehicles. Top speed, straight and clear race day, probably one-forty. The Zip could beat that, given enough time to gear up.

He had no idea if they'd upgunned the engine when they armored that black tank. Didn't really want to know.

Needed to get gone.

Good thing someone had hired a halfway competent wheelman.

He roared off in a scream of howling metal.

Down the side of the building and drift the ass end but not much, because the engine is behind you and most folks don't understand how to manipulate that kind of mass at speed.

The Blue Zip was also mid-engine. Boston was in his element, save that it was an Italian car, so he was sitting on the left like a silly American driver.

Glancing up, he saw the SUV blow by Rollins, who was already going for the truck to get gone. Hopefully, nobody had gotten a really good look at things. That would matter later.

Around the corner, he found the back exit where the lot wrapped all the way around. Going too fast for the driveway, so he dialed gears back down and came in softly.

If he was going to steal a classic, there was no reason to destroy it in the process.

Hopefully.

Side street off a side street, so he bounced left, then left again. Right onto the main street, opposite the way the punks had come, left at the Mexican restaurant he'd never tried.

"Road splits for the bridge over the railroad tracks," Humboldt offered. "Option south on the far side to cut back. Or straight puts you eventually at Southcenter, the transfer station, or the freeway."

He nodded and ignored her. Humboldt was doing her job as spotter, assuming that the wheelman was too busy running like hell to plan where he was going,

Only half right. The Dino had a lot of acceleration, low-slung and powerful. The tank back there could probably catch up, if he stayed straight.

Only a fool made it easy for the bad guys.

That was the problem with a city like Kent. Modern. American. Lots of straight roads, occasionally curving softly around the Green River or the railroad beds, but too squared off for a high-performance sports car to really thrive.

Still, no reason to make it easy for them.

Rear view mirror showed lights. Too far away to be shooting yet. Might not shoot at all, because Boss's prize. Might do it anyway, if the alternative was a car thief getting away.

He bombed madly up and over the bridge, then skewed hard around that first left, running the light because a cop showing up right now to arrest someone would call down all the devils in hell to help.

Kent PD had a rep that went far beyond crazy when it came to militant lunacy.

Road curved. Straightened out. Tank made the left back there and started running hard.

Boston didn't have a gps on the dash, so he had to rely on the one in his head. And the Lineman next to him.

"Past the next intersection, hopping up into the lot," he told her.

"The weird thing with three buildings like some socket lock from space?" she asked.

He'd never seen it that way, but it described that parking lot pretty well. Stupid amount of exit options. Lots of trees. Maneuvering nightmare if you weren't low to the pavement.

He downshifted, drifted, and entered at a speed probably good for a lot of points on his license next time around. Better, any red lights he ran tonight would set off the cameras and mail tickets to whoever owned this sexy beast on paper.

Somehow, Boston doubted that Gari Atorov was the name listed.

Immediate hard left, then drift across several lanes of parking lot as the beast back there SQUEALED around the corner. Probably too much to ask that they clipped a tree or a telephone pole.

Except that they were riding low. Lots of armor around the passengers?

Needed to get crazier to have them roll with all that excess top heaviness.

Useful if so.

Time to find out.

Soft right, around the first of those three weird buildings, ignoring the circular parking lot in the middle where civilized people would have left a park or something.

No way out west side, so he braked savagely, skidded, and snapped a hard left that cut across a greenbelt and into the next lot.

Straight shot across the lot. Stupendous number of low trees around here. Not as solid as French hedgerows, but probably sufficient for his needs. Boston killed the headlights and drove by the glow of Generica.

Hit the street and zip left, zagging with it to the stop sign.

California stop to make sure a semi wasn't about to broadside him, then right.

He had space on the SUV, as long as they had to drive a little more sane than he did.

All that excess mass up top. More than the springs and struts can handle at speed.

There was a reason sports cars sat so low.

Go like hell.

Nobody at the next light. Hard right, listening for oncoming traffic but not slowing down to really check.

Because some nights you have to trust your luck to the gods.

Not too many cars about. Still enough to make this an obstacle course of a drive.

And all the damned buildings around here were long, straight, and square, without any useful corners to hide behind or alleys to duck into, damn it.

"They saw us make the first turn," Humboldt announced calmly. "The trees will blind them for twenty seconds."

Still doing her job.

Time to do his.

Boston took a hard left across traffic that had enough gap. Up a driveway into yet another warehouse complex. Welcome to Kent.

Blasted down a long gap between two buildings with enough side overhang to back 53-foot rigs into place to load.

Only problem was that pulling into one to hide left him trapped if someone came around the corner suddenly and boxed him in.

Ungood.

First gap at the far end he snapped things around left, drifting enough that he would need to put new tires on the Dino soon enough. It was meant to run, but he'd been riding it harder than expected. Plus, he had no idea how much petrol there was in the tank.

And he needed to be quite a ways from here before pulling into a station.

Humboldt was turned halfway around watching their rear as he worked.

"Did they see us?" he said as the Dino coasted out of sight behind the building.

If the fools took that right back there, they should be in the process of blowing west, eventually hitting that long, curving climb back up to the transfer station, with a sudden zag in the middle to put you on northbound Five. Which immediately gave you options of Four-oh-Five and Five-Eighteen as well.

Fellow could vanish, if you gave him thirty seconds lead time.

Main road back there had a soft wobble that obscured sight lines. And enough Wednesday evening traffic that there were distracting lights. Busy part of town, because of the climb out also went to the airport as well as the freeway.

Boston rolled to the far end of the little alley they were in, but stopped short. If someone came out behind them, he could hit the road right in front of him going either way. If they were suddenly right in front of him, a hard left and he was running back up the parking lot the way he'd come.

He counted to sixty, aware that he was breathing heavy, but a five-speed manual in a car chase was a bit of exercise, in an era before serious power-assist steering.

"We clear?" he asked his Spotter.

"Not seeing headlights back there indicating pursuit," she replied quietly. "Nobody out of context in front of us."

Took him a minute to place that, then he understood. Everybody belonged somewhere. They stood out otherwise, like a blue 1972 Ferrari Dino 246 GTS on Kent streets at night.

He gave it another minute, then pulled out and turned left. Risky, if those folks decided to double back, but best way out of here. At the light, right and across the tracks, thankful that the crossguards weren't down and forcing him to run parallel on tiny side streets.

Across and up Easthill, he dialed.

"You okay?" Rollins asked immediately, using the code that said he was safe at his end.

"Headed to your fallback up in Renton," Boston replied.

"The bank?" Rollins asked.

"That's the place."

"See you in ten."

Boston blew out a heavy breath and drove.

～

Left when he reached Petrovitsky. Right into a coffee shop lot next to a chain pharmacy. Coffee shop had been a bank at some point. Recent enough to have drive-thru banking, which was an utterly American thing.

The Dino was still purring as he drove right up behind the flatbed that Rollins had already deployed. Boston killed the engine and held the brake with his foot as Rollins pulled the cable and delicately wrapped the front bumper.

The hollow frame on the flatbed looked like a Pontiac because they could pull the Dino underneath and get it strapped down for transit. Anyone seeing it would see lines that were all wrong. Would miss the surprise underneath.

Shell games. Necessary.

Whatever security system Jones had missed, they might have pulled this trick an hour ago, but Boston was just happy to get out alive.

A few pedestrians watched the whole thing, but unless someone called the cops, all the descriptions would be vague and meaningless. And confusing when the Ferrari turned into an old Pontiac.

They got in the truck and Boston leaned back, letting Rollins drive and Humboldt pretend to be his date.

"Home?" Rollins asked.

"Yes," Boston replied. "We'll send someone after the Toyota tomorrow."

"Got a cousin we can call," Humboldt piped up.

"Tomorrow," he repeated.

Because he had to make another call tomorrow, too.

S ame Italian joint. Less snobbery from the guy up front this time.

Boston still didn't wear a tie to anything but funerals. Hopefully, this didn't qualify.

Same table. Same damned amazing bread. Wine immediately this time instead of water.

Ms. Chan was simply breathtaking when she walked in. If you ignored the goons. Slacks and jacket cut to emphasize lean and long. Hair he assumed was dyed, because he remembered from somewhere that forty was generally the cut-off for women starting to go gray.

He rose. She smiled. They sat.

More wine delivered.

"Gossip mill is all aflutter with news," she observed vaguely.

Boston nodded. He'd heard the same thing. Probably faster than her, because every gearhead in town had been calling each other for updates.

He'd been pretending to watch a tape of Man U getting annihilated by Wolverhampton, which always put a smile on his face.

No criminal mastermind car thieves here, guv'nah.

"Surprised that nobody did something more…violent to the place," he offered.

After all, she'd hired him to steal one car. A statement crime if he ever heard.

"That lacks subtlety," she replied with a compact smile. "Anyone could have hit the place with firebombs."

At that, she was correct, though Boston supposed that such an act might simply be the prologue of a gang war that would make Rollins pull his hair out, even as his bosses were thrilled to watch bad guys removing one another from the scene.

One way or the other.

"I preferred a message be sent," Ms. Chan purred, then paused as food got delivered.

Again, never once ordering, but it had been stupendously amazing last time, and looked it today as well.

She watched him over pasta in white sauce.

"Will the object in question vanish forever?" she asked.

"Found a buyer," Boston replied, not bothering to go into detail about forming a small corporate entity, then loaning it a few bucks to buy said masterpiece from him.

All pretty and crisp, according to one government attorney who hadn't been able to keep from giggling occasionally as she did the paperwork. Rollins had vouched for the woman, and she'd been sworn to secrecy.

She'd apparently done this sort of thing before.

He hadn't asked.

The Dino was safe. Tucked away in a space that accidentally could hold a great deal more, if he was feeling frisky. Or greedy.

"The gentleman in question is furious," she observed blandly. "Thinks the Chinese did it."

Boston kept his opinions to himself. A month ago, he'd stolen a cherry-red Corvette Stingray right-hand, getting himself arrested by Rollins in an act of betrayal that hadn't turned out too bad, all things considered.

Far as Boston knew, those same Mainlander Tong folks were either running for their lives today, or moldering in small, concrete boxes without access to attorneys or consular officers.

Because sometimes, the Feds play a little rough.

"Let us hope he continues to think that," Boston offered blandly.

"What's next for you, Boston?" she asked, those dark eyes still hitting like a cop's desklamp in an investigation.

"A bit of cheer in funding," he answered delicately, aware of just how bloody dangerous this woman was, for all she appeared serene and in complete control of the scene. Any scene. "An upgrade to some of my operations, after a recent stretch where I worried that I might have to pack up and move to Vegas or Los Angeles."

Fools down there were forever stealing cars and needing wheelmen to handle things. Usually amateur hour, but the money would be good.

Provided that he didn't end up in jail when some punk rolled over.

"Staying local?" she asked, eyes suddenly *glittery* in ways that made his stomach flutter. "Available for jobs?"

"That is the intent, madam," he nodded. "Need a bit of time off, as I am in the process of breaking in a new team, but happy to discuss future work if you had something."

He left it trailing off there meaningfully.

She wasn't Seattle Tech Billionaire rich, but those folks had no idea how to use money as power anyway, most of them. They bought sports teams and built rockets.

Ms. Chan owned companies that owned companies. Lots of them. Subtle and quiet and hiding in the woodwork as they generated cash that all got hoovered up and shipped to her.

Everyone in town understood that she was almost legitimate these days.

Almost.

"I have a few thoughts," Ms. Chan smiled. "Things that required a delicate combination of professionalism and violence, if you might be interested."

And he might turn into a criminal mastermind. Well, not mastermind. Team Lead, when the mastermind sat in an office in a tower with a view of the Sound or the Mountain.

Not having any fun with fast cars.

"I might," Boston offered.

Might as well have criminals pay him to do things, knowing that Rollins and his boss would be watching.

He was certain that the Dino would get lonely, after a while.

THE SPY WHO STABBED ME (IN THE BACK)

DAVID BOOP & MATTHEW HELLMAN

THE SPY WHO STABBED ME (IN THE BACK)

C.R.I.M.E. PAYS #1

DAVID BOOP & MATTHEW HELLMAN

"And over to your left, you'll get a stunning view of the Strait of Gibraltar, which separates the Atlantic Ocean from the Mediterranean Sea."

Rylan Doyle said the words that any tourist with half-a-brain should already know, but clearly there were some on his tour bus who had never looked at a map before booking a vacation to Morocco. The locals told Rylan, when he arrived a year ago, that ever since *Casablanca* came out forty plus years ago, Americans flocked to the African coast looking for love, adventure, and mystery. They often went home disappointed, robbed of their cash and jewelry, and never once hearing, "As Time Goes By."

But he didn't care at that moment. All Rylan needed the rubes to do was focus on the harbor to their right for another few moments while one specific tourist, who was, in reality, not a tourist, subtly retrieved a headphone from a hidden compartment under his seat and placed it to his ear. The single earpiece ran to a receiver that had been set to a specific frequency predetermined by the sender. The message that the not-a-tourist heard would be for his ears only. Rylan had no idea what the message contained, or even which side the not-a-spy worked for. All Rylan cared about was being paid, staying alive to spend the money, and never getting involved.

Rylan continued pointing out interesting features of Tangier to the tourists until the not-whatever nodded. By the time Rylan finished his tour guide bit, the headphone had been returned to its place and the definitely-a-spy resumed his guise as a fellow gawker, leaning forward and placing a hand on the shoulder of the person next to him and making appropriate noises as if he'd been watching along the whole time. Rylan had to admit, the agent was good. If the man hadn't said the specific words Rylan needed to hear when he booked the tour, the fixer would've never guessed he worked in some sort of intelligence capacity. Nothing about him suggested spy, or spook, or agent, or consultant or whatever the kids called them these days. The Cold War bred new forms of espionage every day, and Rylan felt fortunate enough to have carved out his own little piece of it as an info intermediary.

However, just as Rylan started up his twelve-seater tour bus, he caught a glimpse of three men approaching in his side view mirror. They were still a block away, so Rylan jammed the transmission into gear.

"Well, folks, if we're lucky, we might just be able to make happy hour down at Sam's bar, where the lovely Chama Tazi will be performing local favorites."

He pulled out from their parking space so fast one man lost his hat, another lady fell into a stranger's lap, and Rylan's spy had the first indication something was wrong. He looked over his shoulder casually to discover what Rylan already knew. The three men were now running after them, guns not drawn but clearly visible in shoulder holsters as their jackets fanned out.

"And I bet, if you tip the piano player nicely, he'll play 'As Time Goes By,' for you. Just...don't tell him I told you that." Rylan had lied earlier. *All* the tourists always went home with

THE SPY WHO STABBED ME (IN THE BACK)

"As Time Goes By" stuck in their ears. It was played at every bar, every night, at least a dozen times, tips or not. It was the only thing that made up for the disappointment and theft.

The road from *Parc Rmilat* wound down a series of switchbacks. No way to avoid it. Tangier had basically been built on the side of a cliff. The pursuing spooks took advantage of their foot chase to cut straight down the hill, keeping them closer than Rylan would like. He didn't care what happened to his special passenger, but he did care about the tourists. Hanging his arm outside the topless bus, he waved until he caught the eye of the spy. He flashed five fingers, and the agent nodded. Then he counted down.

Four fingers.

Three fingers.

Two fingers.

Taking a corner too fast on purpose, Rylan once again distracted the rubes with some local flavor while the potentially soon-to-be-late-spy jumped off the bus the opposite way. The fixer watched him roll, get up, and run. The opposing agents changed direction to follow.

The hounds might still meet Rylan's tour group at Sam's, if they lost their rabbit. They might even pull him into an alley later, push him around to see what he knew about his passenger or the message, but Rylan knew nothing. Because he didn't want to know.

And they all knew that.

The next time, it might be those same three guys asking for him to set an information drop. Rylan never took a side and played both of them. Something he should've learned back in Boston, or he wouldn't be in Tangier driving ugly Americans around and keeping a low profile.

As predicted, three different agents of some foreign power waited for Rylan's bus when they arrived. They afforded him the professional courtesy of allowing his passengers to get inside the bar before they dragged him by the collar around to an alley. Rylan held up his hands in surrender before they could land the first blow to his gut.

"Gentlemen, let me save you the trouble. He jumped out at *Avenue Ahmed Balafrej* and ran south, but you know that. He received a coded transmission of what content *I* don't know. I don't ask. I never ask. You know my reputation."

The three agents looked at each other, then nodded. One took out a wad of folded cash and spoke in a thick accent.

"We vish to make a similar arrangement with you."

Rylan grinned. Two jobs in one day? He'd eat well that night.

∽

Three Weeks Later

"How much?"

Rylan hated asking because it meant that any money he squirreled away would be eaten by the mechanic like last fall's nuts. Wasif clicked his teeth in a way that already told Rylan it wouldn't be cheap.

"Ever since the third-generation bus came out, second-gen parts are getting harder to come by."

"Second gen? Third gen? It's not that old."

Wasif crawled out from under the bus. "Old enough. Did you not buy Cyndi for a ridiculously low price?"

Now Rylan understood. The man who sold him the bus must've already figured out that repairs would increase as parts became harder to get.

"Again, what's it going to cost?"

More clicking, then a number that made Rylan gag.

Cyndi—the affectionate name he'd given the multi-colored

bus because it reminded him of a singer from back in the states — had seen him through several near-death experiences, but she'd paid a price for it. The axle showed enough wear that if he didn't replace it soon, it might fail when he needed it most. The price Wasif quoted was more than he'd saved up even with his "side" ventures.

"How long?"

Wiping the grease off of his hands, Wasif asked, "Until the axle breaks or until I can get a replacement?"

"Both?"

Wasif sucked in a breath through his teeth, clearly doing some calculations in his head. "I'd say the axle, if you take it easy, could last another couple of months, but if you continue to drive the way you do, it might snap in a week or two." He clicked his tongue. "I can start reaching out to see what's inbound, but six months, tops."

The idea of taking it easy on Cyndi versus the need to make money to pay for repairs ran directly opposite to each other.

"Order it. I'll get you a down payment as soon as I can."

His mechanic nodded. The man trusted Rylan as much as he trusted anyone, which was, he'd afford him credit until the first time he didn't pay up. Rylan had been a good customer since he'd arrived in Tangier, plus he gave Wasif "special" repair jobs which made him happy. The young mechanic had a gift for fixing things that integrated well with Rylan's ability to break things.

"Oh!" Wasif suddenly remembered, reaching in over the side of the bus and popping open the secret compartment where the radio receiver lay hidden. "How did this work for your last tour?"

Rylan grinned. "Good, but I think I need to figure out a different configuration. It takes a lot of work to keep the sightseers preoccupied while the client uses it."

"Hmmm." Wasif stroked the seats. "Too bad these are not

third gen seats. Then I could run the earpiece up into the headrest. Then they wouldn't have to bend down to pull the headpiece out."

That's a good idea, Rylan thought. The client then could just lean their head back and get the message they needed. The spy game avoided messages printed on paper as much as possible these days, as they were too easy to intercept. Messages sent via specific radio frequencies made it more secure when the frequency wouldn't be determined until just before the broadcast. The chosen frequency would be given to the agent via a "brief encounter," also in code. Rylan would set the receiver to the right channel and drive the spook to a place where the signal could be picked up through a short-range agent communication—or SRAC, as he'd been told by a client. Rylan understood the tech just enough to make sure there'd been no hiccups so far, but the more obstacles he removed, the smoother the operation would go.

"And how much would it cost to swap out the seats?" he asked, figuring that Wasif had already worked up a cost for him.

Click. Another estimate that turned Rylan's gut. The upgrades to his topless VW bus needed to keep up with these lucrative side jobs. The seats almost countered the funds those jobs brought in.

"Order them. I'll find the money."

Wasif beamed like a birthday boy.

Rylan would have to find a big score to pay for all these repairs, which meant something risky, which put both Cyndi— and him— at risk. He backed her out of the repair bay and headed to the Medina to see what high paying trouble he could get into.

THE SPY WHO STABBED ME (IN THE BACK)

Rylan drove past block after block of new construction. Tangier's economy boomed in the 80s, but not just due to the Moroccanization of industry, which made global businesses partner through Soussis or Fassi investments. Drug cartels from around the world laundered money through the city and real estate was the easiest way to hide ill-gotten gains.

Apartment complexes in various levels of completion may house a few ex-pats, timeshare owners, or vacationers, but the locals would never be able to afford them. Each "palace" had a swimming pool, tennis courts, playgrounds, and community rooms. Even drug lords wouldn't stay in them when they could afford the grandest hotels with twenty-four-seven room service. All these buildings made Tangier look like the "White City" tourists wanted, but Rylan knew the real city, *El Kelba*: The Bitch.

Rylan would find the type of work he required in the old Tangier. Deep into the black soul of the city; the places he dreaded going but needed now.

Rylan passed the Kasbah and turned off the *Rue d'Italie* into the maze of side streets and alleys. He knew which ones would accommodate Cyndi's size, so he navigated the labyrinthine passages until he found a place where he could safely leave her. He'd walk the rest of the way to the Medina.

The aromatic scent of eucalyptus and oranges almost overwhelmed the urine and rotted fish that infused the cobblestone street. Rylan stepped around the various vendors, most of whom recognized him. They didn't accept him as one of their own, choosing to ignore him unless word came down that he'd scored a payday, even if they didn't know why. The citizens of the Medina were knowledgeable and ignorant, as needed.

The Khalij Hotel was not a recommended hotel in the Fodor's Guide, unless they had a section for negative stars. The only people who stayed there were the lost, the hiding, and the ones trying to look lost or in hiding. In other words, intelligence agents. In fact, it was so known in the spy game for being *the* place to get a room that the owners had enacted a "no shooting other guests while on the premises" policy. Any damage done to the property due to gunfire, explosions, or fighting would result in a forfeiture of deposit and possible ban from future stays.

Not that there weren't several hotels like the Khalij around Tangier. Each country, and often each agency within that country, had their favorites. Rylan learned quickly that "open secrets" were common in the spy game. The Khalij stood out from the rest by welcoming all agencies on either side, which is why he did business there. He never wanted to be trapped by only playing one side. That was how someone got disposed of. Plus, he no longer had a country, a home. Someone had made damn sure of that.

The bar, known only for having the worst selection of premium booze in the city, could be counted on to have fixers looking to hire intermediaries, such as Rylan. He often picked up on subtle changes to the spy game. Recently, there'd been a lot of activity, with more spooks coming through the city than he'd seen since he arrived. That was good for Rylan's chances of finding high-paying work, but it also suggested something earth-shattering waited in the shadows.

Taking the stairs to the third-floor bar, Rylan chose a seat that afforded him a view of the Spanish coastline across the Mediterranean. Of all the cities he could've chosen to hide in after fleeing for his life, he was grateful he'd found Tangier. Being near the ocean felt natural to him, and even though nothing about Morocco reminded him of his real home in Nova Scotia, just being near air filled with the essence of Poseidon relaxed him.

Rylan cast his eyes casually around the colonial-style room trying not to appear like someone needing work, while assessing anyone who might be offering work. Brass pendant lights cast the back of the bar in sepia tones, but the summer midday sun brightened and warmed the corner Rylan occupied. Despite the increase in activity, the pickings there appeared slim. No one seemed anxious while nursing a drink. He sipped his own for almost two hours and prepared to give up for the day. Tourists would be ready for an afternoon tour of the city, and while not the money he desired, he still had bills to pay. As he dropped some coins on the table, someone entered the bar and headed directly to him.

No, not someone.

Her.

She flipped the red hair back that had once upon a time draped over him as they lay in bed. Giving him an awkward, lopsided smile, she said, "You look good. You're going by Rylan now, right? Well, you look well, Rylan. The tan suits you."

Stupefied, Rylan stared.

She continued. "Yeah, I know. You said if you ever saw me again, you'd kill me. If I had a dollar for every tim—"

Rylan didn't hear the rest as he'd jumped out the window by then.

～

The awning broke Rylan's fall, which he'd counted on.

He rolled off it and hit the sidewalk harder than he would've liked to, which he hadn't.

Going from hands and knees to an awkward sprint left Rylan unsteady on his feet, but he got his momentum back after a block.

Behind him, he heard the shoving and shouting that came from pursuit. Turning a corner, he caught a glimpse of two men, Feds, trying to catch up to him.

Arica's men, no doubt.

He had no idea how she'd found him or what she wanted, but experience and fear told him he wouldn't like the answers. Cyndi would have to wait. He needed to be clear and fast. Rylan thought about the safe houses he'd established and wondered how safe they really were. If *she* was here, and knew his alias, then she might have been watching him for some time. She might've already worked up a list of his contacts, behaviors, and hidey-holes. That's what she did, after all. Find out everything about her target and then use it against them.

Rylan cursed under his breath. He thought he'd been so careful when he left the States. If she could find him, then maybe *they* would, too.

One place he could think to go. One place he'd kept in reserve for just such a case.

Rylan slammed his way through the Medina, knocking over an oil cart and spilling tomatoes from a vendor's display. Did her men still follow him? He couldn't look back to find out. He'd trust that Tangier's fortune god, *Gad*, would protect him. The city could, if bothered to, close in around him, swallowing him up. He'd disappear into the crowds and his pursuers would be hampered by a sudden curse of bad luck.

He'd scoped out *La Purisima* when he'd first arrived, but never went to mass there. He deliberately went to a different church on the opposite end of the city, so he'd never be spotted around the Church of Immaculate Conception. Instead, he made subtle donations to the church using an alias. The alter boy he used as a courier made sure to give the money to the same priest every time using this alias. Rylan learned this trick from the Patriarca family, which meant *they* could figure it out, but not her. That was too close a family secret.

He hopped down a set of back steps and pounded on the door. He kept at it until his hand nearly bled. Finally, a nun answered.

"*Donc, comment puis-je vous aider?*" she asked. She wore thick, old glasses that matched her skin and eyes. She squinted at him, trying to decide if she knew him.

"I need to speak to Father Renaudin. Please tell him it's urgent."

Rylan's tone startled her, and she took a step back.

"*Qui est à l'appareil?*"

"Tell him it's John. John Winger."

The nun closed the door. Now, Rylan took the moment to poke his head up from the stairwell. He saw no one, heard no sounds of locals being accosted for information. He took a deep breath and relaxed.

The door reopened and the aged nun motioned for him to follow her. The church's basement contained dust-cover crates Rylan was sure were from the crusades. They passed a laundry area where several more nuns washed soiled linens. Rylan realized he'd been lucky, after all. No one might have been down there otherwise.

"Thank Gad," he said.

"*Oui, dieu merci.*"

Rylan chuckled and thought, *Whoever*.

After ascending a series of stairs, Rylan was handed over to a clergyman, who escorted him to the door of an office. The man in white robes knocked on the door. The response, *"Entrer,"* came immediately.

Opening the door, the clergyman bowed slightly as Rylan entered and his heart stopped.

Father Renaudin sat behind his desk, a broad smile gracing his face. The other person in the room also wore a smile, but it was more the cat-eating-the-canary kind.

"There's my brother! Thank God almighty he found his way here."

The redhead jumped from her chair to embrace Rylan in a hug like she hadn't seen him in ages. She whispered in his ear, "John Winger? Really? *Stripes* was the first movie you took me to." She released but held him at arm's length. "You *did* miss me."

The priest joined them putting a hand on each of their shoulders. "I am so pleased," he said with a thick French accent, "that your brother, John, thought to seek our sanctuary when you two were separated by muggers. What a terrible fright you must have had to run in separate directions."

"Yes," the redhead agreed. "John would've fought them, but he only thought of my safety; making the robbers chase him, not me." She leaned forward and kissed each of his cheeks. "My brave brother."

Rylan opened his mouth to say something, to tell the priest she lied, and ask for actual sanctuary from the United States Federal Bureau of Investigation, but she was no amateur. "I hope this donation to the widows' and orphans' funds can be a thank you to God and your church. After all, you clearly know how to help the lost."

The thick envelope she pulled from her jacket removed all doubt in Rylan's mind that he would be leaving with her. Not wanting to burn a bridge, he shook the priest's hands. "Yes, Father. Thank you. May God watch over your flock."

"And you, my son."

But Rylan knew God, Gad, or any deity worth their name couldn't save him now.

A car waited for them outside with a driver and two other agents. Something seemed off, though. The redhead's two agents stood like fish out of water. Their body language indicated a paranoia that Rylan didn't often see in Federal investigators. Especially those run by Arica Riggs.

Arica kept close to him, making sure he got in the back, awkwardly seated between her and one of her agents. The other got in front with the driver. They didn't bother to pat him down. Arica believed he'd never carry a gun unless he had to. Even though he'd been in exile for a year, she must've assumed he hadn't changed that much.

Little does she know.

Maybe he should've run to Cyndi after all. He often packed while on tours, a .45 strapped under the dash for quick retrieval. Tangier changes a person over time.

And she was the cause of it all.

The betrayal of the Patriarcas.

The death mark they put on him.

His fleeing the country to become an ex-pat.

No longer trusting anyone. Always looking over his shoulder.

All because of those eyes. Those aquamarine eyes that reminded him of his mother's. He'd trusted Arica because of those eyes and look where that had gotten him. She'd played him then, and she had him once again.

"So," Rylan said with a cockiness in his tone he didn't feel, "straight to the airport, a hop back to the States to testify against the Patriarca family, and then my death?"

Arica snorted, despite being one of the Fed's best organized crime investigators. To Rylan, it was the only thing that still made her human.

"If I had any intention of making you testify against them, I wouldn't have let you leave the country, would I?"

That puzzled him. "You *left* me tied up...to our bed, as I recall. I had to escape before you collected me and escorted me to jail."

Arica cocked her head, not fully turning in her cramped seat to side-eye him. "I 'tied' you up to our bed to keep you from making that rendezvous with Big Sonny Patriarca. Without his *very able* driver..." She cooed the "very able" making Rylan question whether she was talking about his driving or still on the bed part. "...we wouldn't have been able to bring Big Sonny in. You were just too good...at your job, I mean." She smirked.

She toyed with him. Rylan glanced at the other agent who nervously watched out the window trying to suppress an embarrassed grimace.

"I'm sorry, but if you're not bringing me back to turn state's evidence, why are you here? *If you let me go for a year, why track me down at all?*"

Arica's turn to blush, dropping her eyes. In shame?

"The United States needs your help. *I* need your help. You're the only one in all of Africa I can trust to do this job."

Her words came with sincerity; with an unspoken apology, just as they had when she left him strapped to the metal headboard, gagged and naked.

I need to take down Big Sonny, and you were the only way I could get to him. Your role is over. With me. With them.

He'd been young, in love, and a total fool. He was none of those things now.

"Are you fucking crazy? You must be if you think I'll help you, bitch!"

The agent on his left, who looked as if he'd had his nose broken regularly, elbowed his jaw.

"Watch the attitude, punk."

When the stinging stopped, Rylan spit blood onto the floorboards, glad to see no teeth came with it.

"Okay, let me say it again...nicely."

Arica arched an eyebrow.

"Are you fucking crazy, ma'am? Or did bringing down Boston's top mobster make you think you're a goddamn god now? If you hadn't noticed, this isn't the U.S. of A., Agent Riggs."

Arica held up a hand to keep her teammate at bay.

"I'll explain when we get to the safehouse."

They weren't going to the embassy. He wasn't being exported back to the States.

THE SPY WHO STABBED ME (IN THE BACK)

Wait! Why aren't we going to the embassy? Why a safe house?

Something was rotten in Tangier, and it wasn't three-day-old fish from the Medina.

∽

As Tangier grew over the years, the need for space increased and buildings were built on top of other buildings creating Tangier's almost beehive look. Some would say that there were no bad views of the bay, no matter where you lived.

Apparently, that was not the case in regard to Arica's safehouse. By nature, it shouldn't have a good view, or any view, so it attracted no attention. Spy craft 101. But even for a safehouse, it sucked.

Dank. Humid. Void of anything pleasing to the eye. The room had a desk, some beds, and a toilet behind a folding curtain.

Arica's fellow agents led him to the desk, spun the chair around for him. Sitting, Rylan scanned the room in more detail. Three suitcases, one by each bed, lay open with clothing and toiletries spilling out, a clear indication of an unprepared departure from the US. No charts on the wall. No portfolios on the desk. Rylan didn't even see any communication equipment. Maybe that's why they needed him, but he suspected not.

The four Feds huddled at the back of the room and spoke in whispers, each of the three men furtively peeking out the grimy windows. Voices rose occasionally as the conversation grew heated, but Arica took command and silenced the other three, all of them looking over at him.

Rylan waved.

Arica's shoulder's slumped, and she released a long sigh. She told the others to wait in the hallway; coming over to address their captive.

"Sorry for the cloak-and-dagger stuff."

He didn't waste words. "You're off the books, aren't you? You had a plan, and it went to shit."

She didn't have many tells, which was what made her such a great agent. She'd fooled Rylan back in Boston right up until she stabbed him in the back, but his pronouncement caught her off guard. Her right eyebrow raised a fraction of an inch, and her jaw tightened. He'd only seen her surprised once before, but that moment had burned into his memory; he knew exactly what to look for.

Arica's head hung low for a moment, and she didn't meet his eyes. "The Bureau doesn't know we're here." Then she corrected herself. "I mean, they probably know, but they're taking a wait-and-see stance until we either succeed or fail."

Rylan crossed his arms, leaned back against the chair, and extended his legs out. "Which would they prefer?"

She shrugged. "Fail, probably. If I do what I came to do, it won't win me any favors with the Bureau or the Agency."

CIA? Shit. He sat bolt upright.

The Agency viewed Tangier, as most intel agencies did, as some sort of Broadway theater. Actors came and went, but there was always a show going on. "Bringing down the house," though, had a different meaning here.

Arica went to the desk, opened the bottom drawer, and pulled out a bottle of Irish whiskey. The mahogany color of the liquid matched her hair, and the label went so well with her aquamarine eyes. She opened it, took a swig, then offered it to Rylan.

Reluctantly, he took the bottle but didn't drink.

"Things went crazy in the days leading up to Big Sonny's trial, the worst being he ordered a hit on the Federal judge overseeing it."

Rylan opened his mouth to say something, but she held up a hand.

"He has another judge, apparently, in his pocket, who will take over, only we have no proof of that because the CIA stole my only potential witness."

Rylan started to speak, but she held up a single finger, asking him to wait one more second.

"The witness was on an FBI list of possible Russian moles, but I didn't find this out until after I'd interviewed him. The Agency grabbed him and sent him here to be released to the KGB. They're playing at something and not telling the Bureau what."

Rylan didn't bother to talk as he knew instinctively she had one more bomb to drop.

"And the Patriarcas sent a hitman from Sicily to off the witness, as well."

Rylan finally took a long pull from the bottle.

The Patriarcas.
The CIA.
The FBI.
The KGB.

Rylan couldn't wrap his mind around it. How had he found himself in the middle of a den of killers who'd off him without batting an eyelid? Had his sins been so great that he ended up in a no-win situation?

He returned the bottle to Arica, stood up, and said, "Fuck you." He started for the door.

She blocked him.

"I know. I don't deserve your help."

"Oh, do you think? I'm *here* because of you."

She countered, "You're also not in jail or dead because of me. Have you considered that?"

Rylan had, of course. The takedown of Big Sonny hadn't

gone well. Several dead mobsters. Twice as many agents and cops. There hadn't been anything like it since the days of Capone. Arica managed to bring Big Sonny in alive, though, which should've punched her ticket out of undercover into supervisory agent.

"Why aren't your superiors backing your play?" Rylan challenged.

She waved it off, not looking him in the eyes again. "They don't want to strain their relationship with the Agency."

"Bullshit." Rylan moved around her toward the door. As he reached for it, she called after him.

"You. Because of you."

Rylan stopped, hand in midair. "What?"

He didn't turn around, but the crack in her voice told him what he'd see if he did. Pleading. Submission. The façade of the tougher-than-nails Federal agent dissolving to show the youngest female agent on the force.

"I was supposed to bring you in, too. As his driver, you knew every place Big Sonny was and when." He could feel Arica drawing closer. "We were...I was supposed to offer you immunity for your testimony. Without you, without what you knew, the case would be harder to try." Her words were nearly at his ears now. "But I knew. I knew you wouldn't live long enough to testify. Especially after your fath—"

"Don't!" Rylan spun on her. "Don't you dare."

That was his mistake though. Arica stood right there, looking up at him with those come-hither eyes. She bit her lip in a pout, her cheeks flushed with embarrassment, or something else. Rylan hated himself for letting something long dormant stir inside him.

"I need you. I can't trust anyone else."

But could he trust her?

When she leaned up to kiss him, and even as he returned the kiss, he absolutely knew he couldn't.

THE SPY WHO STABBED ME (IN THE BACK)

Wasif worked on Cyndi again, but this time, under the watch of four FBI agents and Rylan. His eyes spent more time on the Feds than they did on his work, and a scowl contorted his lips. Wasif's glare finally settled on Rylan.

He rolled his eyes at the mechanic. At least they paid cash for Cyndi's mod, Wasif's time, and Rylan's soul. And then some. The number they offered would pay for the parts Wasif had ordered, plus enough for Rylan to disappear, if he needed to.

Arica stepped away from the alteration job.

"You have quite a little bus here."

"Cyndi," Rylan corrected.

She raised an eyebrow. "As in Lauper?"

Rylan gestured at the bus. "Look at her." He'd been right to name her that. The tour bus had so many different parts from so many different vans, she'd become an amalgam of various colors and shades; no telling what her original body color was. Much like the very colorful singer, Rylan's tour bus was one-of-a-kind.

Arica grinned and nodded. "Yeah, I can see it. But didn't your dad raise you on Sinatra and the Rat Pack?"

"I can pick up the Armed Forces Network, and all the bars play stuff like that. It grew old."

She nodded nonchalantly and returned her attention to Cyndi.

Rylan studied her profile. He'd never actually agreed to help Arica, but he guessed the kiss sealed the deal. The three other agents had come along her against direct orders because they believed in her. Arica did that. She made men believe.

In her.

In the future.

Rylan no longer held on to the same beliefs he had a year or two ago. He'd help her, then if he needed to, leave Tangier for another hive of scum and villainy, change his name again, and lay even farther low.

That would be a shame, he thought. He'd just gotten comfortable with the city, its people, and the job he'd chosen to do, but if the Patriarcas got wind of him, Arica's mole wouldn't be the only target on their hitman's list.

"There's not a lot of space under the floorboards. You sure it's going to be enough?" Bent-nose asked.

"Wasif?" Rylan asked.

"Well, given the dimensions of your target, as expressed, when he's lying flat, unconscious, it should be enough. I just wouldn't hit any potholes or go over any curbs."

Rylan couldn't make a promise to either.

"So, you're sure he'll contact *you* when the drop happens?" asked the agent with surfer-blonde hair.

The ex-pat grinned. "I'm the best in town for these types of arrangements, as long as they haven't already gotten wind of you approaching me, so that means, after today, I don't want to see you." He directed his gaze at Arica, "*Any* of you, until I've picked him up."

They nodded.

"And he can't be seen with the CIA, so he'll approach me alone, but they'll be watching, too."

That made the quartet grumble.

"You either trust me, or you don't."

Arica cocked her head. "As long as you follow the plan, to the letter, there shouldn't be any reason not to trust you."

Brakes on an old bicycle squealed as a kid pulled up in front of Wasif's shop. He jumped off, ran to Rylan, handed him a note, and waited for his tip before reversing the process.

They all looked at him., He bobbed his head slightly. "I gotta go meet a mole." Rylan bent down to where Wasif welded away, sending sparks near Rylan's nose. "Will this be done by the time I get back?"

"If I don't have to stop to answer stupid questions."

Rylan gave Arica a look that said that he wasn't trading his soul for a kiss. Only cash. She seemed to understand.

But did he?

Most of the bars were named Sam's, or Rick's, or some variation of Café American, though it'd been based on Caid's. Fat, rich tourists filled the bar, their cruise ship having docked at the port. Rylan inwardly groaned at all the legitimate business he would miss.

Rylan recognized the contact from a picture Arica had shown him. Even so, he went through the motions of going to the bartender, who pointed out a man who wouldn't have stood out from the crowd in any circumstance. That was the thing about spies. Popular film had them as dashing men or super-hot women, but the best spies were flies on the wall.

Thus was the case of Harry Daniels.

Mostly bald with a comb-over, Harry barely cracked 175 and might be a touch under 5'6". He had a seventies' brush mustache, the same brown as the few strands of hair left on his head. He looked at nothing but his drink, ignoring all the revelers around him. That wasn't good.

Rylan plopped down next to him and slid a brotherly arm over the man's shoulder.

"Frank! C'mon, you came on this cruise to forget about her. Stop being so glum." Rylan didn't shout, but talked loud enough so neighboring barflies could hear. He moved in close to Harry's ear. "If you want out of this alive, Comrade, start acting like a tourist."

Harry had tensed, but then relaxed when he understood this must be his contact. He forced a weak smile and hoisted his drink. "You're right. Fuck her *and* her tennis instructor."

Good recovery. "I gotta drain. You comin'?" Rylan asked. Harry downed the last of his beer, and the two pushed their way to the head.

Making sure the stalls were empty, Rylan swung a "Closed for Cleaning" sign over the outside handle.

"When are you supposed to get your message drop?"

Harry looked at his watch. "In about two hours."

Rylan checked his own watch. "That doesn't give us a lot of time. Meet me here in an hour. I'll slide you into my evening tour. Things will move fast."

Harry looked confused. "I'm sorry, but how do you know all this already?"

"I don't. This is how it always is." Rylan had gotten the client before the bus. "I don't ask for much in the way of details, anyway. The less I know, the better."

That seemed to satisfy the Russian mole. "Once I get my message, I'll need to be taken to a specific location. Price is not an object. I have intel—"

Rylan wondered if maybe this guy had been under so long, he'd forgotten basic spy etiquette. "All I need are times and locations. I'll handle the rest."

Harry grabbed a paper towel and scribbled something on it with a pen he pulled from his breast pocket. He handed it to Rylan.

Rylan looked at it and read "19:51" followed by coordinates and a frequency.

He recognized the location of the signal drop as the Interzone at the top of Tangier. The coordinates placed them just far enough from the Kasbah to be "exciting." Tangier wasn't all spies and tourists. They had their gangs, terrorists, thugs, and general ne'er-do-wells like most large cities. The last thing Rylan and the Feds needed was to be robbed by the locals looking for quick cash and jewels on the rubes.

Committing them to memory, Rylan took out a lighter, lit it on fire, and dropped it in the commode.

"Don't be late," he warned, removing the sign.

As expected, there was a crowd waiting for Rylan's bus when he returned. He made his apologies, telling everyone he had a private charter. Luckily, he wasn't the only tour game in town.

To keep up appearances, Rylan hired plants to fill seats on the bus, leaving five open for Harry and the four FBI agents.

Harry seemed concerned. "Who are these people?"

"Tourists," Rylan lied through a scowl. He discreetly held out his hand. The mole slipped him an envelope with half of his fee. No idea if it was CIA or KGB money, but it spent the same.

The Feds arrived in classic tourist wear, Arica and beach-boy agent acting like newlyweds. Worried Harry might recognize her, Arica wore a wig, sunglasses (even thought it was night), and a big, floppy hat.

For a moment Rylan imagined a different life, one where he was in beach-boy's place. But only for a moment.

Arica stumbled up to Rylan as if partially blitzed, while the others took their places.

"Everything good?" she lipped while asking inane questions.

He mouthed back "It's a really tough area."

That didn't make her happy in the slightest. The Russians probably picked the spot since it was a well-known section of town to stay away from.

For appearance's sake, Rylan ran his normal route, but subtly adjusting so they'd arrive on *Rue Tenaker* on time.

As Rylan went through his routine of Tangier's history and flavor, he'd occasionally catch a giggle from Arica that didn't feel faked. She clearly thought his tour guide bit amusing, especially compared to his attitude during his previous vocation. Professional. Even slightly cold. The perfect match to her, until they were alone, and he dropped the mask. He thought she'd dropped hers back then, too, only it'd been just one. She had many.

Too many.

They pulled onto the right street, and Rylan paused to talk about the renovations being done to the Kasbah, not too far away. He gave the signal to Harry, who reached under the seat for the headphone. He listened, nodded to Rylan, and sat back. Message received.

Bent-nose sitting behind Harry, leaned forward and placed a chloroform-soaked handkerchief over his face. Harry struggled, but by then Arica and Beach-boy had secured him.

Rylan gave each of his plants some cash and shooed them off the bus. He didn't want them there for the next part.

Arica popped open Cyndi's new floorboard, and the men dropped an unconscious Harry inside.

She glared at him. "Really? From Star Wars? Don't you ever have an original idea?"

"Don't change what ain't broken, doll."

Getting behind the wheel, Rylan began to drive down the street when suddenly a dozen armed men swarmed around the bus, stopping it flat.

Guns drawn and placed at the head of each passenger, Rylan waited for the leader to step forward and get onto the bus.

"Wallets. Jewels. Bank notes," The burly man demanded with a thick Riffian accent.

"Just do what he says, and we'll be back on the tour shortly," Rylan told them in a comforting tone.

Arica gave him a *Do you want us to take care of this?* look, which Rylan shook off. She put up a good act when they took off her fake wedding ring, which impressed Rylan. Actress to the last.

The men handed over their fake wallets, each with tourist money, keeping their real IDs tucked away, but while reaching for his, Beach-Boy exposed his shoulder holster.

One of thugs shouted "gun" in Arabic, and suddenly the thieves moved with professional efficiency. It took a grand total of ten seconds before the four Feds were dragged to their feet and escorted off Cyndi. Outside, and forced to the ground, they were searched more thoroughly until they'd been disarmed and their real IDs found.

"Feds?" the leader said. "Looks like we have something more valuable than jewels."

Arica spat. "You don't want to know the trouble you'll have if you don't let us go right now. You'll wish you'd just taken my ring."

The gang leader laughed and then walked over to Rylan, who still sat behind the wheel. Rylan handed him the rest of Harry's cash envelope. "Got it from here?" he whispered.

The leader, whose name was Baariq, but everyone called Bernie, winked. "Hold them for an hour, then let them 'escape.' Easy."

Rylan's shit-eating grin filled his face...right until the first shots rang out. Two of Bernie's men went down, as did one of Arica's. Cyndi took two hits to the rear. Bernie jumped off, firing in the direction of the sniper.

"Shit!" Rylan floored Cyndi and fled from the alley as chaos took over.

The Riffians returned fire, but there was no telling how many shooters had ambushed them.

Rylan cringed as he listened to Arica curse his name as he drove away.

Rylan figured it had to be ether the CIA or the Patriarcas's hitman. The Feds wouldn't shoot one of their own, even to avoid an international incident.

Rylan ruled out the Russians. The KGB would pay him double what Arica had offered.

He'd planned it all out, of course. Bernie would waylay the Feds. Rylan would leave with Harry secure and deliver him to the Ruskies. It'd serve Arica right to go home empty-handed. If the CIA deduced his double-cross, they wouldn't stop him, especially if it risked their asset in Harry.

The bet was on the Partiarcas's hitman. Since Rylan was still breathing, maybe the hitman didn't realize who he was.

Yet.

Rylan felt bile rise in his throat. He'd been flushed from cover. If the gunman had found them, he needed to stay a few steps ahead of him. So, he drove out of the city to the desert outskirts of Tangier. Once he felt they were not going to be snuck up on, he opened the compartment and roused Harry with smelling salts.

"Huh? Wha?"

Rylan offered him a hand up. "Things went to hell. You're still alive, and free, for the moment."

Once Harry regained his complete senses, Rylan explained what had happened.

"Too many people want you. At least one of them wants you dead. I played all sides to maximize my money, but now too many factors make it impossible to keep myself safe." The ambush bruised his ego. *I'm supposed to be better than this.*

"Fucking La Cosa Nostra! Fucking CIA! Fucking KGB! I just want to go home, to Russia," Harry admitted, his Eastern Bloc accent prevalent now.

Despite Rylan's rule keeping him from knowing too much, he demanded, "Spill it."

Harry had nothing to lose, so he did. "KGB said if I could get a list of who your government thought were moles, they would let my brother go. He's in prison for criticizing the regime."

"And did you?"

"Sort of."

"Is that why the Agency extradited you?"

"They knew I was a plant and had been funneling me fake intelligence to bring back to the KGB. Big Sonny's trial might've jeopardized that. The mob isn't known for leaving witnesses alive."

"No shit."

"I turned myself in to them, begging them to get me home."

Rylan didn't know everything about how the US government worked, but he knew enough to know that if the CIA had a proven domestic spy in custody they were supposed to give them to the FBI—not send him to the Mediterranean for a vacation.

That left one loose thread.

"What do you have that the Patriarcas want you buried with?"

Sheepishly, Harry withdrew a cassette tape from a pocket.

"What the fuck is that?"

Harry shrugged. "While spying for Mother Russia, I happened to be in a file room when the mob's contact met with a judge they'd compromised. A file clerk had left a radio with tape deck in there, so I secretly recorded their conversation. You know? As an ace. I planned use it in case the Patriarcas got to me before I could get the CIA to take me seriously."

You stupid little spook. They don't bargain.

Rylan leaned back against Cyndi's dash and exhaled. He couldn't let Harry return to Russia with the false information. Once it was discovered it'd been fed to them, they'd kill Harry *and* his whole family. Nor could he let Harry return to the US to testify against the Patriarcas family. Either the mob or the Agency would kill him before he could ever reach the stand.

After a moment, Rylan understood he only had one play. He reached under the dash and pulled out his gun.

Rylan extended his hand for the tape.

"We need to make a copy of this, and then I need you to trust me."

Again, Harry had nothing to lose.

Through his network of contacts, Rylan had let slip the location and time of the rendezvous to the appropriate parties. He'd left Cyndi just inside the town limits but disabled so she'd be less likely to be stolen. They walked the rest of the way to Wasif's. They didn't have a lot of time before the meet.

Returning the mole to Mother Russia had to be the best play, but giving Arica the tape created an equipoise. That just left the CIA's meddling to contend with. He had a plan for that, as well.

"Everything ready, Wasif?"

The mechanic nodded. "Everything is placed where you wanted. It was not an easy task. Much money was spent."

Rylan still hoped to collect two paychecks from his plan. He just had to make sure everyone played their part.

"Let's go."

They got in a Renault 9, a less conspicuous vehicle than Cyndi, and drove to the transmitted spot down by the docks. The KGB would transport Harry by boat until they cleared the Straights and meet with a sub in the Atlantic, where they'd hightail it back to Russia.

Two men waited for them when they arrived. Rylan and Harry carefully exited the car. One of the men walked up to Harry, looked him up and down, and hugged him. "Velcome home, Comrade." He hugged him. A second man stepped forward and handed Rylan a thick envelope. "Any problems?"

Rylan shook his head. "Nothing serious."

"*Da*, is good then." The Spook gave him a warm, yet apologetic smile. "However, ve have one more request. There was only one boat available to rent. Vill you please drive and pilot the boat back for us? That way you can return it after ve depart? Your reputation for skill in driving anything precedes you."

He pointed down to the water where a Fairey Huntsman 28 bobbed gently next to the dock.

Rylan suspected they'd ask such a thing. They planned to kill him once they reached the sub and retrieve their money.

"Sure!" Rylan agreed, as if he had no clue what fate awaited him.

They piled into the boat, Harry wearing a look of concern for Rylan. Rylan drove the Huntsman out into the dark waters. The waves became choppier the farther out they went.

Once they were far enough from the shore, Rylan stuttered the engine to signal Arica and her men it was time to ascend from the forward cabin.

As if magic, the remaining three Feds appeared on the deck, guns drawn.

"Let's make this easy, gentlemen," Arica offered. "No one has to die today." Disarmed, the KGB agents held their hands up. The leader glared at Rylan. "You betrayed us? We understood you never played sides."

Rylan shrugged. "Who says I have chosen a side?" He nodded to Harry, who hugged his comrade before slipping the list of the fake investigations, along with a select one or two real ones provided by Arica. She'd made a call and already had those spies picked up before handing over their names.

Arica motioned with her gun. "Get swimming, comrades."

The KGB agents looked to the water, then to the Feds, then glared at Rylan. One by one, the Ruskies jumped into the water and doggie-paddled back toward Tangier.

Rylan piloted the boat toward Tangier-Boukhalef airport, where the Feds had tickets waiting.

"Sorry about that ambush. Is your man who got shot okay?"

"Like you care. You set that all up."

"Not the ambush. That was the Patriarcas's killer. I didn't think he'd find us so quickly. That's my fault. I'm sorry." He said it genuinely, and it took her off guard.

"He's fine" she answered. "Shoulder wound. Clean shot. The Patriarcas's hitman was trying to separate us. He's only after Harry." After a moment, she added, "Thank you for asking. And the apology."

They sat there, letting the boat's engine fill the silence.

Rylan pulled up to the retaining wall near the airport and disembarked. He explained they'd have to walk the length of the runway to reach the terminal. That time of night, there were not many departures and arrivals, so they followed the asphalt directly.

"Listen, Arica," Rylan started. He stopped and turned to face her. "I'm sorry I backstabbed you. You think I'm the same guy you left tied to that bed back in Boston. But you don't know what Tangier does to you. You can't until you've been here."

The breeze from the ocean wafted her hair in front of her face. She reached up and brushed it away. "So, who are you now?"

"Apparently, a guy who'd betray the woman he once loved…" He gave her an impish grin. He looked at his watch, to make sure he had the timing right. "Twice."

The roar of the helicopter blades preceded its spotlight by only seconds. A second one joined the first, and Arica, Harry, and the Feds realized, exposed as they were, there was nowhere to run, and no one wanted a shootout with the CIA.

Camouflaged men repelled down, their assault rifles trained on the five people, who just raised their hands.

Once more, everyone was disarmed as one of the Huey's

landed. More agents exited and surrounded the quintet. A man in a suit strode up to Arica. "I'm sorry, Miss Riggs, but the CIA can't allow this man to return to the US. We'll take custody of him."

Defiant, Arica shouted over the roar of engines, "He's an important witness in the murder of a federal judge. It's my duty to bring him—"

But the lead spook cut her off. "You're off the books, Riggs. You were told to back off, but you couldn't, could you?"

"Justice needs…" But by then, Rylan had reached over and squeezed her elbow hard. He shot her a look to reassess the situation.

The team no longer surrounded them but had taken up positions on one side. Like a firing squad. Arica's face reflected the understanding that they intended to execute the lot of them.

"Why?" she asked.

"Can't have you go back and report anything about this operation. It's not just a black eye, you see."

Rylan guessed, "Because Harry's not the only mole you've done this with, and you can't have the Feds looking too closely at your ops."

"Indeed."

Arica saw even more problems. "And if you were feeding Harry fake names, then you probably also fed them to us, too."

"Well deduced, Agent Riggs."

The leader pulled Harry from their circle, and two of his men escorted him toward the chopper. "You're a damn good agent, Arica. A testament to the Bureau. You won't give up, that's why we need to stop you."

Harry had almost reached the Huey when the first of the CIA's men collapsed. The shot couldn't be heard over the engines of both copters. Sparks flew off the canopy of the hovering helo, though, as more bullets ricocheted off it. It pulled away, the spotlight no longer encircling Rylan, Arica, and her men.

"Run!" He pushed her head low and urged her into the shadows.

"Rylan? What the fuck?"

Rylan didn't answer, choosing instead to intercept Harry, who, as instructed, ran toward a small airfield to the side of the runway. The CIA wouldn't shoot him. They needed him alive.

The second copter looked for the shooter until he put out their spotlight. The first helo spun up its blades preparing to take off. Two shots through the front window, and the pilot slumped against the dash.

"He'll keep the spooks busy while we get away."

Arica stopped, yanked Rylan around and stuck a finger in his face. "You! You did this!"

He had.

Rylan had funneled a location and approximate time to the concerned parties, effectively providing his own escape route each time. He knew that he'd almost reached the end. One last move. If this didn't work, they were all dead.

She stayed sharp as they progressed through the field. "How are you going to get us out of this?"

They'd lost Arica's men in the chaos. It was just him and her, and Harry who ran a dozen yards ahead of them.

The trio reached the small jet plane at the same time. Wasif waited there by the steps. "You promise? Not a scratch. It's a loaner."

"I promise." Rylan let Harry go up the steps first, then he followed. "Did you get the confession?"

Wasif pointed to Cyndi who sat off to the side of the plane. "You stopped them right by the hidden microphone. It was tough to hear over the sound of the copters, but I think it'll be enough to blackmail them into backing off."

Arica, on Rylan's heels, demanded answers. "Where are we going?"

He jumped into the cockpit and flipped switches. "Up."

By then, Arica's face had turned as red as her hair. "You wanted the CIA to catch us so you could get a confession recorded?"

"Détente. That should get you back in the good graces of the Bureau. They'll give you a cushy job, after that."

Arica wrapped her arms around his neck and kissed his cheek. "You're still a good guy at heart, Rylan, or whatever you want to call yourself."

Rylan, or whatever he wanted to call himself, started the engines. "You better get that door closed before—"

But it was too late. A figure stood at the portal to the plane. His expression and gun said in no uncertain terms, he was now in command.

"Take us up," the man said in a thick Sicilian accent. "No funny moves."

He motioned for Arica and Harry to take seats and strap in, while he remained standing.

Arica tried to reason with him. "We could just let him go back to Russia. The Bureau has what it needs to put your boss away, with or without us."

The man stood unwavering as the plane bumped down the runway.

"I wanted no part of this, you know?" Harry said. "I just want to go home. Your family's business is your own."

Again, the hitman said nothing.

Rylan couldn't get a good look at him, focused as he was on getting them airborne. He could sense, more than see, the wide shoulders, short-cropped hair, and sneer. There had to be a sneer. All of Big Sonny's killers sneered. Rylan was sure that was a prerequisite to being hired.

Rylan wasn't sure what type of gun the man held either. He'd only caught it out of the corner of his eye. The hitman had discarded the rifles, clearly, but what caliber or rate of fire or capacity, Rylan couldn't be sure. He'd just have to chance it.

"This is how it's going to go," began the hitman. "When we reach a certain altitude, I'm going to open the door, and you're both going to step out for some air. Now, you can go willingly, or as a corpse. Doesn't matter to me. I get paid either way."

Arica made a different offer. "What if I could offer you a bigger payday to keep us," she indicated her and Harry, "alive?"

"I don't betray the family." Succinct.

"You wouldn't be." Arica laid on the charm Rylan knew all so well. The seductive voice, the bedroom eyes. He knew what she was about to do, and he couldn't stop her.

"You see, I know where someone who betrayed Big Sonny is, and the price on his head is worth more than our two lives. You'd be doing the Patriarcas a big favor to clear this death mark."

"Don't, Arica. Don't you tell him."

But the hitman's curiosity got the better of him. "Who? Who does Big Sonny want more than the Fed who arrested him and the rat that could expose how deep the family has infiltrated the government?"

Rylan reached the appropriate speed and took the plane into the air. The killer steadied himself, but never wavered his gun.

"Why the very person who allowed me to catch Big Sonny. His driver. Don't tell me you haven't recognized him yet?"

Rylan felt the thug slowly turn, and he didn't need to know which direction the gun pointed. The hitman grabbed Rylan's jaw and forced it around.

"Easy, now. I still have to fly this thing."

"You!"

THE SPY WHO STABBED ME (IN THE BACK)

Rylan watched the altimeter and counted down as the needle climbed.

Almost.

Almost.

The killer boasted gleefully. "Three kills. That'll make Big Sonny happy enough to let me marry one of his daughters."

Rylan asked, "Which one?"

The man shrugged. "Does it matter?"

Arica yelled. "Hey! I thought we had a deal?"

Turning slightly, the joyful goon said, "Now who said we—"

The altimeter hit the number Rylan needed, and he slammed the yoke down.

The Zero-G nature of the cabin left the hitman floating in midair, regardless of his concrete make-up. He instinctively swam.

Arica and Harry, strapped in as they were, stayed put.

Rylan reached under the console, retrieved the .45 Wasif had moved from Cyndi, and tossed it back to Arica. She snatched it and put three well-placed bullets into the thug.

When Rylan leveled off, the killer's dead body hit the aisle.

The federal courts put Big Sonny away for a long time. For racketeering first, then murder of a federal judge. Once the Fed's played the recording for the replacement judge, he turned faster than the cassette. The CIA also exchanged evidence they had on all the Patriarcas in exchange for Arica's silence. The crackdown and subsequent arrests didn't remove the death mark on Rylan, but it would be a while before the Patriarcas reorganized under a new boss.

The lead Agency operative, Rylan never got his name, was reassigned somewhere so remote, no one knew it anymore.

Harry returned to Russia. He freed his brother, and they

were both okay. However, also as part of the deal, the CIA got Harry's family out of Russia for good. Harry sent him a letter saying they were safe under new names in Wisconsin.

Rylan sat on a stool in Sam's as the tourists sung "As Time Goes By" poorly. He'd delivered several of them there having just finished up a legitimate tour of the city. He'd taken a break from info-handling as Wasif fixed up Cyndi with new seats, a new axle, and a few other upgrades the mechanic had talked him into. He still had plenty of money left over from the Ruskies, the CIA, and the Bureau's payouts. Soon enough, though, he'd have to get back to peddling Cold War goods. For now, he relaxed and tried not to listen to the song.

Someone took the chair next to him.

No, not someone.

Her.

Arica flipped scarlet locks from her face and gave him a lopsided smile. "Yeah, I know. You said, *again*, if you ever saw me *again*, you'd kill me."

Seeing there were no windows to jump out of, Rylan made to get up, but she put on arm on his shoulder.

"Wait," she said, her voice with a touch of pleading.

He sat back down.

"Why are you here? After everything I let you take credit for, I figured the Bureau was done with me. Shouldn't you be picking the most choice assignments they have?"

Arica ordered a drink, not saying anything until it arrived. She stared down into it before fessing up.

"I got fired."

That stunned Rylan. "After proving Big Sonny killed a Federal Judge?"

"I went off book. Despite all the wins, the Bureau doesn't like rogue agents. I traded my badge for my men being left alone."

"I'm…I'm sorry."

A shit-eating grin slid to the corners of Arica's mouth. "That's okay. I got a better offer." She reached into her jacket pocket and flashed Rylan her CIA credentials. "Despite the black eye, the Agency liked how I handled myself, and thought I was wasting my skills at the Bureau. They set me up with the 'most choice' assignment for the gathering and distribution of information."

"No."

"Yes."

Arica leaned toward him and kissed his cheek. Barely above a whisper, she told him, "I'm the new spook in town, and boy, am I going to enjoy haunting you."

$100,000,000

NORA B. PEEVY

THE FUNERAL

Hunter and his crew stood at the back of the people gathered at the cemetery. All but the rest. Marco sent them back to Diane's grandfather's house. Judging by the amount of Gucci and Prada at the funeral, he'd had a lot of money. They'd been watching him for a while, unbeknownst to Diane and her fiancé, Ricki. Word on the street was there was $100,000,000 sitting in that house somewhere. A sweet deal.

Diane wore an expensive-looking black pantsuit with minimal jewelry. Her Louis Vuitton heels sank into the muddy ground, but she didn't care. She'd just lost her grandfather. She held a black lace handkerchief to her eyes. Ricki had her left arm around Diane. She wore an appropriate little black dress for the occasion. Both she and Diane held red roses and listened to the pastor drone on about ashes to ashes and dust to dust.

Ricki heard a low voice towards the back of the crowd. She turned and saw a tall man with a jagged scar running halfway down his face. His eye was milky blue. He was blind in that eye. The puckered scar stopped right before his lips. Standing next to him were some of the crew. She didn't know where the others were. Probably off planning another heist she and Diane would help pull off in a few days after Diane pulled herself together.

But where was Marco? He always attended family events for his crew and he wasn't there. She scanned the crowd and didn't see a stout little man with greasy hair anywhere. It came time to throw their flowers onto the coffin and Diane clutched hers to her bust. Ricki unwrapped each finger with loving care and kissed her pinky, where she'd been pricked by a thorn. They threw their flowers on top of the coffin. Then they each picked up a handful of dirt and tossed it into the newly dug grave.

As Ricki and Diane were walking towards the waiting car, a tremendous BOOM rocked the cemetery. The pastor and a few mingling guests went flying. Clods of dirt, grass, and tombstones flew like shrapnel. A wedge of tombstone lodged in one woman's eye and blood started running down her cheek in rivulets. The remaining guests, lucky to be alive, covered in dirt and gravestone dust with tattered clothes, went running for their cars. Car alarms beeping.

"Oh, my god! Ohmygodohmygodohmygod!" Diane shook, white as a sheet of paper.

Ricki slapped her. "Get it together, babe. We have to get outta here now before something else happens."

Ricki ran her startled love, sobbing and screaming, to her car. She tasted thick stone dust and dirt in the back of her throat. The gritty feeling on her skin from the scattered cemetery itched.

People were screaming and fleeing in the cacophony of cell conversations to the police, feet pounding on pavement in a rush to get into their cars, and in the distance, the predictable whining of cop cars and ambulances came fast approaching.

"Wait, a sec." Ricki bent down to check the car for detonators on the undercarriage and then opened the hood of the car to see if anything connected to the engine. Nothing.

She got in the car, praying to Santa Muerte she hadn't

missed anything. On the dashboard was a note. It read: We know.

"What does Marco n' the crew know, Diane?"

Diane was still sobbing, taking in big gulps of air, snot running down her face. She watched the impending chaos outside. People honking their horns at others to move, shouting obscenities, weeping with terror, swearing at slow drivers, not wanting to be stuck at the horrific crime scene. Motors gunning it and driving on the grass as close as they could to the gravestones of others to bypass parked cars.

"Diane! What does Marco know? Have you been keeping a secret from him?"

"N-no. No idea what he's talking about."

At that moment, the creepy guy with the long scar on his face showed up on the driver's side and gestured for Ricki to talk.

"You better not hide anything at the will reading tonight or there'll be more trouble than your grandfather over there. Got it?"

Diane nodded, restraining herself from leaping at his face with her teeth. She was sure Marco's goon had something to do with this.

Ricki gave him the finger and put her window up.

"Let's haul ass back there and make sure the crew are okay. I don't know what's going on, but it sounds like Marco knows about the money. Did you know about the money?"

"Yes."

"Where'd your grandpa hide it?"

"He always said it would be in his will."

MARCO

Marco pried the patio door open with a crowbar. His gang stood behind him as lookouts. The neighborhood was quiet, save for the autumn wind. The sky brought the promise of rain. Marco hated rain. He wanted to get this job done fast before Diane and Ricki came home.

The reading of the will was tonight. Diane's grandfather had insisted on it. What was so important? It was unusual for a will reading on the same day as the burial. This puzzled Marco. He ran his hands through his greasy hair. Where was the money? Marco had a little black book and tracked all their marks. Mr. Winston had been an eccentric, he remembered Diane mentioning once, so he wouldn't have put it in stocks or in the bank.

"I want this place turned over from top to bottom. You hear me? Any of you standing around and not working are going to get a bullet in their foot. If someone farts, I want to know about it. Got it? Now go! We probably don't have much time before the cops show up here asking for answers about the little cemetery showdown."

Did he feel guilty about casing the joint? Not in the least.

They were all family and everyone would get an equal share, even if Diane insisted it was her inheritance. They'd taken a blood oath to always be true to one another.

Marco looked at his watch. Ricki and Diane were probably on their way home after the stunt at the cemetery. This was breaking that oath, but only preemptively. After the money was found, Marco would be sure Diane and Ricki both got their earnings and apologies. So, technically, it wasn't a secret or a lie. Just an advance on payment, is the way he looked at it.

Phan, who was only five two, but had a six-inch imposing blue mohawk, took the upstairs with Tony, a muscle-bound hulk of a man with skin the color of honey and a mouth that could sweet talk the panties off any lady in town. They started with the mattresses, cutting them open with their knives and then attacked the pillows. Feathers rained down on them, making them sneeze.

Tex and Rod were not as bright as the other two. Marco had given them the task of checking for a safe behind every mirror and every painting in the joint. When none of the crew found anything useful, they left, frustrated, their jaws clenched.

Marco growled at Phish, Stan, and Rio. "Negatory. Nothing in the house of value. Got no idea where the old man hid the loot, but I bet Diane knows. And we can get her to talk, if we can get Ricki to help us. And with how doped up Diane is now after her grandpa's death, she's gonna talk real easy. And if she don't, we do it the hard way."

BACK AT DIANE'S GRANDFATHER'S HOUSE

Diane and Ricki returned to a house rifled through, but they knew it wasn't a burglary. No, this had the mark of Marco all over it, the greedy bastard. Diane fumed. Her blond hair was practically smoking with anger. All the cushions ripped open on the leather furniture her grandfather had loved so much and they'd even smashed his collection of Faberge eggs he'd collected with her grandmother. Every anniversary, he had bought her a new one. They had all been stored in a lit glass case that held the pride of place next to the marble fireplace. Even that had been smashed. *Idiots.* As if her grandfather would hide his money inside a marble block. *Total idiots.*

Ricki went upstairs. The mattresses were ruined. There'd be no place to sleep here tonight.

"You can stay with me, babe." Ricki kissed her cheek. "It's awful what they did, but we have to go through with the reading of the will. It's what your grandfather would have wanted."

"But how? This place is a mess. We were going to use his study and look at it. The vultures. They've destroyed everything my grandfather treasured." Diane shook her head, eyes smoldering.

Ricki looked around. All the precious first edition leather-bound books, the antique globes, the cherry wood desk and the drawers smashed. The only thing not touched in the room was the chair, which was odd. Ricki went over to study it.

Why would Marco and his boys destroy everything, but leave this one chair untouched? She turned it over and found a small key wedged into one of the wheels. *Idiots. Total Idiots.* Did they think she wouldn't find it? Or was this some kind of test to see if she and Diane were still loyal to the team with so much money on the line?

The key looked like it fit a jewelry box or was possibly one used to wind a clock, but Ricki hadn't seen any clocks in the house. Diane turned it over in the palm of her hand, studying it. It was warm from Ricki's hand. She put it in her pocket. "Obviously, they either got what they wanted or they split and are coming to the reading tonight. The rat bastards. Desecrating grandfather's coffin like that and his beautiful home where I spent so much time. I'll kill them for this."

"Calm down. We have a reading to go to tonight. We can think about revenge later. Let's go back to my place. You can rest there and we can get something to eat." Ricki led Diane by the arm as if she was a feeble elderly lady. "We'll get someone to clean this up later, baby doll. C'mon, hon."

Diane let herself be led to the car.

THE READING OF THE WILL

Diane looked clean in a pair of Pink© jogging pants and a matching sweatshirt. Who knew what she was supposed to wear to a will read, anyway? Her skin looked pasty white and her lips quivered, her eyes red and puffy from crying all day. Ricki wore a knee-length terry cloth wrap dress. Marco and his crew wore their standard wife beaters with black button-down shirts over them. Ricki had to remind Diane who she was doing this for, as Diane's eyes spit bullets at Marco and the crew, her fists clenched at her sides. She had a hand on Diane's shoulder to keep her from charging Marco.

"You asshole. Look what you did to my grandfather's home?"

"Prove it, sweet cheeks." Marco blew her a kiss.

She rushed towards him, but Ricki pulled back as Marco laughed.

"Good to see you can keep your kittycat in line, Ricki."

Ricki gave him the darkest of looks, stroking the knife on her belt.

The doorbell chimed, and Diane jumped.

"I'll get it," Ricki said.

The man at the door was a mouse of a guy with a drab

brown suit and a bowler hat that looked like it had seen better days. He carried a scuffed leather briefcase. Beside him was a plainclothes police detective. "I'm Mr. Peabody and this is ..."

"Officer Walter. I came to ask a few questions about what happened earlier at your grandfather's funeral, but I see now is not a good time. Here's my card. Call me after the reading, and anyone in this house is not to leave town. You hear me?" He walked into the study and stared at the usual suspects. "Marco and the gang. How nice to meet you again. I've given my number to Ricki and all of you are staying in town. Got it? You run; we'll hunt you down like mountain lions. And we won't be using tranqs. Have a nice evening, everyone. Miss Diane, real sorry for your loss. Your grandfather was a treasure to the community."

The lawyer's eyes popped out so big he looked like a chameleon as he surveyed the study. "Were you all looking for something in here?" He took off his hat and set it on the floor. He sat down in the chair, which immediately fell lower, making the small man feel even more diminished and powerless.

After a few minutes of trying to adjust his chair unsuccessfully while everyone leaned against the walls of the ruined study, he cleared his throat. "Diane, your grandfather asked that the will be read the night of his burial, as you remember. He was very specific about what was left to you. Shall I begin?"

"Yes." Diane squeezed Ricki's hand for support. Ricki winced, but didn't say anything. If Diane had her way, Marco and the gang would be behind bars right now, instead of smugly staring at her tits. Her face was red with anger.

"Ahem." The lawyer cleared his throat and in a quaking voice and glancing at the formidable crew in their wife beaters flanking the two women read the will. "Your grandfather wanted his Faberge egg collection to be donated to the local art museum. But I guess that won't be happening now." He glared at

Marco and his crew, who flexed their muscles, and the lawyer tried to sit up straighter to make himself look taller as the chair sank even lower. "Can somebody fix this damn chair?" He wiped the sweat off his brow with his white handkerchief.

"Sorry. Not a chair fixer." Phan and Rio laughed. Hunter merely remained a stone statue, staring at Mr. Peabody with one milky-blue eye.

"The house was to be sold, and the profits donated to the local park system for upkeep. But I guess that doesn't matter now either, does it?" He looked over the top of his spectacles at the crowded room. Diane was weeping audibly by this point, her shoulders shaking and Ricki was rubbing her back to console her. She dug her nails into the palms of her hands to keep from looking at Marco and his boys.

"The library was to be donated to the local college. Ahem." Mr. Peabody looked around at the flurry of papers and ripped bindings flung around the room like confetti. "But I guess that's not happening either."

"I guess a lot of things are, aren't happening now, are they? Will you just get on to the money?"

"Wait. How did you know about the money?" Ricki turned and glared at Marco and the rest of them each in turn. She tossed her long mane of dark hair in a cloud of anger. Her eyebrows furrowed as she scowled at them.

"'Cuz sweet cheeks, we know every house in the area and how much is in it at every single sec of the day. And I've got a team ready to go at any moment to collect what's due. It's all here in my little black book, 'member?"

"We don't owe you anything." Ricki and Diane growled.

"Yeah? What about the money you stole from the last heist?" Marco scowled right back at Ricki.

"Have some respect. My grandfather is dead. His ceremony and resting place were demolished." Diane looked each of them in the eye, one eyebrow raised, glaring and fuming audibly.

"She's right. Get on with it. Sir." Marco bowed his head mockingly at Mr. Peabody.

Mr. Peabody's voice wavered as he read the last part of the will. "And to my darling granddaughter, Diane, who was always there for me in my time of need and brought me so much joy, I leave $100,000,000."

The room was quiet, and the air was so thick it choked them.

"He left me $100,000,000." Diane shook her head in disbelief.

"Yes. He left you $100,000,000. Your grandfather was quite well off for all his eccentricities and distrust of banks." Mr. Peabody adjusted his spectacles, slipping down his nose with sweat. He couldn't wait to leave her and get a strong martini at Marion's on the east side of town. Perhaps with steak and potato wedges on the side. The thought comforted him under the scrutiny of this scruffy collection of human trash. He felt he'd have to delouse himself before he even set foot in his one-bedroom apartment. It wasn't much, but it was home.

"I believe he left a key in the house from what his will says."

"There's no key. It's gone."

"Hunter, did you take the key?" Marco asked him.

"Nah."

"Phan, did the take the key?"

Phan, who looked naturally nervous most of the time because of the placement of his eyebrows, started sweating and shaking, fearing Marco's wrath more than he feared death.

And well, he should have because Marco reached into his pocket, pulled out a switchblade and after a quiet *snick!* drew the sharp blade across Phan's neck. Blood spurted out in a jet, warm and slick across anyone unfortunate to be in Phan's vicinity. His eyes opened wide in shock just before he slumped to the floor in a spreading pool of scarlet. "That's what happens to any of you that disobeys me. I expect the money you owe in 48 hours, Diane. And make them crisp bills. I hate looking like a bum when I go out somewhere." He grinned at the lawyer, who wanted to fade away into the walls.

"We don't owe you shit," Ricki said, eyes blazing. "Phan and a few of his buddies double-crossed you and that's not our problem."

"Even so, doll, you bring me my money or Diane might take a spill in your nice pool." He winked, grinning around the toothpick he was chewing. Marco was always chewing on toothpicks. He was an anxious guy, and it gave him something to do. "Ted and Tex, you follow them wherever they go. They take a shit I want to know about it. They take time out to skrog, I want to know about it. You hear me?"

"What's skrog mean," Ted asked. Ted and Rod were not the brains of this operation; they were purely muscle and there for effect as needed.

"Sex, you imbecile. Have you had sex before, Ted?"

Everyone except for Ted, the lawyer, Ricki, and Diane laughed. The four of them looked ready to let the house go up in flames, along with the vermin.

SHOES ARE A GIRL'S BEST FRIEND

Marco, his crew, and the lawyer had long left when Diane was curled up in one of Ricki's fluffy robes at her condo. Those bastards. She'd have to fumigate the house. The taint of asshole would still hang in the air after they'd left. How could they?

"What's the one thing your grandfather knew you loved the most?"

Diane sipped her coffee. "Horses."

"No. This key doesn't fit a horse barn. Does it?"

"Nah."

"Diane, think. What else? C'mon, girl. You're smart as a whip."

"Jewelry."

"He give you a strange box before he died?"

Diane's face lit up. "He did. He told me he wanted me to have grandma's jewelry. And I thought it was strange because he said he sold it when someone asked him about at a family get together."

Ricki's eyes lit up as she looked at the key in the light.

"Where's the box?"

"In your closet, but I don't remember it needing a key."

Ricki frowned. "Let's go check, anyway."

They got the mahogany box off the top shelf in Ricki's closet, where Diane had left it for safekeeping. Diane turned the key in the lock and there was a small click. When they opened it, a one karat diamond sat on a cushion of pink satin. "Funny, don't remember this being here before. There was a string of pearls, some earrings, a few vintage pins, but nothing special."

"Well, maybe your grandpa knew more about your real life than you thought."

Diane started crying. She was surprised she had more tears left to cry. Her body felt as dry as the desert.

"C'mon, babe. Think. Think. What else?"

"Shoes. He knew I loved shoes. He used to buy me shoes all the time and when I left home. I didn't take them all with me. And he knew I loved the grandfather clock, which you have here."

The grandfather clock chimed in agreement.

"There were a bunch of shoeboxes tossed around in one of the bedrooms. Nothing in them but shoes. Think they already have the money and know about the diamond somehow?"

"Oh, my god! No! We need to go back and look now!"

"Girl, what you talking about? I love you, Diane, but you know, they have the place being watched."

"We'll create a diversion and lose them. We'll call in the The Wild Girlz and ask for help. Give them $1,000,000 for their trouble." Ricki grinned. "Sheila owes me a favor."

"You're gonna send a bunch of biker hookers to distract Marco and his crew? He seemed pretty serious about getting his dough back, which you and I both know Phan took, and he's dead and can't talk."

"Then, why are we going back to the house?"

"I want to check the shoes, just in case."

"What guy can resist pussy and the promise of money? They'll tell them they know of another heist and the girlz will keep them occupied while we slip inside and check those shoes."

THE SLIP

Sure enough, when Ricki and Diane snuck up to the house, The Wild Girlz were already there in their booty shorts, midriff halter tops, and vinyl thigh boots. You could smell the cloud of sweet perfume from a mile away and the glitter on their bodies gleamed brighter than a new sports car. They were hanging all over the men.

Ricki and Diane snuck inside and found two of Marco's guys they didn't recognize guarding the front entrance. Before they could say anything, Ricki took an elbow to the guy in the red T-shirt. He choked and gasped, his windpipe almost crushed. He then took a roundhouse kick to the head and hit the marble floor. At the same time, Diane pulled out her Glock 9mm with a suppressor, so it was nearly quiet.

"Damn, Diane. You didn't have to kill him." Ricki looked at the guy now splayed out on the floor.

"They blew up my grandfather's grave and destroyed his home. I'll exact revenge anyway I want to." Diane's voice was colder than icicles. She held her gun before her, ready to shoot the next man she saw, but there were none.

"We have to work fast. Marco's crew will start to suspect something's up soon."

Diane and Ricki rushed up the stairs, both with Glocks readied for defense.

Checking rooms as they went and finding no one else, they dashed inside Diane's walk-in closet big enough to hold a small party in.

"Damn, Diane. I knew you were rich, but this place is banging."

The girls started tossing shoes out of boxes. They found nothing. They stared at the shoes and at the same time, their eyes widened as they nodded at each other. They pulled out their knives and started cutting into the soles. One pair had a tiny keyhole on the bottom. That was curious.

"Ricki. Look." Diane held up the key. "Think it fits with ..."

"Try it."

Diane turned the key in the lock and the heel sprung open. Inside was another key. It looked like a key used to wind a clock ... Her grandfather's clock! The one he'd given her! "Ricki! It's the clock! It's the clock at your house! This key opens up a secret compartment."

"We have to work quickly."

Ricki nodded at Diane. Diane grabbed a sequined duffle.

"Wait. We need a distraction while we bail out of here and back to my place. You bring any explosives, with you?"

Diane grinned. "When do I *not* bring explosives with me." She attached an explosive to the closet and then they dashed down the stairs as it went up in flames. Bullets started pinging off the walls. They hid in the doorway of a bedroom and returned fire. Ricki was a better shot than the men on the stairway. They weren't going to be a problem anymore. But on their way down the staircase, they ran in to Phish.

"I knew it. You came back for the cash, and you weren't gonna share it with any of us. Bitches."

"Sssh. Ya help us get outta here and we'll split it three ways. Nobody has to know. What do you say, Phish?"

Phish grinned. He didn't have to think too hard about a third of $100,000,000.

"Okay, the Phish will help you. We got a deal, but you betta pay up, or I'm gonna tell Marco soon as I get the chance."

"Ya got it. Thanks, Phish." Ricki and Phish bumped fists before the two girls ran down the stairs, their Glocks out and ready to fire.

Phish ran out of the house before Ricki and Diane. "Hey, guys! Ricki and Diane are inside right now casing the joint! I think they know where the cash is! Hurry!"

Marco and all his men reluctantly left The Wild Girlz, their guns out for a fight.

After they ran inside, Ricki and Diane popped out of the bushes. They gave a wad of cash to one of The Wild Girlz. "Thanks for the help."

"Anytime, Ricki."

Diane and Ricki were just pulling out of the driveway when Marco came running out onto the front lawn. He shot at the girls' car, but missed, only managing to ding the front passenger door.

"Goddamnit! They're getting away with the loot! All of you stay here, in case they come back. We're gonna get these bitches and end this."

Marco hopped into his Bugatti Chiron 300 and revved the engine. He pursued Ricki's car and ducked as bullets went whizzing through his windshield, almost hitting him. They were going' round a particularly sharp curve when Marco caught up to them and started shooting at Ricki. She ducked and slammed her car into Marco. Marco's car zinged off to the left, but he came back hard and slammed into her car.

"Okay, playtime is over, you bastard." Ricki had an intense

glare on her face. "Diane, keep ya Glock aimed at that car. I'm gonna show this mutt whose pissing ground dis is."

Ricki waited until the next hairpin turn, gunned the motor and banged into Marco's car, sending his Bugatti through the turn rail and down the steep embankment. As the two girls drove off, they waited for an explosion and when none came, they looked a bit worried, but it was possible that Marco died in the crash. They weren't going back to look, though.

They hurried back to Ricki's place and to the grandfather clock. "Diane, hurry and wind it up."

Diane took the key from her bosom and wound up the clock. There was a tiny *sproing!* And then the clock face opened. Inside was another key.

Hunter walked in at that moment. "Looking for something, ladies? Care to share?" He had his Glock trained on them.

"Fuck you, Hunter." Ricki charged him and put him in a chokehold. She took off the scarf she'd been wearing and used it to bind his hands. Then she went searching for some duct tape, which she found in her junk drawer in the kitchen. Before Hunter could get out of the scarf, Ricki bound his wrists and ankles to one of her dining room chairs. She covered his mouth with a piece too.

He seethed, his chest huffing.

"I like a man better when he can't speak. Don't you, Diane? Diane?" Ricki turned to look at her lover. "Ho-ly fuck!" She squealed.

Inside the back panel of the grandfather clock, past where the time mechanism was, was a hidden back compartment stuffed with cash from top to bottom. It was the $100,000,000 they'd been looking for.

Diane reached in and grabbed a stack of crisp hundreds. She walked over to Hunter and slapped him with it. "That's as close as you're ever going to get to this money, asshole."

She and Ricki started putting the money in the sequined duffle.

They had $100,000,000 to hide, and they'd made it out alive with the loot.

Diane, even though her eyes were puffy, and she'd just lost her grandfather was running on pure adrenaline after the gunfight and the car chase, plus the possibility that Marco might be dead, which meant the crew was going to need a leader and she knew exactly who she was going to support. Phish.

They had $100,000,000. *$100,000,000.* They could go anywhere and never have to work another day in their life. They'd be free of Marco and his crew. She couldn't wait to start planning where she and Ricki would go.

SISTER SECRETS

ALISON MCMAHAN

SISTER SECRETS

ALISON MCMAHAN

It had taken everything she had in her to get to this, this award ceremony, in more ways than one: the personal effort to get her sister and her mother to agree to come and to sit at the table and watch her get her award, and the effort to get the award itself.

She wasn't sure which had been harder.

Their table, one of many with silvery tablecloths, was the only one that was all women. The other tables were mostly male salesmen, some with their wives.

The CEO of the company, he of the protuberant eyes, surveyed his audience.

"Let's have a look at those numbers," he said. The image on the screen behind him shifted. A company photograph from the 1983 featuring the usual old guys, a few women scattered amongst the gray suits. Myra in the back, peering over someone's shoulder.

Myra looked over at her younger sister, Rachel. Rachel was studying the salesmen at the next table. She was only her late twenties, very elegant with only a whiff of high maintenance, but somehow looked beaten down. The salesmen didn't give her a second glance.

The next slide showed the sales graphs for 1984, comparing the top three salesmen's sales to the rest. One graph flying forward compared to the others: Myra's.

Myra's mother tapped her arm. "That's you, isn't it?"

Myra nodded.

The next slide showed her with a trophy, and her name, "Myra Silverston, 1984 Salesman of the Year." A few rueful titters from other saleswomen.

"Yeah, I know, I know, we changed it the following year," said the CEO.

But his comment went mostly unheard, as Myra's mother was clapping, nudging Rachel to clap too. Myra thought about making them stop, but what the heck, let them have their fun.

The next slide, 1986, showed Myra at the front of the group of salesmen (a couple new saleswomen in the back). Her suit now sharply tailored, with nice shoulder pads, her hair severely combed. This image clearly labelled, "Myra Silverston, 1986 Salesperson of the year."

Someone tapped her on the shoulder. Bert, the CEO's right-hand man. "Stop staring at your numbers and follow me."

Myra smiled at her mother and followed Bert. He escorted her to a corner behind the curtain separating the multi-media area from the dining area.

"Just wait here until you get your cue," he said, and turned away.

"What's my cue?" asked Myra.

But Bert wasn't going to be helpful. "You'll know," he said.

Myra wondered if he'd booby trapped the path through the layers of curtains, if she would stumble on a cable and knock out all the lights as well as falling flat on her face. She wouldn't put it past him.

She focused on what the CEO was saying. "... and now the

woman with the perfect measurements, I mean numbers, our 1987 Salesperson of the Year, Myra Silverston!"

Myra stepped gingerly through first the blackout curtain and then through something clingy and gauzy, made more clingy by the clouds of steam puffed up from the floor. Dancing colored lights made it hard to see where she was going.

The loudest applause, of course, came from her sister and mother.

The CEO handed Myra her award. She was happy to feel the weight of it. This year the figure was made of plexiglass, not glass. Not something that could easily break.

The CEO moved in to give her a kiss, but Myra was prepared for this. She slid the award under her arm, grasped his hand and shook it, and still shaking hands, took the microphone out of his other hand.

She let go of him and moved right to the podium, so that he couldn't steal her speech time like he had last year.

She perched the figure on the edge of the podium with a loud click. "I just love this little guy," she said, making eye contact with the other saleswomen. That got her a few titters in response.

She turned the figure around and studied him as if for the first time. "But you know, it might be time to give him a sex change."

That got her at least one big laugh and a few chuckles.

"Come on girls, can we do it?" she said.

A few of the saleswomen responded with catcalls, others laughed.

The CEO decided that was enough. He leaned into her microphone, forcing her to shift to the side.

"So, Myra, tell the rest of my sales staff here, what is it that makes you the best?

Myra leaned into the mic in turn. "I'm not the best. I'm not even very good."

A few disbelieving boos. Myra smiled at them. "But I'm better than the competition!"

Ironic laughter.

Myra held up her trophy in a victory gesture. Now she really did get some applause. She stepped out ahead of the CEO so she wouldn't have to accept the arm he offered her.

Bert came towards her. Myra smiled at him, but her main competitor wasn't even looking at her. He would have shoved her except that she did a quick sidestep. He almost ran into their boss.

Something must be up.

"I gotta find Nadine," Bert told the CEO. "Something about her husband."

Myra could have told him exactly where Nadine was sitting, but it was her award night, after all, so she rejoined her mother and sister. She handed her mother the award. "There you go mom. The son you always wanted."

Her mother smiled at them both. "My two girls are just perfect."

Myra noticed she'd hardly touched her dinner, and now she was just picking at her dessert. She felt a cold finger of fear.

She looked away so her mother wouldn't see her expression and saw Bert escorting Nadine out of the dining area. When he pulled the curtain aside for her, she noticed two policemen waiting for her on the other side.

"I wonder what that's about," said Rachel.

Myra shrugged. Some of her colleagues came over to congratulate her and she stood up to chat with them.

The party was over. Everyone spilled out of the hotel. Myra pushed her mother's wheelchair with one arm, while she held up Rachel with the other. She and Rachel were mis-singing the chorus to "Girls just Wanna have Fun," as they wove and stumbled to the car. Myra was stumbling because she was holding up Rachel, and Rachel was stumbling because she was completely drunk.

Other people around them also headed toward their cars. One shadowy figure seemed lost, wandering from one car to the next, but always keeping the same distance to them. Myra unlocked the car. She tenderly helped her mother into the passenger seat. She glanced at the people around them, but they were all people from the awards party. She folded the chair and lifted it into the back of the car.

Rachel leaned against the car, singing for her mother's benefit. *She's actually quite good, once she's warmed up.* Their mother smiled and clapped. Myra joined in the clapping after closing the trunk.

Someone else was clapping too. The shadowy figure, who now emerged into the light.

Myra recognized him. She pushed Rachel behind her.

"Is that what you left me for?" The man said to Rachel. "So you could go out and get drunk and make a spectacle of yourself?"

Rachel was going to say something defensive, but Myra stepped forward, her keys now threaded through her fingers. "Now, Joe, that's closer than five hundred feet."

Rachel grabbed Myra's shoulders. Myra reached back to hand her the keys. "Take the keys, Rachel. Get into the car."

"Honey, listen to me," Joe acted as if Myra wasn't there and just addressed Rachel. "How did things get so bad between us? Come home with me. Let's work things out."

Myra glanced around to see if she could count on help from anyone else. People were watching, but they stayed back. No help there.

"Joe—" said Rachel.

Loudly, Myra interrupted. "The last time she went home with you, you put her in the hospital."

Joe adjusted his stance. He continued more loudly, in an aggrieved tone. "Don't you see it, Rachel? She's using you. Like she did when you were kids. She made you quit your job—"

"It was hard for her to work with busted ribs, Joe." Myra took a few steps toward him.

Rachel made a dash for the driver side of the car. Joe evaded Myra and lunged toward Rachel. Rachel ran back behind Myra.

"Joe, you've been stalking us, and you are about to commit assault. Look at all the witnesses here. Turn around and walk away now."

As she spoke, she inched toward the driver side of the car, pulling Rachel behind her.

Again, Joe acted as if Myra weren't there. "You've got nothing to fear from me, you know that, don't you honey?"

Myra looked around at the bystanders, hoping someone had gone for help.

"Joe, please, just leave us alone," said Rachel.

Joe turned his wrath on Myra. "It's you she should be afraid of!" screamed Joe. "You are a snake, you've sunk your fangs into her, and you won't let go! Now come with me, Rachel!"

"I'm sure somebody here has called 9-1-1 and the cops are on their way."

Joe looked over at the crowd too. "No one will get between a man and the wife God gave him."

While he was distracted talking to the crowd, Myra pushed Rachel toward the driver's side of the car. "Now! Run!"

Rachel got behind the wheel.

Joe dove for the car.

He slammed against the car door just as Rachel locked it. He yanked at the door so hard Myra thought the whole door would come off in his hands, but it held.

Myra reached the passenger side. She tried the door, but all the doors were locked.

"Rachel! The door!" she called.

Rachel stared at the buttons on the door, too panicked to figure out how to open just one door. Joe pounded on the car window, and it cracked.

"Just drive!" Myra yelled, making driving motions with her hands. "Drive! Drive!"

She was suddenly yanked back by her hair.

Rachel and their mother watched, horrified, as Joe smashed Myra's face into the passenger side door.

"I've had enough of you, you goddamn—"

He pulled her back to smash her into the car again.

Myra stepped backward, her heel landing right on his instep, then kicked back, nearly landing one between his legs. He was still yanking her by her hair, but she smashed her elbow into his side. She pivoted under her own hair and landed an upper cut just under his chin.

Joe loosened his hold on her hair and staggered back a step.

"Go! Go! Get out of here!" Myra screamed.

Rachel gunned the engine and peeled away from them.

Joe wrapped his hands around Myra's neck. Myra choked. Joe lifted her almost off her feet.

Myra felt frantically for something, anything. Her hand landed on the award figurine that was sticking out of her purse. She managed to pull it out and awkwardly hit Joe on the head with it.

To her amazement, Joe crumpled to the ground, moaning.

Myra stared down at him, the figurine in her hand.

"If I ever see you again, I will kill you, you understand? Stay away from us!"

"Alright, that's enough," said an authoritative voice. A police officer. Another officer approaching from the other side.

"Oh, thank god," said Myra. "What took you so long?"

"Drop your weapon," said the cop behind her.

For a moment Myra didn't know what he meant. Then she realized it was about the plexiglass award.

She dropped it to the ground.

"Hands behind your back," said the cop.

"Cuff him first," said Myra. "He attacked us. Just ask anyone."

But to her dismay, most of the people who'd been standing around watching had disappeared.

Home. A fashionable apartment building. Myra pulled up in a taxi. She got out, looking around nervously. Hurried into the building. Heaved a sigh of relief when the main door swung shut behind her. Then caught her face in the mirror. A big shiner darkening her cheek, her hair a mess, her clothes torn.

"Guess I won't be going on that sales trip tomorrow," she muttered to herself.

She got into the elevator. Luckily, it was so late that no one else was there.

She let herself into her apartment. It had once been pristine, her haven after dealing with grouchy customers and sour colleagues. But now there was a stack of dirty dishes in the sink, a stack of sixpacks of protein drinks, and a box-column of adult diapers in the corner.

Rachel was watching the news, a mess of chip crumbs and candy wrappers on the coffee table.

"Turn the volume down, Rachel! You'll wake up mom!"

"Nothing wakes her up after she's taken her meds," said Rachel matter-of-factly. "Look at this, can you believe it? I think the woman is the one from your company, the one the cops were looking for at the awards dinner."

That got Myra's attention. She turned to the TV.

The newscaster was telling the story of a home invasion. The image showed a man in his wedding tuxedo, clearly cropped from his wedding picture, as her veil could be seen on the edge of the frame. "While his wife was at a business function, the husband was brutally murdered, beaten to death with his own kettlebell," says the newscaster, now on camera in front of a well-tended craftsman cottage.

"Can you believe that?" said Rachel. "That's this neighborhood. Beaten to death with his own kettlebell!"

"After tonight, I'll believe anything." Myra plopped down on the sofa next to her. She was going to make Rachel look at her if it killed her.

"Hey, my blanket—" Rachel yanked at her blanket and looked at Myra. "Ohmigod, Myra, is that his blood? What did you do to him?"

Myra sighed. "It's mine. I was defending you, remember?"

A police officer was speaking to the camera. "The serial killer seems to only target men, but everyone should be —"

Rachel turned back to the TV. "Did he say, 'serial killer'"?

"You're welcome, by the way," said Myra.

Rachel stayed glued to the TV.

Myra got up. She checked the lock on the kitchen door, the front door, the windows.

She cracked open the door to the one bedroom. It looked like a hospital room: a hospital bed, and IV stand, rows of pill bottles on the table. Her mother was sleeping, sitting up.

She opened her eyes.

"What's the commotion?" she chanted.

Myra smiled, did a dance step and recited: "It ain't no commotion, it's locomotion."

Mom smiled back at her.

Myra noticed the pills on the table. "Mom, you haven't taken your pills. You need these, Mom."

"They make me sick," Moms pulled up the blanket.

Myra teared up. She was at her breaking point. She needed just one thing to go right today. "I need you to take these, Mom. I need you to live."

Mom sighed. She held out her hand. Myra puts the pills in her hand, then refilled her water cup using a pitcher on the table.

Her mom patted her hand, took in her bruises.

"Don't worry. Joe looks worse."

"Oh, for crying out loud, why doesn't she divorce him already?"

"Beats me. Goodnight, Mom."

She leaned over and kissed her mother, gently.

She made her way back to her cot next to her desk in the living room.

Rachel was rummaging around in the kitchen. "Want some aspirin?"

"Please," said Myra, dropping onto the cot.

Rachel handed her two aspirin and a glass of water. "Did it ever occur to you that she's only staying alive for you?" She took the water glass form Myra and added to the pile of dirty dishes in the sink.

"For both of us," murmured Myra, then fell asleep.

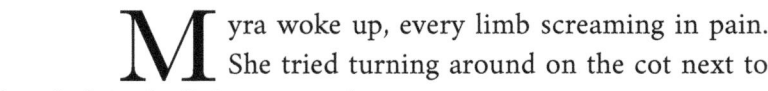

Myra woke up, every limb screaming in pain. She tried turning around on the cot next to her desk in the living room, then gave up.

Rachel, in a fancy negligee, was already up, watching the TV news again. Now a different set of newscasters were talking about the serial killer. *"... police are asking anyone with information to call this number...."*

Myra's eyes focused on the clock. "Did you give Mom her meds?"

"Last night wore her out," said Rachel. "She needs to sleep. I'll give them to her when she wakes up."

Myra sat up in bed with a huge effort.

"She missed her meds. You have to make sure she takes her meds on time," she said. "We need her. How can we handle this mess without her?"

"What mess?" screeched Rachel. "Let me remind you that two months ago I was living in a nice house, with nice dishes, nice clothes —

"And a husband that loved you so much he put you in the hospital once a month," finished Myra.

"He only does that when I make him mad—"

Myra held her hands up. "This is what I mean. I can't stand to listen you talk like this. As soon as you mend from each beating, it's like it never happened. I'm starting to think you are brain damaged."

"You're the one whose brain damaged," said Rachel. "You make me stay here and take care of mom while you get to put on your nice suits, and drive around in your nice car, and have nice lunches at fancy restaurants, while I have to stay here and empty the commode!"

"Rachel, I'm paying all your bills. I paid your hospital bills. And now I'm paying your legal bills." Her eyes widened as light dawned. "Hey, let me ask you something. How did Joe know where we were going to be?" she watched Rachel's face closely. "You're talking to him again, aren't you? Aren't you? After everything we went through to get you that protection order — you aren't supposed to talk to him!"

"You don't understand," said Rachel. "I can't stand to live like this. I want my old life back."

"So, you want your life back. You want to go back to looking like this?" Myra pointed at her own face. "You want to leave Mom, just when she needs us?"

"Just hire someone," snapped Rachel. "I'm not cut out to be a nurse."

Myra sank onto the sofa and covered her face with her hands. "Look, Rachel, you've got to know this. She's running out of time. It won't be much longer. And I have to keep working to pay for all of this. Can you please just stay a little longer? And then if after that you want to run back to Joe and let him beat you to death, I promise I won't say anything. I won't say anything, or do anything, and I'll certainly stop paying all your bills."

"Not everyone is like you," said Rachel. "Not everyone can fight like a man and then get up the next morning and go to work like nothing happened."

"Something did happen—" Myra points to her face. "I don't even know if I have enough makeup to cover all this."

There was a knock at the door.

Myra looked at Rachel accusingly. "Why would anyone knock at our door? They should be buzzing us from outside. You didn't give Joe the building code, did you? Rachel?"

"Oh my god, of course not, why would I do a thing like that?" screeched Rachel.

Myra walked quietly over to the door and looked through the peephole. She immediately opened the door. "Officer, we meet again. What can I do for you?"

The officer stepped into the room. "You again?" He was clearly displeased. He looked around at the room, took in the dirty dishes, the column of diaper boxes and protein drinks. "I'm looking for your sister. Mrs. Joseph Johnson."

"Her name is Rachel. She's right there."

Rachel got up from the sofa and came over, making no effort to put on a robe over the flimsy negligee. "I'm Mrs. Johnson. What is it, officer?"

Myra went to the hall closet and returned with a robe.

Rachel put it on unwillingly.

SISTER SECRETS

The Officer held up his badge. "My name is Officer Burton. You might want to sit down, ma'am."

"What's wrong, officer?"

"Please sit, both of you," said Officer Burton.

"What? Why?" said Rachel.

"You husband's dead, Mrs. Johnson. Murdered."

Rachel puts her hand to her mouth. Her knees crumpled. Myra caught her. Detective Burton was right there with her.

"I know this is difficult," said Burton. "But we have questions we have to ask. It would be best if you two could come to the station."

"How—how—" stammered Rachel.

"He was murdered. That's all I can say. Now I need you to come down to the station."

"We can't both go," said Rachel. "Our mother is very sick. One of us has to stay with her at all times."

Burton turned to Myra. "Then I'll take you down to the station, and Officer Collins — he opened the door to reveal a waiting police officer, tired, rumpled, and sour-looking —"will stay with Mrs. Johnson."

Collins sat down next to Rachel. Rachel recoiled from him and tightened her robe around her..

"I'll be back soon, I promise," Myra said Rachel.

Rachel looked after her, imploringly.

But Myra followed Officer Burton out of the building, resigned.

It was late when she got back. She let herself in quietly. To her surprise the kitchen was clean, all the dishes washed and put away. The bottles of protein drink had been unpacked and put in a cabinet.

Myra went into her room. Her mother was sleeping.

"Don't worry, I gave her all her meds," said Rachel, appearing in the hallway.

Myra stepped back into the hall and closed her mother's bedroom door. "Are there any cops here?"

"No, they all left hours ago," said Rachel.

"Rachel, I need you to help me," Myra whispered. "I need all the cash you have. And anything you have made of gold. Anything I can easily sell."

Myra ran to her own closet and started pulling out jeans, workout clothes, sweatshirts, sneakers and boots.

She looked at Rachel standing there, watching her.

"Please Rachel, come on, I need help."

"Why? Where are you going?"

"I only have a few minutes, Rachel. They're after me." She pulled an overnight bag out of the closet and started stuffing her clothes into it. "Come on, I need cash. I can't risk using an ATM. And I need gold, Rachel, quickly!"

"I don't have any gold jewelry," said Rachel.

"Sure you do!" Myra abandoned her suitcase in the hallway and went into the living room. This space had also been picked up. Two suitcases were open on the sofa, neatly filled.

Myra grabbed Rachel's jewelry box, turned it upside down, and shook it open, grabbing all the jewelry as it fell out.

Rachel wrenched the jewelry box away from her. "Hey! You can't do that!"

Myra crammed what she could into her pockets. She moved to the dining room chair where Rachel left her purse and pulled it open. Yanked out Rachel's wallet. Pulled out a thick wad of cash. "What— what did you do, empty my checking account?"

"I had to," said Rachel. "Because you said you weren't going to help me anymore."

"I said I wouldn't help you anymore if you went back to Joe. But this is my money, you have no right to take it!"

Rachel grabbed for the cash.

Myra slapped her. "This is my money. And right now I need it. The cops are after me. They say I killed Joe."

"What?" Rachel let go of her. "Why would they say that? I thought the serial killer did it."

"They don't think that anymore. It wasn't his M.O. Anyway, I don't have time for this, I have to get out of here, they'll be breaking down the door any moment."

She tugged at Rachel's wedding ring. "Come on, you don't need that anymore."

"That's true. You can have it." Rachel pulled it off and threw it at her. "But I'm not staying here another night, Myra. I'm going home."

"You can't do that, you idiot," Myra snapped. "You have to stay here and take care of Mom until I can prove my innocence."

"Why you? What makes them think it's you?"

"Because of the fight last night. You know, when Joe assaulted you and I protected you? Someone told them I told Joe I would kill him."

"But that was self-defense. He would have hurt me —you— all of us, if you hadn't —done what you did."

Myra went back to her rushed packing. "No, Rachel, when you are a lazy cop out to close a case, that's motive."

"But running away — that's not the solution," said Rachel. "If you are not guilty—"

Myra pulled open a drawer in her desk and pulled out a folder.

"Here is the restraining order, but I can't find his current address, do you have it?"

Rachel frowned. "Why do you need that?"

"I have to clear my name. I have to do some digging. No one else will do it right."

Myra zipped her bag shut. Teared up.

"Let the law handle this," said Rachel. "What will Mother do if you are on the run?"

"I can't take care of her, or you, if I'm in jail. Rachel, I have to do this. And give me the keys to your car."

"My car!" screeched Rachel.

"You can keep mine."

"Your car is covered in blood!"

"Rachel, we're sisters. I rescued you from Joe. I take care of you and Mom. Now I need help. Are you going to help me, or not?"

"She won't help you." It was Mom, standing in the doorway, leaning heavily on her IV stand, panting.

"Oh, Mom," said Myra. "Let me help you back into bed."

"The cops were here," said Mom as Myra got her settled. "She thought I was asleep. They asked her questions. She told them about Joe. About the fight. About how you threatened him."

"I didn't know why they were asking," said Rachel.

Sirens outside. All of them froze.

Myra kissed her mother.

Rachel and Myra went to the window, watched the cops get out, guns drawn, the leader giving them instructions with hand signals.

Myra ran to the hallway and picked up her suitcase. She ran to the kitchen and took Rachel's car keys.

"You can't take those. Those are mine!"

"I don't believe it," said Myra, not letting go. "After everything I've done for you. He nearly killed you!"

"That doesn't make it right for you to kill him," said Rachel.

Myra was hurt before, but this was worse. Really tough.

"Oh, I get it," she snapped. "You're not malicious, just stupid. Do you really think I would throw my life away on your criminal ex-husband?"

"What's so special about your life?" said Rachel. "What about my life? No one ever thinks about my life."

"What about it?" said Myra. She had the car keys now, but she didn't run out the kitchen door like she should have.

"You get to wear the suits. To drive the cars. You are surrounded by handsome men. You get the trophies. What do I get? I get to play nurse."

"Don't let Mom hear you say things like that, Rachel," Myra whispered. "You know it's temporary. She's dying. And you need time to get your life together. That was our deal."

Rachel pummeled her. "My life was together! I had a husband! I had a house! I had it all! And now, now, there's nothing!"

She burst into tears, still hitting her sister. "How could you kill him?"

Myra grabbed Rachel's wrists to stop the pummeling.

"I didn't kill him, Rachel. I couldn't have. I was out cold — you gave me some of Mom's meds. That means you must have done it. And I totally get why you would, Rachel, I totally get that. But what I would like to know is, why. Why try to pin it on me?"

Rachel's expression changed. Myra could see it in her face: finally, finally, finally, she was dropping her act.

It was like night and day.

"I just wanted — reasonable doubt," she whispered. "It always works on TV."

A loud banging sound.

"They're here!" Rachel said.

"No," said Myra. "It's Mom."

They ran to Mom's room. Sure enough, Mom was hitting the bedrail with her TV remote, screeching, "What's the commotion? What's the commotion?"

Rachel turned back to Myra, but Myra was gone.

Myra was outside. She walked toward the police with her hands up. Officer Burton came forward.

"Did you get that?" Myra asked, nearly choking on the words.

Officer Burton nodded. "We got it."

A female officer led Myra to a van and started to remove the wire. "Must have been hard, going after your own sister."

Myra watched Officers Burton and Collins lead the other officers into the building, stonyfaced.

THE PURLOINED LEGACY

E. CHRIS AMBROSE

THE PURLOINED LEGACY

E. CHRIS AMBROSE

Nigel Rowe ducked beneath the tilting lintel of the ancient chapel, electric torch in hand. He didn't quite need it—the golden glow of late afternoon saturated the woods around him and draped the old stone, glinting off the bits of glass still clinging to the window frames. Really, the place looked remarkably good for its age. A fact which he ought to have noticed a long time ago. But one doesn't examine one's own heritage too closely, just like so many people who've lived in Somerset all their lives and never visited Stonehenge. What, that old thing?

So far as he knew, nobody'd studied the old chapel since Donal Cunningham stopped by when Nigel was a lad. Must be a dozen years ago now. Cunningham's visit, and his generosity with his time and talk had partly inspired Nigel's own Oxford studies, so today's excursion in support of a classroom assignment brought him full-circle. In fact, his studies might finally prove of value to his family. They'd been indifferent to him for years, but now he had information vital to their future, just the treat to draw them together. To draw himself back into the fold.

The chapel greeted him damply, cooler than it had been when he arrived an hour ago. He had left his papers inside, then worked his way around the outside, confirming his observations. A peaked roof remained over much of the nave, including the apse and altar and the small choir loft at the far end with its modest bell tower. Near the door, timbers caved in and slate roof tiles scattered. Dove coos echoed from their nests among the eaves. Lichen speckled the walls and floors and soft green mosses took over in the corners of door frames.

A few of the stone slabs underfoot showed engraved lettering alongside well-worn carvings, indicating the traditional burials in the supposedly sanctified space. The empty sockets and gapped mouth of a round form stared up at him. Not merely a shape carved into the stone, but a scuffed to near-invisible skull.

Bits of grass tufted along the old pews. That was another thing. Most churches of this size during the period wouldn't have pews at all. A seat for the prelate, perhaps, but no more, not even for—

"Bit of a mess, isn't it?"

Nigel jumped and spun about, the tumbled beams catching against his back.

Daffyd's laughter boomed around him. "God, Nigel, the look on your face!" His brother clamped a hand over his mouth as if to stop himself laughing, but it didn't take. Instead, his blue eyes twinkled over the hand, his cheeks pink and fit to burst with good humor. "They ought to get you marketing Halloween films."

Charming. Just like Daffyd to try to get the jump on him. He hadn't heard his brother's motor, and surely Daffyd hadn't walked here from the manor. Through a grimy window, Nigel glimpsed one of the estate cars alongside his own old beater. Getting hold of himself, Nigel straightened. "Thanks for coming, Daffyd. Or should I say, my lord?"

"Indeed, you should." Daffyd's voice rang.

"Where's Mum?"

"Just wrapping up tea in the garden with Emma. They've got this tradition on Thursdays, now you're at uni." Daffyd shrugged. "She'll walk down in a few, I'm sure."

Ducking under the tumble of beams, Daffyd entered the chapel, his presence requiring Nigel to move further inside. At least there he could stand upright with less fear of getting feathers in his hair. "P'raps I'll get lucky, and Emma will tag along." Never enough chances to visit with his niece.

"Given the weather, she'll have her books spread out on the terrace. Haven't been down here in ages." As Daffyd glanced around, his nose wrinkled, fleshy lips compressed. "You've not told Emma you're here, have you? It's mid-term and she's got to focus."

Nigel felt a pang. Both of them growing up, apparently. He was in anthropology at Oxford, while his niece had studies of her own, though she was a few years from her A-levels yet. He'd brought her to the chapel when she was so small he had to lift her over the threshold, a thrilling adventure, torches in hand. Even then, she loved to startle the roosting doves and watch them explode into the sky toward the manor. *"The beacons are lit. Gondor calls for aid!"* he cried as white wings beat the air and he aimed his torch through the damaged roof. Then he had to read her the Lord of the Rings so she'd know the reference.

Later, the chapel offered the perfect spot for gothic tales to frighten her and her friends, and give himself a little chill as they walked back to the manor in the darkness. Could explain why he felt a little jumpy now. The place was too damned atmospheric. Nigel shook it off. "I can't stay long in any case, I just needed to confirm a few things, then I felt...well, I thought you should know. Together we can head off a revelation that might prove scandalous."

"What, that the old place is falling to bits? Ought to take it down I guess." Daffy prowled forward, his bulk forcing Nigel to step aside.

"You recall when Doctor Cunningham visited? Years ago, it was."

With a twitch, Daffyd shook that off as a horse shakes off a fly. "Feeling poorly, were you?"

"Not that sort of a doctor. He's a professor, studying Norman-era chapels like this. Said he'd write up his findings, but I couldn't find a copy." Cunningham hadn't published much the last few years. Nigel ought to track him down.

"Doesn't ring a bell. Nor will that." Daffyd pointed toward the little tower. Empty of its wooden floors and ladders, the tower rang only with silence. "Course there's a lot of papers down the archives. Could be in there."

"Could be," Nigel agreed cheerfully. "Sadly your man wouldn't grant me access without your say-so, and I gather you didn't hear from him?"

"I'll talk to him." Daffyd's head tipped toward the uneven mossy slabs of the floor. "You don't suppose there's any bodies down below?"

"If they've not been reinterred elsewhere, then I imagine there are." The empty sockets of the carved skull stared back at him. "If there ever were, of course."

Squatting, Daffyd knocked his knuckles against the slab and Nigel flinched. "Certainly looks like a grave to me, Nigel!" He rose and strode along the aisle toward the darker end where the roof still protected the interior. "Must've been quite a place in the early days of the Rowe family. P'raps we should do a restoration, eh?"

Nigel's metal torch felt clammy in his palm as he followed. "Here's the thing, Daffyd. I think—"he took a deep breath to steady his nerve. "This chapel. I think it's a fraud."

Near the apse, Daffyd swung his head, cocked slightly, then he rested his hips against the altar. "What'd you mean by that?

Doesn't smell like a fraud to me, Nigel. That's pure English muck, isn't it? And the roof's about to come down."

Time to marshal his evidence. "Right. It's likely the beams and such, the fabric of the place, if you will, is genuine, just that it wasn't built here." He cleared his throat. "For us."

Daffyd's furrowed brow shadowed his eyes. "What are you on about, Nigel?"

"Well, to begin with, it's not in the Domesday Book. The well and the original manor are listed, along with any number of monuments hereabouts."

"Domesday's been out of print for centuries. A millennium, isn't it? And it was hardly the height of accuracy at the time."

"Technically, it's only just come into print," Nigel broke off. His brother didn't care for history at the best of times. "You're not wrong about its accuracy. There's plenty of errors and oversights, but the presence of a bit of property in the book is a strong indicator for its age and provenance—"

"Why're we even having this conversation, Nigel? Remind me."

"I've got a personal history assignment from one of my professors. I chose to research the chapel, but I'm afraid what I've found could damage the Rowe family reputation."

"Ah." An expansive sound that encompassed understanding and dismissal in the same breath. "So you've got homework, and you think it could be my problem." Daffyd turned his wrist his cuff edging back to reveal a watch worth more than Nigel's education would be. "I've got to be in London for tomorrow's vote, and I'd every intention of reviewing the documents tonight. Pleasant as it is to spend time with my beloved little brother, this is hardly the key item on my agenda. If you have any hard evidence, you'd best sum it up."

Tomorrow's vote: a parliamentary procedure on the rights of immigrants, and one that Daffyd's position as the hereditary holder of the family lands gave him standing for.

"Understood. Domesday Book merely gave me a place to begin. Manor, yes, chapel, no. Might've been built a little later, in spite of the architectural features suggesting—" a fruitless angle, and Nigel abandoned it. He glanced toward the door, hoping their mother would present herself, else he'd have to go through this all over again. "Not finding it there, I returned here, back in December if you might recall."

A curling wave of Daffyd's hand encouraged him to hurry along, and Nigel did his best to comply.

"I took plenty of photos, using different angles and techniques. On closer analysis, some of the stones don't appear to be properly oriented." He indicated the corbels above them. "The weathering patterns at the exterior windward corner, for instance, don't indicate that level of exposure, not for a thousand years or close to it. A hundred or two, at most. But the opposite corner does, as if the chapel once had a quite different setting. Taken together, they suggest the place has been moved."

"Interesting." Daffyd's face said otherwise.

"Either moved here, or purpose-built some time later. Out of reclaimed stone from other places."

"So. A genuine chapel, built in the wrong place."

"Precisely! Or a chapel fabricated more recently from bits taken out of older buildings." Daffyd's understanding gave Nigel a swell of relief, though his brother hadn't grasped the implications. "But it's not the building that troubles me, at least, not primarily." He walked around the altar toward the narrow cabinets built beneath the old choir stairs. In lieu of a proper vestry, these cabinets stored the priest's garments along with the holy accoutrements of the service. Many churches moldered after Henry VIII's dissolution of the monasteries caused the forcible conversion of a Catholic nation into an Anglican one, but the Rowe family chapel, decrepit though it seemed, concealed a few secrets throughout the years since then.

"You remember the story," Nigel prompted. He set his hand

on the cabinet door, gripping the edges, then tucking the torch in a back pocket to free up his other hand. "How they found the records here, back in the eighteenth century?"

"The family Bible, you mean." Daffyd rounded the altar, arms folded. "The chapel might've been moved for any number of reasons, if you're even right about that. What are you on about, Nigel?"

"The truth, Daffyd. A truth that could disgrace the family." He worked at the door.

"'My lord,'" his brother corrected.

"Sorry, my lord." The door popped open and Nigel tripped back from it. Empty now, but the damp space revealed had once held a family treasure indeed: the manorial record of births and deaths going back centuries, hand-drawn pages bound in with a manuscript Bible. "Where's the Bible now? Your office, I'm guessing?"

"Library, I think. Wherever Da kept it after Gran had that archival box made." He shrugged. "Hold up, Nigel. You're not saying the whole thing's fake—the chapel, the Bible, the works?"

"It's a distinct possibility."

His brother, his liege lord according to that same Bible, stared at him for a long moment as if posing for a sculptor. "Because the building's weathered in the wrong way. You do realize how daft that sounds."

"If that were the only thing, I might presume the gales are broken by that stand of pines, but no. There's no record of our chapel, Da—my lord, but there's meant to be a chapel down the brook at Nether Woodley."

Daffyd snorted. "There's not even a village at Nether Woodley. Hasn't been for ages."

"Meant to be." Nigel held up a finger. "It's gone." He reached for the leather folio he'd set on the altar during his earlier perusal of the chapel and opened it up, placing a photocopy on the altar, then a photo beside it. "Here's an etching from the ruins down there, circa 1850." The chapel stood in a glade behind a couple of ruined houses, abandoned during the Plague back in the fourteenth century, as so many had been. Just the sort of romantic image artists loved to sketch. In the recent photo, the houses remained, much as the artist had shown them, but the chapel had gone—not even a heap of stones to suggest it had ever been.

Daffyd pinched the etching between his fingers, apparently studying it, then he swept his arm around Nigel's shoulders with a hearty squeeze. "You know what etchings are meant for, don't you, Nigel? You find some young lady you fancy, and invite her up to view them. You don't just bandy them about like this." He leaned in close. "Anybody might get a look at your etchings." He dropped the picture on the altar.

"Have a look at the photo—"

"Doesn't have to be a lady, if lads are more your fancy." A curled lip suggested how Daffyd felt about that.

Nigel flushed. "Could you focus for a moment, please? This is important."

"You, trying to discredit our heritage? Here's my advice for you, brother." He tapped Nigel's chest. "Let it go."

"It doesn't bother you? That our vaunted heritage might rest upon a faulty foundation?"

Their eyes met, blue on blue. Daffyd had nine years on him-- with two more brothers between--and about three stone. Photographic evidence suggested Daffyd once looked very much like him. A long time ago now.

"Well, then. Let's find out. If the chapel's been moved, there'd be no bodies, right? Said so yourself."

"You're not proposing—"

Daffyd stalked along the aisle. "How about this fellow?" He shifted a few roof tiles off the grave he had selected.

Nigel trailed after him. "Let's at least wait for Mum. She can't be too much longer."

"Why so hesitant? Isn't anthropology mostly grave-robbing? I recall somebody fresh from first term saying as much at a family dinner. At the least you've become a more engaging meal companion." Daffyd flashed a grin, then moved toward the exit. "There's some tools in the estate car. Won't be a moment!"

"We can't just go about digging up graves," Nigel called out.

Car doors opened and metal grated, then Daffyd reappeared with a shovel and a prybar. "I'm the landowner, aren't I? The ancestral lord of all I survey. You've my permission." He thrust the shovel in Nigel's direction. "It's more than your Dr. Cunningham had."

"So you do remember." The shovel's grip felt smooth and firm in his hands.

"You reminded me." Daffyd set-to, scraping the mossy overgrowth to locate the edges of the black slab.

"There's other ways to confirm my suspicions."

"None faster." He cast a critical eye over his work, then pointed. "Do you know, it looks as if somebody's done this before."

With the leaf litter and most cleared away, the scrape marks stood out against the dark stone, and Nigel agreed. Cunningham, perhaps? That seemed awfully invasive for an historical survey. Unless his inspiration had harbored suspicions of his own. Nigel hadn't been privy to the adults' conversations. Even Daffyd was allowed only because of his recent elevation to the lordship.

"Let's work together, shall we?" Nigel took a position along the nearest long edge, notching the shovel's blade into the gap between the gravestone and the plain flooring adjacent.

"We don't do that often, do we?" Daffyd's eyes softened, almost fondly.

That much was certainly true. As children, the eldest directed them on all sorts of adventures, sometimes rougher than Nigel's taste, to be sure, but the sort of trials that boys were meant to endure, together. Til his training to assume the lordship began in earnest, and Daffyd assumed the mantle of prestige. Their middle brothers took up careers worthy of the Rowe name while Nigel's studious bent sent him ever further from the family embrace.

Now, they stood again side by side, on an adventure brought about by those same studies, an adventure that might redeem him. Daffyd set the pry bar against the gap a little further up.

"Three! Two! One!" Nigel heaved downward on the shovel's handle while Daffyd grunted against the prybar.

With a groan of metal on slate, the slab shifted upward. Nigel's shovel pushed further and he shifted his stance, pushing the slab upward.

"Careful now!" Daffyd barked. He grabbed the edge, and Nigel joined him, the pair of them pivoting the stone higher, straining with the weight, then letting it settle against the old oak of the pews. Nothing like a spot of grave-digging to get a man's heart pounding. Nigel set aside the shovel and wiped his sweaty palms on his canvas trousers. He'd dressed for exploration, at least. If not manual labor. Likely the first time his brother'd done anything like since he'd assumed the lordship on the death of their father. No, Nigel was being uncharitable. After all, Daffyd had been the one to suggest opening the grave. And now Nigel delayed actually looking inside. Right. Nothing for it.

"There, you see now? There's your truth." Daffyd's voice fell suitably low.

Dirt and moss seeped along the edge of the revealed stones. Four more slabs, set edge-on, formed a box inset from the position of the slab. Together, they framed a skeleton, the knees bent to one side, arms folded across the hollow chest. Bits of leathered skin clung to the skull, along with wispy clumps of hair that glinted like pale gold. No smell of rot—no more so than there had been, something he ought to've considered prior to going along with Daffyd's scheme.

"So there is," Nigel murmured. Had he been wrong?

He squatted down, studying the body. Physical Anthropology came together with Introduction to Archaeology during the prior term. He scanned for any sort of grave goods or sign of the occupant's clothing. The fellow might well've been buried naked for all the evidence that remained.

"Guess we ought to cover up this poor chap." Daffyd crossed himself, regarding the dead. "One of our ancestors, isn't he?"

"Or she. It's hard to tell without closer analysis." Nigel cocked his head, then reached out to touch the jaw, gently prying open the mouth of the deceased.

"Nigel..." A warning tone.

As if the dead could speak, the man revealed his own truth: a glint of silver. Not coins, nor rings. Fillings.

"Daffyd, this body's too—" Nigel glanced up as the shadows shifted.

Daffyd's prybar crashed into his temple as he flung up an arm to deflect it. Nigel dropped hard and bones cracked. Fortunately, not his own. Pain burst through his head, his own teeth snapping together with the force of the blow, then the rattling fall. Darkness rushed his vision and nausea wrenched his gut.

For a moment, Nigel swam in the void as if history would swallow him whole. Or leave him beneath the floor to become a relic himself without even the grace of a telltale heart.

Stone scraped and vibrated. Nigel jerked awake to see Daffyd working to release the slab. Nigel caught his breath, but he must've rattled the bones for his brother turned, seizing the prybar.

The dead man took an elbow to the face as Nigel rolled from his brother's next swing, trying to cover his head. The bar clanged against stone.

"Leave it alone, I said, but would you? For God's sake, Nigel, won't you ever just do as you're told."

Nigel grabbed the shovel and the bar rebounded from the handle. The power behind the blow reverberated down his arm. Daffyd had always been on the edge of bullying, but this was madness. Nigel fell back out of the grave, sprawling into the aisle, the shovel held to defend himself. "Daffyd! I only thought you should know."

"Know this--"Daffyd kicked a tile at him, the sharp edge scraping along his back as he tried to roll to his feet—"our history's better left buried."

Scrambling away, Nigel pushed himself up with the shovel. He staggered, the chapel twirling through his blurred vision. Blood smeared the side of his face and his stomach lurched.

"They've got an heir and a spare in myself and Arthur, haven't they? Plus Charlie, and finally you. All because Mum wanted a girl." Daffyd tread carefully down the graveside, weighing the bloodied prybar in his grip. "At least she had the sense to give up after you."

Nigel, the superfluous son, fled toward the altar, where his brother might well sacrifice him for the sake of their name.

Daffyd plunged after him and Nigel's hips struck the altar. He swung the shovel in a desperate arc. His brother leapt back, stumbling, and Nigel aimed the shovel's blade at Daffyd's throat.

"What on earth are you doing, Nigel?" Mother's voice cut through.

Defending himself, though right now, it didn't look it. Nigel withdrew his makeshift weapon, slumping onto the altar. "Mother!" He pressed a hand to his chest, trying to catch his breath. "Thank God."

Dressed as usual in impeccable beige, Evelyn Rowe glowed in the slanting rays of the sun. Her glance flicked between them. "I do feel I'm interrupting."

"Nigel's had a fall."

Nigel wiped the blood back from his eye.

"Onto that prybar, from what I can see." Mum ducked the roof timbers and stepped carefully inside. Her quick eye took in the open grave and the two combatants, her sons. "Surely whatever this is can be settled without bloodshed." A pause, then she amended, "Further bloodshed."

"I think the chapel's a fake, Mother. Moved from elsewhere and given the trappings of Rowe family heritage."

"In which case, there wouldn't be any bodies." Daffyd stood just this side of the grave, the skull and ribs now crushed by Nigel's own fall.

"This one's too recent." Even as he said it the implications clicked together like the last piece of a puzzle dropped into place. A too-recent body, in a grave his brother pegged for exploration. His brother clearly knew the chapel's secrets in more ways than one. Nigel's throat went dry. He blinked a few times. "Let's all head up to the garden and talk this over, shall we?"

"Let's leave here alive and never speak of this again," Daffyd proposed.

"Now, Daffyd, it's a bit much threatening your brother. Has he even grasped what his little fancy implies?" Mum patted the shoulder of her eldest son, then edged by him without looking at the body. From a pocket in her trim pants, she plucked a kerchief and offered it to Nigel. "Is it very bad?"

The cloth hung like a flag of truce. Nigel lay his shovel on the altar at his side and accepted the kerchief to press to his wound. His side ached as well, where the tile had gouged into him. From the doubled vision and churning in his gut, he guessed concussion. "Bad enough, thanks."

At least his mother's presence might inhibit his brother's worst instincts. Their heritage required defending, on that they could agree, but he'd never expected Daffyd to go to such lengths. Or should it be sink to such depths?

"Too recent, you said. How can you tell?" Her face swam in his vision, and the nausea intensified.

"Dental work." He swallowed, trying to control his unruly gut. But when had he ever been ruly? "Also the articulation. The ligaments and cartilage haven't fully broken down." He took a deeper breath. Could help.

Mum nodded seriously. "I'm pleased your studies have had some useful result."

Her praise, even mild as it was, warmed his chest. She would understand the need, and Daffyd would abide by her cooler nature. Surely, he would.

Behind her, Daffyd grunted. "Not so articulated as it had been is it now?"

"Hush, darling."

"When word spreads about this, there'll be a scandal," Nigel said. "If we get ahead of it, if we lead the investigation, we can… mitigate the repercussions."

"And how would it get out, Nigel?" Daffyd asked, his tone all acid, the prybar in his hands. "We might lose our title, our seat in parliament, the reputation we've worked to build through generations. Do you plan to bring us down, just for your academic advancement?"

Generations of what? Liars and frauds. "No! Of course not. I'd never." He pressed the cloth to his throbbing head, the depth of his brother's concern ringing through his skull: was it possible their entire claim to the lordship lay in a fraudulent Bible—that someone had gone through the effort of literally moving a church to prop up the lie? The enormity of it set him reeling. Their entire claim to the nobility rested on lies. "I'm not the only one with questions. If Cunningham's report…oh, God." The last was a whisper. A breath above an open grave, and a body that couldn't be much more than ten years old.

Unsteadily, Nigel slid down from the altar to his feet. His

mother reached to clutch his arm, helping him balance. "Nigel, I'm not at all sure you should be moving."

Neither was he, but he could hardly remain still. He fixed his eye on his brother. "You've killed him, haven't you. That's Doctor Cunningham, isn't it. What's left of him." Transformed into the evidence that couldn't otherwise be found.

"I haven't killed anyone," Daffyd snapped. "Yet."

Nigel flinched, and his mother jiggled his arm. "You're getting wrapped up in your own head, Nigel, just as you've always done. Your brother's not a murderer."

Yet. He appeared more than willing to be the end of Nigel to defend his own rights and privileges. But she sounded so sure, in spite of the scene before her.

The chapel spun around him, a through-the-looking-glass mad universe revolving around the still point of his family. His mother's icy grip on his arm and her utter conviction in Daffyd's innocence. Her lack of surprise at anything he said. He'd thought she would be his salvation. He now saw how very wrong he'd been.

"My apologies." He tried to shrug free of her hand, stepping away. "You're right, of course, I've not thought this through."

"Precisely." Her voice remained clear, cool and calm. "You're dwelling on the past, but it's the future we must consider. What of Emma's marriage prospects, should your wild claims be broadcast? What about your nephews? Not to mention your own brothers. Never mind Daffyd's title, do you think a barrister's career well-served by spouting off about murder, or a financier's by claims of fraud?"

"He won't shut up, Mother, you know he won't. He hasn't stopped talking since birth." Daffyd occupied the aisle between Nigel and the only door.

There must be some way out, some way that didn't involve his direct participation in filling the next grave. He wrenched his arm away and grabbed the shovel, brandishing it before him.

"Nigel! What are you doing?"

Nigel scrambled up the narrow steps to the choir loft, stumbling and barking his knees, then spinning about at the top, defending his tower, such as it was. His bloodied palm slid on the smooth shaft.

"You never have cleaved to family as you should." Her face resolved into its familiar disappointment.

"I'll pin him down, Mother." Daffyd stalked forward. "Get the shotgun from the car."

"Don't be ridiculous, Daffyd. Emma might hear." Mum folded her arms, chin lifted.

Not *"don't shoot your brother, Daffyd,"* never that. Nigel raised his shovel even as Daffyd mounted the stair.

"You wouldn't dare." Daffyd's suitcoat scrubbed the mossy wall.

Nigel slammed the blade of the shovel against the roof beam. The wooden members shivered. Doves burst from their roosts, rushing through every gap in the roof and walls. He pulled the torch from his pocket and aimed it through the tower's empty frame.

"What on earth are you doing?" Mum called.

"Lighting the beacon."

Daffyd shoved his way up and lunged forward. Nigel dropped the light, getting both hands on his shovel as his brother's prybar rushed toward his face. It hooked the shovel and yanked it away, the blood smearing as Nigel lost his grip.

He kicked up a tumble of leaves and Daffyd coughed, blinking fiercely. Nigel pushed his back against the tower wall, hands pressing outward. He got his feet ahead of him, scrambling up the stone chimney and praying the builders—and the re-builders—had built it well.

"Damn you, Nigel!" Daffyd's voice echoed in the narrow space as Nigel got out of reach.

"Mother, please." Daffyd put out his hand, expecting their mother to fill it with murderous potential.

Nigel tried to creep higher, stone scraping his hands and back. The wall in front of him shifted beneath the pressure of his feet. Damnation!

From outside, a girl's distant cry of delight. "Uncle Ny!"

Daffyd froze.

"Nigel! Is it really you?"

"Gondor calls for aid!" Nigel shouted, the tower amplifying his voice for all the world to hear, or at least, for the one person they all agreed they cared for.

"Emma, darling!" Mum called back, hurrying toward the door to head off his savior. "Have you finished your studies?"

Daffyd ducked back out of the tower. "Shit." He strangled the prybar, then shook it in Nigel's direction. "If she hears a word about this. A single word. If anything you've said here gets into the press—swear to God, Nigel, you'll never see her again."

He stomped down the stairs, dropping the prybar into the grave and heaving down the slab. It fell with a thunderous boom, concealing the truth.

Dust and bits of moss danced around Nigel in the tower. His entire body ached as he let himself carefully back to the ground.

"Nigel's just here for his schoolwork, like you. Get back to work," Daffyd ordered from the doorway.

"At least he's got to give me a hug, Daddy. Haven't you always said the most important thing is family?"

Nigel wiped his face with a shaking hand. Time to put the past behind him, and go down to meet the future. To abandon the truth and bow to the lie. For the moment, it just might save his life.

THE BACK NINE

RACHEL AMPHLETT

CHAPTER 1

A rosy tint was kissing the brightening horizon when Curtis Palmer lifted his battered canvas golf bag from the trunk of the eighteen-month-old sedan that morning.

He could hear the *psst-psst* of the sprinkler system soaking the fairway and glanced over his shoulder to see a fine mist lifting into the air from the hoses dotted throughout the course. Another few minutes and they would be turned off, leaving behind a sparkling dew that would quickly evaporate.

Beyond the first hole, an ibis poked and prodded the shallows of the ornamental lake that had been carved into the 18-hole course. The gentle eddy of water carried an undertone of marshland rot while it lapped lazily at the fringes of the course, the flow dependent upon the sprawling swamp that surrounded these parts.

There was no breeze tickling the cabbage palm trees above his head, and a haze clung to the back nine on the far side of the lake. It was already obscuring the flag for the fifteenth hole that lay beyond a sand-filled bunker that tapered towards the water, creating an artificial beach.

The humidity was going to be off the charts today, no doubt about that.

Curtis lowered the bag to the asphalt and slowly straightened, digging his knuckles into his hip where the muscles protested.

The five-hour flight from LA yesterday hadn't helped, not at his age anyway, and the pitiful excuse for coffee that the hotel served this morning had only taken the edge off his bleariness while he'd washed down the painkillers.

He shielded his eyes against the brightening sunrise beyond the clubhouse, then raised his hand as a groundskeeper trundled past in one of the many utility vehicles used to maintain the course.

His was the only car parked in the bays allocated to players at the moment, its rental plates and age marking him as a visitor before he'd even signed in.

Reaching into a side pocket of the duffle, his fingers found a plastic bag that crinkled under his touch as he tore it open, tipping some of the fresh plastic tees into his palm. Those found their way into the pockets of his pants, the rest were tucked away once more, safe.

The clubs were a motley collection of wedges and irons, a well-used driver, and two favourite putters garnered over the years.

Time and again, the professionals at his home club in Santa Monica tried to persuade him to 'upgrade' as they called it.

He scowled.

He was done being screwed by people.

In the distance, the ibis let out an indignant squawk, and he turned to watch while it lifted into the air, leaving behind a series of ripples that chased themselves across the lake. The bird banked, the white patches on its wings reflecting the pink and gold sunrise as it circled above his head with an ethereal grace.

An orange and black butterfly fluttered from a border of

lilies in front of his face, startling him. He raised his hand to bat it away from his face, then stopped.

Jane would have loved it.

It was a crying shame she wasn't here to see it.

He inhaled deeply to calm the grief that rose in his chest.

There was a promise to the air, a freshness that smacked the back of his nostrils, tickled his throat, and sucked a hacking cough from his rotten lungs. He hawked into a nearby oleander shrub, then grimaced as he bent double and spat out the remnant traces of blood.

Bowing his head, he used the shoulder of his pale green cotton polo shirt to wipe away the sweat that bubbled at his brow, then straightened at the sound of an approaching car.

CHAPTER 2

He wasn't surprised to see the gleaming silver paintwork of a two-door sports car that looked no more than a day old.

He couldn't see the driver's face—his features were obscured by the shadows from a large Panama hat—but the man's knuckles sparkled with two diamond-encrusted gold rings, one on each hand that rested nonchalantly on the steering wheel. One of the hands raised in a brief greeting as the car drew closer.

The chrome fender had been polished to within an inch of its life, and its driver took one look at the horseshoe-shaped car park before passing Curtis and parking at the far end.

The engine gave a final soft purr and then died.

Henry Forrester climbed out, keys jangling in one hand and a six-thousand-dollar smile on his lips.

Curtis had recommended the dentist.

His golfing partner of forty years wore his age well, his naturally tanned face surprisingly unlined for a man in his late sixties. And for a man who survived three tours with the Marine Corps, two of which Curtis had witnessed.

After leaving the Corps, Henry purchased a tire sales place near Greenwich, Connecticut, found his niche and had a dozen franchised workshops by the time he quit. He sold the business and now spent a comfortable retirement playing golf in Florida and skiing in Colorado—when he wasn't on vacation somewhere in Europe with his fourth wife, Eleanor (twenty years his junior).

On the rare occasions he was at home in Greenwich, he kept a watchful eye on a part stake in a string of racehorses, all named after Union generals.

"Ready to get your backside kicked?" Henry called as he fetched his bag of clubs from the trunk.

"You wish."

The familiar routine of a three-monthly game, easily remembered after all this time—even if those first holes were plastic cups in the middle of a desert somewhere in the east, far away from the sultry Florida swampland.

For that was what this was, after all.

An oasis in a swamp.

Curtis could smell the rotting vegetation under the green veneer of the manicured fairway beyond the second tee. He snorted under his breath and turned back to the trunk of the rental car. He was aware of Henry walking over before a shadow fell across him.

"Are you still using that beat up old wedge of yours?"

Curtis bit back his first response, fixed a tired smile, and gave a slight shrug before lifting the bag of clubs from the trunk and slamming shut the lid. "It does the trick."

Henry winked. "We'll soon see about that, won't we?"

Any other time, and Curtis would have found that mildly funny, but not today. Still, he chuckled under his breath because it was expected and followed Henry towards the clubhouse.

It was a low-slung red brick affair with gables and a wraparound veranda that hugged floor-to-ceiling privacy glass panes facing the car park and sliding partitioned doors that opened onto the course. A pair of smoked-glass doors with polished chrome handles led into the clubhouse and were kept closed to prevent any of the precious air-conditioned coolness escaping the building.

"How did you get on at the doc's last week, anyway?" said Henry, opening the door for him. "Did you get your test results back?"

"Not yet," Curtis lied. "Apparently, there was a mix-up at the lab. I've got to go back next week."

"Got to admit, bud, that's why I prefer private healthcare over the public system." Henry snorted. "At this rate, you'll be dead before they get an answer, and probably not from what you think you've got."

Curtis stumbled over the threshold, righted himself and shot the other man a wan smile. "We'll see. I've got a few things I'd like to do before I go. Things I'd like to put right, you know?"

Henry wrinkled his nose. "I've never seen the point of that. You've got to live for the moment, my friend. No regrets. Especially now. Jane would have wanted that for you, wouldn't she?"

"I suppose so." Curtis unzipped the side pocket of his bag, extracted his wallet as they reached the reception desk, and handed over his credit card. "We've booked under the name of Palmer."

The pretty girl behind the desk flashed a smile, then promptly swiped his card and removed three hundred dollars from his account, just like that. "Enjoy your game, gentlemen."

"What are the 'gators up to?" said Henry. "Any trouble?"

"No, sir. There are two females out on the number six fairway that shouldn't bother you," said the girl. "We haven't seen Mikey for a few weeks."

"Good." Henry clapped Curtis on the shoulder with such force that his spine shuddered. "Come on, less talk, more golf."

"Thanks." Curtis shot the girl a smile, then hitched the bag up his shoulder once more and followed Henry through the clubhouse and out the back doors to the course.

A hire cart was already waiting for them.

Henry placed his leather golf bag into the back and slid behind the wheel, a predatory smile on his lips. "Ready?"

After using one of the bench seats to change his shoes, Curtis threw his bag beside Henry's and climbed in, barely having time to get comfortable before the other man pressed the throttle.

He squinted at the haze obscuring the back nine holes before aiming a sideways glance at his opponent.

Alligators or no alligators, he was determined to beat Henry Forrester today.

While he still could.

CHAPTER 3

Curtis shielded his eyes, his right hand sweating within a white leather glove, and looked between the palm trees at the flag in the distance.

According to his notes, the sixth hole was a par four with a tricky bunker a few hundred yards from the tee. The river created a dog leg opposite that.

And he needed to do this on a par three if he was going to level with Henry.

The other man leaned against the side of the golf cart, arms folded and a confident smile on his lips. He had teed off first, the ball sailing into the air in a beautiful arc before bouncing onto the green beyond the bunker and rolling to a stop without tumbling into the rough on the far side.

Curtis dropped his hand and clutched the club grip once more, wriggled his shoulders to hurry a trickle of sweat down his spine, and slowed his breathing. His gaze traveled from the ball to the green, from the ball to the green.

The third time, the club met the ball with a satisfying *whack*, sending it high and far.

He exhaled, watching as it found its zenith before starting to fall, and then it bounced on the edge of the bunker.

"Damn," he murmured, his heart lurching.

In his peripheral vision he saw Henry push away from the cart, straightening in anticipation, and then the ball rolled to safety and stopped five yards behind the other man's.

"Lucky," said Henry.

"Yeah." Curtis climbed into the cart and tried to relax for the ride over to the green. They passed the bunker and then an area of rough grass with a fringe of reeds. He sat up as Henry turned right towards the green, then whistled under his breath and pointed. "Check out the size of those two."

The other man slowed the cart as they passed the two alligators lying side by side. The pair of them eyed the golfers with lazy interest as they bathed in the sun's rays.

"Female, I reckon," Curtis said. "About eight feet, no more."

"They won't bother us by the look of it," said Henry. "You'd think they were at an all-inclusive resort, waiting for the next round of cocktails to be brought over to them. All that's missing are the gossip magazines."

Curtis kept his eye on them anyway as the cart sped up again, twisting in his seat until the fairway dog-legged and the green came into full view. "If those are that size, how big is Mikey these days?"

"I don't know, but have you seen some of the monsters on those videos online?" Henry cut the engine and shrugged. "Most are docile anyway. They're too well fed around here. Maybe keep your phone handy. If Mikey does make an appearance, we might be able to film it and sell it to the networks. Go viral, as the youngsters like to say."

Curtis followed him round to the back of the cart and pulled a putter from his bag. "Perish the thought."

Henry had never had kids, but Curtis was well aware of how social media had taken over his grandkids' lives. It was all his daughter, Sophie, talked about during one of their rare telephone calls. He preferred to video call, but there was always an excuse. The house was a tip, she was in a rush, Josh–the second husband–was using the internet, and the connection was too shaky.

They had drifted even further apart after Jane's funeral.

He wandered over the green and waited while Henry made a show of selecting a putter from the collection he had brought with him, each one glinting in the sun as it was extracted from his bag, weighed in his hand and then returned. Finally, the man crossed to where he stood and held up his selected weapon.

"Reckon this one will do the trick just fine," he announced. "Tried it in a tournament back home last week, and it lived up to the hype."

"I'm sure it did." Curtis stood to one side, allowing the other man more room to manoeuvre and line up his shot. It was a difficult one, for sure, and he didn't know if he could pull the same stunt he was expecting from Henry. Because despite the man's bluster, he was a good player, he'd give him that. "Good luck."

Henry looked up, winked, and then chipped the ball with the putter.

It hopped, skipped and then... missed.

"Dammit," said Henry, throwing the putter to the ground. The silence spun out for a few more seconds, and then he retrieved it and fixed a smile to his face. "You can't miss this one."

Curtis plucked a handkerchief from his trouser pocket and took a moment to wipe the sweat from the back of his neck. His hands were shaking, and he knew Henry was right. He couldn't afford to miss this one. He had to level with him, otherwise it would make the rest of the day's play a mere parody.

Taking a moment to ensure his hands had stopped shaking

before tucking the handkerchief back in his pocket, he adjusted his glove and traded places with Henry.

There were only a few yards between the ball and the sixth hole, yet it might as well have been a mile.

His vision blurred for a moment, and he blinked, then wiggled his toes in his shoes, got comfortable, and gave the ball a light tap. Holding his breath, Curtis watched as it parted the manicured grass before rolling into the hole with a satisfying rattle.

"Nice work." Henry dropped the flag back into place and then led the way back to the cart while Curtis followed a few steps behind, some of the tension leaving his shoulders.

"Thanks." He shielded his eyes against the glare from the cart's plastic exterior before climbing in and admiring the view across the fairway to the twelfth green. The fifteenth was farther over, closer to the swamp but prettier. "Jane loved this place."

Henry pressed his foot to the throttle. "She was a fine woman, Curtis. I always had a soft spot for her, you know."

Curtis's stomach twisted, and, for a change, it wasn't because of the cancer.

"I know you did," he said.

CHAPTER 4

"Water?"

Curtis took the bottle from Henry with a murmured thanks and slaked his thirst before handing it back. It tasted metallic, same as everything did these days. Wiping his mouth with the back of his hand, he peered across the fairway to where hole number nine lay, the flag fluttering in a light breeze that did nothing for the humidity that sapped his energy.

The painkillers were in the zip pocket on the outside of his bag, but he couldn't–wouldn't–use them while Henry was watching. Nobody except Jane knew how bad things had got, and so he bit back the agony and jerked his chin at the green.

"What do you reckon?" he said. "Three iron, or…?"

"Four." Henry was already plucking one from his bag, testing its weight while he eyed the course. "I tried the three the last time we played here, remember? It fell short, and I ended up in the bunker."

Curtis remembered all right. Henry's subsequent sulk had led to a sour lunch with little conversation that day until the man had redeemed himself with an eagle on the twelfth and a subsequent win. "I might play the same."

"You sure?" Henry glanced over his shoulder as he made his way towards the tee. "You looked like you were struggling with it earlier."

"I'm okay." Another lie. He took the three instead though, just in case, and waited while Henry fussed around, patting down the grass with his toe, kicking away an imaginary stone before settling his tee.

The man hit a perfect shot. The ball flew into an azure sky before descending, falling gracefully beyond a patch of rough, scrubby grasses and reeds.

Curtis followed suit, his shot leaving the tee with a satisfying *clink* that he felt through the iron and up his arms. He watched the ball, savouring the moment with a faint smile. He could hear Jane laughing with joy.

Beautiful shot, darling.

"Beautiful shot," said Henry.

Curtis frowned, turning back to the cart. "We'll see."

They saw.

Moments later, Henry rolled the cart to a standstill a few yards away and rested his hand on the wheel. "Lucky."

Curtis said nothing, taking a moment to catch his breath while he stared at the ball. He reckoned by the time they turned back for lunch, he'd be peeing blood again. Maybe there would be more than usual after this morning's exertion, but he'd be damned if he'd show it.

That wasn't the Curtis Palmer that Jane Llewellyn married, no sir.

She was pretty when they had met at seventeen. High school sweethearts, the football star and the prom queen, just like in the movies. Two tours in the Gulf, then a successful business, a fairytale wedding, one kid, Sophie–a schoolteacher, who had no idea he was fighting the cancer this past year–two grandkids, then early retirement.

And then…

THE BACK NINE

"Hey. Are you going to take the shot, or what?" Henry demanded. He stood with a hand on his hip, his three iron clutched in his south paw. "I've been and gone while you've been daydreaming."

"Sure. Just weighing up my options." There he went again with the lying.

Curtis stepped up to the tee, placing his little yellow plastic marker just so, then gazed towards the ninth hole. He whacked the ball and watched as it rose into the air with enough force that it bounced safely onto the green and rolled to a standstill a few inches before Henry's, blocking his next shot.

"Well, darn. Don't make it easy for me, will you?" Henry chuckled, turning back to the cart. "Come on, jump in, and I'll show you why I'm this year's champ at the course back home before we get something to eat."

CHAPTER 5

Henry was right, of course. He had executed a perfect shot that curved the ball beautifully, winning the ninth hole easily with a par two, which made Curtis's card an embarrassment to behold.

"Never mind, old friend," said Henry, clapping him on the shoulder again. "We all have off days."

"Right." Curtis grimaced, his thin skin already bruising beneath his cotton polo shirt.

Now, post-lunch, the cart trundled over undulating turf towards the fourteenth hole, the afternoon sun raising the humidity levels to bath water temperature while a haze hugged the horizon. There was no breeze to feather the cabbage palm leaves, no wind to ripple across the reeds that framed the lake separating the course from the swamp, and nobody else around.

Mid-week, the course was empty, devoid of tourists and waiting for locals to finish work.

The only sound came from Henry, yawning from time to time and humming under his breath while he kept the cart at a steady pace. An old Aerosmith number from the seventies, by the sound of it. Curtis couldn't recall the title and was waiting until Henry got to the chorus to see if he could remember the words. Or was it one of those English bands?

"Got the place to ourselves," Henry mused, interrupting his thoughts, and then braked. "Apart from him. Holy moly."

Curtis looked to where the other man pointed and felt his heart try to punch its way through his rib cage. "Damn, is that the one the receptionist called Mikey?"

A gnarly old alligator had emerged from the reeds with a confident swagger to his step and determination in his eyes. He paused momentarily, his thick neck twisting from side to side as his snout tested the air.

"Get ready to hang on," said Henry. "If he comes any closer, I'm not sticking around."

"What about the video you want to go viral?"

The reptile looked at the two men as he ambled across the fairway before continuing nonchalantly towards the reeds on the opposite side, his tail disappearing from sight several seconds after his nose had parted the long grass.

Henry whistled under his breath before easing the cart forward once more. "He's got to be about twelve feet long, right?"

"Reckon so." Curtis rolled his shoulders and turned his attention back to the fairway. "Must be getting on in years."

"Looks well fed, too. Speaking of which, you weren't eating much at lunch. Did you eat breakfast at your hotel?"

"No. I just wasn't hungry." He hadn't been hungry in weeks, months maybe.

He frowned, trying to recall the last meal he enjoyed, then remembered.

It had been a Tuesday night, their usual date night, and thirteen minutes before Jane had confessed her secret.

Right up until that moment, the rib-eye steak had tasted succulent and rich, the red wine sauce was drizzled over the top of the meat just right, and the accompanying vegetables were steamed to perfection. The Cabernet Sauvignon had been picked by the sommelier to accentuate the meal, the tannins teasing his taste buds as he'd brought the crystal glass to his nose to inhale the aromas and peered over at his wife of forty-four years.

The drink had gone to her head of course, it always did, but especially after a martini or two before the meal while they'd been sitting in the hotel's bar. That's why she blurted out what she had kept hidden all these years.

And then two days later, when he had still been reeling from the shock, smarting from the pain, Jane had died in her sleep, message delivered.

The doctors had called it an overdose.

Curtis called it guilt, tinged with a sprinkling of spite.

She had used the last of his painkillers, after all, and the replacement prescription cost him a small fortune.

At least it saved him from having to tell Sophie and the grandkids about the affair though.

Small graces.

"Here we go."

Curtis cast a sideways glance at Henry as the other man rolled the cart to a standstill, stumbled from it, righted himself, and gave an embarrassed chuckle.

"Woah. Guess that second beer went straight to my head in this heat."

"I guess it did."

"I s'pose you can't drink, what with all them meds you're taking for the cancer. Not that it'll do you any good." Henry hiccupped, then blushed. "Well, darn. Sorry. That came out wrong."

Curtis ignored him and walked to the tee to line up his shot. Storm clouds were gathering on the horizon, dark and stained through with yellow like a bruise, and he wanted it over with before the rain came. The humidity on this side of the course was oppressive. Given the fact there was nobody around, he figured most players had taken one look at the forecast, another look at the beer taps glistening with condensation in the clubhouse restaurant and called it a day rather than play this afternoon and risk getting drenched.

Glancing over his shoulder, he saw Henry bumbling towards him, a slight zigzag to his step. When the man drew closer, Curtis noticed that his eyes were unfocused.

As if reading his mind, he gave his cheeks a light slap and smiled. "Beer definitely went to my head."

"You want to quit and go back to the clubhouse?"

Henry frowned. "Hell, no. Only this one and four more to go. Besides, I'm winning."

"Okay".

Curtis took the shot, and it was perfect. Even Henry gave a low, appreciative whistle as it landed with a gentle roll that left it merely inches from the flag.

"Damn, that was good." The other man shifted from foot to foot and almost nose-dived when he bent over to squish the tee into the ground. "Guess I'd better pull something out of the hat, eh?"

He hit the ball.

It went left instead of right, bounced off the tufts of grass lining a bunker at the dog leg in the fairway, and then rolled backwards.

"Shit."

"Want me to drive?" asked Curtis.

"You know what? That might not be a bad idea," said Henry, and gave a tired smile. "You can be my chauffeur, just like the old days. Remember?"

CHAPTER 6

The old days.
Curtis remembered, all right.
Jane and Henry and Louise Forrester (the first wife), all drunk while he drove them back from whatever restaurant they had graced that evening, listening to the conversation. Louise riding shotgun because she always got sick in the back.

He should have realized then.

Should have seen the signs.

The two of them back there, flirting.

Teasing.

But he had been busy. The adjustment to life without the Corps, then the new business, then the arrival of a daughter, then grandkids, then…

Excuses.

Jane's confession had been a sucker punch, all right.

It had hurt worse than the cancer.

He tapped the brake a little on the hard side and saw Henry's head snap forwards, then backwards before the man opened his eyes with a surprised grunt.

"Did I fall asleep?"

"Only for a minute."

He watched while Henry looked around in bewilderment. "Is this the fifteenth already?"

"Three to go."

"Darn it, I don't even remember finishing the last one."

"You won." Curtis lied. He watched as the man who called him his best friend relaxed, his shoulders dipping a little. "You okay to play?"

"Sure am."

He waited until Henry eased himself from the cart, watched as he struggled to pull a four-iron from his bag, and then looked around the course.

They were the only ones out here. Nobody was at the flag on the fifteenth, nobody was following in their wake, and nobody from the clubhouse would see the flag from there.

The storm clouds were churning, and Curtis squinted as a flash of needle-thin lightning scraped the sky in the distance. There was a stiff breeze now, and the cabbage palm branches above the cart rustled, clapping their leaves in encouragement.

Fifty yards away, the sand-filled bunker curved around to the left, its small beach rippled with splats of fresh water that faded as they got closer to the tall reeds lining the green.

He exhaled, forced himself from the cart, and bit back a yelp as the pain in his stomach radiated across his ribs. Taking the three iron–Henry was right, he was struggling with the four these days–he made his way over to where his old friend waited by the tee.

The man was staring at it as if unsure what to do until Curtis reached out to put his hand on his shoulder.

"Don't touch me," he snarled.

Curtis snatched his hand back. "Something wrong?"

Henry hefted the iron in his grip and slowly turned. "You spiked my beer, didn't you?"

"I don't know…"

"Jane told you about us, didn't she?" Henry shook his head and then thought better of it. He wobbled, then righted himself, using the iron as a cane. "I knew she would, one day. Broke my heart when she took her own life after though."

"You bastard," Curtis said, tears prickling. He wiped his eyes. "After all we'd been through."

"Couldn't help ourselves," Henry replied, then straightened, his gaze unfaltering as he swung the iron from side to side. "What were you going to do? Wait until I passed out and then hit me with that wedge? Drag me to the lake and say the alligator got me? Say it was an accident?"

"I don't know."

In truth, he didn't. He hadn't even known he was going to drug Henry until just before lunch. Back then, while Henry had excused himself to go to the bathroom before the main course was brought out, Curtis had simply pulled out the pills, eyed his own glass of water, then Henry's cold beer, and pitched the whole lot into the man's drink.

He had just finished stirring them in with his fork when the other man reappeared at the restaurant's entrance, flirting with one of the young waitresses.

But Henry had known, hadn't he?

"I took stronger stuff than that to get through my third tour in the desert," Henry growled. "It took me six months to get clean when we came back, too, so those little suckers of yours won't harm me. So, what is it? Terminal?"

Curtis nodded. "Got the results four days ago."

"How long?"

"'Bout a month. Maybe two, if I'm unlucky."

"Good."

Curtis didn't have time to react.

Henry was across the grass, and his right hand was swinging split seconds before the punch landed in his rotten guts.

Squealing in agony, Curtis dropped to the floor, clutching

his stomach, pain radiating through his body. He puked, and the remnants of the two breadsticks he'd forced down at lunch splattered the grass. He scrunched up his eyes, clenched his jaw, and wondered what the hell he'd been thinking.

He'd never won against Henry Forrester.

Why should today have been any different?

He opened his eyes to see the other man walking towards him, swinging that damn four iron from side to side, a dangerous smile teasing his lips.

"She meant nothing to me, you know. Eleanor's the love of my life. Jane was…' He left the words unsaid and gave a shrug instead.

"Mine," Curtis wheezed. "She was mine."

"No," said Henry, wagging a finger. "She was her own woman. Made her own decisions. Had her own ideas. Something you never appreciated until she wasn't there anymore. Shame on you. You didn't even notice what we were doing."

"I gave her everything she ever asked for," said Curtis, raising himself on an elbow. "Everything she needed."

"It wasn't enough." Henry kicked him back to the floor. "You're nothing compared to me."

"She regretted it," he persisted. "She told me she wished she'd never met you. Said you were poison, persistent, never leaving her alone. She said she only did it because you got her drunk that day. She hated herself for the rest of her life."

"That's on her, not me."

"I'll tell Eleanor."

Henry froze. His eyes narrowed, and then he raised the four iron above his head. "That's what I was afraid of."

Curtis closed his eyes, waiting for the crushing blow that would split his skull open and end the ceaseless pain.

Then there was a rustling from the reeds, something heavy moving at speed before Henry's scream pierced the air.

Opening his eyes, Curtis stared in horror as Mikey sank his teeth into the man's left calf, the alligator pulling with all its might as Henry tried to beat it away with the golf club.

"Help me," he screamed.

Mikey was already turning, using his weight to unbalance Henry, who tumbled to the floor and raised his arms to shield himself from the inevitable.

Curtis eased himself to his feet, resting his hands on his knees for a moment as black dots fuzzed his vision, then lunged for the four iron Henry had dropped.

The alligator was dragging Henry towards the lake now, heaving him along a few yards at a time while chomping on legs, arms, feet.

Taking a deep breath, Curtis moved around to the back of the reptile, praying that it would be more interested in Henry than in an attack from its flank.

Closer now, he raised the iron, then collapsed on the sand. Fire burned through his belly, the echo of Henry's punch emanating through his kidneys, what remained of his intestines, and his ruined pancreas.

"Help!" Henry screamed.

The alligator was in the water now, and Henry's legs were submerged.

Curtis watched in horror as Mikey's jaw opened once more and then crushed the man's left hip, the sound of shattered bones echoing off the bunker.

The alligator disappeared below the surface, taking his prey with him.

Bubbles.

The last breath taken by Henry Forrester.

Then silence.

Curtis crawled on his hands and knees back to the green, fetched his mobile phone from his golf bag and called the emergency services. That done, he sat against the cart's front wheel, the grassy aroma sweet and soft to the touch while he watched the ripples on the lake.

Movement to his left made him jump, and then he relaxed as he saw one of the black and orange butterflies Jane had adored.

He froze, watching it, mesmerized, as it landed on his hand. Its tiny feet pattered against his frail skin while its wings beat a gentle rhythm, before it lifted into the air and fluttered away.

Curtis Palmer smiled for the first time in months.

THE END

MOUSE AND THE FATE OF
THE WORLD

DAVID H. HENDRICKSON

MOUSE AND THE FATE OF THE WORLD

DAVID H. HENDRICKSON

July, 1943
Paris, Occupied France

The filthy Germans were everywhere. Céline Dupuis knew it shouldn't tear at her soul every time she walked this route along the Seine, the cooling breeze lifting strands of her long blond hair off her slender shoulders. Not after three years. Wounds should scab over and heal. Perhaps leaving a faint scar, but heal.

But the wounds to Céline's soul had never healed, had never even scabbed over, not since the Nazi tanks and goose-stepping soldiers had invaded her beloved city, parading down the *Champs-Élysées*. Polluting the *Opéra Garnier* with their music, the *Théâtre des Champs-Élysées* with their plays, and the very Parisian air itself with their harsh, guttural language that bore as much melodic grace as fingernails on a chalkboard.

No, she would never grow used to this violation of her country.

Céline walked past canopied café tables filled with the vermin, slurping their freshly brewed coffee and gorging themselves on breakfasts of mouth-watering croissants and their own wretched delicacies while she and her countrymen went hungry.

Though her assignments took her throughout all of France, Paris was where she felt the rending of her soul worst of all, the savage wound raw and fresh and deep. Her people would win this city back. Of that, she would never lose faith. She might not live to see the day, though she was but twenty-one years old. In fact, she would almost certainly not see the day. Her code name might be Mouse—all Alliance agents were assigned an animal as their code name—but hers should probably be Cat and one that had already exhausted most of its nine lives.

A misstep on this mission would almost certainly end in her slow, screaming death at the hands of the Gestapo. And that would be far from the worst of it all. Based on what she'd been told, the fate of the entire war could be in her hands. She had to get the secret papers and maps to England or die trying.

Céline shifted the navy blue satchel purse slung over her shoulder. She turned right, away from the Seine, and then after several blocks, left, followed by a maze-light sequence of lefts and rights and lefts, doubling back and circling around, to ensure she wasn't being followed until by the most circuitous of routes she reached the grime-stained ten-story building at the specified address.

No one had followed.

She was sure of it. The usual pedestrian traffic of both Germans and Parisians had thinned as she traversed her route, but there were no faces visible now that were familiar from before. She would bet her life on it.

In fact, Céline knew she *was* betting her life on it.

With one last casual glance over her shoulder, she entered the building, turned right to the stairwell and walked up the five flights of stairs, smelling the stale sweat baked into the walls by the oppressive July heat. Exiting the stairwell to the empty hallway that stretched fifty meters ahead, Céline waited, catching her breath and wiping her brow but more importantly, insuring that no one was following up the stairs.

Silence.

Céline strode almost to the end of the hallway and stopped at the battered wooden door, its white paint bubbled and peeling, to apartment number 549.

Céline wrapped on the door sharply. Once, twice, and then a third time.

"Who goes there?" asked a feminine voice from inside the room.

Céline replied with the specified code words. The voice inside replied in kind.

"*Vive la France!*" Céline said, as was also specified.

The door opened and she stepped into a tiny, single-room apartment. The smell of coffee filled the room. The walls, claustrophobically tight. The air humid and heavy.

Her counterpart stood directly ahead of her behind a wooden kitchen table, eying her warily, hands at her side but apparently grasping a sharp, long knife in each. On the left were a humming white refrigerator, a two-burner stove and oven, and, tucked into the corner, a white porcelain sink. On the right, a bed. Above it, a small rectangular window, closed despite the heat, its curtains drawn. A communal bathroom and water closet were no doubt down the hall. Water stains marred the wall to the right of the small window, extending from the ceiling halfway to the floor. Céline fancifully imagined that the stain traced a map of France, knowing that to be foolishness but taking it as a positive omen nonetheless. On a fateful day such as today, you took whatever positive omens you could get, silly or not.

"Are you Hornet?" Céline asked, thinking that if code names for agents reflected their appearance—surely a dangerous linkage that would never be adopted—this stunningly beautiful woman would be called Peacock.

Céline herself was considered quite the beauty, often an advantage when flirtatious ways could extricate her from dangerous situations but also a danger when it attracted unwanted attention and provoked desire among those men unaccustomed to being denied whatever they craved.

But this woman put Céline's beauty to shame. Blond hair, like her own, and blue eyes, but a high-cheekboned, flawlessly complexioned face that belonged on the movie screen across from Clark Gable. A radiant smile with the most perfect pearly white teeth that she had flashed for only an instant and then was gone. A practiced smile surely used to get what she wanted from men who could not resist its allure.

"Are you Mouse?" Hornet asked, completing the proscribed exchange of words and phrases establishing their mutual identities, then added, "You are absolutely certain you were not followed? You will swear it on your life?"

"Yes, I am Mouse and yes, I will swear it."

"You are far younger… far, far younger than I expected," Hornet said. "Too young! These secrets require someone with far more—"

"I suspect you are no older than I am, and if so, then only by a year or two," Céline said. She had heard the refrain about her youth countless times since joining *la résistance*. "I assure you—"

"You don't understand," Hornet said, anger flashing in her fiery eyes. "I did not mean age. I meant *experience*. The secrets in these documents and maps will change the war. I'm sure even Hitler himself would agree. The secrets cannot be trusted to a young apprentice courier. I have risked everything to obtain this information. I will not entrust it to someone younger even than I. Go back to your superiors and tell them I will accept only their best courier. Nothing less will suffice."

Céline fixed her eyes upon the woman and waited one heartbeat and then a second before she broke the stony silence.

"I am their best."

Céline waited to let the statement sink in. She had no way of knowing if the statement was literally true. No one kept statistics. Isolation was the name of the espionage game. Don't let one agent's capture endanger the entire network.

But Céline knew she was good. Damned good. And if not the best, she was close. Damned close. She'd earned her stripes the hard way.

Death-defying experience.

"I may be young, but I am also the best the network has to offer," Céline said. "I have carried vital secrets many times all across this country and to England. I have never failed. Not once." The statement was admittedly a truism and Céline knew it. *Of course*, she had never failed. If she had failed, she'd either be dead or in a German concentration camp. But that didn't diminish her credentials. She would even add her most shining example despite the risks that came with so much as speaking it aloud. "If you doubt my word, I'd ask you to check with the German officer whose unwanted carnal attentions six months ago threatened to uncover vital documents and maps bound about my waist. But you'd have to search for that officer's gravesite because he paid with his life for his fingertips' proximity to those secrets. I will guard your documents with that same vigilance. I will protect them with my life and the life of anyone who interferes with the completion of my mission."

Hornet glared for long seconds that felt like hours. Then she broke into a warm, bright smile, one Céline knew at once to be authentic, unlike the practiced and artificial one she had flashed before.

"It appears I underestimated you," Hornet said.

"Such is the fate of us young, pretty women," Céline said, responding to her counterpart's warm smile with one of her own. "People see us and assume the only talent we possess is our beauty, the only possible danger our hands might pose is dropping a valued teacup, and our heads are as empty as whatever intentionally banal comments might slip from our supple lips."

"How do you think I obtained these secrets?" Hornet said, shaking with laughter. "I certainly didn't steal them. The officers invited me to their social gatherings where they discussed their work over drinks. I was merely an attractive, harmless piece of furniture. They spoke freely, as if I wasn't even there. But over time, they divulged even more secrets simply to impress me, thinking me harmless, surely incapable of espionage, even as I egged them on, wide-eyed and incredulous. It became almost a competition among them, which one could impress me more."

Céline nodded, impressed at the stunning means by which Hornet had obtained the secrets. But she was anxious to leave.

"I would love to spend hours with you and hear even more, but I must hurry," Céline said. "I wish to leave your delightful presence as soon as possible."

"Of course," Hornet said, all amusement gone from her face, replaced by stony seriousness. "Turn and face the window. Do not attempt to watch me or it will be the last thing you do."

It might be the last thing *one of us* does, Céline thought with suppressed amusement, but she did not delay. She stared fixedly at the water stains on the wall to the right of the covered window, failing now to see the supposedly portentous outline of France in the stain. Instead, she trained her ears on Hornet's actions behind her.

Something heavy skidded across the floor. The small white refrigerator? Wood planking creaked as it was pulled up. Rustling papers were removed. The creaking planking forced back down and into place. The heavy object, almost certainly the refrigerator, skidded back.

"Turn around," Hornet commanded. "The sounds, I am sure, revealed the hiding place, but now it will be upon your body."

A stack of somewhat less than a hundred sheets of paper now rested on the kitchen table.

"Your turn to face away," Céline said.

She did not wait for the slow-to-come obedience, but instead immediately rested her purse on the table, then unbuttoned the top of her navy blue dress, the dark color specifically chosen for its camouflaging benefits. She slipped out of its short sleeves.

She unwound the outer layer of padded white fabric that had been bound about her waist below her white brassiere. She took the papers off the table and fanned them evenly up against the inner layer of fabric that would protect them from sweat on this hot July day. She then wrapped the outer layer back into place, covering the documents, and pinned the fabric tight.

Céline moved toward the door as she was slipping back into the sleeves, then buttoned the dress, doublechecking to ensure proper alignment of the buttons and smoothness of the hidden fabric beneath.

"Go with God," Hornet said, handing Céline her purse off the table. "Protect those secrets with your life."

Céline nodded but said nothing, her mouth suddenly dry.

She'd made no attempt to read even a single word of the documents as she pressed them about her body. It was best that she knew nothing about her cargo. But as she'd fanned the papers to press them against the inner fabric upon her waist, she'd inadvertently seen the detailed maps and diagrams.

Detailed diagrams of what were clearly rockets or missiles of some kind.

Hornet had not been overstating her case. The fate of the war—the fate of the world!—might well depend on the success of this mission.

Céline tried to calm the hammering in her heart.

She could not fail.
She would not fail.
The fate of the world was in her hands.

~

Céline sat on the half-filled northbound train bound for Nanteuil-le-Haudouin, slightly more than fifty kilometers away, begging it to leave the *Gare de l'Est* station.

And of course, it wouldn't. It just sat there. Waiting for her to be arrested.

She sat by the window near the back of the second car, heart in her throat, facing out onto the empty concrete platform, hoping there would be nothing for her to see.

No police. No German troops rushing in from the entrance. And certainly no Gestapo.

Good. So far.

The cabin smelled faintly of soot from the locomotive up ahead. In the window seat on the other side of the aisle sat a middle-aged, bespectacled businessman in a suit and tie with a briefcase on his lap. Both aisle seats were empty.

Train stations had flooded Céline with an overwhelming sense of fear ever since the nightmarish event six months ago when she'd been forced to kill a German officer. Memories of the episode itself were more than sufficient to evoke sheer terror, but the risk of being identified as the killer even after all this time added yet another layer of fear. And of course, the precious cargo she was now carrying upon her body magnified the risk even further.

The fate of the world was in her hands. Or more literally, wrapped about her stomach.

The diagrams of the rockets or missiles or whatever they were called had been labelled *Vergeltungswaffen,* weapons of retaliation. Flying bombs is what they clearly were. Even she could see that, and she was certainly no scientist or engineer. Bombs that required no airplane to fly over its target.

Bombs that could be launched from afar.

If Germany completed development of those weapons and the Allies had nothing to match it, the war was over. Germany could, and would, destroy all of England from the safety of the French coast. An Allied invasion to retake France would become next to impossible. How could any invading force combat such a weapon?

And if for some reason Germany had to retreat to its original borders, it would then destroy all of France. Flatten the Paris she loved so much. Destroy the *Musée du Louvre* and the Eiffel Tower and in the most symbolic strike of all, flatten the *Arc de Triomphe*. Then it would systematically bomb the rest of the country and turn it into rubble.

If she didn't personally deliver to England this astonishing, terrifying secret and the maps which she could only assume pinpointed the locations to bomb, then all would be lost.

The fate of the world... the fate of the world...

Céline maintained her casual, even bored, appearance, idly opening her purse and pretending to look for something, but inside her chest, her heart hammered. Inside her pounding head, she wanted to scream. If this train didn't get moving soon, she would go out of her mind.

Se déplacer! Vite! Maintenant! Move! Quickly! Now!

As if in savage answer to her plea, or in defiance of her demands, a siren outside the station wailed. The sound pierced Céline's heart like the sharpest of knives. She tried to blink away the pain but to no avail. With great effort, she released the clawlike grip with which she clutched her purse.

The sirens wailed louder.

Closer.

Too close.

Was this the end of it all? Had she been discovered?

Entrusted with the possible fate of the world, had she failed before even leaving Paris?

Céline drew in a deep breath, then slowly exhaled. Inhaled normally, as if she had not a care in the world, then exhaled. Inhaled. Exhaled.

Panic amounted to a death knell for any courier. Only with a calm, clear head could she save herself in the face of danger.

Think! There could be any number of reasons for the siren, Céline told herself. Only one of which concerned her.

The pounding of boots thundered, advancing onto the platform. German troops, fifty strong and then perhaps a hundred, swarmed into view. Helmeted. Rifles pointed downward but ready for business.

Icy chills ran up and down Céline's spine. She swallowed hard. Licked her dry lips with a tongue every bit as cotton dry.

But still maintained a calm exterior.

She glanced over at the businessman, wide-eyed and pale. Hands visibly shaking. Obviously a countryman. He appeared ready to bolt.

Their eyes met. Céline gave him the slightest of tight smiles. It was next to nothing but all she could offer.

The fate of the world.

The troops cordoned off the train, ten meters back, then an officer directed pairs of them to the front and back of each car. To Céline, it seemed as if the officer's finger pointed at her and not the rear entrance to her carriage. She turned away from the window and pushed back in her seat as if that might make her invisible.

Behind her and also twenty meters up ahead at the front, doors to the car clattered open. Two soldiers emerged up front. Céline looked away.

From behind, what sounded like two soldiers clomped up the aisle. Practically at her shoulders. Céline dared not turn around.

A soldier reached her row and gestured his rifle in her direction. He was young, even younger than she was, not even eighteen. Impossibly blue eyes simultaneously filled with fear and hatred.

"*Aussteigen! Sofort! Aus dem Zug!*" he commanded. Get off! Now! Off the train!

So this was the end. An end with no possible escape.

Céline's mind raced, searching for a plan. But there was no way out of this. No one woman could overcome a hundred soldiers. Either by brute force, which was laughable, or by flirtatious ways, possibly even more laughable. Any escape would have to be made after this, away from this station, wherever they took her.

Céline slowly got to her feet, the weight of the world on her slender shoulders. She hadn't even made it out of Paris. A heartbreaking failure.

Had she made some mistake? Overlooked some detail? Had someone betrayed this righteous cause? And why had the Germans felt the need to send this overwhelming show of force? Surely a hundred troops were not necessary to subdue her.

But then the blue-eyed young soldier moved to the next row and shouted the same command to whomever sat in the seats in front of her. And then the row after that. And another soldier stepped up from behind and gave the same order to the businessman on the right. And then the row in front of him.

On they moved up the aisle, ordering everyone off the train, until they met the two other soldiers who had begun at the front end of the carriage, shouting the same commands. All four spun around and headed back to the door they entered, prodding stragglers roughly with their rifles to move faster.

"*Schnell! Aus dem Zug! Beweg dich!*" they shouted. Quick! Get off the train! Move! "*Schnell! Aus dem Zug! Beweg dich!*"

Céline didn't need to be told twice.

Standing amidst the other sixty or so former passengers, Céline felt euphoric relief flood over her. A beatific warmth filled her breast having nothing to do with the summer heat. It radiated throughout her body. Even the train station's soot-filled air never smelled so sweet.

She was safe! And more importantly, so was the cargo bound around her waist! The fate of the world remained in her hands. It had not been stolen away after all. She had not failed.

Yet.

The Germans had simply commandeered the train. The two-hour wait she would now have to endure in this station, her personal house of horrors, would be a splendid pleasure compared to what she had been sure awaited her.

As the long seconds and longer minutes dragged on, however, Céline's euphoria predictably waned. She could maintain a calm exterior and show none of her inner torment for as long as the mission required. Twenty-four hours. Forty-eight. Whatever it took. She had claimed to Hornet that she, Céline Dupuis, was the best. And dammit, she would prove exactly that.

But that didn't make the interminable wait any easier. Especially when troops also commandeered the following train. The cargo about Céline's waist began to feel as heavy as the succession of locomotives that chugged out of the station without her.

Every siren, no matter how far in the distance, threatened to be coming for her. Every clomp of a boot threatened to be a soldier prepared to take her away. Even every sideways glance from one of the other passengers threatened to be a look of knowing recognition from a traitor ready to expose her for what she was.

Out in the open on this platform. Vulnerable.

She was willing to die for her country. More than willing. But please let it not be in vain. Let her somehow complete this mission that could decide the fate of the world.

Please!

When she finally boarded a train and it actually chugged ever so slowly out of the station, Céline wanted to weep for joy. She had thought she would never leave *Gare de l'Est*. In time, though, the view out of her window changed from the Parisian cityscape to a countryside of farms with rows upon rows of cornfields.

It was a sight for sore eyes.

But when Céline exited the Nanteuil-le-Haudouin station, something felt wrong. She knew it in her bones. Every instinct screamed danger.

And not just because of the unsetting interrogation she'd just endured at the hands of a stocky, gray-haired, steely-eyed German officer upon disembarking the train. Only five other passengers had stepped off, two couples, one in their fifties and the other likely in their sixties, and the businessman who'd sat in the opposite row on their original train before it had been commandeered.

That he had also gotten off at the small, brick-walled station concerned her. Nanteuil-le-Haudouin was a tiny village with a population of barely a thousand. It made complete sense that only five other people had considered this to be their destination and four of them the older two couples.

But what was the businessman doing here, briefcase in tow? Had he been following her?

Was he a traitor preparing to turn her in for whatever reward he could get? Couldn't be. There'd been no mistaking the sheer terror he'd shown when the German troops boarded that first train. Not even Clark Gable could have delivered an acting performance that convincing. The businessman was a countryman and no traitor.

Céline hadn't lasted this long by misreading traitors for patriots. She wouldn't bet her life on any man or woman other than herself, but she'd wager her next ten or twenty meals that he was no traitor.

Even so, it was a concern.

The officer dispatched the two older couples quickly after little more than a look at their papers, then beckoned for the next.

As Céline stepped forward, the businessman, standing slightly behind her and to her right, shouldered past and handed over his *carte d'identite*.

The officer glared at him in an icy silence that lasted mere seconds but felt like minutes.

"You step ahead of the *fräulein*?" the officer finally said. "Where are your manners?"

"I am so sorry. I thought you pointed to me," the businessman replied. "The train was delayed many times. I am now very late for an appointment. And I thought you pointed to me. That is the only—"

"*I will take you in whatever order I wish!*" the officer snapped. "I don't care how late you are for your appointment. If I wish to make you wait another hour, I will do so! If I wish to make you wait two hours, I will do so! Is that clear?"

"Of course, of course. I am so... so sorry," the businessman said, head bowed. "I meant no offense. I am so very sorry."

Silence hung in the air for long seconds.

"However, as it turns out, I *will* take you first," the officer said. "That is my wish." He glanced at Céline with a leering grin. "I might need additional time with the *fräulein*."

Icy slivers shot up and down Céline's spine. It was just such a situation in Ussel six months ago that had led to her killing the officer to protect the secret papers she carried on her body. She had been lucky to escape alive that time. If this officer likewise decided to take her to a private place where he could paw his disgusting hands all over her body until he inevitably touched the cargo about her waist, then she would again be left with no choice.

She would be forced to kill again. To protect these secret rocket papers, she would do so in an instant. But she didn't like her chances of a repeat escape. She had been lucky once. To expect such good fortune again would be asking too much. And she had to get to the secret airfield where the Lysander would pick her up. She had to personally deliver the documents in England.

As Hornet had made quite clear, the fate of the world quite possibly hung in the balance.

The officer finished with the businessman, then beckoned Céline forward.

She handed him her *carte d'identite*.

"What is your reason for being here?" the officer asked, eying her up and down.

"To visit my ailing mother," Céline said, putting a troubled look in her eyes and a quiver in her voice. She crossed herself. "I pray the blessed Virgin will grant her the miracle of a return to good health."

A sour look came over the officer's face, as if he'd just bitten into a lemon. Céline suspected he didn't appreciate talk of the blessed Virgin interfering with the roaming of his lustful eyes. And yet he continued. Up and down. Up and down.

In her mind, she begged him to stop. *Please! No more!*

Not just because it made her feel dirty, which it most certainly did, but also because every time his eyes roamed up and down, it raised the risk that he might observe some unevenness about her stomach. She had discreetly checked herself on the train, using only a quick glance downward as she got up from her seat, no more obvious than any other woman, especially a young pretty one, checking on her appearance. And there had appeared not even a hint of the papers hidden beneath her navy blue dress and the fabric wound tightly about them.

Even so, Céline made sure to breathe evenly and calmly now every time his eyes passed her midsection. Fortunately, though it filled her with disgust, he fixed his attentions primarily on her breasts and hips until finally... *finally*, he told her to move on.

As she left, he pinched her bottom and laughed with satisfaction when she instinctively yelped, but she refused to give the Nazi pig the satisfaction of her looking back.

Keep walking forward, she told herself. Eyes straight ahead. One more challenge in the gauntlet to England down, several more to go.

Although a part of Céline was disappointed that she *hadn't* been forced to kill him.

The instant Céline she stepped outside, though, she sensed something even worse, something even more foreboding, than what had transpired inside.

The businessman was walking in the wrong direction.

After exiting this small, brick train station, pedestrians always turned right and then when the roadway ended a few hundred meters later, they turned right again and walked along Rue Beauregard into the center of town. Always. To the left, either directly out of the train station or in the opposite direction on Rue Beauregard, made no sense. All that was out there were farms and rows upon rows of cornfields.

And a hidden airfield.

Céline had been here on previous missions. She knew.

The two older couples were heading toward the center of

town, as expected, and would soon be out of her field of view. Why wasn't the businessman following them? To where *the businesses were!*

For what possible reason would a briefcase-carrying businessman head for the cornfields? Or far more ominously, to a supposedly secret, hidden airfield thirteen kilometers away?

Céline reached into her satchel purse and pulled out her compact mirror. She opened it and pretended to check her appearance while actually observing the businessman in the distance. She brushed away imaginary flecks of soot floating in the air, remnants of the locomotive's coal-fired engines, first off her face, then out of her long blond hair, then off her shoulders. She pressed her lips together as if evening out lipstick she was not wearing. She moved one strand of hair back into place and then another. Shaking her head in frustration, she pulled out a brush and combed her hair over and over until it was perfect.

All things a fashionable, pretty young woman such as herself would do. Appearing totally self-absorbed even while tracking the businessman's every move.

What was he doing?

What should she do? That was the direction she should be going, to meet at a rendezvous point about a kilometer away where Agent Magpie would pick her up. He would take her, and potentially another operative or two, to the airfield, which was almost impossible to find in the dark.

But did she dare follow the businessman? She supposed she had to. Already, she was hours behind the projected rendezvous time. Magpie would understand, of course. She had never met the man, but any agent knew that these things rarely followed according to plan. He would keep circling back as unobtrusively as possible until they connected. Still, she didn't want him exposed any longer than necessary. In her experience, most drivers working with *la résistance* were doctors. Unlike most of their countrymen these days, doctors could afford a vehicle. In fact, their profession demanded one. And they had ample cover stories to drive almost anywhere. If Magpie was a doctor, he was taking a huge risk today, albeit the same life-or-death risk they all were taking. If she could minimize it, she would.

And besides, her cover story was that she was visiting an ailing mother. Their family farm coincided with at least heading in the desired direction for six or seven kilometers. It was a flimsy cover story, though. The farm at that location was owned by a loyal French family but not one with the surname of Dupuis. Céline had been able to do no better. The forger she had hoped would produce fake identity papers for her had been arrested by the Gestapo before he could begin work on hers.

She put the compact back into her purse and headed for *Rue Beauregard*. Proceed with the original plan.

Almost immediately, though, a black Citroën approached from behind and passed Céline. It came to a stop and turned left.

Away from the center of town. Toward the cornfields. Toward the airfield.

Even before it turned, Céline memorized the license plate and compared it to the encoded expected value for what would be Magpie's vehicle. It was far too risky to distribute full license plate numbers, of course. Risky to the point of suicidal for the owner of the vehicle. But she had been given an encoding that would not guarantee an identical match, but would safely allow her to reject ninety-nine percent of all plates.

Close enough for espionage, she liked to joke on her darkest of days.

The Citroën's plate number fit into the desired one percent. Perfect! Of course, Magpie would not pick her up this close to the train station. That would be far too risky. Too close to the center of town and observing eyes. And even more importantly, he didn't know her identity anymore than she knew his, apart from the license plate. For Magpie to accept her as genuine, she would have to be in the designated location and say the specified code phrases, as she had done with Hornet. If not, Magpie would leave.

Céline was just about to turn left onto *Rue Beauregard* and head for the rendezvous point when she stopped, horrified at what she was seeing.

The businessman was waving down the Citroën! *What was happening?*

The car slowed, then pulled away. But the businessman chased after it, briefcase in tow, waving his free hand as frantically as a husband with an expectant wife about to deliver would beg for a ride to the hospital.

The Citroën slowed and then stopped.

No! Céline wanted to scream. *No! Get away!*

Instead, the businessman wrapped on the passenger side window, mouthed some indecipherable words, then climbed into the car.

No! Magpie, what are you doing?

Céline was shocked at the breach of protocol. And if the businessman had fooled her with his better-than-Clark-Gable fear of the German troops and was indeed an enemy to the cause, Magpie would soon be paying the price. She halfway expected to hear the sound of a gunshot from within the Citroën.

Céline heard nothing but received an almost immediate confirmation of her fears that was every bit as conclusive. From a position hidden to her around the corner, a position closer to the center of town, two black Mercedes roared into view, accelerating almost instantly to top speed.

They bore down on the Citroën.

Gestapo. Without a doubt.

Magpie! No!

Céline felt an immediate and overwhelming hatred for the businessman—the traitor!—who had apparently set some trap for Magpie. And Magpie had fallen for it! A sour, bitter taste filled her mouth.

The two Mercedes caught up to the Citroën, pulled alongside, and angled it off onto the side of the road.

Magpie was a dead man.

Or worse.

Céline turned right onto *Rue Beauregard* and headed into town.

∽

She ducked into the first thicket she could find and sank down to think, out of view. What could she do now? Was there *anything* she could do now?

Was the entire operation compromised? How could it not be? Magpie had been captured. Wouldn't he inevitably surrender under Gestapo torture and give them all away? If eventually he did crumble—and who could withstand such savage agony?—could he hold out long enough for this one last Lysander flight out of the airfield? This one last flight with the papers bound about Céline's waist that could potentially decide the fate of the world?

Céline didn't like the odds.

But the odds had been stacked against her people ever since the German invasion and occupation of the country. And weren't the long-term odds always stacked against anyone in the espionage business? Last she checked, Alliance wasn't offering its spies and couriers a retirement plan.

It really didn't matter how bad the odds were. She had to get to that airfield come hell or high water before midnight, climb aboard the Lysander, and get the cargo about her waist to England.

Or die trying.

After waiting ten minutes for the coast to possibly clear,

Céline got back to her feet and stepped through the thicket and onto the side of *Rue Beauregard*.

She headed away from the center of town. Toward the cornfields and the airfield.

The fate of the world.

By the time she got to where the two Mercedes had maneuvered Magpie's Citroën off the side of the road, all remnants of the three cars were gone, save the tire tracks on the side of the road. Likewise, all remnants of the businessman-turned-presumed-traitor, Magpie, and the Gestapo were also all gone, save for thick droplets of blood next to the tire tracks.

Céline grieved for Magpie for a brief moment even though she had never even met the man. She grieved for all the agents who had been captured and killed these past few years. And she grieved for her country.

But she never stopped walking. Never slowed down. Because the cargo she carried might decide the fate of the world.

It was thirteen kilometers to the area outside of the secret airfield. Céline recalled that number because so many people considered it an unlucky one, a number to be feared. But every previous time she had traversed those thirteen kilometers, she'd been blessed with nothing but good luck. Stunningly good luck.

And so she remembered the number as a lucky one. Lucky thirteen kilometers. Calibrating that distance in her head as she walked, Céline counted down the remaining kilometers. Eyes and ears open for approaching cars or bicyclists, from ahead or behind.

Springing into the surrounding thickets at the beginning, staying hidden until she was sure she hadn't been discovered. Then the thickets briefly gave way to woods. And finally, to cornfields as the roads became almost entirely empty, especially after darkness fell.

Céline hid from one and all. She trusted no one. She could not allow herself to be discovered.

She could not fail.

In the end, blanketed in a darkness broken only by the full moon, Céline almost missed the narrow side road. She recalled taking a side road during her two previous trips, a side road filled with hellacious bumps that had threatened to tear out the undercarriage of the cars transporting her.

But was this the correct side road?

As owls hooted and crickets created their symphony of sound, she debated the point. Didn't all side roads look alike in the near-pitch-black darkness? Or most of them? By her estimate, she was still half a kilometer short of the full thirteen. So should she keep going on the main drag and wait for the next side road? Or had they on those previous trips driven on this side road for a half kilometer and the anticipation of almost being there made it seem so much shorter?

Instinctively, this side road felt right. So she took it.

The cornfield was newly threshed on both sides, making it look oddly barren in the moonlight. After a time that was quite likely close to half a kilometer, she reached a towering pile of corn stalks. Céline navigated around the mountainous pile and came to a small moonlit clearing. She detected a mounted flashlight at the two ends, shadows moving about them.

The airfield! She'd found it!

Céline heard the distinctive, chilling sound of the racking of a shotgun. From off to her right, fifteen meters away.

"Who are you and what are you here for?" demanded a low, raspy male voice.

"I am Mouse and I bear gifts," she said, using the euphemism for secret documents.

"I am Grizzly," the raspy voice responded, giving the code name of her expected airfield contact, completing the identification sequence. "Where are the others?"

"Others? I know only of Magpie," Céline said, sadness piercing her heart. "He was arrested before our rendezvous."

"You are sure of this?"

"I saw it from just outside the train station. Gestapo. In two Mercedes." A bitter taste again filled Céline's mouth. "Some fool businessman convinced Magpie to pull over just a short distance from the train station. I don't know why he broke protocol to give the man a ride. I can only guess that Magpie is a doctor, like so many of our drivers, and the businessman somehow appealed to those Hippocratic instincts."

Grizzly swore. "What did this businessman look like?"

Céline gave her description. Middle-aged. Glasses. Wearing a suit and tie. Carrying a briefcase. A businessman.

Grizzly swore again.

"That was Pigeon. One of ours. Well positioned to be useful, but high strung. Not quite a rookie but close. Panics at his own shadow."

Céline's jaw dropped. The businessman had been an Alliance agent? Him, an agent? Impossible!

But of course, it all made sense now. His abject terror upon seeing the soldiers entering the train. His total loss of nerve when dealing with the German officer because he was so late. Even his panicked rookie move to get Magpie to pick him up so close to the train station.

It all added up. The delay of several hours making him late for his rendezvous sent him off his rocker.

And then it struck her.

"If the Gestapo has him," she said, barely able to get the words out, "And the Gestapo most definitely does have him. He'll crack in seconds. He'll give us all away."

Céline spun around, scanning the path she'd come from

around the pile of corn stalks, halfway expecting a pack of Gestapo agents to emerge. Seeing nothing, she spun back around.

"These documents I carry must get to England! *I* must get to England. On the Lysander tonight. Before he cracks—what was his name, Pigeon?—before Pigeon cracks and gives us all away."

"This is bad, but not as bad as you think," Grizzly said. "Pigeon does not know this location. He cannot give us away. Only Magpie knows it and he will not betray us. Hold it! Wait! How did you get here? How did you find us?"

"I walked, hiding off on the side of the road whenever anyone approached," Céline said. "I found you here because I've been here twice before, and I pay close attention."

"I should say," Grizzly said, finally coming close enough to see, a bearded mountain of a man in his twenties. "So if you're such a veteran, help us get set for the landing."

The flight was predictably turbulent with the winds buffeting and bouncing the tiny, single-engine aircraft as though God himself was trying to shake it into pieces. The Lysander was used for these missions because it could rapidly land and take off from small, makeshift landing strips such as the one they'd just left, but it contained no navigational equipment. The pilot, equipped with nothing but a compass and a map, could use only moonlight to locate the landing fields, which themselves were lighted only by the mounted flashlights Céline had spotted earlier.

The Lysander also contained room for only the pilot and two cramped passengers. Céline sat alone now, facing backwards, hands gripping tightly onto both the sides of her seat as the craft bucked and rolled. The only other seat, the seat to her left, was empty.

It had been intended for Agent Pigeon.

When they landed, Céline felt relieved that they had survived the nerve-wracking trip through what amounted to enemy territory. They'd have been sitting ducks if spotted by enemy fighter planes or anti-aircraft batteries.

But she felt even greater relief, coupled with overwhelming satisfaction, when she handed over the precious cargo to her superior, a man she knew only as Agent Armadillo. Tall and lanky, he was somewhere between forty and fifty with salt-and-pepper hair, sunken eyes, and a perpetually beleaguered, tired look on his face. Agent Armadillo thanked her and told her to wait for an update with her next assignment.

So she waited.

And waited.

And waited.

She inquired as to the fate of those at the secret airstrip amidst the cornfields and was assured that all the agents were well and by all accounts, the secret remained a secret. Céline felt great relief at that news.

But when she asked about Agents Magpie and Pigeon, she was told that nobody knew for certain. Neither of the two had reestablished contact.

Céline didn't need that one translated. They were dead or in concentration camps. Most likely dead after unbearable hours of Gestapo torture. That was hard to take even though expected. You always hoped for a miracle.

But what of the rocket secrets? Hornet had painstakingly accumulated them at great personal risk. Then Céline had transported them, also at great personal risk, not to mention the risks of those at the cornfield and the pilot. And sadly, Magpie.

Céline was told not to ask.

She wasn't sure what to make of that even though she often was left in the dark as to the eventual outcome of her missions. It was Standard Operating Procedure, actually.

But if Hornet was to be believed, and Céline believed her with all of her heart and soul, the fate of the war was quite likely in those documents and maps. And with that, the fate of the world. Certainly, those in the high command were taking action.

Weren't they?

Hearing no answers, Céline grew restless to return to France. She was doing no good here. All she could do was obsess over the rocket secrets and the Germans getting closer every day to being able to launch them at will. She needed something to get her mind off the flying bombs, the *Vergeltungswaffen*.

What she needed was her next mission. She needed to get back to France and get back to work. It felt like she'd been here in England for years, not weeks.

She knew better than to complain, though. The Lysanders could fly only during the two-week window centered around a full moon to provide the required illumination of a landing strip, not to mention additional limitations imposed by inclement weather. It seemed miraculous the pilots could find the landing strips through the thickest of clouds as often as they did. She would just have to bide her time.

Finally, on August 18, she was summoned to Agent Armadillo's office. It was a small but tidy room with a bookshelf on the left filled with four rows of important-looking books. Céline sat in a plain wooden armchair and faced Agent Armadillo, seated behind his immaculately neat and clean, dark wood desk.

"I want to thank you again for your extraordinary work," Agent Armadillo began. He steepled his hands. "It may seem that we've moved slowly to respond, but I assure you that is not the case. Some in the highest circles found Agent Hornet's claims hard to believe. Fanciful exaggerations at best."

Céline felt tempted to ask if that had been because they came from a pretty young woman, but held her tongue.

"In the end, however, those documents—those stunning, terrifying documents—were very much believed," Agent Armadillo continued. "Down to the last extraordinary detail. And so a response was put into place. As forceful a response as possible to this gravest of threats."

He leaned forward as if to emphasize the gravity of his next words.

"Last night, almost six hundred British aircraft, virtually all of the RAF Bomber Command's frontline units, bombed the rocket development facilities described in those documents you carried, using the maps you carried. Wave after wave of bombers. Explosive bombs. Incendiary bombs. We inflicted great damage. *Enormous* damage. This was a catastrophic blow to the German rocket program, setting it back countless months, and at the most critical time possible.

"They will rebuild, of course. They have to. It's too devastating of a weapon. But the months they have lost may spell the difference between the success and failure of an Allied invasion of Europe. And with that, the outcome of the entire war.

"If we go on to win this war, as I trust we will, you and Agent Hornet will have altered the course of history. A grateful world thanks you."

Waves of emotion cascaded over Céline. They took her breath away. She blinked back tears.

Will have altered the course of history. A grateful world thanks you.

"Thank you," Céline finally managed in a quivering voice. "Thank you."

Agent Armadillo wasn't done.

"The head of the entire Alliance network had planned to give you this news herself," he said. "She wanted to congratulate you herself, but unfortunately an emergency beckoned, as they so often do." He gave a tight smile. "There is, after all, still a war to be won. But she wants you to know that my words of gratitude come from her as well. And when this war is over, she hopes to thank you over a fine meal and a glass of wine."

Céline touched a hand to her chest. She could not believe the words. Could not breathe.

"I... I... I am so..." She swallowed hard. Tried to calm her hammering heart. Finally managed to draw in a gulp of air. "... so honored! Thank you! Please tell her thank you!"

Agent Armadillo nodded, then drew in a deep breath himself.

"As for your immediate reward," he said, "it is that you will board a Lysander bound for France in two days and will once again put your life in mortal peril."

"That is truly a wonderful reward!" Céline said. "Thank you!"

And she meant it.

THE END

ALL EYES FACE INWARD

M.L. BUCHMAN

"These Three Women" have met before in TRM #2: *No W.W.M. (Western White Males)* and TRM #5: *Sisters-in-Arms*. They've done this despite coming from three separate series set in three distinctly different storylines. *Three Makes a Crowd* centered on Kate Stark's world of the Dead Chef series in which, yes, a chef dies. During *It Takes Three*, they met at Henderson's Ranch in the Night Stalkers world of Major Emily Beale. This time, Miranda Chase takes them on quite another adventure.

ALL EYES FACE INWARD

"Andi thought this would make a good place for a girls' outing." Miranda climbed out of the car and moved to the overlook to inspect the grassy valley that was to be their home for the next five days.

She was careful not to use the word *vacation*. Her two prior attempts at vacations had become unmitigated disasters: one in which she was kidnapped to Russia, and the other had nearly killed her whole team as they were hunted by supposedly friendly forces across the Australian Outback. She had *not* enjoyed either experience.

The Faroe Islands, deep in the North Atlantic, were at a such a high latitude that the sun never rose very high. Even now, four hours to sunset, it hung low enough to shine rose gold on the underside of the long-streaked clouds reflecting off the smooth waters of the big bay. The mountaintops snared and tattered them as they passed. It was both foreign and yet, somehow, familiar.

She, Kate, and Emily had decided to get away together, with no crises. Miranda didn't have many friends, and Andi had convinced her it was a reasonable way to expand her horizons.

Also, they had each been headed to different parts of the European continent for their own reasons and the Faroe Islands had been deemed a convenient waypoint.

"If you aren't going to trust your girlfriend, who would you trust?" Emily Beale came up to her right side to look at the view as well.

"But I do trust her. That's why we're here. Because she said—"

"Oh, my God." Kate Stark came up to her left. "I'm so not in the back seat for the next leg of this trip." Miranda hadn't thought about the heights of the two other women when she'd rented the Mini Cooper.

Instead, she'd thought of how much fun it would be to drive the all-electric version of Andi's car. And it had been. The combination of high performance and low noise had been very pleasing despite the country's generally low speed limits, which she followed assiduously. The Faroese sheep had a deep-seated belief that the islands' grassy slopes were theirs and roadways were no exception.

They could hardly be blamed for that attitude. The Faroe Islands had more sheep than people. They also had lived here longer. The monks who originally imported the sheep midway through the first millennium CE had all died out. The Vikings, who landed several centuries later, had discovered the hills alive with sheep. Miranda wondered briefly if that was like being alive with the sound of music, but decided that was silly.

She was also the driver because the other two women weren't. Kate Stark lived in Manhattan and rarely drove. Emily confessed to rarely driving anything other than horses or helicopters since retiring to her mother-in-law's Montana ranch. Miranda's assessment of vehicle appropriateness had proven flawed, by relegating one of the two taller women to occupying the cramped back seat.

Unsure what to say about her miscalculation, Miranda followed her usual practice and kept her words to herself.

Whenever the two women stood to either side of her, which extended observation had proven to be consistent positioning for over eighty percent of occurrences, Miranda always felt so small. It was silly. She was five-four—statistically average for a US-born woman, though her light frame placed her in the twelfth percentile nationally—but Emily and Kate both stood five-ten.

Long white-blonde hair to her right and long black to her left. She kept her own mouse-brown hair trimmed exactly to the length her mother had cut it shortly before dying, just reaching the lower edge of Miranda's jaw. Even a few centimeters longer and it felt all wrong as it touched new places on her neck. Certain aspects of her autism were not worth arguing against; her hair length was one of those.

The other two were such…womanly women. She was so slender and they were…

"Amazonian? Are you both Amazonian? You're the same five-ten height as Gal Gadot, who was chosen to portray a Princess of the Amazons in *Wonder Woman*. Though her eyes aren't blue and both of yours are…so maybe not."

"They're mythical, Miranda."

"Your eyes?" She'd never heard of mythical eyes.

"The Amazons."

"Oh, right."

"I don't know, Emily, I'm okay with being an Amazon princess." Kate snapped her fingers together. "Boy, boy. Three mimosas on the double." Then she looked around as if expecting a boy to show up on a Faroese cliffside bearing glasses, orange juice, and a bottle of chilled champagne.

A sheep who'd been napping in the nearby grass did raise its head to inspect them but showed no inclination toward delivering mimosas. She'd be surprised if it did, or if a waiter boy showed up. The three of them stood alone at the viewpoint above the tiny village of Elduvik at the northern end of Eysturoy Island—the second largest and second most populous of the eighteen major Faroese islands.

The village lay below in a small cove fed by a wide stream that wandered northward along the grassy valley to the east. That was only proper as *vik* meant cove or inlet. *Eldu* meant fire. Perhaps the original Vikings had lit a fire by the stream and named it Fire-cove.

She could see why Andi thought she'd like it. The houses were clustered neatly in two groups on either side of the stream. There were only a dozen year-round residents, growing to just forty during the summer holidays. Most of the houses were small and traditionally tar-painted black with grass roofs. A small white church with a tall steeple was the largest building in the village. It looked very friendly.

High ridges, also grass-covered, towered six hundred meters in all directions as if hugging the town close by the wide bay that, in turn, was largely guarded from the sea by the high terrain. A simple place to enjoy with her two almost friends.

She'd rather enjoyed the challenges of driving in a new country. The Faroe Islands weren't actually their own country, rather an autonomous territory of Denmark. But she'd never driven in Denmark either, so it still counted as new. In her *Personal* notebook, she had to flip around for several seconds before she found the *Countries Visited* page; she hadn't been to a new country in months. Having been to Copenhagen in the past, the Visited column already had a date and time, but Driven In acquired a new entry. She still hadn't slept in Denmark, or the Faroe Islands, but looked forward to making an entry in the third column soon; their long flight across two-thirds of the Atlantic was catching up with her.

They'd reserved a guest house for the five days and Miranda looked forward to quiet days and pleasant walks along—

The sharp ring of Miranda's phone made Kate jump. Emily, of course, barely blinked. Rising to the rank of major in US Army Special Operations had made her nerves steadier than Kate could credit—or ever manage. Kate's past role as a Secret Service protection agent was too far in her past, she ran a cooking television network now.

"This is Miranda Chase. This is really her not a recording of her." She'd answered the phone on speaker.

"Ah, Miranda," the speaker had a strong French accent, "I am so pleased to have reached you. This is Général Pierre Vachon. Perhaps you remember me?"

"The NATO department head for Article 5 investigations." Miranda said it as if by rote, including a French accent. Probably the precise way Vachon had originally introduced himself at their first meeting.

Kate glanced over at Emily and raised her eyebrows in question. Emily returned the slightest shake of her head. Emily was a childhood friend of the retired two-term President of the United States. Kate herself had cooked for a meeting of the G-7 heads of state—and saved her President's life. But Miranda was connected to strange places in ways neither of them could follow.

Article 5 of the NATO treaty stated that if war was declared upon any member nation, it was effectively a declaration of war against all the nations of NATO, including the US.

"We have a problem, Ms. Chase, *d'une urgence extraordinaire.*"

"I'm currently on vacation in the Faroe Islands."

"*Oui.* This is the reason I am calling you. There are no crash investigators who are residing in the Faroe Islands. The nearest one would take many hours to arrive there, and you already are present."

"I am."

Kate sighed. It seemed their vacation was going to become tramping around a plane crash together. They'd done it once before, and the memories still gave her chills.

"Do you know where the village of Vestmanna is?"

"One hour away by car. Fifty-nine minutes, as we're one minute outside of Elduvik."

"How did you do that?" Kate couldn't help asking.

"You are on speakerphone?" The Frenchman sounded thoroughly outraged.

Miranda didn't answer. Instead, she held her phone farther away and began looking about a little frantically. As if…

As if she was looking for someone to hand it to—quickly.

Kate plucked it from her fingers and Miranda visibly relaxed. "Yes, she is on speakerphone. Deal with it. Besides, I asked my question first. She hates doing things out of order. Now be quiet and control your temper or I'll hang up on you *for her.*"

Emily gave her a thumbs up. Miranda had clutched her hands together and showed no interest in recovering her phone. Instead, she appeared to be inspecting the sheep who had stood up in the grass to gain a better view of them.

Miranda reluctantly turned from watching the sheep. "You did ask first, Kate. Though I often find it more expedient to answer multiple questions in reverse order, as it allows me to dispose of them in a retrograde order rather than cycle through them all. But as you already answered the latter question, I'll proceed to yours." She pointed southwest. "I looked up a variety of tourist attractions in case you or Emily became bored with staying in Elduvik. The list of the truly exceptional locales is limited and therefore easy to remember. One of the most impressive is the sea cliffs of Vestmanna, which is precisely one hour from Elduvik in that direction at posted speeds. And Elduvik lies a minute that way." She pointed at the village below. "I thought the math was rather straightforward."

"It was. It was your already knowing all the rest of the details I found puzzling."

"The rest of which details?"

Kate opened her mouth but closed it when she didn't have a ready answer. "Why don't we find out what the general wants? Are you calmer now, Vachon?"

"Who am I speaking with?"

"A friend of Miranda's. Now what's the problem?"

She waited him out. He didn't take long to crumble. Officious people in a hurry often did in her experience.

"There is a plane down at this Vestmanna. It was carrying certain data that must be recovered."

"Didn't we just go through this?" Emily grimaced.

"Who are—"

"That was so last year," Kate whispered while Vachon blustered about yet another voice on the line.

Vachon cut himself off. "Extreme urgency, Ms. Chase. I need your assistance."

"But I am on vacation with two almost friends and I don't wish to be rude by preempting their expectations."

Emily rested a hand on Miranda's shoulder. Kate did the same from the other side, remembering to do so firmly as Miranda, like most autistics, found light contact very upsetting.

"It's okay. We'll all do this together." Emily raised her voice. "We'll head out now. Later, General Vachon." And nodded to Kate.

She hung up the phone and returned it to Miranda.

"Almost friends?" Emily had been through life-and-death situations any number of times while flying helicopters for the Army and a few times as an airborne firefighter. But in her private life, she'd only been through two—both with these two women.

By slowing down as they returned to the car, Kate ended up well ahead—who rolled her eyes at Emily when she caught on, but folded herself into the backseat.

"There's no appropriate word in the English language," Miranda answered once they were all seated in the car. "I have a girlfriend, who is far more than a friend, but there is no word for her relative importance to me. I have teammates who I know as well as I know anyone, so I choose to consider them friends though they are technically coworkers. Does my therapist, who was my governess after my parents died, count as a friend or a guardian? I know the Chairman of the Joint Chiefs of Staff and his wife very well, but that doesn't seem to make them friends in any way I understand the term. I barely know the two of you."

She took several deep breaths with her hands clamped firmly on the wheel. Enough that Emily realized Miranda was attempting to calm herself, and Emily felt sorry she'd brought it up at all.

"Relationships can be very confusing."

"Yes!" Miranda burst out. She thumped one hand on the steering wheel. "*This* car I understand. A well-engineered machine with a specific purpose and role in my life that has so far fulfilled those admirably. People are…"

"A mess," Kate stated and shoved a knee hard enough against the back of Emily's seat to jolt her forward.

"Yes!"

Emily resisted the temptation to tilt her seat back onto Kate's lap. "Don't sound so put out, Miranda. We all feel that way. You just do so more intensely."

"I guess that's a relief. Oh no!"

"What?"

Miranda put the car in Drive, looked carefully at each of

their seatbelts, then poked the accelerator hard enough to spin gravel toward the sheep who'd come to graze along the side of the overlook. "I lied to the general. I told him it would be fifty-nine minutes, but we've spent at least three minutes talking since I hung up. I failed to account for that."

"I won't tell. And neither will Kate."

"Promise?" Miranda begged.

Feeling a bit ridiculous, Emily made a gesture that she hadn't used since she was a little girl. She drew a crisscross between her breasts. "Cross my heart. Hope to die."

She regretted the words as soon as she spoke them.

But Kate said the same.

And Miranda made the same gesture herself.

Miranda felt great relief when she arrived at the crash precisely fifty-nine minutes after Kate had hung up on the general. She *had* followed the speed limit with great care. And they'd been blocked three times by sheep wandering across the road, their wool shining brightly when the low sun caught their coats. It was after nine p.m., did that make it a *night* sun? It was still two hours to midnight, so it wasn't a *midnight* sun; it would set twenty-seven minutes before it could be that. But there wasn't time to ask.

Upon their arrival, she saw that the crash lay on the near side of the bay. That saved the distance/time to circle around the head of the bay and navigate to the center of town, making them precisely on her promised schedule.

The two-lane road was half-blocked by an array of vehicles with flashing lights. They tried to wave her on by. When she pulled over, a policeman came stomping over to her window and began speaking in a foreign language that she could only assume was Faroese.

Miranda was unsure what to say to that, especially as the man appeared quite upset.

Instead of leaning over to speak to him out Miranda's window, Emily climbed out of the car. "Do you speak English?"

"Of course. Most Faroese are at least trilingual with Danish and English. Now move along. You can't stop here."

Now Miranda knew what to say. "I'm Miranda Chase. Investigator-in-Charge for the NTSB. We're ready to begin."

"I do not care if you are the Queen of Denmark; you can not park here. Move along."

"I would suggest that you consider your next words very carefully." Emily had moved up beside him.

Miranda winced in anticipation. Her team member Holly, as tall and almost as blonde as Emily, would now be preparing to violently disarm and subdue the policeman. Holly was one to act first, with surprisingly little concern for longer-term consequences.

Emily did *not* do a Holly. Instead, she kept her voice soft. "We're here under NATO orders to investigate your plane crash and it would be better if we didn't disturb your Prime Minister at this late hour."

The policeman eyed Emily cautiously, though not as if he was in fear of bodily damage. "Do any of you have identification?"

Miranda held out the card identifying her as an IIC for the National Transportation Safety Board. He didn't look impressed; at least that's how Miranda interpreted his expression—narrowed eyes but no down-mouth frown. The card Emily produced earned a very different expression. Miranda could just see that it was marked with a top-secret clearance and named her as *Colonel* Emily Beale in the US Army.

"I didn't know you were promoted."

"It happens," Emily noted.

Kate handed over her Cooks Network business card, which said, *Owner / President.*

The policeman barked out a short laugh, then inspected the three of them again. "Nobody could make this up. Fine. We have placed descent ropes by the lead truck."

Miranda waited a moment longer, but Emily's method hadn't included disarming or damaging the officer. She'd have to tell Holly there were other methods for handling obstinate officials. Or at least this one. She lacked sufficient evidence for a wider range of conjecture.

Miranda inspected the slope. From the road downward, the water lay perhaps a hundred meters below. But the grassy slope was over sixty degrees, with only a small section at half that. The steep pitch explained the ropes' necessity for a safe descent even as a sheep wandered up to a middle section and sniffed it to check for edibility before moving along.

A Gulfstream G280 bizjet lay crumpled against the base of the steep cliff. It had come in over the water and skimmed across the surface before riding up onto a small sloped meadow at sea level, then impaling itself on the steeper section.

She opened the car's trunk, took off her light jacket, and pulled out her NTSB site investigation vest. After putting it on, she shrugged on a small backpack. No one spoke as she checked each pocket to make sure none of her tools had shifted or fallen out. Selecting a fresh notebook, she labeled it appropriately, then measured the wind speed, direction, and other atmospheric details.

Next, Miranda measured the final flight path with a compass and began drawing.

"What's that?" Kate and Emily had come up to either side of her. But in her investigation vest, she didn't feel so small between them. Did that mean her height was both physical *and* psychological? Was such a thing possible? She noted that in her Personal notebook before answering Kate's question.

"If you look out there in the bay to the northeast, see the large circular rings? Those are aquaculture rings with approximately twenty thousand salmon in each." A grouping of fourteen fifty-meter diameter rings lined this side of the bay. "I note that the above-water structure of the seventh one in the first row is slightly damaged, as if struck a glancing blow by the descending aircraft. Enough to twist the angle of the flight to impact this point of land rather than skim alongside it. That gives a final heading of one-zero degrees for the aircraft. Almost due south. Because of the headland we're standing on, that makes a pilot very unlikely to attempt such a heading. Impact with this cliff face would be unavoidable."

"Meaning the pilot wasn't in control." Emily nodded.

Miranda shrugged. "I don't know. I never understand people's intentions." No matter how she tried, they eluded her analysis. "But I expect that the flight path, intentional or not, proved fatal."

Miranda showed no emotion that Kate could see at that statement. Even as she watched the crumpled mess below, a pair of body bags were being lifted out of the plane and set on the rough rock. Nausea twisted in her gut; the twisted wreckage was the same model as her own jet. Kate wished she could focus on something, anything, else.

The town—a hundred times the size of Elduvik, twelve hundred rather than twelve—was still smaller than anywhere she'd been in years. Her food network employed that many people. And the headquarters staff and studios only filled a double handful of floors in the towering Rockefeller Plaza building. Though it was less picturesque. The cliffs surrounding the town and the long, tapered bay rose in eight-hundred-foot leaps from the dark waters of what must be called a fjord.

"I hope they took photographs before removing them." No question about Miranda's focus. Straight down.

Kate was simply glad that they wouldn't be looking at the bodies—this time.

They had to wait for others before they descended the ropes backwards. The rappelling harnesses kept them walking rather than tumbling down the steep slope. The three of them reached the still-sloped bottom just as the rescue teams were preparing to haul the body bags upward. Numerous rescue workers in their Hi-Vis vests milled about the plane. Miranda then delayed the bodies being winched up the cliff while she insisted on inspecting them herself and talking with the forensics specialist. Apparently they *did* have to look at them. Both looked surprisingly normal, as if they slept...though their heads weren't quite—

"It appears that they died of broken necks from the force of the crash," the man reported. "One was the pilot, still strapped into his seat. The other sat in the seat closest to the emergency exit door, perhaps hoping to escape the wreck if he survived." He sent a number of photos to Miranda's phone.

Kate glanced at the grisly images, then looked away quickly. Emily did little more. Miranda zoomed each one to look at it in minute detail.

"Was anything found on his person?" Kate asked.

"Passport and wallet. Fifty euros in cash. The pilot had much the same."

Miranda sorted through their personal effects quickly. Emily took more time inspecting those.

"What are you looking for?" Kate looked over Emily's shoulder to distract herself.

"The general said there was a message. I'm looking for a memory chip or SD card."

"You won't find anything." Miranda set off around the plane.

"Wait, how do you know that?" Kate was getting a little tired of being left three steps behind.

Without looking up, Miranda pointed at the right side of the plane and continued picking her way zig-zag fashion down the final slope to the water. The other rescue workers had to dodge around her to avoid getting run over by the small juggernaut that was Miranda Chase on the job.

Kate had learned the hard way, that zig-zag was how Miranda searched for the edge of the debris field at a crash. Now it was, thankfully, a lesson for others.

"Do you see what she meant?"

Emily was shaking her head.

The plane's nose was flattened back to the lower edge of the windshield. Its instruments and radar, or whatever filled the pointy nose, had been crushed. The main windshield was sufficiently star-cracked to be opaque but remained in the frame. The fuselage was surprisingly intact, though the wing was badly torn and twisted. Above the remaining stub of the starboard wing, the side emergency escape hatch was open.

"They wouldn't open that in flight..." Emily said carefully.

"...unless they were throwing something away." They both turned to look out at the dark water.

"She's a little spooky."

Emily offered a brief laugh. "Only a little? I had a mechanic who I thought was the limit. Miranda is her times ten."

The evening breeze—she checked her watch, ten at night—the night breeze rippled the water. The sun had disappeared into a cloud bank, but much of the sky remained bright blue. It was a good thing that her body was still on East Coast time. In response, her stomach grumbled for dinner.

"Dream on," Emily whispered. "Does Miranda even think to eat during a crash investigation?"

Kate's sigh answered her question.

Montana lay eight hours to the west. Emily either needed lunch too, or a snooze button on her body clock.

They circled the plane to find Miranda as she hadn't reappeared around the other side. She was mostly inside the aft luggage compartment, only showing from the knees down.

"Planning on flying as cargo for your next trip?" Emily teased her.

"I think it would be dark and uncomfortable. However, as this aircraft, like most others, flies with a pressurized luggage compartment, it would not be untenable." Miranda slid back out to stand in the grass. "But to answer your question, no." She'd forgotten that Miranda was not adept at following jokes and took most of them at face value.

"Then what were you doing?"

Miranda held up the bright orange flight recorder. The Black Boxes were called that for their contents, not for their easy-to-find coloring. She quickly extracted an array of equipment from her backpack. It required a series of three adapters to attach the Black Box to her computer tablet. Seconds later, she had voices emanating from the speaker.

"Voices of the dead," Emily whispered to Kate in a sepulcher tone.

Kate shuddered visibly. "Trust me, it's worse when you catch it on film."

Emily decided that perhaps Kate had won that round. They crowded together to listen, and to stay clear of the few rescue workers still inspecting the plane.

F*lame-out on Engine One...*

What! A second voice shouted.

There goes Engine Two. Fuel gauges both show full. No sign of hydraulic failure. No alarm prior to engine cutoff. The pilot continued to work through various scenarios.

Can you get us down safely?

We're too low. Vágar Airport is out of range. The choice from here is flying into those houses, a cliff, or a water landing. I'll try to skim us on the fjord's surface.

Could it be sabotage?

There was a brief pause. *That would fit.*

I have to get rid of something. There was a sound like a releasing seatbelt. Then the second voice spoke very clearly and loudly, as if the speaker wished to make sure he was understood. *There is a copy. All eyes face inward.*

There might have been a few hummed notes of a tune, they gave Emily the chills—one of those diminished chords or something.

Those were the last words on the voice recorder. Past that, a snapping sound like a metallic whip, which must be the strike against the salmon enclosure's structure. Then a single brief scream, or perhaps a cry of pain as the plane impacted the shore.

Miranda studied her screen. "The emergency exit door was opened nine seconds after the person left the cockpit. The flight impacted the aquaculture ring at twenty-two seconds and the cliff at twenty-nine."

"Was it..." Kate paused and swallowed audibly, "...sabotage?"

"Oh yes," Miranda began packing up her equipment. "I thought that was obvious. Didn't you see the condition of the wings?"

Emily had. Both were badly damaged; the starboard one was barely recognizable as more than scrap metal.

"But—" Kate started.

"No jet fuel," Emily finally caught on. "There should be a fire. Or at least the smell of kerosene." She turned to look at the water. No rainbow sheen. No flattening of the small waves stirred up by the wind. The lowering sun, now kissing the far horizon, appeared to sparkle off the waves reflecting the reddening clouds.

"The pilot said the fuel gauges read full," Kate pointed out.

"He did." Miranda held up a mechanical arm with a ball and a piece of string on the end. "Quite simple, really. They tied the string to the fuel gauge's float, and then trapped it in the fuel tank cap to hold the float up. I would conjecture that the fuel was drained prior to attaching the string; it would simplify the task."

"What's the distance to Vágar Airport from here?"

Miranda only had to blink once. "Forty kilometers by car, ten kilometers by air, directly southwest."

Emily traced the flight backward in her mind. Then she tried tracing it forward but her attempts to picture the plane's destination if it followed a Great Circle Route starting out from Vágar Airport and passing over Vestmanna…

"Oh, I see." Miranda nodded and began packing her equipment.

"Well, I don't," Kate sounded annoyed.

Emily shook her head. "We're even on this one. Where were they headed, Miranda?"

"Almost certainly an Arctic route passing above Norway and Sweden. They were headed to Russia. The long way around to reach Moscow without passing over any Western airspace, not even over the Baltic. The Gulfstream had plenty of range if its tanks had indeed been full."

Emily leaned back against the hull. "So, someone sabotaged a plane bound for Russia. Once they figured that out, rather than being caught with the *goods,* he dumped them in the ocean."

"Or maybe," Kate stared out toward the deep waters where the evidence must lie, "they were afraid of it falling into the wrong hands if they wound up dead."

Emily nodded. She often took the most obvious answer, but Kate's fit the scenario better. Why else would he have recorded the message of where to find the backup?

"It would be unlikely to have any other Western Europe or Icelandic destination along this flight path." Whereas Miranda moved straight down a topic until she had it beaten into submission. "I'm unaware of any local air traffic requirements to require a late turn if departing for Europe. No, they were on their intended course. The Gulfstream G280 doesn't have the range to reach over the pole to China, even if they passed over Siberia. Russia is the only logical destination. There was no sign of tampering with the directional equipment."

"So, they're carrying a secret to Russia. From the Faroe Islands of all unlikely places. And someone at the airport sabotaged the plane to stop whatever data General Vachon is so worried about."

"But," Kate held up a finger, "that NATO general calls us *after* the plane crash. *After* his plan failed?"

"Actually, he called me," Miranda stated.

Emily was too used to team-based thinking, and Miranda clearly struggled with the concept. She let it go and decided to rescue Kate. A sense of sisterhood taking hold before Kate put her foot in another Miranda logic-snarl.

"Right. He called you—*after* the crash. Because…" And Emily couldn't connect the pieces.

Miranda shook her head. "I warned you; I have no skills regarding other people's agendas."

"What's the plausible story?" Kate asked, then began answering her own question. "General Vachon had the plane sabotaged so that it couldn't take off before he could get someone here to the Faroes to deal with the messenger and the secret data. But the sabotage wasn't perfect. Perhaps intended to have the plane start, but die as it approached the runway, making for a whole scene and a lot of questions that would delay their departure. But there was enough fuel remaining in the tank to depart Vágar and fly ten kilometers before failure."

"Technically, to fly seven kilometers. Following a normal departure profile, in the first ninety seconds they'd have climbed to fifteen hundred feet before loss of fuel." Miranda tapped her tablet computer a few times. "This is corroborated by the flight profile on the Black Box. From flame-out, they had fifty-two seconds of glide time before reaching sea level and that would have covered the last three kilometers." Again the tapping. "Confirmed."

"You know your planes."

"I do."

Emily waited for more, but for Miranda it wasn't being humble or bragging. It was a statement of—

"Except it's not my plane."

—fact. Pure fact. Perhaps being an *almost friend* with Miranda Chase placed them closer than many people she herself called friends.

Once Miranda had satisfied herself about the plane, they climbed the cliff. With the aid of the ropes, it was slow but not arduous. The traffic up and down the slope continued, but had thinned significantly since their arrival.

Back at the car, Emily was reaching for the door handle—it was about time she gave Kate a turn at the front seat—when Miranda called out, "Wait."

Emily froze with her hand a mere inch from the car.

∽

"There's a scrape in the paint by the hood latch." Miranda pointed.

"Doesn't look like much," Kate leaned in close, forcing Miranda to lean away. She couldn't tolerate someone so deep in her personal space except Andi, her more-than girlfriend.

"It wasn't there when I rented the car. I was most careful to inspect the vehicle for any signs of damage before accepting the insurance terms of the rental agreement. I didn't want to be liable for any pre-existing damage. That damage was not pre-existing." Miranda pulled out a flashlight to inspect it more closely. "It's consistent with a screwdriver being leveraged into the hood release."

Emily grabbed her wrist tightly as Miranda reached to test the extent of the damage. "Don't touch it just yet."

But Emily wasn't looking at her. She was inspecting the crowd, though most had left while they'd been talking down at the plane.

Miranda did the same, after Emily let go of her.

The ambulance and the coroner had departed. A single fire truck remained at the road's edge. Two policemen were chatting with the firefighters. In between mouthfuls of grass, six sheep looked down on them from where the steep hillside turned into a cliff above them. She was unsure if they'd been there previously. An oversight, but of what consequence she couldn't be certain.

The policeman who'd initially accosted them walked over. "Did you learn anything interesting?"

"We learned that the plane—"

"Did you see anyone approach our car?" Emily cut her off.

—*was sabotaged,* Miranda completed the sentence for herself. She hated unfinished statements; they always felt so...prickly with their cut-off ends.

"If they did, I didn't see them." Then he squinted up at the sheep as if perhaps they'd seen something. "I do recall your car hood being raised at some point. I didn't think much of it."

"Do you have a bomb squad?"

"Here? In Vestmanna? There's just me and Herta," he pointed at the female officer who noticed and walked over to join them. "Did you see anyone working on this car?"

"*Nei.*" She shook her head.

"They want the bomb squad to come up and look it over. It has a small scratch and I might have seen the hood up." He sounded...

Miranda leaned closer to Kate and whispered, "Is that skeptical or is it—"

"You got it. With a little bit of dismissive mixed in."

"Oh." She hadn't much considered the combination of multiple voice tones when trying to study speech inflection. Worse, only a little of one and a lot of another? This would make for a much more complex analysis matrix. Her initial grid-based approach would be wholly unable to account for such variables. Extending to three dimensions was little better because what if any tone could be mixed with any other tone? The ramifications approached infinite complexity. If skepticism and derision could coexist, could sadness and joy do so as well? Terror and sadness, perhaps. But terror and elation seemed an unlikely combination.

She would have to give this thought far beyond any prior consideration.

Herta looked carefully at the scratch, then down at the wrecked plane below. Then she looked intently at Miranda.

Not liking that, she tried to shift behind Kate without being rude about it.

"Einar," who must be the male policeman, "checked and you are apparently *the* top investigator for the American crash people?"

"She is," Emily answered for her. Saving Miranda from leaning out from behind Kate.

She turned back to Einar. "Might not be such a bad idea to call the bomb squad in."

"But—"

"You're the boss. Do you want to be the one blown to pieces checking out their car for them? I won't be the one to tell Tórhalla. Your wife would not be happy with me if I told her you were coming home in teeny tiny pieces."

He grumbled but placed the call. Miranda might not have recognized it, but his reaction was similar to what she'd just felt. Apparently Einar's commander had applied that same mixture of skeptical and dismissive to his tone—or was that a false assumption and it had merely been a *similar* admixture of intonations? This was getting harder rather than easier the more she thought about it.

After hanging up, Einar grumbled out, "A pair of techs will be here in under an hour."

From her position behind Kate, Miranda gave her a small nudge.

Kate glanced over her shoulder and nodded, before turning back to the police. "I'm afraid we can't wait that long. We'll need a ride."

Kate could get to like this. She'd managed to get the front seat this time, though it wasn't a huge win as the *Politi's* VW station wagon offered much more comfort to its rear passengers than their abandoned Mini Cooper. Unlike American cars, there was no screened cage between the front and back. Pity.

Einar had been very unhappy, which Kate was fine with. Herta had taken under thirty seconds to convince him she was taking the car, by stating that she'd take the consequences as well. But it was the lone police car. The firemen had left while they were talking.

Which left Einar to pace back and forth at the top of the cliff until the bomb squad arrived from the capital of Tórshavn—almost the opposite corner of Streymoy Island. The sole road south from Vestmanna was a narrow two-lane that hugged the cliff's edge. The shoulder and guardrail buffer was far too narrow for Kate's liking.

"So, Miranda. Where are we going next?" She asked to distract herself.

"I have no idea."

Herta jammed on the brakes hard enough to make the car skid. Once stopped—and she dared breathe again—Kate eyed the sharp drop-off close by her side of the car. They'd climbed to at least twice the original height above the sea as they'd taken the only road south, but the ocean lay no farther away. She was looking *down* far more than *out* to see where water met land. And the shoulder's width...

Kate carefully turned her back to the view and looked toward Miranda in the rear.

"But you solved all of those clues about the plane's sabotage."

"*Sabotage?*" Herta shouted. "No one said anything about sabotage of the plane."

"Should I have?" Miranda's innocent question stumped Herta into silence.

Though Kate could see her knuckles whiten from grasping the wheel so tightly. She looked to be seconds from dumping them all off the cliff and turning around to beg forgiveness from her boss.

Miranda explained. "Someone sabotaged it so that it wouldn't reach Russia. It was what led me to suspect sabotage of our vehicle as well."

"Why you? Why didn't we see them?"

A glance at Emily, and Kate knew there would be no immediate help there. Emily Beale was a helicopter pilot by training; her thinking was tactical. Miranda's thinking was… Kate didn't know what. But her own was strategic. It had served her past in the Secret Service and her present in creating the largest food-based television network in the business.

"Okay, Herta. How far until the first decision point?"

"About three seconds!"

Kate laughed as if it was a joke, but that cliff edge felt very, very close by. "Let me rephrase. How long to the first place we have to decide which way to go."

"About ten minutes. Except for the islands still isolated by ferries, you can cross the whole country in about ninety minutes. We don't have all that many roads."

"Okay, let's get started."

"Is Einar safe? We left him alone back there."

"Precisely. Alone. Whoever tampered with our vehicle may have merely tampered with it to delay us. Or added a tracking device. Though I'm not willing to bet that there *isn't* a bomb, I think it's less likely. If their intent was to kill us, they'd have stuck around to make sure it worked. We're behind them, wherever they're headed, but I can't predict by how much."

Herta began driving again.

Emily had thought she was done with missions like this one. Sent into action under-informed, with no clear strategy until they could directly observe the battlezone.

"If they left, they know something that we don't. Otherwise they would have stayed to gather the intelligence directly from us."

"Maybe they were close by us at the plane and overheard us

listening to the recording. *There is a copy. All eyes face inward.* " Then Miranda hummed a few notes of a tune.

Emily had forgotten there was music after the words.

But Miranda kept humming more than had been on the message.

No—Herta was humming it.

"You know that tune?"

"Yes. It is in the Jellyfish Roundabout."

"The…what?"

Again it was Miranda who explained. "It was one of the other options I researched for us if we needed to get away. There's an eleven-kilometer-long tunnel that connects the nation's capital on this island to two widely separated sections of Eysturoy Island to the east. They connected the three parts in an underwater roundabout that looks like a jellyfish. It's the only underwater roundabout in the world."

"*Ja,*" Herta agreed. "And those notes, they are the ending notes of the Voice of the Tunnel."

"The Voice of the Tunnel?" That was a new one on Emily. "Do we meet the Ghost of Christmas Past there too?"

"No, silly," Miranda spoke like she was addressing a small child. "This is June. There won't be a Ghost of Christmas Past for at least six more months when the *Scrooge* reruns are broadcast."

"So, what are the eyes that face inward?"

"Oh!" Herta didn't explain. Instead, she turned on the car's flashing lights and accelerated hard.

"Don't hit any sheep!" Miranda cried out.

That analyst woman definitely needed to work on her priorities.

∼

Herta didn't slow.

She didn't know what was going on, but she came from a long line of Faroese fisherman, everyone in Vestmanna did. They might fish the aquaculture nets now more than the open ocean, but that too continued.

And the Russians had forced a damnable fishing treaty upon the Faroese. In exchange for ten thousand tons of fish taken from the Barents Sea, the Russians were permitted to rape eight times that amount from Faroese waters. There was not a fisherman who understood the arrangement, especially not now with their attacks on the Ukraine and their threats to nuke NATO.

Any sheep between her and the Eysturoyartunnilin had better stay off the road.

She grabbed the radio and keyed the headquarters' frequency. "Close the Eysturoy tunnel! This is an emergency! Close all three entries and exits! No one in or out!" It was a crazy order that command would ask a thousand questions about before implementing, by which time it might be too late.

Unless…

She hoped she was right.

"We have a potential bomber headed for the roundabout. I'm bringing in a specialist team. Be ready to let me through."

She covered the thirty-three kilometers to Tórshavn in a startling eleven minutes—without killing a single sheep. It was midnight-twilight. The animals must have decided it was night and time to sleep. The sun wouldn't be rising again for another three hours.

Three kilometers shy of the tunnel, she spotted the bomb squad truck headed the other way. The speed at which she passed them would hopefully get them moving faster to Vestmanna before Einar did something stupid like try to inspect the car himself.

When they reached the tunnel, the *Landsfúti*, the chief

constable, stepped forward to flag her down. It was a good thing that he was nimble on his feet as she didn't slow one bit. Once in the tunnel, she really opened up her speed. The seven kilometers to the roundabout passed so quickly that her nerves only had time to escalate and none for her to capture control of them.

Herta had turned off the flashing lights when she entered the tunnel. Now, as they approached the roundabout, she doused the headlights, and turned off the engine to coast the rest of the way downslope.

"Whoa!" Kate whispered from the front seat with the proper amount of awe as she stopped in the tunnel's shadows, but with the roundabout chamber visible. It was a great toroidal shape, twenty meters high that could allow two lanes of traffic to circle the entire central pillar. Like a donut turned inside out, the pillar swelled and curved up over their heads to the round ceiling. Lights of blue, green, and red washed over it in a mottled pattern like being inside a rippling jellyfish.

She tried not to think about the thirty-three meters of rock and twenty-four meters of water that pressed down on them from above.

"See the dancers?" Silly thing to say, they were impossible to miss.

Life-sized steel cutouts encircled the pillar. It created an outline of people of all sizes standing shoulder to shoulder as they would in a dance. They stood back from the pillar just enough for the lights behind them to shine upward on the stone. The colored lighting came from the center; the dancers were in stark silhouette.

"This is a very old and very traditional chain dance. Everyone holds hands. We dance and sing the great Faroese ballads. This we do at weddings, Christmas, and especially on Ólavsøka, St. Olav's Day. That is our National Day next month, in July."

"A bit of nice history, but why is this the place?"

Miranda answered from the back before she could. "When they dance in a circle like this, all eyes face inward."

They climbed out of the car and Herta eased the trunk open. Neither Kate nor Emily hesitated when she handed them each a weapon. Their gestures showed their easy familiarity with firearms.

Miranda declined with a whisper, "I only use a gun to put down injured animals."

Herta found that to be much harder than the two drug runners she'd had to shoot over the years. The animals had no way to know what was about to happen.

They split into pairs and eased up either side of the tunnel: she and Kate to the right, Miranda behind Emily to the left.

In the roundabout, a single car had parked with two wheels up on the sidewalk. As she watched, a man circled around from the far side of the central pillar. He leaned in over each pair of shoulders and looked down inside the circle.

She waited, until he had come too far to run back and shelter around the other side of the roundabout, before raising her weapon and shouting.

"Freeze right there! Hands up!"

He slowly raised his hands, turning one toward her oddly. Even in the dim blue aquatic light, she could see that he didn't hold a gun. Rather some device in his fist.

"You won't like it if you shoot me. This is a dead-man switch. That," he nodded toward his car, "is a bomb big enough to shatter this tunnel and let the ocean come pouring in. Now you help me to find what is hidden somewhere here. Then you make a way that I get out of tunnel safely."

"You've got him, Herta?" Emily asked from the other side of the tunnel.

"Dead in my sights."

"Okay then." Emily tucked her sidearm in the front of her pants, stepped forward, and heard the soft shuffle of Miranda following in her wake. She stopped five meters away and folded her arms. "This is an interesting problem, isn't it?"

The bomber offered a smile. "It can be simple. Do not make it more of a problem."

Emily nodded. Calm and rational. No hysteria, panic…or doubt. He was a professional operative and not likely to make mistakes. Emily would prefer that he wasn't. It was a more dangerous play, but with a professional there was unlikely to be a play at all.

Kate stayed three steps behind Herta and kept checking her six—rearguard. The kicking in of her old Secret Service training actually gave her a bit of vertigo. But no one coming down the tunnel. No one in the other tunnels. The five of them appeared to be the only ones underground, and underwater.

Manhattan's tunnels, both car and subway, ran beneath rivers not fjords, but she'd been a New Yorker her entire life, except for the five-year aberration of the Secret Service. Being underground didn't bother her in the least.

Being a hundred and ninety feet down with a mad bomber, however, only her old training and conscious effort kept her from having a flop sweat that would make the Glock she'd taken turn slick against her palms.

Miranda had studied the engineering of the Eysturoyartunnilin in detail. Her expertise was airplanes—how they were built and how they broke—but this must have been a fascinating challenge to design and build. She would have to find the engineers before she left the Faroes because there were so many aspects of the design to discuss: strata composition, shear and fracture coefficients of the native rock, ratio of rebar to shotcrete to seal and smooth the walls.

She still wore her site investigation vest. She tugged out a notebook and began listing her questions as she inspected the tunnel, its art, and the lighting effects.

The lights shifted, blues and greens trading places, reds and yellows muting and shining forth somewhere else. An elegant design on every level. She wished she'd thought to turn on the car's radio to hear the Voice of the Tunnel. The composer had used the actual construction sounds—blasting, digging, spraying the concrete slurry, even the paving equipment—to generate a living, breathing soundtrack.

The steel figures in silhouette did indeed appear to all be facing inwards, toward those lights.

She spotted a blemish in the light show on the pillar when the colors shifted again.

One of the steel figures was hinged, a service gate to the inner ring of lights. She stepped through and there, on one of the LED instruments, rested a three-and-a-half inch hard disk drive. It had slid enough for a corner to intrude over a part of the lens, creating a distinct aberration in the projected light. Otherwise it would have remained effectively invisible because of the light directly from the fixture.

A brief inspection revealed that there were no surprises in the wiring of the lights. Cable housings disappeared into the shotcrete. They must continue along the pillar and over the ceiling to exit out one of the tunnels. No controls here, they were all centralized, probably back at the capital in Tórshavn.

When she stepped back out with the hard drive in her hand, no one had moved—but now the bad man was smiling.

"Well done. I must have missed that three or four times. You can just give it to me and we'll move on to the next stage of this operation."

"What's on it?" Emily asked

Miranda hadn't thought about that. She put away her notebook, then pulled out her tablet computer and an adapter to match the SATA connection on the hard drive.

"Don't! I swear I'll blow this place up before you can access that drive." The man's shout echoed angrily around the circular chamber in ways that were difficult to predict.

"If you know what's on it, then you don't need it," Kate kept her voice far steadier than Miranda felt inside.

She also didn't follow Kate's logic but decided that making the man even more angry at her wouldn't be good. Miranda put the adapters away.

Yet General Vachon had directed her to retrieve this drive. And someone else was trying to smuggle it from the Faroes to Russia.

Could it contain proof that Russia was indeed in violation of NATO's Article 5 and had already declared war on one of its member nations?

That seemed unlikely or the Russians would have simply destroyed it rather than creating a copy and hiding it so carefully.

Was it stolen and would lead to a war if the Russians knew what was on it? If so, that meant that General Vachon knew there was proof of illegal activity on this hard drive and had been willing to sabotage a plane to get it.

But he hadn't wanted it destroyed; he'd wanted it recovered.

Hadn't he?

Whatever information everyone wanted, must exist only upon this drive.

Which meant…

And that's where Miranda's suppositions fell apart.

"I'll never understand people."

But she knew one thing.

From her vest, she extracted a thick glove, then reached into another pocket.

~

Emily hadn't dared look away from the Russian operative. That deadman switch was worrying her.

But she must have been worrying him as he had glanced aside only momentarily when Miranda had foolishly discovered the drive. Perhaps not foolish, instead predictable. Miranda could only ever function in a straightforward and logical manner.

Or perhaps it had been for the best. While Miranda had been wandering about the tunnel, taking notes and whatever else she was doing, Emily had made no progress in swaying the operative's guard—a hundred percent pro.

Then something happened behind her that swung all the man's attention away from her. Something Miranda—

"No!"

Whatever made the man cry out, it was all Emily needed.

During their conversation, she managed to move from five meters away to four, well inside Tueller's Radius. At twenty-one feet, six-and-a-half meters, an aggressor with a knife can charge and attack before a defender can draw and fire a sidearm—a measurement first made by Sergeant Tueller of the Salt Lake City Police and confirmed many times since.

From four meters, Emily hoped she could grab the agent's hand before he'd think to release the switch.

She drove toward him somewhere between a full sprint and a lunge.

A blinding light came from Kate's right.

Herta glanced that way then cried out and raised an arm to cover her eyes.

Kate's training, though long out of date, held. She didn't turn to be blinded by the explosion, leaving her unable to chase a perpetrator.

Except it wasn't an explosion.

A dazzling white light continued washing away all the muted colors of the Jellyfish roundabout. By its light, she could see Emily tackling the Russian agent's hand.

But she could also she him reaching around for the back of his belt.

As his hand swung once more into view, the last of the actinic white light glinted off the six-inch blade of his knife.

Emily's body blocked most of the agent's body.

Except—Kate could only hope that her shooting skills hadn't decaying too much.

He raised the knife high, ready to plunge it into Emily's side.

His motion froze for an instant at the maximum distance—and Kate took her shot.

Herta, though still badly dazzled, had called for help.

The Faroese police had come racing down all three branches of the tunnel.

Once Emily had extracted the deadman switch from the man's grasp, Miranda had disarmed it. The police, when they arrived, didn't appear inclined to believe her. Though they seemed happy enough to arrest the man, binding his shot hand only after they had him fully shackled.

Nor were they impressed by the small puddle of metal, that

had once been the hard drive, that Miranda had melted into the road's surface.

"What the hell is that?" the chief constable shouted at her.

Miranda shifted behind Emily.

Emily turned to her but spoke softly. "What *did* you do, Miranda?"

She pulled the rubber handle out of her vest and a fresh cartridge, a three-inch piece of stainless-steel rod. "It's a thermite torch used for cutting through steel. Each cartridge lasts about two seconds but burns at five thousand degrees Fahrenheit. It will cut easily through any grade of steel up to a three-quarter-inch rod or half-inch plate. Military and law enforcement use it for breaching locks or removing window or jail bars."

"And what the hell was that?" the chief constable's voice echoed about the chamber as he jabbed an angry finger toward the melted drive once more, sending Miranda scooting behind Kate this time.

Miranda wondered at the thought; could a finger be angry? She inspected her own that she'd used to pull the device's trigger but it didn't either angry or complacent.

"That," Emily pointed, "is now no one's problem."

They'd arrived at Elduvik at sunrise. Which should have been at 3:35 a.m., but the high mountains blocked the northerly sun from the deep valley until 6 a.m.

The three of them sat out on the porch of the small house Miranda had rented for them. Several sheep were wandering along the still quiet streets, sampling various plants that had ventured past a nearby garden's wire fence. She, Kate, and Emily sipped mimosas and ate fresh *kleinur* that they'd picked up in Breyðvirkið bakery before departing Tórshavn. Their new car—thankfully—had plenty of room in the back seat.

Miranda was always cautious about new foods, but the fried cake twists filled with cardamom and raisins were very comforting after the long night. They went very well with the mimosas.

"Seriously nice move, Miranda." Kate slouched in one chair with her feet propped up on another. Emily refreshed their drinks with the last of the champagne.

"You seriously cooked that drive." Emily hesitated, then reached for another *kleinur*. "Why not? I'm on vacation. So, Miranda, I didn't get to hear why you chose to burn it."

"Was I wrong?"

"I don't know. What was your reasoning?"

"Everyone wanted it intact. If there were other copies, no one seemed to know about them. NATO, Russia, Article 5. I knew I could never straighten it out but isn't Europe already enough of a mess as it is? No one acted as if the contents of that drive were going to make things better. So, I decided to remove it from the equation."

Kate held up a hand palm out. "Well done, you. Melted it right into the roadway. They had to pry it out with a tire iron."

Miranda high-fived Kate's hand even though she felt bad about the hole she'd melted deep into the nice clean pavement. "I closed and covered my eyes as I didn't feel there was time to find safety goggles. What happened?"

"When you distracted him, Emily here," Kate toasted her with her mimosa glass then drained it, "tackled his ass."

"No, I tackled his *hand* with the dead-man switch to make sure he didn't release it."

"With all her focus there, she couldn't see him pull a knife with his other hand."

"So, Kate shot him."

"Just a little."

"In the hand. Nice shooting, by the way."

"Thanks. You were blocking his center of mass. But I figured if he stabbed you, it would seriously mess up our vacation. Busy night for the bomb squad between the crash site and the tunnel bomb."

Their car had merely had its control computer smashed, but the load of C4 in the man's car might well have caved in the entire tunnel.

Miranda liked how comfortable Kate and Emily appeared to be with each other. That's how friends should be.

"What did General Vachon have to say to you?" Emily asked.

Miranda shifted uncomfortably in her chair. "He was very upset at the loss of one copy and the destruction of the other. I…" She felt the heat rushing to her cheeks. "I was unconscionably rude. I…hung up on him!" She finished in a rush.

This time it was Emily who held up her hand to high-five and repeated Kate's earlier comment. "Well done, you."

Miranda was less certain about it than Emily was, but slapped the offered hand anyway because it would be rude not to. Once in a day was once too many for her.

Kate had slouched too low to easily raise a hand, but she did offer a thumbs up, making Miranda feel a little better about her decision. Maybe some secrets were best if no one had them.

"Not bad work for a group of *almost* friends," Kate mumbled, mostly asleep stretched out in the morning sun.

Miranda considered. What was a friend? Someone you liked and trusted? Perhaps how *long* she knew someone was of less consequence and the *feeling*—always a tricky concept for her—counted for more? She liked the way that sounded. Besides, she'd know them much better after their remaining five days together.

"Not bad work for a group of *friends*." She tried out the word.

ALL EYES FACE INWARD

Emily toasted her with the end of her *kleinur* before eating it.

Kate offered a very soft snore.

Miranda pictured herself in a circle dance with Kate to one side and Emily to the other. A Faroese dance of unity with all eyes facing inward toward the light.

Yes, she liked that idea very much.

U*SA Today and Amazon No. 1 bestseller M. L. "Matt" Buchman is the author of 75-plus action-adventure thriller and military romance novels, 200 short stories, and lots of read-by-author audiobooks. PW says: "Tom Clancy fans open to a strong female lead will clamor for more." Booklist declared his romances were: "3X Top 10 of the Year." A project manager with a geophysics degree, he's designed and built houses, flown and jumped out of planes, solo-sailed a 50-foot sailboat, and bicycled solo around the world...and he quilts.*

NEVER MISS AN ISSUE!

S ign up for the Thrill Ride Magazine newsletter HERE###

www.ingramcontent.com/pod-product-compliance
Ingram Content Group UK Ltd.
Pitfield, Milton Keynes, MK11 3LW, UK
UKHW030800170325
456354UK00001B/92